then, now,
Always

MONA SHROFF

then, now,
Always

HQN

HQN

ISBN-13: 978-1-335-01318-7

Then, Now, Always

HQN
22 Adelaide St. West, 40th Floor
Toronto, Ontario M5H 4E3, Canada
www.Harlequin.com

Printed in U.S.A.

Recycling programs
for this product may
not exist in your area.

To Anjali

Always believe in love.
It'll make your dreams come true
as mine did with you.

then, now,

Always

CHAPTER ONE
MAYA

New York, 2012

IF SAM WERE HERE, Maya wouldn't have to go to this meeting alone. She jogged the last few blocks in a lame attempt to be less late for her meeting with the vice principal of her daughter's high school. The woman had called this morning and scheduled an emergency conference, with no regard for how long it really took to get from Queens to Manhattan.

Maya barely even registered her thoughts about Sam as she drew in cool air and finally approached the school. Thoughts of Sam were like the flour and eggs in a cake: always there, but not what she concentrated on.

Besides, the fact that Sam wasn't there was her own doing.

The school was set back from the street, and usually, Maya would take a few minutes to admire the beauty of the architecture in old New York City, but on this day, the pit in her stomach made her blind to her surroundings. She ran up steep steps that led to a sidewalk before she approached the covered doorway. She wiped sweat from her upper lip, grateful for the crisp fall chill while she waited to be buzzed in. She tried not to glance at her watch, but failed. She should have been in the meeting ten minutes ago.

Her heels clanked on the tile and echoed in the high ceilings as she took the longest strides her legs would allow. Large, tall windows let in the sun. The dark wood of the doorframes gleamed from recent polish, and the absence of graffiti gave the impression of a Fifth Avenue office building rather than a high school.

She approached Mrs. Pappenberger's office and found a school security officer at the door. Panic made her jog the last few steps. The vice principal's secretary was leading a woman and young blonde girl holding an ice pack to her lip into the outer office where her daughter, Samantha, waited. Maya recognized the blonde as Brittany Stevenson and suppressed a groan.

Beside Brittany, an immaculately dressed woman in a black pencil skirt, cream silk blouse and coordinating black blazer teetered on four-inch stilettos. Maya pulled her coat tighter, grateful she had removed her *Sweet Nothings* apron before leaving her coffee shop-slash-bakery. Her daughter was also standing, arms fiercely folded across her body, dark curls tamed into the ponytail Maya had seen her in this morning. Despite the angry glances she was throwing at the mother-daughter pair, Samantha's face was pale, making her dark brown eyes look almost black. The woman glared at Samantha as she delicately adjusted the ice pack on her daughter's lip. Both girls wore the standard school uniform, but while Samantha's skirt was decidedly knee level, Brittany's skirt definitely challenged the school dress code.

Maya's heart sank as she analyzed the scene. "Samantha." It was a strong effort, keeping her voice neutral. "What's going on?"

"I'll tell you what's going on, Ms. Rao," the woman said, turning ice-cold eyes on Maya. "Your hoodlum daughter took a swing at my poor Brittany." She had a slight accent that Maya couldn't quite place, and she pouted full red lips against camel-colored skin. "It's not enough that she throws outrageous accusations at her—now she has to physically assault her!" She actually ran her hand along her daughter's blond tresses as if petting a dog. It was all Maya could do to not roll her eyes.

"Listen, Mrs. Stevenson," Maya fired back. "My daughter is not a hoodlum." She took a step closer to Mrs. Stevenson, and, through a tight smile, continued, "If Samantha took a swing at Brittany, you may want to investigate Brittany's behavior."

Mrs. Stevenson raised her chin. "How dare you suggest that someone of my daughter's stature would stoop to anything unsavory?"

Maya couldn't believe what she was hearing. "Didn't that shop owner press shoplifting charges against your daughter?"

"Only because your daughter somehow convinced him of her own innocence. So my daughter was left taking the blame."

"Because Samantha apologized and worked after school for two weeks to pay off what she took."

Mrs. Stevenson arched an eyebrow. "As if a Stevenson would work in a shop."

"Just tell your daughter to lay off mine."

"Maybe," she said, shaping those bright red lips into a sneer, "if *your* daughter had a strong *male* influence, she could be kept in line. I honestly don't understand how people with your…"

"With my *what*?" Maya spoke slowly through gritted

teeth and took a step into the other woman's personal space. "Brown skin?"

Mrs. Stevenson's mouth gaped open, her eyes wide in horror. "I was going to say *'lack of stature'* are allowed admission to an institution such as this."

MAYA SMIRKED AND took a step back. "Well, you're here, so clearly, they'll let anybody in." It shouldn't feel good to watch this woman squirm, but it totally did, and Maya didn't even try to hide her satisfaction.

"You'll certainly be hearing from our lawyer." Mrs. Stevenson turned on her heel and stalked away. "Come, Brittany." Brittany glared at Samantha and Maya before she stomped off behind her mother like a duckling.

Samantha's brown eyes were filled with anger, her nostrils flared with the effort of trying not to cry. Maya sighed and pulled her daughter in for a hug.

Samantha succumbed to her mother's embrace, much as she had when she was a little girl. "Mom!" Her voice cracked as the tears were set free.

"Seriously, sweetheart?" Maya hugged her tight, keeping her voice low. "Did you have to hit her?"

Samantha pulled back and wiped her eyes even as she set her jaw. "Mom, she deserved it! She—"

"Ms. Rao. You're late." The voice was familiar, as was the slow and mocking tone. Maya turned to face the vice principal.

"Mrs. Pappenberger." Maya forced her mouth into an overly polite smile and bit back a retort about the flying broom that Mrs. Stevenson must have used to make it on time. "So sorry."

The vice principal's precisely colored lips formed a thin pink line, and she raised one eyebrow. "Yes, well.

We do have a problem, don't we?" She tossed a cool glance at Samantha as she opened the door to her office. A tilt of her head and a glance down her nose the only indication that they should follow.

Mother and daughter were greeted by the warm scent of cherrywood and leather, although the warmth extended only as far as that scent, despite the two large windows behind Mrs. Pappenberger's desk that let in the autumn sun. To Maya's left was a wall lined with plaques, all bearing the vice principal's name. The opposite wall was lined with bookshelves holding old yearbooks and what appeared to be classic literature. Surely the bookbindings were a facade, filling the shelf space with impressive covers but blank pages.

They sat down in the two leather-bound chairs facing Mrs. Pappenberger's desk and waited, grim with expectation. Samantha positioned herself poker straight on her chair, while Mrs. Pappenberger took a seat on her side of the desk and got right to it. "It seems we have *once again* found controlled substances in young Ms. Rao's possession."

Maya whipped her head to Samantha. "What?"

"It's not mine." Samantha's voice was surprisingly firm considering the amount of trouble she was facing.

Mrs. Pappenberger pursed her lips, her voice matter-of-fact. "So you say. However, the fact is that it was found in your locker."

"But I didn't put it there."

"Then how, Ms. Rao, did it get there?"

"The same as last time—Brittany, or one of her gang—put it there." Samantha moved closer to the desk, to the very edge of the chair, almost as if she were afraid of what would happen if she got too comfortable. "I was minding my own business. Brittany and her gang were giving me sh—bugging me—while I opened my locker." She clenched her fists. "They do it all the time." There was blood on her knuckles.

"So, you open your locker and they just *happen* to be there and out pops this bag of marijuana? And so you decided to punch Ms. Stevenson?"

Samantha maintained eye contact. "Well, it's not the first time she did this—she's been trying to get me expelled ever since…ever since…last time." Her eyes flicked to Maya, then back to the vice principal.

"Could you please tell me what's going on here?" Enough with the twenty questions. Maya didn't care if she appeared unfriendly as she turned to the vice principal, she'd had enough of her daughter being harassed. "Why is there a security officer here?"

"Standard school procedure when there's a fight." Mrs. Pappenberger gave Maya a tight smile, then addressed Samantha. "You understand who you are accusing?"

"What difference does that make?" Maya leaned forward in her chair. "If Brittany planted it in—"

"Ms. Rao." Mrs. Pappenberger leaned in toward Maya, her perfectly manicured hands folded in front of her, and spoke to her as if she were one of her students. "That girl is Byron Stevenson's daughter. As in the Parker-*Stevenson* Library."

Maya felt the blood drain from her face. That library used to be called the Parker Library. She wiped cold sweat from her upper lip with clammy hands. Byron Stevenson was a Columbia Law School grad who had made his fortune by marrying into one of the wealthier families in the city. If Maya weren't so panicked, she'd take a moment to relish how it must grate on Mrs. Stevenson that they had to share the library name with Parker.

"The Stevensons will be pressing assault charges," Mrs. Pappenberger continued. "There will be a possession charge, from the authorities. And we will be discussing the possibility of expulsion, per school regulations." Maya could have sworn the woman was smirking.

A wave of nausea caused Maya to hesitate a moment before finally speaking. "What does that mean?" She jerked her head toward the officer in the outer office. "She's not being arrested!" She squeezed her daughter's arm, as if that were all it would take to protect her child.

Mrs. Pappenberger stared at Maya, her ice-blue eyes cool and impassive. "No," she said, sounding almost disappointed. "Not today. Today, you will take young Ms. Rao home, as she is suspended from school for five days per school policy in these cases. We will be in touch with you regarding the legalities." She shuffled and stacked some papers to indicate that the meeting was over, releasing Maya and Samantha from the now-stifling air of the office.

Mother and daughter were in shocked silence as Samantha gathered her things from her locker. The tension in the air followed them outside, where even the bright sun seemed to mock them.

"Talk to me." Maya was calm but firm. They should walk a bit before returning to the roastery. Her mother could handle things there for a while.

"Brittany put that pot in my locker, I know it!" Samantha's brown eyes filled with fire, and instantly reminded Maya of Samantha's father.

It wasn't the first time Maya had seen Sam Hutcherson in her daughter. She ignored the hiccup in her heartbeat. Flour and eggs. She dismissed the thought almost as quickly as it came. Almost.

"I'm sure they have cameras that can show—"

"Mom!" Samantha screeched. "Didn't you hear Mrs. P? Brittany is a *Stevenson*. The only reason she even got into trouble for shoplifting last time was because that shop owner had no idea who her mom was." She wiped her eyes and softened. "It doesn't matter what the cameras show."

"So you hit her? What does that solve?"

"Nothing—I know! But she can't keep getting away with that! Brittany has been trying to get me expelled since the whole shoplifting thing." Samantha's righteous fury petered out, and her voice became very small. "Why did I ever think I needed to be friends with her, anyway?"

Maya inhaled as deeply as she could, the crisp, cool air clearing her head. "Do you understand that her parents are going to press assault charges? And the school might expel you? These people have influence that I don't."

Fear filled Samantha's eyes and shook her voice. "You're not going to let them put me in jail, are you?"

"Oh, honey, of course not!" Maya stopped and pulled her daughter into a tight hug. "I believe you. And I'll do whatever I have to." Her heart fell even further into her belly as she realized exactly what she needed to do.

Maya was going to have to wake the past.

CHAPTER TWO
SAM

New York, 2012

SAM HUTCHERSON CLOSED the last document on his screen, pushed himself backward in his chair and stretched his long legs out on the desk before him. He leaned back and closed his eyes for a moment. He had been in meetings, dealing with environmentalists and oil companies, all day. It was good work, but now he needed the gym. The familiar buzz of his cell phone zapped his moment of Zen. Paige.

"Hi, sweetheart. I was just thinking about you." A yawn escaped him as he sat up and smiled into the phone.

Paige giggled at the other end. "Liar. You were thinking of a way to sneak out to the gym."

Sam laughed. "Busted."

"I have an appointment to look at linens for the tables. And I found an Indian chef who specializes in Indian fusion cuisine. I think your mom will love him." She paused. "I don't suppose you want to tag along?" Her smirk came through the phone.

"Not if I can help it. How about I take my beautiful fiancée to dinner instead, after I skip the linen thing?"

"You *are* going to show up at the wedding, aren't you?" Paige teased.

"Two hundred forty more days. The only question is, how will I wait that long?" Sam smiled as he envisioned his fiancée twirling a well-worried segment of her red hair. "It's just that you have such an eye for linens and dishes and flowers. It seems a shame to mar all that with my lawyerly opinion."

"Spoken like a true man of the law. Speaking of which—" her tone became serious "—how about that info from the environmental group?"

Sam ran a hand through his hair, dark curls thoroughly dislodged, and sighed. "Compelling. Now we'll have hard evidence against the gas company. They won't be happy." He tried to disguise his eagerness, but to no avail. He was pumped. "This could be the break I need, Paige. I'll finally have a chance to do some good here at the firm."

"Sam, I love that you're trying to help people, but let's not lose track of the big picture. Make sure you win. That'll put you where you need to be." She paused. "Ethan Felton sure as hell is going to try to beat you."

The edge in her voice was usually paired with an eye roll. Probably better he couldn't see it. "He can try. But he won't win." His sense of satisfaction from a job well-done today quickly faded. "Helping people, Paige, is a good thing. It *can* get you elected."

"Yes, yes. Fine." She sounded detached and seemed to have lost interest in the conversation. "I'll take you up on that dinner, so go. Enjoy the gym."

"Yeah, okay." He closed his eyes against the creep of agitation.

"Love you."

"Love you, too."

He hung up and stared at his screen saver. Maybe

she was right—nice guys don't always get elected. And he did need that congressional seat.

Sam's mother, Hema, had introduced him to Paige three years ago at a fund-raiser held in the art gallery Paige owned. Sam's father, John, had seemed to like Paige, and despite the fact that his mother was the one making the introductions, Sam had been quite taken with Paige. And that hadn't happened in a long time.

Paige was as intelligent and ambitious as any woman he'd ever known, and since they'd been together, she had been his partner in every way—she always made sure he saw the big picture and didn't stray from his goal, which was ultimately a seat in Congress and beyond.

Without conscious thought, Sam pulled a well-worn coin from his pocket that he always carried, and flipped it in the air. It landed with a small thud in the palm of his hand as it always did, the weight of it a comfort. Paige was right: maybe he should look out for his own interests more. He returned the coin to his pocket.

His phone buzzed again. *Dad.* Sam answered, a smile on his face. "Hey, Dad."

His father's smile came right through the phone. "Hey, Sammy. I need a favor."

"Sure. What do you need?"

"I went to that nursing home today to do a few house calls—and something's not right there. I'm thinking neglect—and maybe some of the employees are stealing. Is there something you can do about that—legally?"

Sam inhaled as if taking in patience from the very air around him. He fielded at least one of these kinds of requests from his father every couple months. "Dad, I'm not that kind of lawyer—I've told you."

"Yes, but these people have nobody looking out for

their interests. Their families are too busy, and no one really notices—"

"Dad, I'm in the middle of a huge case—and anyway, that's in Maryland, what do you want me to do from Manhattan? Isn't there someone else you can ask?"

"I'm asking you."

"But I'm not that kind of lawyer."

"Well, maybe you should be." Disappointment oozed through the phone as readily as the smile.

"Dad…" Sam tried to assuage his guilt by pointing out the obvious. "I can't be. Not if I want to run for office." He needed the big profile cases, not the little ones that didn't get noticed.

"Never mind. I'll figure something out."

John disconnected before Sam could say anything else. He stared out the window at the busy street below, and his mind wandered to that nursing home and its residents. Those poor people. But why was it his problem? Didn't he just decide it was best to take care of his own interests? He turned his attention to his phone, which was heavy with his father's request.

With a sigh, he sent his father a text. Send me the name of the place. I'll look into it and see if my friend Janice from law school is still in that area. Maybe she can help.

The response from his father was almost immediate. I knew I could count on you.

"Yeah, yeah," Sam said out loud. He shut down his computer and gathered his things, gym bag included. As he slipped his phone into his pocket and peered out the window down to Lexington Avenue, he made a mental note to research that facility. It was already dark, and Manhattan was lighting up for the evening. People pulled their coats tighter against the fall chill as they navigated the always vigorous New York City streets.

Sam put on his coat and headed down in the elevator. He nodded good-night to the night watchmen in the lobby and pushed the door open to the cool evening air outside. A brisk walk to the gym would be a nice warm-up, so he picked up his pace.

Thoughts about the case, the new evidence he'd found and the nursing home claimed his attention. So when he heard his name, in *that* voice, he started, nearly bumping into someone. He hadn't heard that voice in sixteen years, but it was never too far from his memory. As he turned, he knew he was being summoned by his past.

CHAPTER THREE
MAYA

New York, 2012

DESPERATION HAD MAYA waiting for Sam against the office building. A Google search had easily told Maya that Sam worked in this building as a corporate lawyer. Maya wasn't surprised, just disappointed.

Maya stayed in the building's shadow as she decided what to do. If he saw her first, he might just walk away, and that would not do. A review of her finances had confirmed what she knew: there wasn't any money for a lawyer. She fiddled with her pendant of *Ganesha*, the remover of all obstacles. *Well, here is a huge obstacle. Remove it.* She shivered in the evening chill.

She had considered making an appointment with Sam under a false name, but then everyone on his staff would have seen her. She didn't need that. He certainly didn't need that. All she needed was for him to take care of Samantha's situation and she'd be on her way. She had gone home with Samantha this morning and distracted herself with work until she could find an excuse to return to Manhattan. She guessed that Sam would leave the office sometime after six, and planned on waiting in this spot until he came out.

The office door opened, and her heart hammered in

her chest as if it recognized him before her eyes did. She could tell it was him, just from his walk. Confident without being cocky, Sam had the stride of an athlete. He was wearing a long coat over his suit, which did nothing to hide the fact that his shoulders were broader than she remembered. Not for the first time, she wondered how else he had changed in the past sixteen years. He turned his head slightly, and Maya swallowed hard as she took in his strong jawline and the weak-knee-inducing smile she remembered so well. Not to mention that dimple. Maybe this wasn't such a good idea. Maybe there was another way. What was she thinking, dredging up the past like this? He started walking away. No, she needed him for Samantha. Maybe she should have at least put on some lipstick.

Maya jolted back to reality. "Sam! Sam Hutcherson!"

He turned at the sound of her voice, and Maya's breath caught. She remembered how the brown of his eyes could blaze as if lit from inside, or smolder as if made from melted chocolate. She quickly flashed to the last time she'd seen them—hard as coal, red-rimmed, wounded. Tonight, his eyes were sharp. He dropped his bag.

"Sam, it's me." Her stomach fluttered.

Sam opened his mouth, but paused before he spoke. "Maya?" It was barely a whisper. "Maya." In an instant, his voiced changed, becoming stronger, cooler—indifferent. "What are you doing here?"

The sound of his voice, without the warmth it used to hold for her, was familiar and foreign all at the same time. Like a favorite song she hadn't heard in a long while, but to which she still knew the words. She took a few steps closer to him. Had he always been this tall?

She took in air to steady herself. "Sam." She held her hands palm-up, as if trying to calm an unpredictable animal, her voice soft but determined. "I know it's been a lifetime. I just need to talk to you."

He darted his eyes from his gym bag to her and back to the gym bag.

"Please, Sam, I know I have no right." She risked another step closer. "Trust me, I wouldn't be here if I had another choice." Her voice trembled, despite her confident words. The all-too-familiar burn built up behind her eyes as tears threatened to fall. She blinked them away.

"Trust you?" He turned the hard-as-coal eyes on her as he shifted his weight and crossed his arms in front of him.

"I'm desperate, Sam." It was from instinct rather than conscious thought that she waited for him to drop his hands to his pocket and tap his coin like he used to. He kept his gaze fixed on her, but sure enough, he released his arms and tapped his pocket. She met his eyes. Maya had seen Sam flip that coin countless times, always with the words, "Heads, we do this, tails, we do that." Though the last time she'd heard those words from him, she had left him.

He clenched his jaw and she could almost feel the heat radiating off him in waves of mistrust and suspicion. Understandable. She fought to maintain eye contact with him. With a pang of sadness, she realized that his face, once an open pathway to his emotions, was now unreadable to her. He shook his head and sighed, mumbling something to himself as he rubbed a hand over his mouth and chin. Did his hands still hold the calluses she remembered? Was his touch still as gentle? She flushed. Sam huffed and adjusted his bag.

"Fine," he said, finally. His tone was terse, but something about him had softened. "Coffee. I can do coffee." He indicated that she lead the way and they fell into step together.

Maya peeked at him through the corner of her eye as they walked in silence. Milky latte. She rolled her eyes at herself. She couldn't help it. The coffee roastery was her life-blood, so colors and scents came to her in terms of coffee. Sometimes even chai. She glanced at him again. Yes. His skin was the color of a milky latte and he had a slight five o'clock shadow.

She had expected that he wouldn't be thrilled to see her, but she hadn't expected him to still be so angry. It had been sixteen years, after all. She glanced up at him again and noticed something was different. His nose, maybe?

"Did you break your nose?" Small talk. Innocent enough, though she cringed at the idea of making small talk with *Sam*. They'd gone from lighthearted jabs to deep conversation on their first date.

Sam stared straight ahead and though they weren't touching, the air between them charged with tension. "You could say that." He grumbled at her and lengthened his stride.

Maya cleared her throat and looked away. She couldn't afford to be distracted by her reaction to him. That would only make this harder.

They ordered their coffees and Maya pulled out her credit card to pay.

"I got it." Sam stepped in front of her and handed the barista a twenty. When he had reached into his wallet to get the cash was beyond Maya. Some men just had that knack. Turned out Sam was one of them.

"No, it's fine. I came to you…" Maya placed her card in front of his bill.

Sam barely afforded her a glance. He moved his twenty in front of her card and flashed the barista a small smile. That did it. The barista flushed and took the twenty.

Maya rolled her eyes inwardly and put her credit card away. "Well, thank you."

They found a table in the back of the coffee shop and settled in with their coffees. Chatter spilled from nearby tables of professionally attired people conducting after-hours meetings. From the coffeehouse speakers, Taylor Swift adamantly proclaimed that "we are never ever *ever* getting back together." Sam sat back, his arms folded across his chest. Words froze in Maya's throat.

She shifted in her seat, noting Sam's tight jaw and tense muscles. She straightened. Now or never. "You seem to have done well." She brought her cup to her lips and took a sip, allowing the hot liquid to warm her.

"I get by."

"No, I mean—you being a lawyer—you're not doing exactly what you said you would be doing, but you seem to be doing well." Maya faltered, and quickly added, "I'm not here for money."

"I didn't think you were." Sam removed the lid from his cup and blew on the hot liquid.

"How's your dad?"

Sam sipped slowly. "Fine."

"And your mom?" Maya's voice cracked.

"What do you want, Maya?" Sam snapped at her.

She tensed. "I need your help with a legal matter."

Sam reverted to silence. He replaced the lid and took another sip of coffee.

"I know you're well connected, and I also know you're engaged to be married and that you're on your way to a congressional bid." Maya paused for a sip of her coffee.

"Google." Sam's response was terse; his gaze did not waver.

"Yes, well." She flicked her eyes to the table next to them as a woman in business attire pushed her laptop aside and placed her hand on top of her companion's. Maya shifted again in her seat. "Anyway, I want you to know that I'm not trying to disrupt your life in any way. I know we left things badly, but I'm desperate."

"We?" Sam raised his eyebrows at her.

Maya sighed. "Me, I—whatever. Not the point."

It was Sam's turn to sigh. "What *is* the point, Maya?" He gestured with his coffee cup; he was half finished.

Maya took a deep breath. *Just do it. It's for Samantha.* "The point is that I have a daughter who is being wrongly accused of drug possession and assault," she began. "The authorities and some parents want to press charges. The school may expel her. She was already in trouble for shoplifting, so I can't have anyone press charges." She paused for breath.

Sam furrowed his brow. "You have a daughter?"

"She's a really good kid. Just made a mistake, and ended up in the wrong place at the wrong time."

Sam said nothing.

For the first time, Sam leaned in toward her. But his face was still a mask. "When did you get married?"

Maya gulped her coffee and crossed and uncrossed her legs. She glanced at the neighboring table. The man reached out to the woman and tucked back a stray lock of hair that had come loose. She smiled at him. Maya cleared her throat. "I didn't."

Sam followed her gaze, and then quickly turned back to her, looking at her, for a moment, just as he used to all those years ago. Their eyes accidentally locked and the moment evaporated. He spoke slowly, as if yellow caution signs surrounded her. "Where's her dad? Why can't he help?"

Sweat beaded on her upper lip and forehead, and Maya fought the urge to wipe at it while still avoiding Sam's eyes. "He's not around." She rallied and took the offensive. "Why else would I come to you, after all this time?"

Sam stared at her, biting his bottom lip and shaking his head. Maya tucked a piece of hair behind her ear and opened her mouth, prepared to beg him for help.

"This is not my area," Sam said, his voice matter-of-fact. "Not to mention my fiancée would have a fit if she knew we were even talking." He stood, pulled out his wallet and handed Maya a card. "Give this person a call. Mention my name. She'll help you out."

Maya looked up at him, her heart racing and speech failing her. What was happening?

"No, Sam, wait!"

He put on his coat.

Panic made her voice squeak. "An attorney implies that I need the charges dropped. Can't we just get them never started?" Her stomach churned as Sam picked up his bag.

Sam shook his head. "No, Maya. Sorry." He studied her face for a moment and Maya caught a glimpse of something warm in his melted-chocolate eyes. It was gone as fast as it came. He started out the door.

Maya was momentarily frozen in her chair. Sam was her only option. Samantha could not be arrested. She grabbed her phone and chased him outside. He was almost half a block away. The sun had set completely and the fall chill had turned bitter cold, but she barely noticed it as she ran to catch up to him.

"Sam! Wait!"

Miraculously, he did.

"Look," Maya spoke quickly, lest he walk away. "I run the bakery. Well, it's not so much *just* a bakery anymore, it's—never mind, the point is that I don't have—the *funds* for an attorney right now."

"Maya, I'll call her, give her a heads-up that you'll be calling. I'll ask her to waive—"

"No, wait." Tears of desperation burned behind her eyes. *Don't cry. Don't cry.* "If they press charges, there's a good chance she'll have to go to juvie—"

"No, she won't. This person is very good at—"

"No, Sam, you don't get it!" Maya almost shouted at him as she fumbled with her phone. She was shivering and her phone wouldn't respond immediately to her touch—it was taking forever to get what she wanted on the screen.

"I think I understand the law," Sam said with exaggerated patience. "It'll be fine."

"Sam! Just stop talking and look!" She finally found the screen she wanted and shoved her phone in front of him. "This is Samantha. She turned *fifteen.* In *April.*"

Sam's features slowly froze as he took in the picture. His eyes held an expression Maya had never seen and couldn't define. Samantha's eyes were a dazzling chocolate brown, and she had curly, chestnut-colored hair. Her skin, like Sam's, was the color of a milky latte. Maya's heart thumped as she watched him turn pale and meet her eyes. *He knew.*

But she still had to say it. "She's yours, Sam. Samantha is our daughter."

CHAPTER FOUR
SAM

Maryland, 1996

SAM HASTILY LIFTED himself out of the pool when he heard the doorbell and grabbed a towel to dry off. The DJ on the radio announced he'd be playing the song that had inspired the latest dance craze, the Macarena, and his little cousins cheered. He did a couple quick steps with them and was still laughing when he opened the door.

The towel slipped from his grip and fell to the ground.

She was standing in the unseasonably sweltering Maryland heat in full business attire, sweating, but subtly. Her eyes widened in surprise as she looked from him to the towel and back. She stared, not speaking, into his eyes. Sam's heart raced.

He managed to pick up the towel and toss it over his shoulder as he folded his arms across his chest to gather himself and buy some time. It was her eyes that threw him. Honey-colored against her brown skin, they were shy and self-conscious. They turned slightly darker, and looked bolder, as she spoke.

"Hello. I'm Maya Rao. I'm here to see Mrs. Mehta regarding the nanny position." Her voice was confident and had the remnants of a British accent. Sam's mouth was suddenly unable to take direction from his brain, and so he remained silent.

"Ahem. Um, excuse me?" She furrowed her brow and leaned in toward him. "Are you all right?"

"Oh, I'm fine." Brain and mouth reinstated communication and he leaned as casually as he could against the doorframe, as if it had been his intention to be silent. He grinned at her in what he hoped was a slow and confident grin, as opposed to an idiotic gawk. "I just had to hear that accent again," he said, finding himself at last. "It's as beautiful as you."

She raised her eyebrows at him, her eyes going cold. "If you could just let Mrs. Mehta know that I'm here."

Sam uncrossed his arms and turned his body to step aside and make room for her to pass. "Come in. She's my aunt." Maya brushed by him, bringing with her the scent of honeysuckle, sending an electrical current through him.

Wet footsteps and a chirpy voice announced the arrival of his girlfriend, Bridget. "Hey, Sam." She wrapped a possessive arm around him. "What's going on?"

When Sam didn't move or speak, Maya turned to Bridget. "Hi, I'm Maya. I'm here about the nanny position."

Bridget pursed her lips into a smile. "Oh." Sam felt her arm tighten around him as she waved her free hand toward the back of the house. "Mrs. Mehta is back by the pool." She glanced at Sam fondly. "He's helping his uncle with renovations." She turned to Maya, her voice hard again. "But he doesn't live here."

"I'll take you back," Sam said, at last able to speak and move at the same time. He unwrapped himself from Bridget and led Maya to the pool, Bridget pointedly trailing behind. "Monica-*mami*, there's a nanny candidate to see you." He felt Maya looking at him as he addressed his aunt, but when he turned to face her, Maya's attention was on Monica-*mami*. It happened from time to time. He didn't really look Indian, so people just didn't expect him to use Indian terms for family.

His aunt looked up from where she had been reapplying her daughter's sunscreen, her blond ponytail bouncing along with her smile. "Hello." She extended a hand to Maya. "Monica Mehta. Nice to meet you."

Sam stood by, mesmerized by Maya's smile. A silence fell over the area and he realized all three women were staring at him. His aunt's green eyes held a smirk in them. "Sam," she said, "could you and Bridget play with Ben and Niki while I speak with Maya?"

He flushed and hastily turned to Bridget. "Sure, c'mon, Brig." Sam grabbed a grudging Bridget's hand and they headed for the pool.

BACK AT HIS parents' house, Sam found himself sitting out on the deck in the middle of the night holding an untouched glass of cold milk. He had considered a beer, but he was starting the bathroom remodel tomorrow at his uncle's and had to be at the hardware store early the next morning, and he already wasn't sleeping. The incessant chirping of crickets barely registered and he started, as the glass, wet with condensation, nearly slipped from his grip.

He had stayed at his uncle's house, long after Bridget and Maya had each left, to have dinner with Ben and Niki. His cousins had been unable to talk about anything but their new nanny, whom Monica-*mami* had hired on the spot. Maya had won awards in swimming.

Maya lived in Queens, but she was living here with her uncle and aunt for the summer—and how *cool* was that? Maya had an amazing accent, didn't she, Sammy? Sam had remained silent, simply nodding his head, trying not to be thrilled by each additional piece of information the children gave him.

It was the accent, he told himself. Two days of listening to it and she'd be just another pretty face. That was it. What else could it be? He tried to ignore the little voice in the back of his head that insisted that no other girl had ever kept him up in the middle of the night—unless she was in his bed.

He set the glass down next to him and stared out at his battered old childhood play set. He and his brother had climbed on it and jumped off it as children. It would be nice to still have a brother to talk to, but the accident had changed everything. The play set was rusted, with a fraying rope and dented slide. The swing was simply two chains; the seat had long since broken off. He couldn't convince his parents to get rid of it. Mostly, it was his mother who refused to part with it. After all, Arjun had played on it.

He chugged the milk and went to bed.

SLEEP HAD NOT come until close to sunrise, so he yawned as he entered his uncle's house and perked up at the scent of brewing coffee. "Sudhir-mama," he called out to his uncle, "I'm really sorry. I know I'm late but there was a line—" He froze as he entered the kitchen and found Maya mixing something in a large bowl.

She flicked those liquid-honey eyes at him over the bowl, and Sam's pulse quickened. "Your uncle already left for the office, but said that you knew what to do."

She shook her head at his blank stare. "With the bathroom remodel?"

The kitchen let in a good amount of light, so despite the dark wood cabinetry, mornings here were sun-filled and bright. The addition of Maya to this place unnerved him so much it was like the simple and automatic act of breathing required thought. Her T-shirt and shorts grazed her curves in the most tantalizing way, and her hair was trapped in a ponytail. Sam had to tame his urge to free her hair from its imprisonment. The silky-brown of her skin contrasted so pleasantly with the honey in her eyes that Sam didn't even care that there was a taunt in them. Inhale. "Um, yeah sure. I mean I do. Know." Exhale. "I do know what to do." He didn't move.

A wisp of dark curl had escaped the ponytail. She tucked it behind her ear as she furrowed her brow in irritation. The action was simple, just tucking away a flyaway piece of hair, but everything about it had Sam entranced, from the graceful movement of her hand to her face, to fingers grasping the dark, silken curl as they pushed it back and over her ear.

"So go do it then."

Right. He turned and nearly bumped into the doorframe. Real smooth. When had he become such a dork?

CHAPTER FIVE
MAYA

Maryland, 1996

MAYA OPENED THE oven and released the deep, rich aroma of freshly baked chocolate chip cookies.

"Mmm, that smells amazing." Sam's voice was almost as mellow as the melted chocolate.

Maya did her best to ignore Sam. But how did he manage to make chocolate chip cookies sound sexy?

She had an *awareness* of Sam's presence, as if her senses were suddenly heightened when he was around. Which was annoying, because the fact that he had flirted with her within five seconds of meeting her while he still had a girlfriend did not impress her in the least. Maybe some boys thought they were good-looking enough to get away with that, but Maya wasn't buying it.

There probably wasn't a functioning brain to go with that body, anyway. Not that she'd noticed Sam's body. Or his hair. Definitely had not noticed the knee-weakening smile.

She'd only ever had one boyfriend, which might have been unusual for your average twenty-two-year-old college graduate, but it wasn't necessarily unusual for a twenty-two-year-old first-generation Indian girl. Especially if her mother was Sunita Rao.

Maya had dated Vinay behind her mother's back for about two months in her junior year of high school. She'd made the mistake of kissing him on school grounds on the day that her mother had parent-teacher conferences. When her mother caught them, she lectured Maya for days about her priorities, the dangers of falling in love so young and the fact that boys were not to be trusted, anyway. Sunita had made it abundantly clear that she would be the one to find Maya the proper mate—so Maya need not concern herself with it. She also called the boy's parents and insisted that they rein in their son and keep him away from Maya, lest she call the authorities. Maya became the joke at school. As a result, she simply avoided boys and focused her energies on her studies, continuing to do so all through culinary school.

Ultimately, this was fine with Maya, as she had plans. She was getting out of the bakery. Her mother had opened it when Maya was about ten, a couple of years after Maya's father had left them. The bakery had become their livelihood as well as their home. But while Maya loved baking, she wanted more from life than just running a small hometown bakery. So as for her mother finding her a husband, she figured she'd deal with that when the time came.

Sam continued to flirt with her as she placed the cookies on the cooling rack. Her back was to him when the thumping of rapid footsteps made her turn.

Niki emerged in the kitchen in her *Blue's Clues* nightgown, running as fast as her little feet could carry her. Her dark hair hung in her eyes, wild from sleep.

"Maya! Sammy! Ben says he doesn't feel good. He says his tummy hurts."

Sam was at the steps before Maya could move. She gathered Niki and followed close behind. Ben had been in bed with a fever since Maya got to work. Niki must have woken up and gone to check on him, as was her habit.

"Ben," Sam called out as he reached Ben's room. "Hang on, buddy, I got you." Sam leaned down and picked up a very green-looking little boy. "Hold on, okay? We have to use the bathroom in your mom and dad's room."

Maya and Niki cleared a path, but Sam had taken no more than three steps down the hall before Ben started to heave. Sam quickly ducked into the hall bathroom— the one being renovated—just in time for Ben to vomit all over the both of them and the unfinished tile job.

Maya froze.

Niki held her nose. "Ugh, Maya. It's stinky."

Maya put down the little girl. "Go wait in your room." Niki scampered off and Maya grabbed a paper towel roll and a couple bath towels from the hall closet. When she returned, she found Sam sitting on the edge of the tub, Ben still in his arms. The vomiting had stopped, but Sam continued to hold the boy, and spoke in slow, soothing tones.

"Feel better, buddy?" Sam said.

Ben nodded. "I'm sorry, Sammy. I got it all over you." Tears of shame filled his eyes.

"Oh, come on, now. That was some awesomely gross throw-up. Nothing to cry about." Sam's voice was soft and playful.

Ben smiled through his tears. "It really is gross, huh?"

"Trust me, I know!" He turned and caught Maya watching him. He flushed and promptly returned his attention to Ben, but in her surprise, she was unable to look away from him.

Sam picked up Ben. "Let's get you into the tub."

Maya reached out to help him.

"Stop." Sam shook his head. "You'll get it on you. I'll just clean us both up in the tub."

There wasn't a trace of the playful or flirtatious Sam she'd known for the past few weeks. "You sure?"

"Yes. Just leave all that stuff here. I'll take care of it." He looked her in the eye. "Thanks."

Maya put the paper towels and the bath towels where he indicated, but remained frozen to the spot.

"Are you going to watch me take my clothes off?" Sam winked. Ben giggled.

And he was back. Maya threw him a glare and turned on her heel.

"Maya, did you bake? I smell cookies." Niki was waiting in her room.

"Well, how about if we get you dressed and maybe you can have one?" Maya brushed aside some hair and found the little girl's giggling face. "There you are!" Niki grinned.

This was Maya's favorite part of the day. As Niki opened her closet, Maya leaned against the doorframe for a fashion show, keeping close tabs on the sounds coming from the bathroom.

"I want to wear a pink dress."

"Sure. Pick one." The girl had at least five pink dresses.

Niki could have been Sam's little sister, as opposed

to just a cousin, as they had the same skin tone, ready smile and soft chocolate brown eyes. Jeez, Maya really needed to get a life outside the bakery. Niki proceeded to try on each of her pink dresses, asking Maya for her opinion on each one.

"Which one, Maya?"

"Whatever you want."

"Does that go for me, too?" Sam's breath grazed her ear from where he stood—too close behind her.

Maya tried to ignore his clean scent as well as the heat from his body and focused on narrowing her eyes as she turned to face him. It seemed easier to not look at his face, what with his silly grin and laughing eyes. Not to mention the damp curls. But he was wearing an old concert T-shirt that was almost worn through, and had conformed nicely to the muscles in his arms and chest over time. She readjusted her gaze to his face and swallowed hard. *That dimple!* There was nowhere to look at him that was safe. "Sure, you can wear the pink dress if you want. It might be a step up from that T-shirt."

He feigned hurt and shock. "What's wrong with Hootie?"

Maya rolled her eyes and walked into the room to help Niki with her chosen dress.

"Seriously, Maya." His voice was soft, almost hesitant. "Go out with me." Like he was afraid she would say no like she had every day for the past two weeks. Valid concern. The amusement had left his eyes and was replaced with—hope? "What do you say?"

That was new. She smiled sweetly. "I'd love to, Sam."

"You would?" He sounded as if he couldn't believe his luck.

"Sure, except for the fact that *you still have a girl-*

friend!" She glared at him, doing her best to convey the disgust she felt at him actually asking her out—repeatedly—while he was dating Bridget.

"So, if I didn't have a girlfriend, you'd say yes?" He frowned, considering this.

Maya shrugged. "Sure? Why not?" What was the likelihood of that happening?

"He doesn't have a girlfriend." Niki's muffled voice came from under her dress.

Maya's heart pounded, and she fought to keep her face calm. "What?"

She kneeled to undo the buttons so the dress would go over the little girl's head. Once Niki's head was through, the girl continued. "Sammy doesn't have a girlfriend anymore. They broke up *ages* ago." Niki paused dramatically and gave an eye roll worthy of a teenager. "We didn't like her. We like you." She leaned in toward Maya's ear. "And so does Sammy."

"So it's a done deal." Victory colored his eyes a dazzling brown as he grinned like a little boy. "I'll pick you up at seven."

Niki laughed with glee and ran to Sam for a high five.

"Is she your wingman?" Maya attempted indignation at being tricked, even as her heart lifted.

Sam was unapologetic. "She's great at it!" He picked up Niki. "Two cookies for you, kiddo!"

CHAPTER SIX
SAM

New York, 2012

AT THE RESTAURANT later that night, Sam pushed at his shrimp and rice, not really seeing it, not really caring to eat it. He made the appropriate sounds when Paige paused in her diatribe about the latest debacle in the wedding plans.

"Hey." Sam started at Paige's hand on his. "Where are you?"

"I'm sorry." He squeezed her hand. "It's that case... and my dad wants me to look into possible nursing home fraud..." He sat up and pointedly focused on her, as if to make up for the lie. "But I'm back—you were saying?"

Paige shook her head. "Honestly, I love your dad, but doesn't he understand how important your work is? You can't be running around doing pro bono stuff—"

"It's fine, Paige. I really don't mind. Now, you were saying?" Arguing with Paige about small-time lawyering was not going to help his distraction.

She sipped her wine and continued her story about being sent the wrong linens, and how the centerpieces wouldn't work now. They were trying to combine a Hindu ceremony with a Catholic ceremony, which, as it turned out, was no small feat. Luckily, Sam's mother and Paige both loved a challenge, as well as each other, so Sam let them be.

Sam's insides trembled, and his thoughts drifted again, making it nearly impossible for him to follow Paige's story. A daughter? He and Maya had a daughter? Maya had offered to bring him Samantha's birth certificate as proof of her date of birth, but he didn't need it—he knew she was telling the truth. Sam forced himself to participate in conversation with Paige until they got home.

Paige immediately attended to paperwork and phone calls for the gallery, so Sam tried to do some research on that nursing home in Maryland, but he found himself staring at the graphic of a soccer ball bouncing around on his sleeping computer screen. He shook the distractions from his head, recalling the skills he had used to focus on his studies after Maya had left him.

Hours later, he lay in bed and, without work distractions, thoughts of Maya and Samantha surfaced once more. How could it be that he had a daughter? How could Maya have kept this from him all these years? Anger mixed with his confusion. She must have been pregnant when she'd left. Further conversation with Maya had ended in only more questions. She'd deftly avoided answering them by focusing on the details of Samantha's troubles.

He flipped the pillow over and lay on his back, staring at the ceiling. Even the sound of Paige's rhythmic breathing couldn't drive away thoughts of Maya.

Sam quietly got out of bed so as not to disturb his fiancée. He pulled on an old and worn Columbia Law sweatshirt against the night's chill, and ambled to the kitchen to stare into the open fridge for the cure to his restlessness. Not finding it there, he went to the bar and poured two fingers of bourbon.

Sam sat in the chair by the floor-to-ceiling window, twenty-three stories up, and stared out at the vibrant, moonlit city below. The first sip of bourbon warmed him but failed to soothe. Maya had texted him Samantha's picture, and he pulled it up on his phone. She undoubtedly had his eyes and coloring, but Maya was there, too. Subtly, in the cheekbones, maybe the chin. More likely in that intangible way that mothers and daughters look alike, even when their features don't match.

He closed his eyes and took a second, larger sip as he sank into the plushness of the chair. The alcohol reached into his fingertips as well as deep into memories long suppressed. He hadn't made Maya any promises, he'd only said that he would see what he could do. One thing was for sure—Samantha was definitely their daughter.

By the third swallow from that glass he knew sleep would not come, so he surrendered to memories.

A warm hand on his shoulder pulled him from his reverie. "Hey, you. Can't sleep?" Paige's red hair was tousled in the most becoming way. It was almost as if she made it look that way on purpose.

Sam grinned at her as he turned the screen of his phone away from her and took her hand. "Yeah."

"Bourbon? In the middle of the night?" She yawned and came around to sit on his lap. "Must be serious." Her green eyes were filled with sleep. She curled up and rested her head on his shoulder. "What's going on?"

Sam looked down at the top of her head and clicked

off his phone screen. "It's just work. Nothing really."
He stroked her strawberry-scented hair. "Come. Let's
go to bed."

CHAPTER SEVEN
MAYA

New York, 2012

MAYA HAD THE giant mixer started by 3:00 a.m. Might as well get some work done, since she wasn't sleeping anyway. Lyrics from her earbuds taunted her, telling her that now she was just somebody that he used to know. She turned on the roaster and added the coffee beans. This October had been cooler than most, boosting coffee sales, and come November, things would soon get crazy-hectic at the bakery. The coffee shop. Maya shook her head at herself. She had changed the focus of her mother's business from pure bakery to bakery plus coffee shop over ten years ago, but she still thought of Sweet Nothings as *the bakery*. To be fair, baking still happened, but only a couple cookie varieties and specialty cakes. Maya now served specialty coffee as well as specialty tea. Specifically, traditional Indian chai, in all its variations. As it was, she had more cookie orders this year than any year previous. And the specialty cake orders were increasing. She needed more space.

Telling Sam he was Samantha's father had never been part of the plan. She had hoped he would help her out for old times' sake. Asking him was risky, she knew, but unless she won the lottery, or sold part of the business, there was no way she could come up with the money for a lawyer. Not to mention the damage the charges would do to Samantha's life.

The giant mixer churned hard. She added chocolate chips and the motor waned a bit under the added struggle.

"Come on," she urged the mixer. "Don't fail me now." As if responding to her, the mixer stuttered, then whirred into rhythmic motion. "Good girl." She patted the side of the mixer as if it were a favorite pet.

"Are you talking to the machinery again, *beta*?" Her mother always teased her about this, but Maya had caught her mother doing the same more than once over the course of the years.

"Mum, you know how it is—whatever it takes." She grimaced. "There's a fresh shipment of cinnamon for the chai masala in the cupboard."

She checked on the roaster, grabbing a bean to taste. The instructions always specified a certain amount of roasting time that was optimum for flavor, but nothing was as good as her palate. She hadn't been the star pupil in culinary school for nothing.

Maybe it was because she'd just seen Sam, or maybe it was because she was waiting for his answer, but the sweet smell of chocolate chips and vanilla, mixing with the butter, flour and sugar of the cookie dough, all carried on the aroma of roasting coffee beans, took her back to that summer in Maryland. It took her back to Sam.

Maya finished the cookies, allowed the beans to cool, and moved on to her next project. Samantha finally awoke and came down from their apartment, which was located above the shop. She took care of the customers, while Maya ground the coffee beans and the remaining spices for the ginger masala chai, and her mother took over the baking. The day passed with still no word from Sam.

Maya started the closing process. She checked her phone—again. She had called Sam twice already, but he hadn't called back yet. She finished the sweeping, locked the door and set the alarm. Still no response from Sam. She tightened her lips at the phone. He had specifically asked her not to leave a voice mail. He promised he would get back to her.

She leaned against the counter and looked around her shop. Her mother had started this bakery shortly after moving to the States as a single mom. She'd been determined to never be dependent on a man again, so she'd learned how to run a business and provided for herself and her daughter. Maya and her mother had worked hard for every nail, every tile, and every piece of wood in this bakery-turned-roastery. There was a time when Maya had had bigger dreams. But all that had changed. And now all her dreams for herself and Samantha were dependent on the success of Sweet Nothings. Well, most of them. In any case, she really couldn't sell any portion of it.

She dialed Sam's cell again. Forget their agreement. She needed an answer. This time she left a message.

CHAPTER EIGHT
SAM

Maryland, 1996

THE ENGINE OF the '89 Honda Civic didn't exactly purr, but to Sam, it was the sweet sound of hard work paying off. He had saved up for this car and he loved everything about it, from the powder blue color to the hatchback trunk. He didn't even care that the passenger-side door occasionally stuck. It was nearly seven years old, but the previous owner had cared for it, so the car ran beautifully.

The clock said 6:55 p.m. when he stepped out of the car and gently closed the door, looking up at Maya's uncle's house. A wraparound front porch with a swing, chipping white paint and a fairly well-cared-for lawn. He absently patted the car, as if it were doling out confidence, before approaching the two steps to the front porch. He fingered the coin in his pocket while he rang the bell.

The sound of giggling reached him from behind the door. A teenage girl with a lovely smile and bronze skin opened the door and continued giggling, stopping only when she introduced herself. "I'm Sejal, Maya's cousin," she said gesturing for him to come in.

Sam startled at his own reflection in an ornate hall mirror and quickly shifted his gaze to a pink-walled dining room to his left. A pink tablecloth covered the table, and in the center was a stainless steel tray holding two small jars. It looked just like the one his mother left on their dining table. The jars were home to spicy lime or sweet mango pickles that everyone had with every meal.

His attention was diverted back to the giggling girl as she called out. "Maya! He's hee-ere!" The young girl stood and watched him, her eyes sparkling with delight, but there was no sign of Maya.

Sam was starting to sweat when a stern-looking man, old enough to be his father, ambled into the hallway. The man looked Sam up and down with suspicious, bulging, black eyes. After seeming to determine that it was safe, he thrust out his hand. "Deepak Shah. I am Maya's uncle." His Indian accent was mild, and his tone was firm and decidedly unfriendly. "Her mother is my elder sister."

Sam clasped the man's hand firmly and smiled, hoping that his hand was dry. "Sam Hutcherson, sir. Nice to meet you."

The older man grunted. "Hutcherson?" He seemed to repress a smile. "Not John, is it?" He placed a brown hand on his healthy belly. "You are not *Dr.* John Hutcherson's son?"

Sam shifted his weight. Where was Maya? "Yes, sir, I am. I believe you might also know my uncle, Sudhir Mehta?"

This time, the uncle's smile made a small appearance, and then disappeared behind another grunt. "Of course, I know Sudhir." He did not elaborate. Endless silence floated between them, making Sam's stomach clench. The uncle continued his assessing stare.

The familiar aroma of onions and garlic sautéing

with mustard seeds and cumin reached him from just beyond the pink room, and calmed him enough to break the silence. "Are you also an internist, sir?"

The older man grunted. "Cardiology."

Great. He'd just borderline insulted the man. Sam turned to the cousin. "What high school do you go to?"

She giggled again, but she obliged. "Wilde Lake."

"Oh yeah? I graduated—"

Apparently, knowing where Sam had graduated high school was not at the top of Deepak Shah's priorities, as he chose that moment to bellow, "Maya!"

A breathless Maya came bustling out of the kitchen and into the foyer. "Hi!" Her cheeks were flushed in a most pleasing manner. Sam had to stop himself from staring.

"Sorry," she said, apology in her eyes, "but all of a sudden, my aunt 'happened to need' my baking expertise." She made air quotes and cast an accusing glance at her uncle. "Know anything about that, Deepak-mama?"

Deepak looked slightly abashed and his demeanor softened. "Truthfully, my sister is very intimidating, and if I am to allow you to go—" he jerked his head in Sam's direction "—I need to check him out, no? You are like a daughter to me, beta, after all." He shrugged slightly. "I know his father and his uncle. They are good people." He put his arm around Maya and gave her an affectionate squeeze. "Go, if you must." He looked at Sam and pointed a firm finger. "Midnight."

"Yes, sir." Sam intended to make the most of the next five hours.

Ten minutes later, they were still laughing at Deepak-mama's strictness, and his fear of Maya's mother as they pulled into the crowded lot at the movie theater.

"My mom is a force—so if you turn out to be a serial killer—she'll blame Deepak-mama for not properly researching you."

"Well, I'm not a serial killer, so your mama is safe."

"Isn't that what all serial killers say?"

She was smart and funny. Sure that his grin was idiotic, he changed the subject. "How about *Mission: Impossible*? I haven't had a chance to see it."

"I saw it." Her eyes lit up. "Tom Cruise was amazing. Sorry." She didn't sound apologetic. She laughed.

"How about *Dragonheart*? Can't go wrong with Sean Connery."

"But how about actually seeing Sean Connery, as opposed to just hearing him? As in *The Rock*?"

"You like the blow-up-stuff movies, huh?" A girl who shared his action-movie obsession? Sam bit the inside of his cheek to contain his excitement. He opened his door then turned back to her. "Don't move."

Sam hopped out of the car and in a few strides was on Maya's side. She shrugged as he opened her door. "I like all kinds of movies." Her nose wrinkled adorably when she smiled, and her mouth turned up just a little bit more on one side than the other.

When she stood he noticed, as he had before, that she needed to tilt her chin up to look at him.

"Thanks," she said as he shut the door behind her. "But I wouldn't mind seeing Sean shoot at things."

"But dragons and swords and honor? How can one resist?"

Maya's grin was friendly, but there was no mistaking the firmness behind it. "Well, then it seems we're at an impasse."

"I have a suggestion." He pulled the coin from his pocket. "We'll flip for it."

"Are you serious? You begged me for a date, and now we're going to flip for the movie?"

"I did not beg." Sam couldn't suppress his smile. "I was *persistent*. And yes, we're going to flip for it, unless you want to give in?"

"Flip your coin."

Sam did his best to appear serious. "This coin was a gift, and it has never steered me wrong. Heads, we see Sean shoot things. Tails, we listen to Sean as a dragon." He flipped the coin and caught it in his palm.

Maya leaned in to see. He could feel the heat from her body and his heart raced at having her so close.

"Oh! Heads!" She looked up at him, victorious. "Sean shooting things it is!"

Sam narrowed his eyes at the coin. "This coin has never failed me…"

"Ha," Maya laughed. "Until now." She took a moment to gloat. "C'mon, or we'll miss the beginning."

Sam entered the theater behind Maya, unable to believe his luck at actually being on a date with her.

Maya, it turned out, whispered to herself at the movies. She became so completely entranced by the world on the screen that she was almost oblivious to the immediate world around her. She gasped in horror, whimpered in terror, dropped her mouth in outrage, and whispered, "No way! That is so wrong."

Sam watched her as much as he watched the movie. He watched as the light from the screen darkened and he could just make out her profile. She sat erect in her chair in anticipation. He watched as gunfire made her jump and she dropped their popcorn on the floor.

"I'm sorry," she whispered as she bent down to get the bucket. Her bag fell from her lap just as she reached for the bucket, knocking it over and causing it to roll away under the seat in front of her.

From the darkness came a few shushes.

"Oh, no." She looked wide-eyed at Sam. "I should've mentioned that I'm a hazard at the movies."

Sam's body shook with suppressed laughter. He didn't trust himself to speak.

"Are you laughing at me?"

Sam cleared his throat as silently as possible and held up his hands in surrender. "No. Of course not. You just seem so graceful in everything else…"

"It's an act." She twisted her mouth and shrugged. "I'm actually clumsy—all the time. That's the dirty truth of it."

A few more shushes. Maya widened her eyes and put her index finger to her lips to shush Sam, who wasn't even speaking. "The movie." She winked at him and returned her attention to the screen.

Sam sat back in his chair. He spent the rest of the movie watching Maya. She was beautiful and clumsy and her smile was sudden and unexpected. She twisted her hair absently as she concentrated on the screen, shifting forward and then leaning back in her seat from time to time. Sam smiled to himself. She could not sit still.

Every so often, she would turn toward him and catch his eye. In those moments, Sam should have flushed with embarrassment at being caught staring at her, but she would flash her eyes or grin and all thought of trying to be cool and smooth left him, and he was bared open to her.

"That was amazing!" Maya laughed as they exited the theater. She bumped his shoulder. "You have to admit it was fantastic."

Sam opened his mouth to protest, but found she was right. He laughed with her. "Yes, it was fantastic." He looked at her sideways. "I told you that coin never fails me."

"Next time, we'll see your fantasy flick," she said. "I actually enjoy dragons and swords and honor."

His heart flipped. Did she say next time? Sam turned to catch her eye. His next words were just loud enough for the two of them to hear. "Next time, then."

He tried to hold her gaze, but Maya flushed and looked away. "I thought you said something about great places to eat in Columbia? Didn't you mention a place with excellent tacos?" She shrugged. "Let's do that."

Sam pulled out his coin. "Heads, we have tacos, tails, we do pizza."

Again, Maya was forced to move closer to Sam to see the result. Her long dark hair fell in waves and smelled of summer. A soft, rebellious piece brushed Sam's hand as she bent down closer to see the coin in the dark. She tucked the flyaway strand behind her ear and looked up at him, victorious once more. "Heads again! Tacos it is. Are you sure this coin never steers you wrong?"

Her face was close enough to his that he could feel her breath. He couldn't help the crooked grin that took over his face, as he looked her in the eye. "I'm sure."

Maya cleared her throat and took a step back from Sam. She fidgeted with her bag. "Well, let's go then."

The place was a hole-in-the-wall reputed to have authentic food. The best chorizo taco ever, in Sam's opinion. "So, I forgot to mention that there isn't a place to sit," he said, as they walked out of the restaurant. "I know exactly where to go." He tried to look mysterious. Didn't girls like mysterious men?

Ten minutes later, he pulled into a lot facing a lake. "Lake Kittamaqundi." He beamed at her with a glint in his eye. "Don't move."

He got out of the car and walked around to her side. She followed his movements and he thrilled to know she was watching him. He opened her door.

"Thanks again," she said. "You know, it's not every guy who would open a car door for a girl, when she's perfectly capable of opening it for herself."

"What have I been trying to tell you?" Sam stepped back to open the hatchback. The spicy aroma of salsa greeted them. "I'm not every guy." He picked up the food and a couple blankets. "And it's not about whether a girl is capable of opening the door herself."

Maya peeked into the back of the car. "A first aid kit, jumper cables, a couple jugs of water and an umbrella." There was a twinkle in her eye as she teased him. "It's almost like you're a Boy Scout."

He raised his eyebrows. "Not almost. I actually am an Eagle Scout."

She smiled wide, clearly impressed. Hmm. Impressing Maya Rao was a heady feeling. He'd have to try to keep doing that. She took the blankets and indicated that he lead the way. "So what's it about then?"

"What's what about?"

"If it's not about whether the girl can open the door herself?"

"It's about respect." Sam stopped at the place he'd planned, waiting for Maya's approving nod. When he got it, he helped her put down the blankets. "And honor." He took out the fragrant disposable boxes of chorizo tacos, beans and rice, while Maya arranged all the smaller sauce containers in a logical and organized fashion. It was his turn to be impressed. But everything about her was impressive.

"It's about—" he shrugged his shoulders as heat rose to his face "—being nice." He cleared his throat and almost mumbled, "And sometimes the passenger-side door sticks."

Maya smiled, but did not laugh. "Ah."

"But mostly the being nice stuff."

They sat at the top of a deep amphitheater, with broad grass steps that looked down on a central stage. Behind the stage was the lake, black glass in the moonlight. There were no events at the amphitheater tonight, just a few families and couples having a late picnic as they were. Electronic beeps and bongs from a Nintendo mixed with the sounds of crickets and soft laughter. A few feet away, a streetlamp shed a mild glow of light around them. The night was humid, but a light breeze from the lake cooled them as they ate their spicy meal.

"You're right." Maya paused between bites. "This is incredible."

Sam was trying—unsuccessfully—not to make a mess of his taco as Maya fell silent for a moment. She had finished eating and sat with her knees bent and legs shifted over to one side. She opened her mouth as if to speak but then closed it, as if keeping the words from escaping.

"What?" Sam grimaced at her. "Am I grossing you out?"

"No, not at all." Her smile was automatic.

"What? Just ask away." He tried to hold his hands

out to indicate that he was an open book, but failed to complete the action because he needed both hands on the taco. "That's what first dates are about, aren't they?" He looked her in the eye and softly stated, "And we are on a *first* date."

Sam continued to navigate his dinner, as Maya appeared to contemplate her question. Finally, she inhaled deeply and let the words out. "Your uncle. You call him 'Mama,' like I call my uncle. He's Indian."

"Yeah, he's my mother's brother, like yours." Sam ate the last bite and wiped his hands on napkins, resisting the urge to lick his fingers.

Maya shifted her position. "Well, your last name is Hutcherson, which isn't Indian. So I was just wondering..." She trailed off.

Sam glanced over at her, a smirk playing at his lips. "Wondering what?" He leaned into her and whispered, "Half-Indian wouldn't be enough?"

Her eyes widened in horror and she started to protest, but stopped. Instead she pursed her lips at him. "Or maybe too much."

This girl was too much. He lifted his cup to her, laughter on his lips. "Touché."

She lifted her cup to his and focused those honey eyes on him. "Well...?"

He put his cup down and sat back, legs outstretched, and leaned back on his arms. He loved telling this story. "My mom is Indian, from Gujarat. My dad is not Indian," he explained. "My mom had come to the States for college, which is where they met." Sam paused as he imagined his father as a young man, smitten. The image always made him happy. "My dad insists it was love at first sight. So he learned a few lines of Gujarati before he even attempted to speak to her." He turned to face Maya, pride in his voice. "The first words he ever said to her were in Gujarati."

"Well?" Maya nearly squeaked with suspense. "What did he say?"

"He asked if he could walk her to class. She was so taken aback, she said yes." Sam chuckled. His parents had their moments, like any other couple, but no one could deny they loved each other. Sam only wished to be so lucky. "They fell in love and she never looked back. Sudhir-mama joined her in America a few years later, also to go to college. He met my aunt, Monica-*mami* there. The rest is history." Sam looked at Maya, who seemed charmed by this true-life love story. Maybe his wish was coming true.

Sam checked his watch. "Speaking of mamas, we're getting close to your curfew," he said. "And as you have already promised me a next time, let's not mess that up."

When they arrived at her uncle's house, Maya invited Sam to sit with her on the porch steps. "I'm early," she said.

Sam glanced toward the door, half expecting her uncle to be standing there, a sentry guarding his niece's virtue. The door was shut.

Maya showed him her watch. "Ten 'til midnight. Plus, technically, I'm home."

He didn't even bother to try to hide his pleasure, eager to be in her presence, excited to prolong their evening.

Maya turned her head up to the night sky and sighed. "What a perfect summer night." Sam loved how her neck and jaw were exposed when she tilted her head and her hair fell away. She had no idea how beautiful she was. He had to hold himself back from reaching over to trace her jawline. Unwillingly, he tore his eyes away from her to follow her gaze.

It *was* the perfect summer night, but it had less to do with the warmth of the night and the clear sky displaying the stars than with the fact that he was sitting beside a girl whose company he knew he would crave when he didn't have it. After a moment, he felt her eyes on him, and he turned to face her. She did not look away. "Ben and Niki look like you. Except Ben's eyes. He has his mom's eyes." She bit her bottom lip. "You're really good with them."

Sam puffed his chest out. "Ah, well. It comes naturally." He laughed at himself. "They're amazing kids. It's easy to love them." His voice softened as he leaned toward her, resting his elbows on his knees. "They're as close to siblings as I have now."

Maya nodded. "They did tell me that you were their only big brother—now."

Sam tensed and flicked his gaze to her. "Did they?"

Maya's words tumbled out quickly, as if trying to erase what she had just said. "They did, but I shouldn't have said anything. It's really none of my business. It's just you pulled out that coin, and I got the feeling it was…"

Sam remained silent. Maya was watching him, waiting patiently for his answer. What was it about her that made him want to tell her about something he hadn't spoken of in years? He nodded, then gazed back up at the stars. "You're right. It's from my older brother. He was killed in a DUI, ten years ago. I was thirteen."

Sam continued looking at the heavens, lost for a moment in the memory of his brother, when he felt Maya's hand on his. Her skin was soft and smooth, her hand strong. She gently squeezed his hand but stayed silent.

"My parents took it pretty hard." He almost whispered his words. "To this day, my mother doesn't even say his name." Maya's body was nearly touching his. It was...comforting. "I think it's easier for her that way."

Sam felt Maya study his face for a moment, and when he didn't offer anything more on the topic, she turned back to the stars. They listened to the crickets in comfortable silence.

"Well, okay then." Sam broke the silence. "Your turn. What's your story? Any siblings? I mean, besides the cousin you have here, who is probably the giggliest thing I've ever seen."

Maya laughed. "Oh, Sejal. And you're right, cousins are like siblings. She does that in front of—" Maya paused "—in front of really handsome boys." She left her gaze on the stars, but Sam once again enjoyed the flush on her cheeks.

"I don't have any 'real' siblings." She turned to face him, chagrin on her face. "My *parents*," she said the words with some sarcasm, "met in India. My mum was working in the cafeteria of the college my father attended. They met—" she tilted her head and Sam was distracted, again, this time by the curve of her face "—and fell in love. However, their parents did not approve. Not having an arranged marriage was unheard of, not to mention they were from different parts of India. So, having seen one too many Bollywood movies, they decided to run away. They married in secret and left India for London."

Maya gazed off into the distance at something Sam couldn't see. "Things were fine for a bit, but when my father heard his parents had become ill, he went back to care for them. He never returned." She paused. "I was eight." Maya sat back and shrugged her shoulders, as if she didn't care. But the rest of her body language screamed that she did. "My mum was alone with a child, so she came to the States to stay with her brother until she got on her feet."

"Your Deepak-mama?" Sam had never seen her this vulnerable, and for a brief instant, the Maya before him was an eight-year-old girl. The hurt her father had caused when he'd abandoned her seemed to flicker behind her shrug. Something vile boiled up inside Sam. What kind of man abandoned his family like that?

"Yes." Maya smiled. "We stayed with him for a bit, but my mother became fiercely independent and refused to stay with him indefinitely. Baking and cooking came naturally to her, so she taught herself how to run a business. She ended up opening a bakery in Queens. And that's where we live now." She leaned back onto her hands on the step. "I've been busy with school, so I haven't had a chance to visit my cousin in a while, so I came for the summer." The pain left her eyes, replaced with their natural warmth.

"Excellent for me." Sam leaned back so he was level with Maya. "How come your mom didn't just go back to her parents?"

Maya sat up and turned her gaze away from him. "She was from a small village. You know how it can be." She turned back to him, a small fire in her eyes. "Marrying outside what was considered acceptable was not tolerated." She paused and the fire cooled. "My uncle doesn't believe in those old notions. He supported my mother when she was at her lowest. He helped her become the force of nature she is today." She chuckled. "And now he's afraid of her!"

"So how does she feel about you dating?"

Maya pressed her lips together before responding. "She is not a fan. She's convinced that she will arrange my marriage when the 'time comes.'"

Sam's heart dropped. "What did you tell her about us?"

Maya grinned at him, her half smirk that he loved so much, as she leaned toward him. "Well, until now, there wasn't really much of an 'us.'"

"Is there now?"

Maya shrugged and her smirk slipped a bit. "If I tell her, she'll make me come home."

Sam sat up and placed a tentative hand on top of hers. She did not pull away. He took her hand and fixed his eyes on hers, which seemed to glow with a light from within. He was just bringing her hand to his lips when the door opened.

"Maya?" Her uncle leaned out, his deep voice thick with sleep resounding in the still air.

Maya pulled her hand free of Sam's with such speed, he thought he might have a friction burn.

"Yes, Deepak-mama." She bolted up onto her feet, and spoke hastily. "I've been home. Just enjoying the summer evening."

"Enough enjoying. Come in." He shut the door and went back in.

"Yes, Deepak-mama." Maya turned apologetic eyes on Sam. He was already on his feet. He drank her in for a moment and fought the urge to reach out and touch her.

"You're different than I thought you'd be." Her smile was suddenly shy.

"Is that good?"

"It's really good." She bit her bottom lip and the flush on her cheeks made him weak.

"Until next time, then." There was no suppressing the stupid grin on his face.

She nodded. "Next time." She took a step toward the door.

It looked to Sam that she was stalling. Excellent. "Good night, Maya." Sam turned and walked back to his car, lest he dawdle as well and get her in trouble. He had one hand in his pocket, clutching the coin. He smiled to himself. "Hasn't failed me yet."

CHAPTER NINE
MAYA

Maryland, 1996

"HE HASN'T GOT a prayer, Maya-*didi*," Sejal said, using the term for older sister, as she admired her older cousin's reflection. Since neither girl had siblings, sisters they were. "That boy is going to fall for you." She crossed her hands over her heart and pretended to swoon.

Sam had called that morning and invited Maya to an outdoor concert that night at Merriweather Post Pavilion. The invitation had both surprised and thrilled her, so she'd accepted without hesitation. If her best friend, Ami, were here, she would probably lecture her on the hazards of seeming too available. Whatever. She couldn't explain it, but she had tossed and turned all night after their date the previous evening, her belly spinning with anticipation of seeing him at work today. But he'd been busy picking up more tile and supplies, so Maya's belly continued its churning.

Sejal had been horrified when Maya had simply put on jeans and a T-shirt to go to the concert. "Are you kidding, Maya-*didi*? This is a date. A *second date*." She spoke slowly, as if Maya were a child. "You have to dress nicely, but not *look* like you're trying to dress nicely."

Maya had rolled her eyes. "That's ridiculous."

"No, it's not," Sejal had said, handing Maya black capri pants and a lime-green blouse. "How can you have graduated from college and not know that?" She leaned closer to Maya and whispered, "Just because my parents don't let me date, doesn't mean I don't." She put her hands on her hips. "Put that on."

Maya pursed her lips at her younger cousin. Of course Sejal was dating behind her parents' back. Deepak-mama was almost as strict as her mother. He might have supported his sister when she was in dire straits, but he certainly didn't want his daughter to end up pregnant and alone—which is what both brother and sister assumed dating would lead to. Maya did an internal eye roll at the thought. "Who's the guy?"

"Not important." Sejal blushed, and Maya made a note to pursue this later.

The fact that Maya was a college graduate was what allowed her even to go on a date. That and the fact that Maya let her uncle believe that her mother allowed it.

In any case, Deepak-mama made her keep that midnight curfew. It made no difference that she was twenty-two years old. Maya had simply shaken her head at her cousin and obediently put on the outfit, much to Sejal's approval.

At precisely seven, the doorbell rang. Sejal squealed. "He's here!"

Maya's stomach lurched, and she reprimanded herself. This was Sam, whom she had spent three weeks avoiding and turning down. Why, all of a sudden, did her heart quicken, and palms get sweaty when she was about to see him? She leaped to her feet to answer the door.

"What are you doing?" Sejal squealed at her like she had suddenly gone mad. "My dad has to do round two of his interrogation."

"What?"

"C'mon." She grabbed Maya's hand and put one finger to her lips. She quietly led Maya to the top of the stairs, just out of view from the front door.

They heard Deepak-mama grunt and open the door. Maya peeked her head around the corner and caught a glimpse of Sam standing just inside the doorway, clean-shaven and beaming. He flicked his eyes around, looking for her, and she flushed, grateful that he couldn't see her. He was simply dressed in khaki shorts and quite a nice-fitting T-shirt the slate blue color of the ocean just before dusk. The color did amazing things for his skin and eyes. Maya peeked around the corner again to see just how well the T-shirt molded around the muscles of his shoulders, grazed his chest and hung loose just past the waistband of his shorts.

Sam exuded energy as he extended his hand to Deepak-mama. "Uncle!" Maya noted that Sam used "uncle" to address Deepak-mama, rather than "Mr. Shah." It was what Indian kids did: it showed respect, but maintained familiarity. It was different than the titles like mama and mami, which indicated a blood relation. She grinned to herself. *Half*-Indian indeed. "How are you?"

The confidence in his voice reverberated all the way up the stairs.

The older man hesitated as he took Sam's hand and

shook it, a bewildered look on his face. "Great," he said. "And you?"

"You know, it turns out that my dad does know you," Sam said.

"Oh?"

"Yes." Sam made eye contact, and his smile was genuine. "He remembers meeting you at a medical gathering a few months ago. Apparently, internal medicine and cardiology shared a conference…"

Deepak-mama tilted his head. "Yes, I do remember that. Your father is too modest. He spoke at that meeting. Very impressive. Dr. Hutcherson has a wonderful memory." Deepak-mama's mood turned amiable, as if Sam's father's ability to remember him made them all old friends.

So much for round two.

Sejal finally nudged Maya. "Are you going on this date, or is my dad?"

Maya smoothed out invisible wrinkles in her clothes and went down the stairs. She caught Sam's eye over her uncle's shoulder before she hit the last step and he paused midsentence, breaking into a wide grin. Deepak-mama turned to follow his gaze, and Sam took advantage of the moment to wink at her, as though they shared an intimate secret. Between the grin and the wink and how he looked in that T-shirt, it was all Maya could do to simply smile back in response.

She took the last step down. "Hi." She forced her voice to sound as casual as possible. "I'm ready when you are."

She watched as Sam turned his eyes to Deepak-mama. Her uncle leaned over and kissed her on the cheek. "Okay, beta, have fun."

He turned back to Sam, his voice once again stern, though this time Maya heard a hint of amusement escape his lips. "Midnight."

Sam nodded, his demeanor relaxed and comfortable. "Absolutely. Yes, sir." Maya was unable to tear her eyes away from him.

The door had barely shut behind them before he leaned toward her, eyes ablaze, and whispered, "Hey, you look amazing." His breath tickled her ear, sending shivers down her spine. He took the two porch steps down in one stride, and turned to Maya. She was eye to eye with him, and he reached out and took her hand as if they had been holding hands for years. His hand was warm and firm, and the way their fingers intertwined made her feel safe.

As he started the car, she breathed deeply in an attempt to gather herself and failed miserably when she was filled with his clean scent mixed perfectly with something that was uniquely Sam. *Say something!* "Nice handling of my uncle."

Sam wrinkled his brow. "I wasn't 'handling' him. My dad really did remember him." He gave her a crooked smile. "And besides, he's 'in charge' of you this summer, right?"

Maya nodded.

"Well, I'm really hoping this isn't our last date."

Heat rushed to her face, making her sweat despite the air-conditioning.

On the ride over, Sam explained that Merriweather Post Pavilion was an outdoor concert venue and that over the years, any number of big and little bands had passed through. He had seen at least one concert there every summer for as long as he could remember. He told

Maya that the best times had been when his brother was still alive and the two of them, along with their parents, would bring a picnic and enjoy the lawn seats.

When they arrived, Maya got out and leaned around to peek in the trunk. "You packed a picnic?" She grinned at him. "Impressive."

"I'm trying." His smile was almost as shy as it was proud.

Her heart did a little flip at the idea that he was still trying to impress her. No one had cared enough before to bother. She got lost in the grace and strength of his movement. He caught her staring again and raised an eyebrow at her. She snapped out of it and grabbed the blankets, hoping that the heat that rushed to her face didn't show.

The evening was warm without being humid, but a breeze would have been nice. They laid out their blankets and opened a couple beers, just in time for the first notes of the opening band. Sounds of laughter and people singing drifted in the air. Cigarette smoke wafted from all around and mixed with the scent of grilling meat and the sugary-fried aroma of deep-fried funnel cake. A group of what appeared to be high school kids in the audience were singing an Ace of Base song about it being a beautiful life. At that moment, it really was.

Maya sat side by side with Sam. He was close enough that she could have touched him by simply leaning her shoulder into his. The scant inch between them was charged with electricity, and a few minutes into their conversation, she leaned toward him and closed that gap.

Sam had one of those smiles with a dimple on one side of his face. His perfect teeth were framed by lips that curved into a smile when he looked at her. Maya got light-headed every time she saw that smile, because it didn't only come from those amazing lips. There was a touch of amusement and maybe even admiration that came from his eyes. His whole face seemed to light up when he looked at her, and when he smiled, she felt like it was meant just for her. He turned this smile on her as her shoulder met his arm, and Maya blushed as if he could read her thoughts.

He appeared to study her for a moment. "Well, now." His voice was soft. "This is pleasant."

Through his dark lashes, his soft chocolate eyes were warm. His smile was crooked, but it held no taunt this time. Maya's heart was pounding so loud it was a wonder to her that Sam couldn't hear it. She let her eyes wander to his full, soft lips. What would they feel like?

He leaned closer to her, his gaze shifting to her mouth. Her body took over and she leaned closer to him. She could almost feel his lips on hers…

"Hey! Coach Hutcherson!" A young boy's voice called out from nearby. Maya sprang away from Sam as he closed his eyes and exhaled deeply.

Three young teen boys approached from a few rows in front of them. Sam turned to the boys with exaggerated patience and forced enthusiasm. "Hey, guys. How's it going?"

"Great." One of the boys glanced at Maya, then back at Sam. "How about you?"

"I was better about ten seconds ago." He squinted up at them into the setting sun.

Blank faces greeted Sam and he groaned only loud enough for Maya to hear before he turned to her. He addressed Maya, apology written all over his face. "Maya, these are the youngest of the goalkeepers I coach over the summer. Boys, this is Maya."

The tallest of them elbowed the boy next to him, his face flushed and covered in a ridiculous grin. The boy he elbowed then elbowed the boy with glasses standing next to him. The three boys snickered, and Sam looked mortified. Maya bit her lip to keep from laughing.

"I know!"

"Shh. She's sitting right there."

"Totally hot. Coach is one lucky bas—"

"Boys!" Sam finally spoke. The sniggering continued. "Anand. Manners!"

"What, Coach?"

Sam opened his mouth to respond, but shook his head instead. "Who's here with you?"

The boy named Anand spoke up. "Coach Mike brought us. He's over there." He waved absently in the direction of the stage, stealing another glance at Maya.

Sam looked over their shoulders. "He's looking for you." The boys turned, and sure enough, their coach was summoning them back to their seats.

Grumbling and goodbyes ensued as they returned to their area. "Total hottie, Coach!" The tall one called over his shoulder.

Sam closed his eyes and pinched the bridge of his nose before turning to Maya. "That—" he sighed the sigh of a parent "—is part of my soccer team."

"Charming." She burst out laughing. "Adorable." The boys clearly idolized Sam, just like his cousins.

"What? Them?" He shook his head in disbelief.

"No," Maya said. "You with them." She shrugged and tilted her head. "You're good with kids."

"Yeah, probably because they're not mine!" Sam

chuckled. "I do private goalie sessions with them," he explained. "Mike is the assistant coach, but he'll start med school in the fall, so someone else will have to take over. They'll miss him." He paused. "In fact, this will be my last year coaching them for a while, too. I won't be coming home."

"Law school beckons." Maya nodded. Of course.

"Yeah." Sam pulled at the grass and seemed to get lost for a moment.

"What? Law school not everything it's made out to be?" Maya brought her knees in and leaned on them.

"Huh? Oh no." He stopped pulling at the grass and came back to earth. "Columbia is great. Law school is actually fantastic." He didn't seem able to meet her eye.

He'd had no problem telling her about his brother, but something was holding him back today. Maybe encouragement. "But…"

He sighed and opened his mouth as if he wanted to say something, but remained silent. Maya waited as his eyes grew dark under a furrowed brow. Sam clenched his jaw as he searched her face. Maya wasn't sure what he was looking for, but she had never seen him like this before, and what passed and didn't pass between them was more intimate than if he had kissed her right then.

When he finally spoke, his voice came slow and heavy. "Big plans have been made for me, Maya." Instinctively, she remained silent. With closed eyes, he tapped the pocket of his shorts and shook his head. When he opened them again, his face relaxed, and the warmth was back in his eyes. "Not tonight." He took her hand. "There's a time to talk about that, but not tonight."

He stood and gently pulled Maya up with him. When he smiled at her, she knew that he was unaware of anything else around them, and that all he could see was her, and she forgot all her reasons for ever having fought her feelings for him. The top of her head just grazed his chin, so if she rested her head on his chest, she would fit in that secure area between his cleanly shaven chin and muscular chest. He held her close enough their bodies touched, and the light musk from his cologne relaxed her. She fit in his arms as if she belonged there.

"Tonight," he said, "we dance."

They enjoyed the music in silence for a few moments, and Maya was wondering how it would feel to rest her head in that secure place on his chest, when Sam spoke.

"What about you? You just graduated. What now?"

She tilted her head up to meet his eyes. "That's easy. I'm looking for a job in a restaurant. I'll need some extra training, but eventually, I'd like to be head pastry chef in a five-star restaurant." Maya smiled. "It's all I've ever wanted."

"Maybe it's all you've ever known."

Maya pulled back a fraction. "What does that mean?"

Sam frowned. "Just that it seems like you've worked in that bakery all your life. You've never done anything else but bake."

Maya narrowed her eyes at him and stiffened. "That bakery was survival for my mum and me. My father left her with only their scant savings, which was enough to get us here, and not much more. She worked nights as a cashier in a twenty-four-hour corner market with me asleep behind the counter." Those days, her mother's only priorities had been Maya and making a life for them both. Maya had always taken pride in the fact that her mother had been able to build that life from flour and eggs, sugar and butter.

Maya pulled away from Sam as she spoke, all thought of that shoulder wiped from her mind. "I think I knew how to bake and decorate a cake from scratch before I hit middle school." She was proud of that, too. She took a deep breath and looked him dead in the eye. "It may not be glamorous like the law. And it may well be the 'only thing I've ever known.'" She did the air quotes with as much disdain as she could muster. "But that doesn't make it the wrong choice for me. And in any case, you don't know me well enough to know if it is or isn't." Honestly, who did he think he was?

Blood pulsed in her head and she paused again for breath. "It's honest work and it makes people happy."

Sam pressed his lips together, the nonchalance with which he had downplayed her bakery gone from his face. He met her eyes with something like regret or shame, as he sat down and indicated that she join him. But she wasn't about to sit next to him. "And to be quite honest, I'm really good at it."

Sam gazed up at her with innocent eyes in what was now light from the rising moon and the stage. "Okay." He shrugged and patted the ground next to him. "You're an excellent baker."

"Pastry chef," Maya corrected him from between clenched teeth as she continued to glower at him. She did not sit. He didn't seem to get it.

He smiled up at her, eyes wide, apologetic. "Pastry chef. I'd like to apologize, but it'd be easier if you were sitting next to me." She folded her arms across her chest and cocked an eyebrow at him. That smile had her heart racing, but she wouldn't give in that easily.

The smile faded, replaced by something else. Was it amusement? Admiration? Irritation? Maya couldn't be sure. But in the next instant, he was standing a head over her, his face contrite, looking almost ashamed. He reached out a finger and gently tilted her chin up to face him. "I'm sorry I offended you," he said. "It can't have been easy growing up without a father—I had no idea what you or your mother had been through."

"This has nothing to do with my father! I don't need *pity* from you." She wouldn't take pity from anyone. So she'd grown up without father. Worse things happened all the time.

He bit his bottom lip and continued, his voice low and sincere. "I'm not pitying you, I promise. If anything, I respect your mom for standing on her own two feet. You're right, I don't know you well enough to know what you should be doing with your life. And trust me, I'm the last person who should be making that judgment, anyway. I'm sorry."

His eyes searched hers, she had the sense he was hoping for forgiveness. She unfolded her arms.

"And I certainly am not one of those people who thinks the law is glamorous and better than everything else. But you don't know me well enough to know that, either." Sam leaned in close and whispered, "That's something I would like to change."

His breath on her ear made that whole side of her body tingle. Maya did her best to ignore the sensation, and continued to glare at him for a minute longer. His apology was real, and it broke down her anger. She became conscious of the fact they were the only ones standing, and the headliner was about to begin. "We should sit— we're in the way." She sat down first, but glanced up at him and scooted over to make a spot for him.

"You know, you never asked what my mom does," Sam said.

"Okay." She indulged him, a smile prickling at the edge of her lips. She couldn't help it. "Sam, what does your mom do?"

Mischief took over his eyes and he started to chuckle. "She's a lawyer." Sam threw his head back and laughed.

Maya threw grass at him and shook her head, fighting the laughter that bubbled up inside her. It shouldn't be so easy for her to forgive him. But his laughter was so real and so free, it became impossible for her not to smile.

"See, I told you I'm in no position to judge." He wiped a tear from his eye as Maya finally stopped laughing. "Now, do you think we can be done with the 'yelling at Sam' portion of the evening?"

Maya leaned her shoulder against his in answer. He put his arm around her, and didn't remove it for the rest of the concert.

SAM DROVE SLOWLY and chose the long way back to her uncle's house, and it thrilled Maya that he was trying to prolong their time together. Her curfew had never bothered her before, but tonight, she truly resented it. She was old enough to vote *and* drink, after all. Just because her mother wanted to choose who she spent her life with…

They were lost in conversation when he finally pulled in front of the house.

"But, Sam, if your father is a doctor and your mother is a lawyer," she asked, "why take all those loans and extra jobs?" They had long since passed topics that were off-limits. "I mean, can't they help you?"

"They could. I mean, they certainly wish that I would take their money." He turned off the engine and held out his can of soda to Maya. He tilted his head back and finished it when she held up her hand in refusal. "But it's their money, right? My mother insisted, and they did help out with undergrad. But for law school, I just felt I…"

"…had to do it for yourself." Maya caught his eye and nodded her head. This guy just kept impressing her.

"Exactly!" He beamed at her as he checked his watch. "Two minutes." The look of disappointment on his face mirrored her own feelings. What would happen if she just sat here in this car with Sam? She flushed at the thought.

MAYA WAS KEENLY aware of the warmth of Sam's hand on the small of her back as he escorted her to the door. It was protective and intimate, and she found comfort in it. His touch sent a welcome thrill up her spine, making it difficult to focus, resulting in silence on her part as she failed to come up with even one thing to talk about. Only the sounds of the summer night were between them as Sam was also quiet.

Maya turned to face him when they stopped at the porch. He was close enough for her to feel the heat from his body. The night had turned humid and silence hung between them thick as droplets in the air.

"Well, you should probably…" He motioned toward the door before shoving his fists in his pockets. "You know, before the giggly one comes out."

"Yeah, right. Okay." Maya willed herself to turn and take the first step up. She could feel Sam still behind her.

"Maya."

It wasn't anything more than just a hoarse whisper. But it held desire and longing and everything else Maya wanted to hear.

She didn't think. She spun around and wrapped her hands around his face as she leaned in and kissed him. His surprise lasted only an instant before he kissed her back. His lips were soft and insistent, and she closed her eyes and let herself go. He tasted sweet like the Coke he had been sipping in the car, and he smelled like the concert: a touch of grass, a hint of smoke and a lingering trace of his cologne.

Sam's body was strong and she relished how his muscled arms felt wrapped around her as he deepened their kiss and pulled her close enough that she could feel his heart pounding hard against hers. It could have been days or minutes or seconds. Maya had no idea. She let herself get lost in his mix of sweetness and warmth and strength.

Somewhere, almost as if from a tunnel, came the sound of a door opening and a small voice disrupted her bliss. "Maya-*didi*! I swear I'm not looking, but Papa fell asleep waiting for you and it's after midnight."

Sam stopped kissing her but did not pull away. "It's the giggly one." His lips were near her ear as he whispered into her hair, causing her to shiver despite the heat. "She really does have her eyes covered."

"Pretend she's not there." She opened her eyes enough to see Sam's lips curve into his smile as she leaned up and took his mouth again.

"Maya-*didi*! If you ever want to see him again, Papa can't know you were late." Sejal's voice was worried and urgent. "And if he catches you *kissing* him…"

"What will happen if I catch her kissing him?" The familiar deep voice rolled out to them.

Oh, shit!

Maya jumped back from Sam, her heart hammering somewhere in her belly, and nearly fell backward onto the porch. Sam caught her before she fell, easily lifting her back to standing, his face grim. But he didn't step away from her, or even let her go. Instead, he drew his gaze over her and to Deepak-mama. She turned to follow his gaze and face her uncle, Sam's hand still supporting her arm, his chest secure against her back.

"Uncle, I'm sorry she's late. I meant no disresp—"

"Didn't you?" Deepak-mama narrowed his eyes and slowed his breath. He barely moved his mouth to speak. "That is not true, considering what I just saw."

Behind him, Sejal's eyes were huge and filling with fear. "Come, Papa. Everything is fine." She tugged on his shirtsleeve.

Without shifting his gaze, Deepak-mama addressed his daughter. "Sejal. Go inside. Now." Sejal took a step back from him, but remained in Maya's line of view.

"Sir." Sam's voice did not falter. "I—"

"Stop. Talking." Deepak-mama barely moved his lips.

Sam did as he was told, but Maya felt his muscles tighten while his heart thumped wildly against her back.

"Maya. Come."

Maya did not move. "We didn't do anything wrong." Maya surprised herself with the strength in her voice.

"Your mother will disagree."

Still, Maya did not move.

"Come. Now." Deepak-mama's simmering anger was getting ready to explode.

Sam loosened his grip on her arm, and almost imperceptibly, nudged her forward with his body. Maya straightened her shoulders and took the last step onto the porch. "Good night, Sam."

His lip twitched. "Good night, Maya."

Maya turned back and glared at her uncle as she passed him into the house. Deepak-mama followed her and shut the door without a word to Sam. He attempted to stare Maya down. "I'll call your mother in the morning. Go to bed."

"I went on a date, Deepak-mama. What did you think was going to happen?" Maya didn't care how mad he was. She hadn't done anything wrong.

"I thought you would conduct yourself in a respectable manner."

Maya rolled her eyes. "There was nothing not respectable about that."

"What will your mother say?"

Maya was silent. Her mother was going to be pissed. And not just because kissing was "not respectable," but because Maya was breaking her cardinal rule: no boys. Her mom was going to get a bunch of news in the morning.

Sejal tugged at her arm. Maya followed her up the stairs and into the room they shared. Sejal shut the door and sat down next to the window. "Well?" Her eyes twinkled as if nothing had just happened downstairs.

Maya could not suppress her smile. "Looks like I'm in trouble—but totally worth it!"

Sejal glanced out the window, and then stood up to get closer. "Maya-*didi*, come."

Maya peeked over Sejal's shoulder. Sam was leaning against his car, flipping his coin in the air. He looked up and saw them in the window. Maya wiggled her fingers at him. He waved back and watched her for a minute before getting into his car.

Sejal displayed all her teeth and all her sass, as she turned to Maya. "I *told* you he didn't have a prayer."

CHAPTER TEN
SAM

New York, 2012

SAM STUFFED HIS gloved hands into the pockets of his woolen coat, buried his chin inside his scarf and headed out into the blustery cold. Suddenly, October was behaving as if it were January. He decided against using the company car and instead walked a good five to six blocks from his office before hailing a cab.

Sam removed his gloves and loosened his scarf to settle in for the trip from Manhattan to Queens. He hadn't told Paige about his daughter yet. He just wasn't sure how she would take it. He gazed through the window as the city passed in a haze of buildings and cars and his thoughts drifted back, once again, to that summer in Maryland.

The cab ride to Queens was surprisingly uneventful, and before he knew it, Sam was drawn back to the present. He paid the driver and traded the warmth of the cab for the bitter cold of the day.

Sam found himself standing in the cold, a smile plastered on his face. Of course this was the place. Though there was no real reason to be surprised. He'd had faith that anything Maya was involved with would be incredible. But it was so much more. Sweet Nothings was classy and refined, not just a place you'd go for a simple treat. This was where you came because you required something extraordinary.

He fingered the coin in his pocket, barely even aware that he did so. What would Arjun have said of this particular predicament? Sam would've given anything to have his brother to talk to right now, as opposed to just his coin.

In place of a door jingle when he entered, a soft bell chimed. The rich aroma of roasting coffee beans, mingled with the enticing scent of freshly baked chocolate chip cookies, was overwhelming, creating a pit in Sam's stomach he thought he had long ago eliminated. Familiar orange undertones in the coffee jolted him back to a time of flickering candles and soft sheets. He shook his head as if to dislodge the memory. *This* was the coffee she served here? He should have just called her.

"Hello! Welcome to Sweet Nothings! How can I help you?" A young woman with a bounce in her voice and a lovely smile greeted him pleasantly from behind the counter.

Sam started at the girl's voice as he was once more pulled back to the present. "I'm here to see Maya Rao." He flashed a warm smile, attempting to hide his distraction. She blushed as she turned to get her boss.

Behind her was an observation window that allowed customers to watch the artistry in progress. An automatic coffee bean roaster took up a corner of the window, the small brown gems tumbling about—proof that the roasting was done on the premises. The rest of the window revealed two women in hairnets and chef's whites, working on a three-tiered cake. The woman with her back to him was painting a city scene on the side of the cake, while the other attached some kind of flower to a higher layer. Maya had always worked well with her mother.

Maya caught his eye, and nodded in the direction of the door. She quickly put aside the flower, and appeared behind the counter.

"Sam!" Maya was breathy and panicked, her eyes darting toward the window. "What are you doing here?" Rather than wait for his reply, she turned to the young girl at the counter. "Julie, can you see if the cupcake order for the Kantharias has been boxed yet?"

Julie flicked a quick look at Sam before excusing herself, leaving Sam and Maya alone.

Maya grabbed a paper towel from behind the counter and wiped her hands as she came around the front of the counter, leading Sam to a table in the far corner. When she finally spoke, it was almost a hiss. "I thought we decided not to meet at workplaces."

"Well." Sam turned his back on the observation window and followed her as he took off his gloves. "Since you went ahead and left me a voice mail, I figured we were ignoring the rules."

Maya pursed her lips at him and managed to look slightly abashed. "Well, fine. Okay, you're here." She tilted her head. "Are you going to help me?"

Sam fidgeted with his gloves, trying—and failing—to not look at her. Her chef's whites, unbuttoned at the top, were stained with various colors. Her hair was trapped in a net, and there was most definitely colored icing on her cheek. Any other woman dressed like this would have conjured up nightmares of the lunch lady from school, but not Maya. Maya managed to make you wish you were the cake.

His gloves lay abandoned on the small table between them. A small voice in the back of his head kept telling him to look away. Or at least say something. She gasped—it was a small thing, someone else might have missed it—and then her hand was at her head as she yanked off the offensive hairnet. Sam swallowed hard as dark hair fell in soft waves around her shoulders. It was time to look away.

"I, uh… I just came to say that I can help you out," he said. "Byron Stevenson and I went to law school together."

Maya smiled expectantly, and Sam remembered why he had wanted to do anything for her back then. "You're friends?"

"Not exactly. He was kind of an ass in law school, so in helping out your…our…" He paused at the word.

Maya finished for him. "Daughter."

"Daughter. Yes. I'm still getting used to it." He shook his head and sighed as he watched Maya. "So, in helping our *daughter*, I will get the added benefit of annoying Byron, so…"

"Oh, Sam!" She beamed as she stepped closer, almost as if she were going to throw her arms around him. She stopped midway, and grabbed his hands in hers in an awkward, backward, two-handed handshake. "Thank you!"

She glanced down at their hands and dropped them as if struck by electricity. "Oh, sorry, you—have—uh, well green icing on the edge—well—it'll come off."

Sam scraped dried icing from his cuffs, but his hands still held the memory of her touch. For a split second he had thought Maya was going to hug him. Their nonembrace lay thick in the air between them, forcing Sam to remember what it had felt like to hold her, making him wonder how it would feel to hold her now.

Sam cleared his throat and willed his body to squelch that memory. He was engaged to another woman. "Uh, no problem." He was treated to her blush. "I don't like this coat anyway." He smiled at her. "But before you're too grateful, you should know that I do have one stipulation."

"Fine," she said quietly, giving a sharp nod.

"How about some coffee?"

"Um, sure." She gestured toward a table.

Sam came around to her side and pulled out a chair for her, before removing his coat and sitting down opposite her. The table was next to a window, and the noontime sun sent warmth from high in the sky.

"Julie, could you please bring us two coffees?" Maya nodded her thanks to Sam as she sat down. "Just a splash of cream and one sugar for Mr. Hutcherson here."

"And just a splash of cream and no sugar for your boss." Sam grinned.

Julie seemed a bit confused until Maya nodded her away.

"You remember." Maya's voice was gentle, no sign of irritation or demand.

"I remember lots of things." Though he tried not to, his gaze lingered on her. "Like the coffee you have here."

He waited for her to make some sort of excuse to justify using that specific coffee in her shop. Some reason why she would have bothered to learn how to roast and flavor *this* particular coffee. She shifted in her seat and looked away, saying nothing.

"Do you remember that Honda Civic I drove that summer?" Sam broke the silence.

Maya gave her slightly lopsided smile that Sam remembered so well, and let out a "humph." "Of course. Powder blue, if I remember correctly. And the passenger-side door stuck from the inside." She sat back in her chair and raised one eyebrow at him.

Sam dropped his gaze and chuckled. "You do remember."

"Whatever happened to that car?" She caught his eye.

"Totaled it."

"What? Were you hurt?" She sat up in her chair and leaned in toward him.

"Nah." Sam shrugged. The sweet scent of flowers and sugar coming from her drew him in closer. "I was lucky. The car actually saved me." He looked her in the eye. "I notice your sign is the same color as that car."

Maya sat back. "Is that so?" She shrugged. "Coincidence."

Her eyes didn't quite meet his.

The coffee arrived and Sam stared at it for a moment, knowing that one sip of that coffee was a trip to a past he had fought to forget. He took the sip. The richness of the coffee was balanced with just a hint of orange flavor. Even though he knew it was coming, he nearly choked on it. "It's been a long time since I've had this."

"Yeah." Maya busied herself with her coffee.

"I can't believe you serve it here," he said, not bothering to hide his irritation.

"What? It's a coffee shop. We serve specialty coffees." She waved a dismissive hand, her focus on her mug. "Don't look too hard into it."

Sam pushed the coffee aside and leaned in toward Maya. "You know what I would like to look a little harder into?" He was close enough to whisper aggressively in her ear. "I would like to find out why I was never told you were pregnant."

Even as he said the words, a knot formed in his stomach and an unfamiliar hardness tightened his throat. He leaned back enough to look her firmly in the eye, but remained close enough to feel the panic in her breath. "I want to know how it is you turned me away from your door that day." He nearly growled his next words. "When you *knew* you were pregnant with our child. That's my stipulation to helping you. That, and I want to meet Samantha."

"I'll tell you what you want to know, but let's not bring—" Maya stopped short and her eyes filled with alarm as footsteps announced someone behind him. Sam turned around and all the tightness in his body released. There before him was the girl who had been painting the scene on the cake.

The girl he had only seen in a photo.

"Mom," the painter called to Maya, "since when do you go around having coffee with strange men?" She nodded at Sam, and her eyes widened as she took him in. She sighed and placed her hands on her hips in an almost maternal gesture. She turned her attention to Maya. "No matter how good-looking they are?"

Sam looked to Maya. Her eyes locked on to Sam's. The blood had drained from her face. This was why she didn't want him here.

CHAPTER ELEVEN
MAYA

New York, 2012

MAYA'S HEART POUNDED in her ears as she shifted her gaze from Sam to Samantha. They weren't supposed to meet. *They weren't supposed to meet!*

For his part, Sam looked as pale as Maya felt. Samantha opened her mouth as if to speak, but closed it again. Odd. Samantha was many things, but at a loss for words was not one of them. She couldn't possibly *know*.

Could she?

Sam's gaze darted from her to their daughter and back. The silence was endless. What was he doing, coming here, anyway? All dressed up in that perfectly fitting suit, wielding that dimple as if he had no idea what it did to her. The fact that he actually had no idea what it did to her made it worse. The remnants of whatever musky cologne he wore did nothing to hide that clean scent that was essentially *Sam*. Combine that with the coffee, and it was no wonder she'd almost hugged him, and it was all she could do to not touch him again.

The pounding did not cease, but Maya forced calm into her voice. "Samantha." She nearly tripped over her chair as she scrambled to stand behind her daughter.

"This is Mr. Hutcherson. He's a lawyer and he's just come by to tell me he can help us out." Maya nudged her daughter to prompt her manners.

Samantha threw her mother an irritated look before turning to Sam. She smiled and wiped her hand on her apron before offering it to Sam in greeting, a robotic "Nice to meet you" emitting from her lips. Her daughter's behavior was odd and surprising, but Maya's full attention was on Sam.

He simply stared at Samantha, his eyes darting around her face, studying her. For a moment, Maya forgot why she had ever left Sam, and allowed herself to drink in his wonder and astonishment at seeing his daughter for the first time. She quickly squelched that warm and happy feeling, reminding herself that father and daughter meeting each other was not good for any of them.

A beat or two stretched between them before Sam regained himself and shook Samantha's hand. But before he could gather himself to speak, Maya stepped in front of Samantha.

"Well, Mr. Hutcherson, thank you for stopping by." Her own voice reminded her of the vice principal at Samantha's school. "Feel free to call me for any details you require."

Samantha's glare pierced the back of Maya's head as the silence built again.

"Yes." This time Sam broke the silence. "Nice to meet you, Samantha." He looked around Maya at Samantha. The way he said her name, Maya knew he wanted to say more. She turned her body, forcing him to look at her.

He lowered his head toward her, his voice soft and

intimate. "I'll be in touch regarding that other matter." If Maya had melted into his voice in any way, his words set her straight. More than a touch of warning was directed her way.

"Anytime," Maya said, louder than was necessary, as she guided Sam to the door. "Thanks so much for stopping in. Very kind of you." She all but pushed him out into the street.

With Sam gone, Maya faced her daughter with a smile plastered to her face. "Well, nice of him to stop by and let us know he can help out, huh?"

She ignored Samantha's narrowed gaze and started for the kitchen. "Yeah, it was." Samantha followed her mother through the door to the kitchen. "I'm sure he's a busy man. Why wouldn't he just call?"

Maya found a hairnet and resumed work on the gum paste flowers. "How would I know? Maybe he was in the neighborhood." She picked up her utensil and sighed. "Don't you have a cityscape to finish?"

"A guy like him?" Samantha pointed to her finished cityscape and rolled her eyes. "Seriously, Mom."

Maya glanced at the finished cityscape and turned her back on Samantha to work on the flowers. The girl worked fast. And she was still talking. "Did you not see the suit he had on? He obviously works on Lex. Not way out here in Queens."

Alarms blasted in Maya's head. "How do you know he works on Lex?"

"I found him on a Google search," she mumbled.

"What were you looking for?" Maya snapped her head around, and in doing so, crumpled the current flower she had been sculpting.

Samantha paused and made eye contact before spitting out her reply. "I was looking for my dad!"

Maya was treated to the full teenage head-shake that stood in for the word *duh*. She stepped away from her work area and closed in on her daughter. "What do you mean, you were looking for your dad?"

"Exactly what I said! I can figure things out, you know!" Samantha did not waver under Maya's anger. She took a deep breath. "And that man is my father."

Oh God. Maya's hand flew to her *Ganesha* pendant. *Obstacle! Do something!*

"Oh, honey. Stop searching for your dad. We're fine. Finding your dad will only lead to—" she looked down at the crumpled flower somehow still in her hand "—confusion. Can't you just be content with me and your grandmother?"

Samantha gaped at her, anger blazing in her eyes. It was Maya's turn to stay firm. She tossed the crumpled flower and stood. "Tell you what, since you're all done painting, you can work on making these flowers. Might as well make the best use of that suspension."

"Are you saying he's not my dad?"

"I'm saying Mr. Hutcherson has agreed to help us so that you won't have a record, and for that, we should be grateful." She inhaled, summoning the strength to remain calm.

"You're not answering the question."

"Listen, we've done fine without your dad all these years, and we'll continue to be fine without him. I'm done with this conversation." Maya put on her best "stern mother" expression. "Get the flowers done. I'm going for a swim."

Samantha glared at her but remained silent as she

snatched up clean gloves and started work on the gum paste flowers. Maya sighed and grabbed the keys to the van.

"Well, you needed him now, didn't you?" Samantha mumbled, just loud enough for her to hear.

Maya pretended she hadn't heard as she let the door slam behind her. This was far from being over.

CHAPTER TWELVE
SAM

Maryland, 1996

THE LIGHT WAS still on at Sam's parents' house when he pulled into the driveway after the concert. He inhaled Maya's lingering floral scent. He could still feel her lips on his, and the way her body had shaken as she'd faced off with her uncle. Maybe he should go back and check on her. That phone call in the morning with her mother was going to suck. He knew Maya's mother was going to forbid her to see him. What if Maya listened to her mother? His stomach clenched at just the thought. She wouldn't. She couldn't.

"Here he is." John Hutcherson lowered the volume on his game as Sam entered.

"Hey, Dad." Sam sat down in his seat, giving wide berth to the middle cushion. No one sat there anymore. It was Arjun's seat. "Mom." He ran a hand through his hair.

His dad was comfortably ensconced in his chair, while his mother curled up at her end of the sofa, reading under a lamp.

"How was your date?" John studied Sam's face.

"My date? My date was amazing. *She* is amazing."

"So what's the problem?" John took off his glasses. His mother looked over her own half eyeglasses at her son.

"Her family is—very conservative Indian."

John side-eyed his wife. "I've been there."

Sam's mother shook her head. "Oh, come now, John. I took care of my family. And now they love you and Monica."

Sam's thoughts wandered back to Maya and their kiss, and the look on her uncle's face when he'd seen them.

"Sam. Sam, where are you?" There was a twinkle in his father's eye and a smirk on his face.

"Right here, Dad."

"Your mother asked who the girl is."

Sam flushed a bit as his father studied his face. "Her uncle is Deepak Shah, the cardiologist I asked you about," he said. "Her name is Maya."

His father's eyes crinkled as he began to chuckle. Sam looked at him, surprised. "What's so funny?"

"You." He shook his head at his son and turned to his wife. "Our son is in love."

His mother deepened the wrinkle in her brow. "What? How could you possibly know that?" Hema Hutcherson still had her Indian accent, so her *W*s sometimes came out as *V*s, and this was the source of more than one joke in their family.

"Besides, how many times have you seen her, anyway? You've had two dates?" She frowned. "That's nothing."

"Dad said he knew the first time he met you." Sam turned to his father for support.

John's support and enthusiasm were apparent from his vigorous nod. "That's true."

Sam's mother rolled her eyes at them both, but Sam caught her blush and winked at his dad. She waved her hand at the both of them. "Crazy."

"Ma, she's Ben and Niki's summer nanny. Monica-*mami* told you, remember? I see her every day at your brother's house." And he hoped he would still be able to after Maya spoke to her mother.

Hema frowned. "That baker's daughter?"

Sam ignored the frown and managed to smile at his mother. "She's been to culinary school, and she's going to be a pastry chef," he said, pleased with himself.

John chortled and looked back at his wife. "Oh, yeah. He's done for."

Sam considered again the wisdom of going back to see Maya tonight. No, he'd be better off waiting until work tomorrow. She had to go to work, right? The thought of losing what he only just gained prevented him from noticing his mother's continued frown as she put her glasses back on and returned to her book.

SAM ARRIVED EARLY to his uncle's house to wait for Maya. He hadn't really slept, so getting there early was easy. He brewed coffee and worked on the tiling while he waited. He kept checking his watch, but the minutes passed slowly.

"Sam?" Sudhir-mama called out to him.

"In the bathroom." Sam stepped down from the ladder as Sudhir-mama entered. He'd been working for an hour that felt like a whole day and had successfully placed all of two tiles.

"Maya just called."

Sam's stomach plummeted. "Yeah?"

"She's running late. Can you hold down the fort with

the kids until she gets here? I have a meeting in half an hour, and Monica left already. They won't be up for a while."

"Yeah, sure. No problem." Sam started back up the ladder.

"Is everything okay, Sammy?" His uncle glanced at the two tiles.

Sam shrugged, ignoring his uncle's gaze. "Yeah. Everything's fine."

"Okay." Sudhir-mama furrowed his brow. "You just seem… I've never seen you like this before."

You mean you've never seen a man wait to find out whether the love of his life might leave him because her mother was making her?

"I'm good." Sam picked up a random tool and had no idea what to do with it.

"Okay." Sudhir-mama eyed the tool. "Not sure why you need a screwdriver to tile, but you go for it."

"Sure thing." Sam came down the ladder.

"Let me know if the kids are a problem."

"Uh-huh."

Sam continued working for the next hour. Just as he debated getting the kids ready to go with him to Maya's uncle's house, he heard a car pull up. He washed up and waited in the kitchen. Sam poured two cups of coffee, adding just a splash of cream to Maya's.

Maya rushed into the kitchen, and looked startled when she saw him standing there. "You're here early. I didn't think…"

He grinned with an ease he did not feel. "Of course I'm here. Somebody has to do your job when you show up late." His relief at seeing her had him almost giddy.

But her eyes were swollen and red, her hair was trapped in its ponytail and she was fidgeting.

She shook her head. "Of course, the kids, and the tiling…of course you'd be here." She faked a smile, but it didn't hide the question in her face.

"Maya, I'm here early because I didn't think it was a good idea for me to come over to your uncle's house. But if you hadn't shown up, I was coming to get to you."

"Oh, I thought…after last night…you wouldn't want…" She threw her hands up. "I mean… Deepak-mama's unreasonably strict, but he's just doing what he thinks my mom would want…"

He crossed the room and was by her side in an instant. "You thought I'd bail because Deepak-mama glared at me?" He couldn't believe Maya thought there could ever be a reason he wouldn't want to be with her.

She met his question with a small shrug and big, questioning eyes. "It's not easy, going out with me."

"That is true." He cupped her face in his hand. "But since it took me weeks to get you to go out with me, I can't waste all that work."

A small giggle escaped and her body relaxed. "True, you did beg."

Her laughter calmed the storm within him. "Persistent. I was persistent." Sam handed her the coffee. "Drink this. Tell me what happened." Sam took her hand, enjoying the perfect fit of it in his. He led her to the sofa, and when she sat down, he pulled her legs onto his lap.

Maya sipped her coffee. "Perfect. How did you…?"

"I pay attention."

Sam was rewarded with a small smile before she stared down into her coffee. "Sam—" she flicked her gaze at him before returning to her conversation with her coffee "—my mother has pretty much forbidden me to see you. Like, ever. Like I have to quit this job, ever."

The roiling in his stomach returned with a vengeance. "She can't do that…"

"Well, she can." Maya lifted her chin, her lips forming a tight grimace, but her eyes blazed. "But I don't have to listen. And that's what I told her." Her face brightened. "You have to understand—my mother was hurt very badly by my father. So her way of protecting me is to try to keep me from making her mistake. Which basically involves her deciding when and who I'll be in a relationship with." Maya paused for a sip of coffee. Her crooked smile took over her face.

"She wouldn't pick me?" He smirked, already knowing the answer.

Maya shrugged. "I told her you were different. She insisted it was a mistake for me to be with you."

"Maya, I would never do anything…"

"I know." She brought his hand to her lips. "I told her you were my mistake to make." She searched his face. "I don't know where this is going, but—"

"I can't give you up." The words fell out of his mouth, but it was the truth.

"I can't give you up, either."

"What are you saying, Maya?" Sam had to hear her say it. His heart was quite literally paused, waiting for her to either push Play or Stop.

"I'm saying that I told her I was going to continue seeing you and that I wasn't quitting my job, and that I would be home at the end of the summer, like we'd planned. She can't keep me sheltered my whole life.

She's not happy with me." Maya shrugged. "But she'll deal."

"Are you okay with that? I mean, you and your mom—you're so close…"

"What's the matter, Sam? Trying to get out of this?" Amusement colored her words.

Relief washed over Sam as he rested his hand on her face and leaned in and kissed her, picking up where they had left off the night before. A soft moan escaped Maya's throat. He pulled back. "What do you think?"

"I think if you're trying to get out of this, that kiss is not helping your case."

"What about Deepak-mama?" Sam tucked back a flyaway lock of her hair.

Maya dismissed him with a wave. "He'll do what my mom says. She told him to keep an eye on me. But apparently my cousin has a secret love life, too. So… whatever."

"Why do I smell chlorine?"

"I went for a swim this morning after my mom called. It's stress relief."

Sam pulled Maya closer still, and pressed his lips to hers once again, and was rewarded with her ready response. The scent of chlorine on Maya was new, but not unwelcome. "So is this."

"Eww. Sammy, are you *kissing* Maya?" Ben's voice was filled with all the disgust his eight-year-old body could muster.

Sam groaned as Maya jumped back from him. "These interruptions have got to stop."

AFTER WORK, AND after stealing a few more kisses with Maya when the kids weren't looking, he made his way to the mall. Excitement put a bounce in his step as Sam realized he was taking his future into his own hands for the first time. He paused at the jewelry store, where glass cases gleamed with all things gold, silver and diamond. Sam absently fingered the coin in his pocket before walking in. There was no question. This was what he wanted.

He searched the cases until he found exactly what he was looking for. When Sam pointed out what he wanted to see, the jeweler paused and drew his gaze over Sam, taking in the worn jeans and old T-shirt. Sam did not waver; he simply met the jeweler's gaze, and pointed again at what he was interested in.

"Tell me about it—" Sam scanned the jeweler's nametag "—Charles." He tapped his fingers on the glass while he waited.

Charles shrugged and opened the case. He appeared to be in his midforties, with a ready smile and slight question in his eyes. After an almost imperceptible hesitation, he spoke quietly. "Well, you have great taste," he said. "On your first try, you picked a very high-quality diamond in an eighteen-karat gold setting, and at just shy of one karat, it's a reasonably sized engagement ring."

"How much?" Sam bit the inside of his cheek when he heard the price. He could probably squeeze in a few more goalie training sessions per week and finish his uncle's remodel ahead of schedule so he could get another job. At his silence, the jeweler showed him a smaller ring, of lesser quality.

Sam shook his head at him. "No. It's the first one. That's the one." Sam leaned his elbows on the case and spoke softly. "I'll just need you hold it for a bit, until I can—"

Charles held up a hand to silence him. "Not a problem, son. We do it all the time." Sam left his name along with a deposit and headed out, light and happy, on his way to see Maya.

CHAPTER THIRTEEN
SAM

Maryland, 1996

"Come on," Sam said. "It'll be fine. I promise." He kissed the soft underside of her wrist to reassure her and spoke against her skin. "My parents don't bite."

"Yeah…" Maya's hand went slack from his kiss, and goose bumps appeared on her arm. She shifted her gaze to the house. They were sitting in the Civic, in front of his parents' house. Those honey eyes were—nervous. "I thought we were going to a game."

"We are." He loved the idea of being the one who gave her goose bumps, but right now didn't seem the time. Instead, Sam squeezed her hand. "It's just that…" He turned in the driver's seat to face her. "It's just that my dad really wants to meet you."

Her brows knit together. "Why?"

"Why?" Sam chuckled. "Seriously?"

Her blank stare made it apparent she had no idea.

"Because." Heat crept up his neck, but he ignored it. He cupped her cheek in his hand and focused on her eyes. "Because he knows I'm in love with you."

Her small, lopsided grin made an appearance as she leaned her face into his hand. "What?" The word came out on a breath.

He knew she'd make him say it again. It didn't matter: he'd say it as many times as it took. "I love you."

She smiled at him for a moment before her face clouded over. "So, he wants to check me out? See if I'm good enough?" She was spewing words so fast, Sam had trouble keeping up. "Oh my God!" She pulled out of his reach, and covered her mouth with her hands. "So I'm like *meeting-your-parents* meeting your parents?" She turned on him. "You could have warned me!"

Sam stared at her, trying to figure out what was happening. Had she even heard what he said? She must have, because she was freaking out right now. "Maya." Sam spoke as if he were trying to calm a cornered animal. "It'll be fine. *I* love you. They'll love you, too. I promise." He took both of her hands between both of his and held them steady.

She nodded, her breathing became more even and she turned to look at the house. Sam released her hands, and she tucked a flyaway piece of hair behind her ear, revealing her jawline and neck. She bit her bottom lip. He couldn't help himself. With a low groan, he leaned over and kissed the corner of her jaw, just below her ear.

He heard her gasp and felt her smile as she tilted her face close to his.

"You do deal with Deepak-mama every time you come over."

He grinned into her cheek as he kissed her again. "Mmm-hmm. I do." He felt more than saw her goose bumps, so he kissed her again, moving closer to her mouth.

"Sam…" Her breathless giggle only encouraged him to continue. He could feel her words on his mouth. "We're sitting in front of your parents' house!"

"So?" He held her gaze with his.

"So…" Her hands were soft and cool when she took his face in her hands and kissed his lips. Sam leaned over the gearshift to her side of the car and deepened their kiss, like a man starving for her. Which he was. Maybe they could skip the game…

Maya pulled away, leaving him wanting more. She closed her eyes as if summoning strength. "Okay, if you can do it, so can I."

"Great." He leaned over to continue their kiss.

She pulled back and rested her forehead on his. "Sam."

"Mmm?"

"We really should go in."

He really needed to be closer to her. He brought his mouth to hers and spoke against her lips. "I really do love you, you know." He reached around to grab her by the waist and pull her to his side of the car, but she pulled away from him.

Maya bit her bottom lip again, putting him at arm's length. Her eyes filled with mischief. "Well, good."

Sam's eyes widened as he shook his head back and forth. "Maya…"

She laughed and pushed him away. "Your parents are waiting."

Sam groaned as he got out of the car and came around to open her door. He laced their fingers together and led her to the house. His father stood in the doorway just as they approached.

"Sammy!" His father greeted him with a jovial slap on the back and then turned his attention to Maya. "You must be Maya. Come in, please!" He stepped aside and proffered his arm. "Take my arm, young lady, I will introduce you to my lovely wife." His father's grin lit up his face as he turned to wink at Sam.

Maya took his arm and smiled. "Thank you," she said, and she sounded calm. "It's wonderful to finally meet you."

Sam breathed easy at how relaxed she was. His dad really did have a way with women. His mother would be another story. He lagged behind as his father led Maya to the kitchen where the scents of sizzling garlic and onion told him that his mother was making dinner.

"So nice to meet you, Auntie." Maya offered a warm smile and stepped toward his mother as if to give her a hug.

Sam's mother offered her hand. "Nice to meet you."

Maya recovered smoothly and shook his mother's hand. Sam glared at his mother from behind Maya. What was she doing? Having her over here was in part her idea.

"We have heard so much about you, but Sam seemed reluctant to bring you to see us."

Maya turned amused but accusing eyes on Sam.

Sam's mouth gaped open. "No, I was…"

"Oh, Sammy was probably afraid we would try to scare you off," Hema whispered loudly to Maya. "That's what he thinks we did to his other girlfriends. It is a new one each month—"

"Mom!" Sam popped his eyes at her, trying to figure out if she was teasing him or serious. "Why would you say that? So not true."

His mother shrugged. "Well, maybe not *every* month. In any case, we're not trying to scare anyone off. Why would we do that? All we want is for Sam to find the right girl." She granted Maya a huge saccharine smile before turning to her husband. The smile never really reached her eyes, making Sam wonder what was up. "Isn't that right, John?"

His father had his hand over his mouth, his expression held a hint of alarm, but he quickly rallied. "Well, I suppose that's true." He turned a twinkling blue eye on Maya. "*You* are special."

Heat crept slowly but surely up Sam's neck. "Dad."

Father turned innocently toward son. "What? I promise not to take the baby pictures out until next time." He winked in Maya's direction.

"Baby pictures?" Maya bit her bottom lip. "Why wait until next time?" Amusement flashed in those honey eyes, and even that weakened him.

"Maya needs to see the house." His father offered his arm to Maya again, and led her out of the kitchen, away from his mother. Sam threw his mother a questioning glance and followed his father.

His dad gave Maya the whole tour, ending up in the family room.

"Okay, Dad. You've met Maya. We need to go if we're going to catch that game." He took Maya's hand and gave it a squeeze, immediately drawing comfort from her warmth.

His father held up his hand. "All right, just hold on a second. I'll get your mother."

Sam sighed his acquiescence. "Hurry." He turned to find Maya studying a very old family portrait of the four of them.

She rested her gaze on him with a touch of sadness in her eyes. "You look like your brother."

"Nah." Sam didn't even need to look at the picture.

He had studied it himself many times. "Arjun looked like my dad."

"I see why you think that, the blond hair, the beautiful blue eyes. But you have his smile—even that one dimple—though I think you're probably taller."

Sam shrugged. "Maybe."

"His name was Arjun?" Maya asked, while furrowing her brow. "It's a very strong name. You know in Hindu mythology, Arjun is…"

"…a great warrior," Sam spoke as if reciting from text. "One of the five warrior Pandava brothers. Those brothers had a bond that was beyond reproach. And Arjun was most known for his bravery and skill in every facet of life, from swordplay to dancing."

"You know the stories. Then you also know it's a difficult name to live up to."

"But he lived up to it." Sam looked into Maya's eyes, not sure what he was looking for. It wasn't so much that he was jealous of his brother, as much as it was hard to compete with his ghost. Arjun had been the perfect son.

Sam drew a deep breath and continued. "He was headed to Columbia as an undergrad. The plan was Columbia Law after that. Then he was going to work for a huge firm and get recognition before finally entering politics. Arjun was as charismatic as they come. He would've done it. But he, well…he died a week before he was going to leave for college."

Sam shifted his gaze to the portrait, his voice almost a whisper. "I adored him. As a big brother, he was everything to me."

Maya stood next to him, their shoulders touching. She leaned her head on his shoulder. "I'm really sorry you lost him."

Whether it was Maya's proximity or gentleness, he didn't know, but Sam's muscles relaxed and his breath came easier. A serenity fell over him that he hadn't even known was missing. "It's been a long time."

Suddenly, Maya lifted her head and turned to look at him, curious. "You said 'big plans have been made for me' and you went to Columbia as an undergrad, and you're at Columbia Law School right now."

Sam hung his head. He dragged his toe across the carpet for a moment before looking at her with chagrin as he spread his arms wide. "Well—" his words were tinted with sarcasm "—I'm living the dream."

Maya faced him, her hand on his chest, concern narrowing her eyes and pursing her lips. "You're doing everything he was going to do? But—you've never talked about going into politics. Is that what you want?"

Sam opened his mouth to speak, but Maya suddenly yanked her hand away as if burned. She stepped back and became keenly interested in the closest painting on the wall. Before Sam could ask what had caused this reaction, he found his mother behind him.

"It is in fact what Sam has always wanted to do." His mother carefully placed a hand on her son's shoulder. "He will make this family proud as he changes the world." She gazed up at him fondly.

"Hema, we should let the kids get going. They'll be late for the game." Sam's father came in right behind his wife.

"Of course." She released Sam's shoulder and he kissed her cheek.

"See you later, Ma." He caught Maya's eye and nodded his head toward the door.

"Well, Auntie, Uncle." Maya turned to his parents.

"It really was lovely meeting you. I see where Sam gets all his fine qualities."

Sam's father walked them to the door and gave Sam a side-armed hug. "Have a great time at the game." The enthusiasm in his voice seemed forced to Sam. But his next words to Maya were genuine. "Maya, it's truly wonderful to have met you. I can see why my son has fallen for you."

Maya blushed.

"Dad!"

"Oh, come on now, Sammy." He waved off his son's embarrassment. "You should've have told her by now. And if you didn't, I just helped you out." He winked at Maya.

Maya smiled warmly and flushed as he kissed her hand. Sam's father beamed at him. "Sammy, I really like this one." He looked at her affectionately. "Baby pictures, next time."

"If there is a next time." Sam's mother came up behind her husband.

Sam caught his father's eye and found his father's jaw clenched. He gave an almost imperceptible nod to Sam to just go. Sam bit the inside of his cheek and guided Maya out the door with his arm.

He settled Maya into her seat and jogged around to his side and sat down. "What?"

Maya was staring at the house.

"Your dad is super sweet." She faced him, a small grin on her face. "I see where you get your charm."

"He really likes you." He started the car and pulled out.

"Your mom seems like a really good cook. The smells from the kitchen were amazing!"

Sam grinned. Diplomatic. "She is." He glanced over to see Maya staring out the window again. He reached over and squeezed her thigh. Maya put her hand on his and turned to face him. He grabbed her hand and kissed it. "Don't worry. She'll come around. Mom isn't really a people person." He cleared his throat and concentrated on the road. "And I've never really brought a girl home before."

This time, Maya kissed his hand. Her lips were soft, and full of promise. "So I was the first?" The warmth in her face, and the way she looked at him—she loved him, he knew it. Why wouldn't she say it?

"Mmm-hmm. I told you. I'm in love with you." He didn't even hesitate. He loved her, and the more he said it, the better he felt. And the more he loved her.

Later that evening, Sam reached into his shorts' pocket and found an envelope. Puzzled, he opened it to find five hundred dollars in cash, along with a note in his father's handwriting. *Charles, the jeweler, is a patient of mine. Hope this helps.*

CHAPTER FOURTEEN
SAM

New York, 2012

IT WAS UNTHINKABLE to Sam that he go back to the piles of briefs and motions on his desk, after having laid eyes on the young lady who was his daughter. This person who existed partly because of him, whether he knew about her or not. His stomach was in knots and his thoughts bounced from elation at having this child, to anger at not being told about her, to confusion as to why Maya had kept the truth from him.

Rather than dealing with deadlines and paperwork, he called his secretary and told her to reschedule his meetings and send some files to his apartment. He'd look at them tonight. Right now, he needed a game. Someone would be at the soccerplex.

The soccerplex was bustling with activity. He hadn't played a game in weeks. A recreation team made up of men in their late twenties was warming up to play. The team was set for keeper, so he decided to play striker. Just as well—he needed to run. And kicking a ball could be quite satisfying.

For most of the first half, there was no Maya, no Samantha and no Paige. *Paige.* Thoughts of his fiancée distracted him and he missed a pass. He needed to tell her, and soon. Samantha was his daughter, and no matter what Maya said, his phone call to Byron Stevenson and the juvenile courts would not be the last thing he did for her.

This realization hit him just as the opposing team's keeper kicked the ball back into play. The ball was airborne and coming in his direction. Sam deftly brought the ball down, noted the keeper's weak side, and kicked the ball directly into that corner of the net. The keeper dove, but too late, and missed the save, as Sam had anticipated. Goal scored.

His thoughts turned to Maya as the game continued. His stomach was roiling with nerves, his concentration was off and he started missing plays.

The younger guys started cracking jokes about "the old man," until he finally stepped off the field.

Back at his apartment, he opened the door to find Paige pacing the length of the apartment as she spoke on the phone. Her side of the conversation was fraught with words like *centerpiece*, *classic* and *fix it*. As she hung up, he opened a bottle of Paige's favorite red wine and poured two glasses. He handed her one and kissed her cheek as they clinked glasses and drank.

She rolled her eyes. "So sorry—but I'm trying to get all that linen stuff fixed and I was super busy at the gallery today." She put her arms around him and looked him in the eye. "Mmm, don't you smell great? Soccer today?"

"Yes. Soccer today." He tried to keep his voice casual. Paige knew that he usually played when he needed to clear his head. "Did some files come for me?"

She nodded her head toward the table. "Right there." She stepped back from him, her hands still in his. "Everything okay?"

Sam fingered her engagement ring. They had shopped for it together so she could have the most perfect and unique ring. It had to be different from what her friends had, yet big enough for them to envy without being garish. She'd chosen a ring with a four-karat diamond in a custom platinum setting. It was unique in every way.

"Yeah, fine. Everything is fine." His voice sounded forced, even to him. He needed to tell her. "Actually, you won't believe what happened today."

"What's that?" Her eyes grew cautious with concern, as she searched his face.

She already knew that Maya was his girlfriend from his law school days. But that's all he'd ever told her. That's all he ever knew. What would he say? *So, remember I told you how Maya broke my heart when I was in law school? Well, turns out she was pregnant when we broke up, and she never told me. And I just met my fifteen-year-old daughter.*

"I found out…" He paused. Innocent curiosity filled her eyes. This news would rock her world, just as it had his. It wasn't time. He should wait until Samantha knew who he was. "I found out that there is something sketchy going on in that nursing home my father asked me about."

"No way!" Paige's eyes widened as she sipped her wine. "That's terrible! I know I said it's a drain on your time, but that needs to be addressed."

She continued to speak, but Sam interrupted. "How

about I order us some sushi, and I'll tell you all about it over dinner?"

She smiled wide and she was beautiful. He'd tell her later.

CHAPTER FIFTEEN
MAYA

New York, 2012

NOT FOR THE first time, Maya found the shop stifling. Having her two worlds collide had definitely caused a small explosion within her. How would Samantha even know where to begin a Google search for her father? *Sejal!* Maya's cousin in Maryland would have been easy to pump for information. When Maya ended up pregnant, the romantic in Sejal could not understand why Maya wouldn't tell Sam or why the fact that he was the baby's father had to be kept secret. Samantha probably only had to ask a few vague questions, and Sejal would've offered up more than was necessary without even knowing it.

Maya glanced at the time as she removed her chef's whites and left the shop to Samantha's loud mutterings. Whatever. Two hours until that cake needed to be delivered. She would only need one.

The smell of chlorine in the locker room was as calming to her as any balm or yoga class. She changed into her swimming gear and found an empty lane. Goggles over her eyes gave her the sensation of being alone as she sat on the edge of the pool and dangled her feet in the water for a moment. Maya slowly lowered herself into the pool and dunked her head in. The coolness of the water shocked and refreshed her and she pushed off the wall to begin her stroke.

The softness of the water and the familiar rhythm of her stroke cocooned her in comfort. Her breathing calmed as she matched her breath to her stroke. Even as a young girl just learning to swim, Maya had always felt at home in the water. Chlorine had been in everything she owned, and the smell of it on her skin always brought her contentment.

As she finished her warm-up, she pushed herself harder as she started her set. One hundred yards as hard and fast as she could go, followed by one hundred easy yards for recovery, then repeat. She might not be quite as fast as she was in high school, but she hadn't lost too much. With each stroke, a little more tension was released. Before long, her mind was empty of everything but her swim.

She relished blissful thoughtlessness. But when she paused for the next set, the raucous laughter of teenage boys floated toward her and the past attacked her again. She had spent the better part of the past sixteen years stifling any memory of Sam that surfaced. She was not going to go through all that again. She couldn't. Time to shut down those old feelings. They had no place in her life right now. She immediately began the next set to push away thoughts of Sam.

It was a losing battle.

Maya was halfway through her sets when she checked the clock. Slow today. She pulled her right arm across her chest in a stretch while she caught her breath. The boys were still enjoying the pool near the high dive. She stretched her other arm. The lifeguard had turned on an oldies station on the radio. The lyrics floated over to her just as she started her next set. It was an old Ace of Base song about a beautiful life. For an instant she caught the mixed scent of cigarette smoke and grass and *Sam*, as if he were standing right in front of her, and her heart ached with the memory.

Unfortunately, the swim had failed to clear her head. Fine. Once Sam made those phone calls and went back to his life, it would be easier to put those memories away for good. For now, images of Sam continued to invade her thoughts. She was still on edge when she returned to her apartment from delivering the wedding cake that Samantha had quite adeptly finished.

It was Friday, the night she and her mother usually cooked together. She found her mother sitting at the kitchen table, looking at old pictures. Maya closed her eyes in an effort to find patience. She inhaled deeply to prep herself and nearly gagged.

"Why do I smell lavender?"

Her mother nodded in the direction of a bouquet of flowers that sat on the table.

"What the…?" Maya marched over to the offending flowers. There was a card. *"The Colombian roast you suggested was a hit! Best, Leo."*

"Where did this come from?"

"That man who always asks you out. He brought them by the shop while you were at the pool." Her mother shook her head. "Samantha went up to my apartment to get away from the smell."

"I don't blame her," Maya muttered. She tossed the flowers in a plastic bag and tied it tight. She hadn't been able to stomach the scent of lavender since she was pregnant. Interestingly, Samantha had never liked it, either.

Maya gently placed her hand on her mother's shoulder. "Raju-kaka proposed again today, I take it."

While Sunita had been in the process of purchasing the bakery, she had needed to go to various suppliers for inventory—baking supplies, ingredients and the like. Not having a car, and not always feeling safe on the subway at night, she met Raju-kaka when he was her cabbie one night. Their friendship had been almost instantaneous, as they were from neighboring villages in India. After that, Raju-kaka saw to it that he was always available when Sunita needed a ride. Over time, he became an important part of their family in Queens— taking Maya to dance practice or a friend's house on occasion. When he fell in love with Sunita was anyone's guess. All Maya knew was that there had never been a time in her new life in Queens that Raju-kaka was not there. In fact, it had been she who gave Raju-kaka the honor of being called "kaka" as opposed to "uncle"— maybe because she hoped in some way that he really was her father's brother, even though he was not.

He was as close to a father figure as Maya had ever known, and Maya knew he waited for the day that Sunita would acknowledge her love for him, as well. Maya had repeatedly warned him that day would never come—Sunita was too bitter. Nevertheless, he persisted.

Sunita nodded but didn't look up. Maya picked up one of the pictures. She had seen these many times before. Every time Raju-kaka proposed, in fact. The one in her hand was a yellow-tinged black-and-white image of a much younger Sunita holding an infant. She stood beside a handsome man with a mustache and light-colored eyes. The man was smiling and relaxed, seemingly happy with his little family. This picture used to warm her heart, give her hope. But those feelings had long since been quelled into submission. She avoided looking at the other pictures, but even the fact that they were there caused cracks in her heart.

The other pictures were of Maya as a little girl in braids, filled with adoration as she looked at her father, while he tossed a ball to her. In another faded photo, little Maya laughed as her father swung her through the air. And the one that Maya tried to forget the most was that of herself at eight years old, proudly standing next to her father after winning a ribbon at a cake-baking competition. Even back then, her father had believed she could be a world-famous pastry chef, and because he had believed it, so did she. The worst part of this memory was the love and pride with which her father gazed upon her. All that love. All that pride and affection. He'd left the following week, and Maya never saw or heard from her father again.

She used to stare at this picture and will him to come back to them. She had been sure that he would return. Her mother spoke so lovingly of him; Maya couldn't understand how two people who loved each other so much could stand to be apart. Maybe he didn't love her, but surely he loved her mother.

As the years passed, however, Maya had watched her mother's love and hope turn bitter. Over time, her mother seemed to realize that her "true love" was not going to return, and she lost faith in love and in men altogether. She had made it her mission in life that Maya never suffer her fate.

"You know, in India," her mother said tersely, "it is

widely believed that people with light-colored eyes are not to be trusted."

Maya tightened her lips and shook her head. "My eyes are light." She no longer wished for her father's return. In fact, Maya had done her best to keep her own daughter from the disappointment of parental abandonment. At least, until Sam had met Samantha today.

Truthfully, until recently, the only emotion she afforded this picture was indifference. Now it made her angry. Her mother brought these pictures out every time Raju-kaka proposed, to reinforce her reasons for turning him down.

"I don't mean you, beta. You are very trustworthy."

"Am I?" Maya sighed deeply. "Raju-kaka's eyes are the deepest darkest brown there is." She tossed the picture on the table. "What was it this time?"

Her mother stared into space. "Oh, you know. The usual. 'I love you. I'll wait.'" Her hand trembled as she picked up the picture that Maya discarded.

"You know he will." Maya opened the fridge to start dinner.

"No. He'll leave." Her mother sighed sadly. "They all do."

Maya took out vegetables and chicken, and started chopping onions. Her mother gathered up the pictures and returned them back to the metal box they'd always been in.

It had been close to thirty years since Raju-kaka had found his way into their lives. Maya wanted to tell her mother that if he hadn't left yet, he never would. But they'd had that discussion and it always ended with her screaming, and her mother in tears.

Her mother picked up a knife and started to chop

tomatoes. Sounds of chopping and sizzling joined the aroma of onions cooking with garlic, tomatoes, cinnamon and cloves. Mother and daughter worked in companionable silence, each preoccupied with her own thoughts.

"Samantha did a wonderful job on that cake, don't you think?" Her mother sounded like her old self.

Distracted, Maya simply nodded.

"I hate to say it because of the circumstances, but it *is* nice having her around during the day," her mother said. "She's very talented."

"She's not going to run the shop, nor will she spend her life baking for it." Maya's voice was firm.

"I didn't say she was." The older woman put up her hands in surrender. "But if she doesn't get back into that school, she has a backup."

"She's going back to that school."

"Only if you send her. There are plenty of other schools." She paused. "Did you find a lawyer?"

"I did. In fact, he told me today that things would be taken care of."

Her mother turned to face her. "So I heard."

Maya shifted her body away from her mother and toward the stove. She closed her eyes and chided herself for being so distracted that she'd fallen into this conversation. "Hmm."

"Yes. Samantha told me she met the lawyer today. That he came to the roastery."

Sweat started to bead on her upper lip. She stirred the pot and tasted the chicken. "Needs salt."

"A Mr. Hutcherson." Her mother's inflection said it all.

Maya could feel her mother's glare boring holes into the back of her head. She sprinkled salt straight from the canister and added a small handful of chopped cilantro before stirring the pot again.

"Can you pass the lemon juice, Mum?" Her hand shook as she took the bottle from her mother without turning to face her.

"Not a very common name."

Without even looking, Maya knew the set of her mother's jaw.

Maya cleared her throat. "Actually, there's a young actor Samantha has a crush on with that same last name." She forced a chuckle. "Haven't you seen the poster in her room?"

"She gave me a full description of the lawyer. Complete with details of how the two of you shared coffee." Her mother grabbed Maya's arm to face her. "What have you done?"

CHAPTER SIXTEEN
MAYA

Maryland, 1996

MAYA AND SAM had been together for a month, and it was all Maya could do to focus on anything but him. She wasn't sleeping well, and so many happy butterflies had taken up residence in her belly, she found it hard to eat. She'd always rolled her eyes at girls who claimed no appetite and no sleep because of a boy, but now she was thinking maybe they weren't so crazy. *You just don't get it if you're not in it.*

"Look what I found." Sam stood behind the sofa where Maya was sitting and handed her a brochure. She was babysitting Ben and Niki for the weekend while his aunt and uncle took a well-deserved weekend away to celebrate their anniversary. Which really helped, because it meant sleeping over at the Mehta house with the children, and a whole weekend away from her uncle's overprotectiveness. Sam had a free hour before his next shift started and was spending it with her.

Maya put the brochure aside. She turned slightly and reached for his hand over the back of the sofa. "Why do you have to have three jobs, Sam? You're running yourself into the ground." Dark circles under his eyes and a stifled yawn proved her point.

He kept his gaze on the TV as he absently answered, "I'm just saving up for school expenses." Sam picked up the brochure again. "Look! I found it on the desk." He leaned over the back of the sofa, his face was next to hers and Maya lost herself in his clean, masculine scent.

She forced herself to focus on the brochure, which advertised a bed-and-breakfast in Virginia, a mere three-hour drive from Maryland. Her heart raced. "Are you serious?" *A bed-and-breakfast?*

He was all wide-eyed innocence. "What? You said we should spend more time together." A mischievous grin broke through, sending butterflies free in Maya's belly. "And I happen to agree." He opened the pamphlet. "See, there's hiking and horseback riding. And I can get the weekend off." He gently nudged her cheek with his, his scruff scratching her cheek in the most intimate way, sending a thrill all the way to her core. "And did you also see there's breakfast?" He cleared his throat. "And a bed?"

Yes, she had seen that there was a bed. It was really the only thing she saw. Warmth traveled the length of her body and she bit the edge of her bottom lip, as she flipped through the brochure, purposefully avoiding his eyes.

"Yes, I did see that." She looked at him sideways and laughed. "Hiking and horseback riding sound great."

He kissed her neck, sending tingles all the way down that side of her body. "Or you could let me come over after work and...stay."

She pulled back just enough to whisper. "Probably not a good idea. Because there are children in this house, and I'm working."

Sam deftly vaulted over the back of the sofa so he was

seated next to her. His eyes were darkened with desire, making her heart pound. "The rug rats are sleeping now."

There was no reason, and no way to resist that low and husky voice. She closed her eyes and leaned closer to him as he pressed his mouth against hers, deepening their kiss.

"Maya!" Niki's voice cut through their moment. "Maya!"

Maya stiffened and started to push away from Sam. He didn't release her. "Pretend you can't hear."

She glared at him. "Sam!"

He released her with a groan. "Virginia, Maya." He nodded at her. "Virginia."

Maya smiled as she gathered herself from their interrupted kiss and called to Niki. "I'm coming." She started for the steps and nearly ran into the little girl. Niki was clutching a blanket and a teddy bear in one hand and rubbing her eyes with the other. "Oh, hey, sweetie. What's the matter?" Maya knelt to look Niki in the eye.

Niki stopped rubbing and squinted at Maya through a screen of hair. "I had a bad dream." Her voice was small and scared. "Can I stay here with you and Sammy?"

"Oh, sure you can." She flicked her eyes at Sam as if to say, *"See what I mean?"*

"Come on, monkey." Sam called out to his cousin, patting his lap. "Tell us all about it."

Niki curled up into his lap and Maya sat down next to them as Niki began a detailed account of the monster chasing her in her dream. Niki fell asleep just after describing how the monster had fur all over his body and huge eyes and thought Niki would taste good in soup. Sam held the little girl close.

Maya reached her arm over and absently played with Sam's curls. "Let's go to Virginia."

Sam's eyes lit up. He whispered over Niki's head, "What about your uncle?"

Maya pressed her lips together and looked past him. "I need a plan to sneak out." She leaned over and kissed his cheek. "I'll call Ami. She has two older brothers. If anyone knows about sneaking out, it's her."

BY THE TIME Maya's car tires crunched onto the driveway of the bed-and-breakfast, it was past 11:00 p.m., and she was grateful to see a light on. She grabbed her bag and headed up the porch steps as quietly as possible. Her skin was sticky from the thick mid-July humidity, and she willed herself not to sweat. When she reached the door, she found it was locked. She knocked lightly.

A man close to her uncle's age greeted her with a warm smile. "Hello!" The man's voice was just above a whisper. "Let me get that." He took her bag and stepped aside to let her in.

Maya let out a breath of relief inside the coolness of the house. "I'm Maya, and I'm awfully sorry for the late hour. The traffic was terrible."

"Not a problem," he said. "We understand." He continued to smile as he waved off her concern. He offered her his hand. "I'm Dave. That DC to Virginia traffic drives us all crazy. That's why we live here now."

Dave's manner reminded Maya of Sam's father and as she shook his hand, she was immediately at ease. "Thank you, Dave." She stood in a small foyer that opened to a family room of sorts on her left. There were sofas and cozy, overstuffed chairs. To her right was a dining table large enough for twelve people. In front of her was a staircase. She caught the lingering scent of coffee and something sweet, like baking cookies. There was no Sam. Her heart dropped. "I'm, uh...supposed to be meeting someone here. Sam Hutcherson?"

"Oh, of course. He waited for a while, but he's gone up to your room." He indicated the staircase to Maya. "He said to just bring you up when you got here."

She smiled, relieved. Of course he was here.

"Shall we?"

Maya nodded and followed Dave up the carpeted steps. There were three doors on the second floor. Dave led her to the farthest one and handed her bag to her.

"This is as far as I go. Good night."

As Dave's footsteps faded away, she faced the door and contemplated what was waiting for her on the other side. She took a deep breath before she picked up her bag and turned the knob.

The room was bathed in the soft glow of candlelight. Candles were on the windowsill to her left, and also covered the bureau to her right. A small tea table with two cushy chairs in the back corner hosted more candles, some of which were barely still flickering. The wardrobe next to the tea table set had a small ledge with a few candles placed there. The effect was calming, romantic. Maya put down her bag and shut the door quietly. To her left was a four-poster bed of cherrywood.

On the bed, handsome as ever in the glow of romantic candlelight, lay Sam. He was fully dressed to go out and stretched out on his back, fast asleep. Maya didn't realize that she had been holding her breath until she saw him. His creamy skin showed off its brown undertone in contrast to the stark white of the pillow. He took up almost the whole length of the bed. Even in sleep, when people were at their most vulnerable, Sam emitted an aura of strength that immediately put Maya at ease. She finally released her breath and then sighed deeply with—what? Disappointment? Relief? Maybe a little bit of both. She took off her shoes and blew out the candles. A sliver of moonlight lit her way back to the bed.

She climbed onto the bed and lay down next to him. He didn't move. She found comfort in the familiar scent of his cologne and the warmth of his skin. Maya kissed his stubble. He shifted a bit, but didn't open his eyes. She snuggled down and lay her head on his chest. Without waking, he brought his arm around her and pulled her close. She fell asleep listening to the sound of his heartbeat.

When Maya woke, the sun was up and Sam was gone. Puzzled, a bit groggy and still in yesterday's clothes, she took a shower. She took advantage of the floral-scented lotion she found and then wrapped herself in one of the plush robes provided by the inn. Her hair still damp, she stepped out from the bathroom just as Sam entered the room.

He was fully dressed in khaki shorts and a T-shirt, but his feet were bare. The rich aroma of coffee followed him into the room and mingled with the clean scent of her shower and the waxy-floral fragrance from last night's candles. Sam's presence filled the small room, and Maya became acutely aware of the fact that all she had on was a robe.

"Hi." She spoke quietly and brought her arms across her body, trying to meet his eyes, but instead noticing how well the T-shirt formed around the muscles of his chest, and how his slightly damp curls touched the nape of his neck. When she looked away from him, her gaze found only the bed. She swallowed hard.

Sam was frozen in place. "Hey." He openly stared at her, lips full and slightly parted.

Maya pressed her own lips together. Silence banged around between them.

Maya pulled the robe tighter and finally met his eyes. They looked a bit glazed. "Um, is one of those for me?" She indicated the two mugs in his hands.

"Huh?" Sam continued to gawk at her and then apparently seemed to remember he had hands. He looked down. "Oh, uh, yeah." He started to hand her one then the other. "I don't remember which is yours."

Maya crossed the room and took one of the mugs. Her fingers grazed his and sent a tingle up her spine. "The sweet one is yours." She closed her eyes as she inhaled the unique aroma of orange mixed with coffee. She took a sip and her taste buds flooded with the sweetness of the citrus and the slight bitterness of the coffee. The combination was intoxicating. Or maybe it was just being here. In this room. With Sam. "Yours." She switched mugs with him.

"Okay, good." He had been watching her this whole time. "I feel like I haven't seen you in a week."

She backed over to the chairs and carefully took a seat as she tilted her head and motioned for Sam to join her. "Five days. But who's counting?"

Sam had small, dark circles under his eyes, and he stifled a yawn.

"Did you get yet another job?" Maya asked. "Sorry I was late." She started rambling before he could answer. "The traffic was ridiculous and Ami didn't mention how things get clogged up on that highway."

Sam seemed to relax, and his crooked grin, complete with sexy dimple, reappeared on his face. "I thought so." He sat down in the chair next to her. "Sorry I fell asleep." The small tea table was between them, but their feet could touch. Even that felt electric. Mischief made his lip twitch, made his eyes glint with amusement. "Though I will say that I didn't think my first night sleeping with you would end up with us *actually* sleeping."

Heat rose to her face as she caught his eye. The amusement left his eyes, leaving behind what Maya could only guess was longing. She cleared her throat. "This coffee is incredible." She took another sip. "I've never had…the orange taste…with coffee…" It was impossible to look at him and speak at the same time. She brushed her upper lip with the back of her hand. Was it warm in here?

"Hmm-mmm." Sam sipped again and Maya became mesmerized with the way his lips gently touched the mug. His molten-brown gaze never left her face. "They get it specially made."

The heat continued to rise up her neck, but now it started to spread throughout her body. She nervously crossed her legs and the robe fell open, revealing her leg almost to the hip. She hastily uncrossed her legs and readjusted the robe, but was forced to lean forward and caught Sam staring at her, frozen again. He swallowed hard. Maya tensed and automatically sat back up again.

More silence.

Sam finished his coffee. Maya watched his hand shake slightly as he placed his cup on the table between them.

"The candles were a nice touch." Her voice cracked. "Very romantic."

He leaned forward and placed his elbows on his knees, while he covered his face with unsteady hands and inhaled all the way down to his toes, holding his breath for just a beat, before finally dropping his hands and emerging. He let out a quiet chuckle.

"Maya." Sam's deep, smooth voice was soft and familiar. He leaned toward her and touched her hand. She stiffened. "It's okay." He hesitated for a fraction of a second before putting his fingers under her chin, lifting her face. This close to him, Maya was enveloped in the aroma of coffee mingled with his soap. She was able to appreciate the smoothness of his skin where he had recently shaved, as well as the welcome roughness from callouses where his fingers touched her chin. "Dave tells me there's excellent hiking here. Get—" he cleared his throat "—dressed. We can check it out."

Maya stared at him. There was amusement and understanding in everything about him. From the warmth of his eyes, to the crookedness of his smile; from the strength in his jaw, to the words he was saying. Everything about him shouted that he loved her. Even his hand under her chin was gentle and strong, but not demanding. He had been saying it, but she hadn't really understood that until now. Now that she did, it was clear to her that she loved him, too. Why hadn't she seen this before? Her whole body relaxed. She put her mug next to Sam's as he stood. She looked up at him. "Where are you going?"

Sam laughed as he gave a deep sigh. "To take a shower."

Maya wrinkled her brow and assessed him. Wet hair. The smell of soap. "You already had a shower."

He inhaled deeply and rubbed his hand over his mouth and jaw as he mumbled, "Cold shower, Maya. Really cold." He started toward the bathroom.

She grabbed his arm. "Are you sure you want to do that?" It was more than a whisper, more than a question. Just speaking the words made her heart pound.

He wrinkled his brow in confusion. "Maya, we don't have to…"

He stopped when she rose to face him. She stood on the tips of her toes and tilted her face to him. She was close enough to feel his breath on her lips. She looked at him from under her eyelashes. "The thing is, I love you and…"

He cupped her face in his hands and leaned down to look her in the eye. His grin went from lost to found, his excitement barely contained in his face. "What did you say?"

Maya pressed herself closer to him, still looking into his eyes. "I said that I love you." She couldn't suppress her own small smile as she took his hands from her face and held them in her own. She brought her lips close to his and softly continued, "If you want to celebrate that with a hike, I can get dressed." His heart pounded against hers and his breath was getting shallow.

"What's my other option?" Sam's voice was soft and hoarse and his words touched her mouth.

She concentrated on his lips as she whispered back. "*Not* hiking…" She flicked her eyes in the direction of the bed. "You could check with the coin."

"No need." She barely heard his words because he let go of whatever restraint he had left and wrapped his arms around her as he pulled her to him. His lips were on hers and he kissed her as if she were a craving, and he just couldn't get enough of her. He tasted like orange and coffee and she pressed even closer to him, kissing him fiercely, as if she couldn't get enough of him, either.

He paused for breath, and she felt soft, full lips on her eyes and chin, before he took her face in his hands again. She half opened her eyes as his lips lightly grazed hers. He looked at her and whispered, his voice heavy with desire, "I'm yours."

She stood on tiptoe and brushed her lips along his jawline toward his mouth. She stopped just short of touching his lips with hers, grabbed a handful of his T-shirt and led him to the bed. "I'm yours."

CHAPTER SEVENTEEN
SAM

Maryland, 1996

SAM WOKE HOURS LATER, the sun in the afternoon sky and Maya asleep next to him. She had rested her head on his bare chest, her long, dark tresses sprawled across them both. The scent of honeysuckle from her hair wafted around, enveloping him as he absently stroked her hair. Clearly, he'd been wasting his time with other girls. Maya was the one. That he felt this way about her in so little time was not the norm for him, but he knew in that moment that he would never love anyone like he loved Maya.

No, that wasn't quite true: he had known after that first date.

"Hey." Maya's sleepy voice interrupted his thoughts.

Sam smiled and turned on his side to better see her. "Hi."

She rested her head on his arm, brushing her soft, sweet-smelling hair away from him.

He traced a silken path from her shoulder to her elbow and back. "You were right." Her skin was smooth in contrast to the rough calluses on his hands, and for a moment, Sam considered pulling his hand away. But she hadn't complained yet. In fact, she snuggled her body closer.

She smiled. "You'll have to be more specific."

"Remember when you said that maybe I didn't know anything else except what my mother wanted for me?" He traced a line from her shoulder to collarbone and toward her neck. He smiled in satisfaction as goose bumps appeared on her skin.

"Well, I didn't say that exactly," she said.

"Well, you were right. It *is* all I have ever known. Since my brother died, it was like an unspoken rule that I would do everything he would've done. It seemed to make my mom—well, less sad." He continued tracing his finger from her elbow to her hand, brought her hand to his lips and kissed it. "If I had my way—" He couldn't say it. It felt almost wrong to voice his own hopes and dreams, when Arjun no longer had his.

"If you had your way, what?" She spoke softly, almost as if she were afraid that if she spoke too loudly he would stop talking. He wanted to tell her that would never be the case.

Sam dropped his gaze on hers and let it rest. She was beautiful, inside and out. A sensation had come over him that he hadn't experienced since childhood. He felt light and free, and he was happy. He couldn't understand how he could feel this carefree while still being connected to this one person. He'd simply been going through the motions of life, doing what was expected, but now, he knew what he wanted. And she was lying right here in his arms. She looked at him with such pure love, he knew he was completely lost to her. Her eyes were soft and golden, and her cheeks carried a pleasant flush that he had put there.

"After my brother was killed, there was a trial. The defense tried to make it look like Arjun was a reckless teenager and was equally at fault. They said that even though the other driver was over the blood alcohol limit, if Arjun has stopped *completely*, there wouldn't have been an accident. Our lawyer was smarter and came up with all kinds of evidence that proved that theory wrong. We ended up getting justice for Arjun and our family. It made a big difference for us, in helping us move on." He looked at her fingers, entwined with his. "At least for me and my dad." Sam hazarded a glance at her. She smiled when he caught her eye, waiting for him to continue.

"So ever since then, I thought how incredible it would be to help out families like that, to make a difference in people's lives during a time that's difficult for them. If had my way," he continued, "I'd open my own office and do just that—forget all that corporate crap." He watched her, waiting for her expression to change. But when it did, it wasn't with the disapproval he feared, instead she beamed at him, clearly impressed.

"That's amazing! God knows half our neighbors in Queens have been taken advantage of simply because they couldn't afford to pay a fancy lawyer." Her face glowed with pride and love, and she made small circles on the back of his hand with her thumb. "You should totally do it." She snuggled closer and kissed his neck with those soft, plush lips. *Oh, God.*

He closed his eyes. "So, I had made a promise to my mom that I would fulfill Arjun's dream of corporate life and politics, and I'm keeping it." He surprised himself with the resentment that showed up in his voice. "That's my map to my future. And there aren't any detours."

Maya's hand on his face made him open his eyes. "Maybe you could do both." This was just another thing he loved about her—her sense of hope. She clearly did not know his mother, and there was no way to explain Hema to her.

"It doesn't matter. What matters is being here with you." Sam's anger vanished as he pushed aside the soft tresses that cascaded over her shoulder and focused on Maya's beautiful, bare, brown skin. He leaned over and kissed her shoulder. *But why couldn't he have the life he now knew he wanted?* She reached out for him. *One that included Maya and his own dreams? They could live in the city. Maya could become a world-famous pastry chef in any restaurant in New York, and he could have his practice.*

"Hey, where'd you go?" Maya ran her fingers along his jawline, and down his neck to his chest.

"Hmm?" He closed his eyes and gave in to her hands. "Nowhere." He opened his eyes and locked her gaze. "Maya?"

"Yes." Her eyes were soft and loving, and Sam was positive he was the only man alive who felt this way about a woman. Surely he was the luckiest man on earth to be locked in her loving gaze.

"I've never told anyone about my dreams. I always thought my dreams were…secondary. But…you make me feel like anything is possible. I love you, Maya. And I meant what I said before, I belong to you. Only to you."

She bit her bottom lip, and her eyes lit up. "And I belong to only you. And I always will." Her expression became playful as she kissed his lips and face. Just as he reached around to take her back in his arms, she whispered, "We need food."

"No. No, we don't." His voice was husky as he placed a hand on her bare hip to pull her closer.

She laughed and pushed him away as she reached for her robe. "Yes, we do. At least some more coffee." He reached out to pull her back to the bed. She continued to laugh as she escaped his grip and donned the robe. "A shower first."

Sam threw himself back onto the bed with a groan and watched as she walked into the bathroom. *Time to live the life he really wanted. He'd talk to his parents when he got home.* She threw the robe out and poked her head out. "You coming or what?"

CHAPTER EIGHTEEN
SAM

New York, 2012

SAM EXITED HIS office building with his phone to his ear. Cold wind and honking cars made it difficult for him to hear the voice mail. He and Maya had been playing phone tag all day, the last one from Maya sounded final. He'd gotten Byron Stevenson as well as the authorities to agree not to press charges against Samantha. He had also convinced the school that expelling Samantha was not in anyone's best interest. Maya had thanked him and, apparently, dismissed him back to the past. He had called her back right away, but she hadn't picked up or returned his call. Irritated, he left another message. "Maya, call me when you get this message. I'm on my way to the coffee shop. I want to be a part of Samantha's life. I can't just make a few calls and forget I have daughter. But I think we should tell her together."

No sooner did he tap his phone to disconnect than he was stopped in his tracks. A young girl with long dark curls, wearing a camel-colored woolen coat but no hat or scarf, sat by the fountain. Sam could not imagine why she would be here, but his pace increased as he approached her. *Maybe he'd tell her himself.*

"Well, hello."

Samantha started at the sound of his voice, but recovered quickly as she stood to face him. She reached out a bare hand to tuck her flyaway hair behind her ears. "Hello." She wiggled a couple fingers at him in greeting.

The silence between them was solid enough to be another person. But neither moved away. "So, everything okay?" Sam spoke first.

"Yes." Her hands were shoved into her pockets, but she could not seem to stop studying him. It was as if she was trying to memorize him. "You're the lawyer."

If Sam was not mistaken, she rolled her eyes in that small eye-roll way teenagers had when they felt self-conscious. Niki had done this a lot.

He caught her eye and responded with a smile. "We met. The other day…" Sam wanted to say more, but he was trying to catch up with the fact that he was actually looking into eyes that were the same as his. "Why are you here, Samantha?"

"Mom and I were called to see my vice principal yesterday." She started to walk.

"And how was that?" He buttoned his coat and put on his gloves as he joined her.

"Well, Mrs. Pappenberger hates me. So I totally expected her to throw every book at me that she could."

Sam tensed. "Is that what she did?"

Samantha frowned, her eyebrows raised. "No. She called me and Mom to the office and made a big show of how she's so important, and how I don't really belong at that school." Samantha shrugged. "But in the end, she let me go with a warning. Apparently, no charges will be filed, and now I have a clean slate." She paused.

"Thanks to you." She granted him a sideways glance. "So, thank you." It was almost a whisper.

Sam relaxed and nodded. "Not a problem. Just a couple phone calls." He was trying to decide if she sounded like Maya. He thought she did. "As I told your mother, the added bonus was sticking it to Byron Stevenson." He laughed the nervous laugh of a teenager and he could almost taste the cigarette smoke in the wind as it mixed with the aroma of fried food wafting from nearby restaurants. People passing them on both sides muttered irritations under their breath, but father and daughter seemed oblivious of all this as they concentrated on one another.

"You're not just the lawyer, are you?" She stopped, almost midstep, and spit out the words quickly as if she were afraid they wouldn't come out otherwise. "You're my dad."

The words hit Sam with the force of a blow to the belly. She murmured something he couldn't quite make out. They stopped and were silent as the crowd flowed around them, two boulders in a creek of people.

Sam opened his mouth to speak, but nothing came out. He paused and took a deep breath as he looked past Samantha at the neon lights of the city, brilliant around them. Relief mixed with confusion. He wanted nothing more than for her to know who he was, but how had she found out?

When he opened his mouth a second time, speech had, thankfully, returned to him. "Excuse me, I didn't get that last part."

Samantha looked up at him with cold brown eyes as she raised her voice. "I said, 'or at least the sperm donor.'"

A passerby sniggered, and while Samantha reddened, she did not break eye contact. Sam simply raised one eyebrow at her. "Okay. Yes, I am your dad." Then with some degree of awkwardness said, "But the second part, it wasn't like that."

Sam leaned toward her. "I'm surprised your mom told you. She all but kicked me out of her shop the last time I saw you."

A look of victory crossed her face and realization kicked in. "She didn't tell you, did she?" He sighed. "Nicely played." He bowed slightly to acknowledge her win. "How did you figure it out?"

"Well." She hesitated, but she managed to look abashed and proud all at the same time. "It wasn't hard to figure out. She never has coffee with the customers. Like, *ever.* And you saw her that day, she couldn't wait to get you out of there, which made no sense, since you'd agreed to help me. At the very least she could've sent you home with cookies." Her cheeks flushed with excitement and her words tumbled out, engulfing Sam like warm water. "But when I want information," she said, "I use the internet."

Her voice softened. "I started looking for you about a year ago. I wanted to know about you, and she wouldn't ever say much. She also never came to Maryland with us to see Sejal-*masi.* She only sees them when they come up here. So, I was alone with Sejal-*masi…*"

"You asked Sejal?"

"Yeah, you know her?"

Sam grinned. "I used to know her." Visions of a giggly young girl with her hand over her eyes, swearing she wasn't peeking at them kissing, popped into his head. When he didn't offer more, Samantha continued.

"I started with Sejal-*masi*, because she's great and all, but sometimes, she lets things slip." Samantha tried, but failed, to hide the pride in her smile. "Like the fact that Mom was a nanny in Maryland the summer before I was born, and had dated someone who went to Columbia Law. She didn't even realize she said your name." Samantha bit her bottom lip. "Google did the rest. I was narrowing it down, but you were the right age, and your name is Sam." Her voice lowered. "I always wondered why I was named Samantha—as opposed to something more *Indian*. Made sense."

"You—you're amazing," Sam said, with what could only be pride in his child. He shivered in the wind. "I notice you're taller than your mother." Sam tilted his head to the side. "By more than an inch."

A smile played at her lips and she offered him another small eye roll. "I suppose I have you to thank for that, too."

"Yeah, I suppose so." He leaned in close to her. "But that sass—that comes from your mother." He stood back and laughed. "Or your grandmother." He looked around as if Sunita might be lurking. "But don't tell her I told you that."

He offered his hand in a handshake. "Let's meet, officially."

Samantha just stared at his hand.

Sam pressed his lips together and returned his hand to his side. "I thought you came to find me so we could get to know each other."

"Yeah, well. That doesn't change the fact that *I* had to come find *you*." She glowered at him.

"Well, I've been playing phone tag all day with your mom so I—"

"Why is that?"

"Why is what? Phone tag? Because your mom won't—"

"No, why did I have to come to you, instead of the other way around? Where have you been for fifteen years?"

Her anger was like a punch and the fire in her eyes reminded him so strongly of Maya, it was as though he were transported back in time. He was speechless for a moment as he took in the rage that emanated from her. "Samantha, I never knew about you. When your mom and I broke up, she—she never told me she was pregnant."

Samantha stared at him, her mouth agape.

"I swear. I had no idea you even existed until a week ago."

Samantha closed her mouth. "You're lying."

"No." Sam stepped closer to her. "No, I'm not. Your mom told me about you when she asked me to help you." *When she needed something.* Sam clenched his jaw in anger and frustration. "You have to believe me."

"Sam! Sam? Is that you?"

Sam froze at the familiar sound of Paige's voice. What was she doing here? He threw a nervous glance at Samantha before turning to face Paige. "Hi, honey! What's going on?" His casual tone sounded forced, even to him.

Paige approached and kissed him on the cheek as she linked her arm with his. "I was just coming to the office to see you, and here you are."

"Yeah, here I am." His eyes flicked to Samantha, who shuffled her feet and folded her arms across her body.

Paige looked from Samantha to Sam in the silence

that followed. She extended her hand to Samantha. "Hello. Paige Doyle, Sam's fiancée. Are you the new intern?"

"Yes, she's the new intern." A knot built in his stomach.

Samantha's eyes widened, then narrowed at Sam as she shook Paige's hand. His stomach tightened, and he was vaguely nauseous.

"Oh, that's great." Paige smiled. "Nice to meet you." She gazed at Sam, then turned back to Samantha. "He may be a tough boss, but he means well—don't let him get to you!" She turned to Sam. "How about a drink? We're close to our bar."

"Um, yeah. Sure." He turned to face Paige. "It's freezing. Let me finish up here, and I'll meet you."

"Sounds great!" She quickly kissed him and waved goodbye to Samantha.

Before Paige got even half a block away, Samantha was yelling at him. "Nice, *Dad*. Can't even acknowledge me to the woman you're going to marry. Mom was right. We *were* fine without you. I should've listened to her." She wiped angry tears and stomped off. Stricken, Sam followed.

"No, it's not like that. Listen, we just met—you're all grown up and I didn't even know I had you. I can't just spring that on my fiancée in the middle of the street. Listen, I'm going to tell her, but right now is not the best time. What about your mom? Did you tell her where you were? That you were coming to see me?"

Samantha stopped walking.

"Yeah, that's what I thought." Sam softened his voice. "I get it, you're angry and you have no reason to believe me. I *really* did not know about you. But if I had…" He stopped as his anger at Maya threatened to erupt. "Just believe me, now that I do, I would really like to get to know you—maybe be part of your life. No matter what your mom says."

Something flickered in Samantha's eyes, and hopeful, Sam continued, "Just think about it. Ask her—she has to tell you the truth."

Samantha gave a barely perceptible nod and turned away from him as she headed for the subway station. Sam stared after her, and his heart ached. Every time a woman walked away from him, she managed to take a piece of his heart with her. And he never got it back.

SAM MET PAIGE for a drink at her favorite place, The Dream Bar. He knew he had to tell her about Samantha, but she greeted him with a huge smile and a kiss and started right in about wedding plans, and he couldn't find the right moment. She seemed to have reconciled the issue with the linens and tablecloths and was going on about this fabulous wedding cake designer she had found out about.

"We have an appointment with her next week. Okay, Sam?" Paige squeezed his hand. "Are you with me? I want to you to come and help me choose the cake."

Sam sipped his drink, making forced eye contact with his fiancée. Her lips were moving and sound was coming out, but Sam could not seem to focus on her words. Glimpses of the pain and anger in Samantha's face flashed before him and his mind wandered as he wondered how he'd get to see her again. He hadn't gotten her cell number, so he had no way to contact her, save going to the coffee shop—which was not ideal, as

Maya had made it clear she wanted Sam to have nothing more to do with Samantha. He'd give her a couple days.

"Sam? Sam, are you with me?" Paige was smirking at him. "Cake tasting. Next week."

"Of course." Sam grinned at Paige and focused on her. "Whatever you want."

CHAPTER NINETEEN
MAYA

New York, 2012

"What the hell, Maya?" Ami said, scolding her friend. "I leave town for, what, not even two weeks, and S-A-M is back in your life."

Maya watched as Ami took a sip of her martini and expertly placed it back on the wooden table without spilling. Extra dirty with three olives, same as hers. They had sat in this very bar at this very table countless times over the years. They had sat here to celebrate getting into the colleges of their choice. They'd drunk to their broken hearts and toasted their accomplishments. It was here that they sat when Maya had told Ami she was pregnant. The smell of smoke still lingered in the bar, despite the smoking ban a few years ago. The scent was a comfort to Maya, as were the familiar sounds of clinking silverware and chatter and laughter. Ami used to try to sneak them both in here when they were in middle school. It never worked: the staff knew who they were and how old they were. Not to mention who their parents were.

Ami narrowed her dark eyes at Maya and shook her head in disbelief. "And he knows about Samantha and he says he wants to be part of her life?" She took another sip and held up a finger to Maya. "Don't even get me started on what your face looks like every time I mention him. It's like you're twenty-two again."

"My face is fine," Maya said, "and that's what he says in his voice mails. I'm not returning his calls."

Ami had been traveling for her job as a fashion journalist and had just returned from some exotic locale. After receiving the bazillion texts and voice mails Maya had left her, she'd come straight to Queens.

Ami tapped the table. "So, you think that just because you don't answer his calls, he'll just give up and forget that he has a daughter? *With you*."

"Well, yes." Maya squirmed in her seat and sipped her martini to avoid the look on Ami's face that said she was a nutjob.

"Have you considered what Samantha might think of all this?"

Maya shrugged, trying not to remember the look on Samantha's face when she'd asked if Sam was her father. She'd looked hopeful, like she thought it might be nice to have a dad. Maybe, until he left. And he would leave. Just like Maya's father had. That's what men did. God knows Sunita had made sure Maya never forgot that. "It doesn't matter. We've been fine without him all these years, and we'll continue to be fine without him."

"Have you really been fine?" Ami sniffed.

"What's that supposed to mean?"

"Well, you've never really dated—not seriously—"

"What was the point? To have a man come in and be a part of our lives until he decided he didn't want to anymore? I was protecting my daughter. And FYI— it's the twenty-first century! Women don't need men to be happy."

"We may not need men, but they sure are nice."

Maya took another sip of her drink. Ami was a pain.

"Trust me, this is your daughter we're talking about. If you don't give her permission to see her own father, she'll just do it behind your back."

"No, she won't." But Maya shifted again in her seat.

"You did plenty of things behind your mom's back." Ami smirked. "Or did you forget?"

"How could I forget?" Maya stifled a chuckle. "Samantha is living proof."

THE MOON WAS high as they made their way back to Maya's apartment from the neighborhood bar. Maya caught Ami as she tripped over air molecules. "Come, say hi to Mum."

Ami teetered a bit but pulled free of Maya. "Sure. Did she cook?"

"You know she did." Maya had treated herself to a second martini, so her head was swimming. Ami, however, had downed three, so she was pretty much drunk. Luckily, her kids and husband had come to Queens to stay with Ami's parents, so she only had to walk two blocks from Maya's. It wasn't that late, but at 9:00 p.m. on a Sunday evening the streets were empty, except for stragglers such as themselves.

"Maya. Maya." Ami stopped. "Do you remember the plan?" Ami was still sober enough to catch Maya's glare. Ami shook her head. "Of course you do." She laughed. "It was great. 'The Sneak-Away-For-The-Weekend' plan."

Maya smiled in spite of herself. "Yes. How could I forget?"

"How lucky were you that I was actually at University of Virginia for that summer?" Ami started to walk and stumbled again. The sidewalk had cracks and breaks that it hadn't had in the days when the two friends were younger. It had become unfamiliar terrain. Maya grabbed her arm again.

"Very lucky." Maya led Ami to the back of the shop to the apartment entrance.

"I mean, can you believe they all bought it? That you were going to the beach with me, instead of you-know-where with you-know-who." Ami laughed at herself. "To do you-know-what!" She stopped, as if having a revelation. But Maya had heard it all before. "See? If it weren't for me…" She giggled again.

Maya rolled her eyes and sighed deeply as she redirected Ami to the stairs. She *had* had to sneak out of Deepak-mama's house back then. There was no way he would've let her go away for the weekend with Sam— or any boy, for that matter. The fact that she'd ended up pregnant out of wedlock was beyond scandalous to Maya's family, but Ami had stood by her. Ami had been the one person who didn't judge or find fault with Maya. She knew Maya loved Sam, and that despite the options available to her, her decision to keep the baby was grounded in that love—reciprocated or not.

"I thought you said there was food."

"Is that Ami I hear?" Sunita called from the top of the stairs, her voice muffled as she turned her head. "Raj, Ami's back."

Ami winked at Maya as they made their way past the door to Maya's apartment and up to Sunita's. "Auntie, do you have a man up there at this hour? About time! You have been stringing poor Raju-kaka along for too long."

"Oh, Ami." Sunita flushed, clearly trying and failing

to keep her voice firm. "Is that any way to talk to your auntie? Besides, Raj had stopped by to pick up some food. He still doesn't cook, you know."

"She is right, Sunita." Raj's deep voice boomed from somewhere inside the apartment.

They reached the top and Ami hugged Sunita with both arms. She imitated Raj's accent, but spoke in a drunken stage whisper. "See? He *is* here! Why do you fight him?"

Maya's mother's cheeks reddened even as she tightened her lips. "Why don't you stop at one martini?"

Raj hugged Ami. "Ah, *beti*, good to have you back. But I am only here to get food, eh? I must be sure to never learn to cook." He winked at her.

"You must have come for food, as well," Sunita said to Maya and Ami.

"Of course." Ami stumbled into her seat at the small kitchen table. This apartment was a bit smaller than Maya's. There was only the one bedroom, and an eat-in kitchen that opened to the living area. Maya sat down next to Ami and glanced into the living room where Samantha stared at her laptop, earbuds in, face sullen.

Maya caught her mother's eye, who simply shook her head in an I-have-no-idea gesture. "She helped me make the chutney tonight and she seemed fine." Her mother furrowed her brow for a moment. "Although it was odd that she didn't complain or even roll her eyes when I told her to use 'some' lemon juice and 'just a bit' of salt."

"You know, Maya." Ami was momentarily coherent. "You never like when I say this, but this whole thing could've been avoided if you had just trusted you-know-who…"

"Okay, Ami. Put food in your mouth. This always happens when you've had that third martini." Maya's voice was loud and firm as she glared at her friend.

Sunita placed homemade samosa on the table with sweet chutney made from dates, and spicy chutney made from cilantro. "Aww, Auntie! You remembered my favorite!" Ami was loud and slightly teary eyed.

Maya rolled her eyes and shook her head in her mother's direction. Sunita jumped in. "Beta, it's been two weeks. Not a lifetime." She cupped Ami's chin in her hand and gave her a quick shake. "Eat."

Ami bit into her samosa and glanced over at Samantha. Maya joined her.

Ami shook her head back and forth and finished chewing. "What's her problem today?"

"Her *problem* is that she knows Sam Hutcherson is her dad!" Samantha burst out with full-on teenage irritation as she stalked into the kitchen and plopped herself down next to Ami.

Maya clenched her jaw as Ami's mouth dropped open. Sunita brought her hand to her mouth with a loud gasp and Raju-kaka quietly retreated back to the sofa.

Ami broke the silence. "You told her?"

Maya glared at Ami and shook her head while Samantha grinned in victory. "No, Ami-*masi*, you just told me." Samantha had always called Ami *"masi"* because the bond Maya and Ami shared went beyond friendship and into sisterhood.

"Fine." Maya clasped her hands together. "So you know. So what now? You think he's going to be a dad to you? He's a busy man—he's got his own life—"

"Ami-*masi*." Samantha turned away from her mother. "Just answer me this."

"Samantha!" Maya pulled out her best warning tone.

Samantha spoke quickly, keeping her back to Maya. "Ami-*masi*, did he know about me? Did he know Mom was pregnant when he left?"

Maya's heart fell into her stomach. This was too much. She was asking too many questions. Before she could do much more than silently beg her friend to be quiet, Ami answered.

"No, Samantha. He didn't know anything about you when your mom left him." Ami's voice was suddenly quiet. Maya looked away as Ami reached for Samantha's hand.

"Mom left *him*?" Samantha was clearly surprised by this information. The pit in Maya's stomach grew, and it had nothing to do with the martinis. She pressed her eyes closed, as if doing so would erase the scene unfolding before her. It did not.

Ami nodded. Samantha sat back, her shoulders drooping, her eyes darting all over the room. A moment or two passed while she seemed to digest this information. Then, her face cleared, and she sat up, a smirk on her face. "Well, no wonder he looks at her like that."

That was it. Maya slammed her hand on the table. "That's enough. Time for bed!" She stood and leaned forward on the table to add weight to her words.

Samantha gaped at her, disbelief her shield against Maya's motherly powers. "You're not even going to tell me why you left him? While you were pregnant?"

"Bed. Now." Maya's heart was beating rapid-fire, and she fought to keep her voice from shaking. This was not supposed to be happening. Her daughter could not be asking these questions. Not yet. Not now. She was still too young. Too impressionable. She'd never understand.

Samantha would never forgive her.

"It doesn't matter. He's not going to stick around." Maya continued to stare down her daughter, her stomach clenched. She couldn't allow Samantha to believe that Sam might really be a part of her life. Sure, he might think he wanted to right now, but what about after he married and became congressman? Where was the guarantee that he'd still want to be a father then?

And what about Sam's mother? A wave of nausea came over Maya as she considered the possibility of seeing Sam's mother again.

"You don't know that. He made all those phone calls!" Samantha got up, still glaring at Maya, and replaced her earbuds as she grabbed her phone, sharply turned on her heel and headed for the door. She let it slam shut behind her.

Ami closed her eyes and shook her head. "What is it about you Rao women that you are unable or unwilling to trust a man? Are you actually afraid to be happy?" She bit her samosa and pointed the remainder at Maya's mother's back. "There's your mom, the queen of misguided loyalty and bitterness, then there's you—" she pointed at Maya "—so full of abandonment issues, you couldn't even see what was in front of you. Are you going to damn Samantha to that same fate? Let her see him—he *is* her father—and find out what happens."

"And your answering Samantha's questions for me helps how?" Maya directed her last bit of anger and fear at her best friend. "Thanks for nothing." That wasn't what she was doing to Samantha, was it? She opened her mouth to speak again, but just then—the doorbell rang. It was Ami's husband, Ajay, come to claim his wife. Ami and Ajay had been high school sweethearts, so Maya had known him most of her life.

Ajay entered just as Ami polished off the last samosa. "Ahh...there she is." He was tall and lean, and he currently wore a T-shirt stained with baby food. He approached Ami with a grin so filled with affection, it warmed Maya's heart, and she wondered if this was how Sam had looked at her. She squashed the thought before she even finished it.

Ajay bent down and kissed his wife's cheek. "Drunk as a skunk. Just how I like her." He grinned at Maya. "I thought she was supposed to get you drunk?"

Maya shrugged her shoulders and went over to hug Ajay. Ami's words had opened a pit in her stomach. "She tried, *bhaiya*." If Ami was like a sister to her, Ajay was as close to a big brother as Maya ever had, and she called him bhaiya with all the respect and affection that the word implied. She wrapped her arms around his middle and buried her head in his chest, relishing a moment of serenity in her "brother's" arms. "But you know how she loves a good dirty martini. Or three."

Ajay's bear hug calmed her stomach, but Ami's words still nagged at her. Ajay pulled back and grinned at Maya. "So, the baby daddy is back, huh?" He chuckled, dodging Maya's smack, but she landed a blow on his arm. He wrinkled his brow, feigning pain, his demeanor all innocence. "What?" He made a show of cracking his knuckles. "Isn't it my job to kick his—"

"Yes, yes, you're very macho, sweetheart." Ami rolled her eyes and waved at Maya and Ajay to get their attention. She fixed Maya firmly with her gaze. "You think about what I said." She turned to her husband. "Take me home, honey. I think we've both done enough damage here for one night."

Maya helped her friend to the door. She playfully narrowed her eyes at Ajay as she gently punched his arm again. "Behave!"

Ajay bent down to kiss her cheek. "I think I can take him."

Maya rolled her eyes at him as she reached over to give Ami a hug. Ami whispered in her ear, "It was a great plan."

Maya chuckled, her anger gone. "It sure was."

CHAPTER TWENTY
MAYA

Maryland, 1996

"Is THAT YOU, SAM?" A familiar—yet unwelcome—voice screeched at them, as Maya sat holding hands with Sam on the bleachers while they waited for his team to arrive for training. "Are you fucking kidding me? You're with her now?"

Maya cringed as Bridget made her way toward them. Sam swore under his breath as he turned to face his ex-girlfriend. "Hey, Bridget. What's going on?"

"What's going on?" Bridget sounded incredulous as she stopped in front of Sam and glared at them both. She flicked her eyes toward Maya but did not address her. She leaned into Sam. "Why haven't you returned my calls?"

"I told you, Brig, it's over. It's been over two months since we broke up. Look, we had a great time, but—"

"But now you're with her." She glared at Maya.

"Goodbye, Bridget." Sam placed his hand on Maya's knee, as if to protect her from Bridget's mean-girl vibe. His voice was firm and, for the first time, unkind.

"Look, I've been calling you because—" She flicked her eyes toward Maya, and Maya was surprised to see tears.

"Why don't I take a walk?" Maya grabbed her purse and started to get up. She didn't need to sit here. Sam grabbed her hand.

"No. It's all right. Whatever Bridget has to say, she can say with you here. I'm not hiding anything."

Maya sat back down next to Sam and entwined her fingers with his. Whatever Bridget had to say, it wasn't going to be good. Tall and slim with bouncy blond hair, bright blue eyes and legs that went up to *here,* Bridget was classically beautiful. Not for the first time, Maya wondered why Sam would give up Bridget for her.

Right now, though, Bridget looked like she was going to cry. Sam did not reach out to comfort her.

"Whatever, Sam."

"Spill it, Bridget."

Bridget spoke, her voice thick with tears. "I'm late."

Silence, as the two of them soaked up this information. Maya's heart thumped hard against her chest, before it fell into her stomach. Bridget thought she was pregnant? With Sam's baby?

Sam released Maya's fingers, and his expression softened. "What? But how…we were—" He seemed to remember Maya was sitting next to him and stopped abruptly.

Great.

"Nothing's 100 percent, Sam." Bridget sniffled.

He tensed and turned away from Maya, leaning toward Bridget. "Did you take a test?"

Bridget flicked her eyes in Maya's direction, then back to Sam. "No."

Sam shook his head, visibly relaxing. "Well, maybe do that before you freak out."

A tear escaped Bridget's eye, and Maya looked away. It felt invasive to watch her struggle.

"I'm scared, Sam." Her voice cracked, and she continued, her speech getting louder by the second. "What if I am? I don't have time for this right now—my parents will be pissed. What if I have to drop out of school?"

"Hey, hey calm down." Sam stood and held her arms. Maya's heart dropped even as she saw green. "Brig, it'll be fine. We'll figure it out." His words were hushed, as if he didn't want Maya to hear. She turned her head away to give them a semblance of privacy. She felt like an outsider, and that's what she was.

"Take the test, and see what it says before you freak out." He dropped his voice further, but Maya could still hear. "We were always careful—I'm sure you're fine."

Maya did not care to be reminded about the fact that Sam had slept with other girls. He was hers now. At the same time, it couldn't be easy facing an unwanted pregnancy. Maya waffled between jealousy of and sympathy toward Bridget.

She heard Bridget sniffle again, and Sam murmured words of comfort before saying goodbye. Maya turned her head back in time to see Bridget descend the bleachers.

Sam sighed and shook his head, as he sat down next to Maya and took her hand in his again. "It's always some kind of drama with her."

"Drama? You think a pregnancy scare is drama?"

"No, I think true pregnancy is something to deal with. But right now, she just wants attention. Let her take the test. Besides, I'm always careful."

There was that "always" again. Exactly how many girls had there been? "What about us?"

Sam grinned and leaned in closer to Maya, all the gentleness and warmth that she loved so much, restored. "*We* are different." She felt his breath on her. "*We* belong to each other." His lips met hers and everything made sense. He loved *her*. She put Bridget out of her mind.

CHAPTER TWENTY-ONE
SAM

New York 2012

SAM HAD BEEN waiting in the Manhattan café for twenty minutes. He walked outside and to the corner and back. No sign of Samantha.

Maya's return was conjuring up all kinds of suppressed memories. Like how he had wanted to open his own practice and help people in the community. He remembered the conversation with his parents. His father had been supportive, as expected, and his mother had been wary, but she had seemed to come around. But when Maya had left, and his mother was diagnosed with cancer, her one request had been for him to continue along his original path. He was her only remaining son, she liked to remind him—it was his duty. What choice did he have?

He hadn't given any real thought to his dreams in years. Sure, he took on the occasional case his father mentioned, and yes, he pretended that those cases distracted him from his real job, but the reality was that those cases made him feel like he was making a difference, like he was making good use of his life.

He checked the time on his phone. Samantha had reached out to him for this lunch. It was today, right? He checked his calendar. He called her. Straight to voice mail. He left a message. Shoved the phone back into his coat pocket.

Sam paced the block again and peeked inside the café. Nothing. He pulled out his phone. Nothing. He started to scroll, looking for Maya's number. Not that it would help—she hadn't answered or returned any of his calls all week.

"Don't call my mom. I'm here."

Sam sighed in relief and turned toward the sound of Samantha's voice. "You came. I was getting worried."

Samantha shrugged. "Are we eating or what?"

"Sure." Sam eyed her warily and opened the door. "Is this okay?"

"Yeah, great."

They found a table by the window and ordered food.

"Since you're here I take it you believe me?"

"Yes." Something about her softened just then. "I asked Ami-*masi*, and she told me that you had no idea Mom was pregnant. And that *she* broke up with *you*."

"That is true."

"She *really* dumped you?" It seemed hard for her to believe. Well, that made two of them.

Sam shifted uncomfortably in his seat and bit into his sandwich to avoid her eyes. "Yes."

"Why?"

"She said—she said she didn't love me anymore." Why was it still so hard to say those words?

"Did you believe her?"

"At the time, yes. She was very convincing."

"That sucks." She pursed her lips and cocked her head.

Sam smiled. "Yes, it did."

Samantha looked at him with what could only be sympathy and sighed deeply.

"What did your mom say when you told her you were meeting me?"

"Not much." Samantha had a sudden interest in her food.

"You didn't tell her." He was harsher than he meant to be. "How'd you get my number?"

She rolled her eyes. "Mom's phone, duh." And there was the famous Rao sass. "Did you tell Paige?"

"No, but I'm not a teenage girl secretly meeting a man, father or no. You have to tell her." Sam tried to stare her down. "Or I will."

Samantha took a bite of her sandwich in response. No sooner did Samantha take one bite than she started making a clicking sound with her tongue. Her eyes widened, and she started rummaging through her bag.

"What?" Alarm bells went off in Sam's head.

"I'm allergic..." She coughed and looked dizzy.

Sam didn't think. He grabbed her backpack and began rummaging through it. Phone charger, phone case, lipstick, books, all the contents of a teen backpack were pushed to the floor so Sam could locate the EpiPen.

"Dad." At the thickness in her speech, Sam's heart pounded. Somewhere in the back of his mind he registered that she'd just called him "Dad," but he'd never felt more unprepared for that role than now. He unzipped all the compartments and unceremoniously dumped the contents of her backpack. Hands shaking, he sifted through her belongings, the action calming his own mounting panic.

He finally located the EpiPen and showed it to Samantha for verification. Her eyes half closed, she nodded. He leaped to her side and nearly knocked over his chair in his haste. He opened the case and rammed the needle into her thigh.

"Samantha. Samantha. Talk to me!" He pulled her close, helpless to steady his own hands or slow the rapid thudding in his chest.

"Sir? Sir!"

Sam looked up at the employee addressing him.

"We've called an ambulance. Is there anything else we can do to help?"

"No. Thank you." Sam pulled Samantha closer. She was conscious, but her breathing was labored.

The employee squeezed his arm. "Your daughter will be fine."

Sam could only nod his gratitude. How quickly he adapted to that term.

"So sorry, sir. But we didn't know she had an allergy. She didn't mention it."

Sam nodded his acknowledgment. He hadn't known, either. How could he? Even in his fear for Samantha's life, his anger toward Maya built. If he'd had the chance to raise his daughter, he'd have known about her allergy, and about so much more. He grabbed his phone to call her. She did not pick up. He used Samantha's phone. Maya picked up on the first ring.

"Samantha, where are you?"

"Maya, it's Sam."

"Sam? Why do you have Samantha's phone?"

"She's here with me. We met for lunch."

"You what? Behind my back?"

He ignored that. "Maya, she had an allergic reaction."

"Oh, God! Is she all right? Were you with her?"

"Yes, I'm here. I used the EpiPen. Listen, the paramedics just got here. Meet us at the hospital." Sam paused in a valiant attempt to steady his voice. "Maya," his voice cracked, "she's breathing, but I don't know…" He'd only just found his daughter. Losing her was not an option.

"Yeah, okay. I'm coming."

As he climbed into the back of the ambulance, his phone buzzed. A text from Maya. How does she look?

He looked over at Samantha and smiled. A feeble attempt at hiding the new and terrible fear that found a home in the pit of his stomach. Samantha's skin was pale—no sign of that creamy hue right now—but she was breathing, albeit with an oxygen mask on. She smiled back at him. He turned to the EMT. "How is she?"

The EMT raised his eyebrows. "She'll be fine. We'll be at the hospital in five minutes. Try to relax, Dad." The EMT turned back to his patient to check her vitals. "Every girl deserves a superhero dad."

Samantha nodded her head in agreement. Sam couldn't have felt less like a superhero if he'd tried.

Sam's phone buzzed again. Maya. Sam???

He responded right away. They say she'll be fine. Be at the hospital in five.

K. See u there.

He found a place to sit where he could hold Samantha's hand. It was as much for him as it was for her.

CHAPTER TWENTY-TWO
MAYA

New York, 2012

MAYA OPTED TO take the subway to the hospital, since Raju-kaka was with a fare. This way, she could also keep her mother at the coffee shop and not have to deal with Sunita's distaste for Sam. But the train seemed to be moving slower than usual, so Maya paced. She was getting some stares, but she barely noticed, and out of the many things that occurred on New York City subways, nervous pacing was pretty benign.

This had happened once before when Samantha was about six. There had been cashews in something she'd eaten at a birthday party, and her tongue had begun to swell within a minute. There had been no time for panic. At that time, Maya had been there, and had that EpiPen out and had injected her daughter within seconds. Panic hadn't set in until later, when she'd had Samantha at the hospital and out of danger. Sam might be in that spot right now.

But, seriously, what was he doing with her, anyway? Maya had tried to make it abundantly clear that Sam was to forget about them and return to his life. She didn't want or need anything from him more than the phone calls he had already made. He didn't seem to like taking no for an answer any more than Samantha did.

Maya rushed into the emergency room, bringing the cold air with her. She sent Sam a text while she impatiently waited her turn at the intake desk and was finally directed to Samantha's room. The door was open, but the curtain was closed, and she was about to walk in when she caught snippets of their conversation.

Sam's low rumble sent a jolt though her body. "You play soccer?"

"Yeah, I was starting keeper three years in a row." Samantha was clearly happy to talk to Sam about something she was proud of.

"Was?"

"Um, yeah. I'm not playing this year." Her disappointment was obvious, and Maya felt a pang. She'd had to make that choice for Samantha. With the tuition at this new private school, Maya couldn't afford the soccer fees.

"Why not?" Sam asked.

"Oh… I'm just super busy with school." Guilt stabbed Maya at hearing her daughter lie. "But I saw *your* soccer awards online."

A beat passed before Sam responded. "Yeah, I guess you did. I played some. Was a decent keeper back in the day." He laughed.

He started a conversation about keeper strategy, and he and Samantha were soon speaking a language that, while familiar, Maya did not understand. Much like hearing an old song on the radio could take you back to a moment in time, so did the sound of youthfulness in Sam's voice. Maya's thoughts were flooded with images of concerts and picnics and stolen kisses.

She suppressed those past images, which were better off forgotten, and stepped into the room, opening the curtain. Sam cleared his throat and stood as he stepped back from the bed. Upon seeing Maya, his expression turned grim, his eyes wary. Sam's suit jacket had been tossed across a chair with his tie, and his shirtsleeves were rolled up, revealing corded muscles. Maya chided herself for even noticing his muscles at a time like this.

"Hi, Mom," Samantha said apprehensively. She knew she was busted.

Maya walked in and addressed her daughter first. "You okay?"

"Yeah—the hidden cashew again. In the nut butter. I forgot to ask." She rolled her eyes, and followed it with a torrent of words. "Are you mad? Don't be mad. I know I should have told you I was meeting him, but I just knew if I asked, you would say no. And I wanted to meet with him—he is my dad."

Maya cut her eyes to Sam, expecting to see accusation and defiance. What she found instead gripped her heart. Rather than being hard and angry, his eyes were soft and pained. She turned back to her daughter. "I'm not mad." She side-eyed Sam. "Really, I'm not." And she wasn't. Her daughter was okay, and if Maya knew nothing else, she knew Samantha was safe with Sam.

He exhaled, and Maya felt the tension leave his body. She nodded toward the door. "Can I talk to you?"

Samantha rolled her eyes again, but laughed. "It's okay," she told Sam. "She won't bite."

Maya started as Sam gently placed his hand on the small of her back to guide her to the hall. The warmth of his touch was achingly familiar.

He came around to stand and face her. The white in

his shirt contrasted with the creamy brown of his skin. He set his jaw and gripped her in his gaze. "I had no way of knowing she was allergic, and until she showed up, I didn't know she was coming behind your back."

Maya nodded. "Yes, I know. She kind of does what she wants sometimes." Maya shook her head. "In any case, thanks for coming and staying. I'm sure you have work to do. I'll stay. You can go."

Sam looked at her, incredulous. "I'm not going any-where." He peeked into the room. "I'm staying right here until we know she's okay."

It was Maya's turn to be incredulous. "What? You don't have to—"

"I may not have to, but I want to and I will." There was no room for negotiation.

Maya couldn't help smiling. "Fine. But she's going to make you watch soccer videos."

Sam smiled, showing that dimple, and laughed softly. It was a deep, low rumble, and Maya's stomach did a pleasant flip at the sound. "Twist my arm." He placed his hand at the small of her back again as they headed back in the room. Maya took a deep breath to calm her pounding heart. After all these years, why was she re-sponding to him this way?

Just before they reached Samantha's bed, Sam leaned down and whispered to Maya, "Let's not forget that you still haven't told me why you left. I'll be stopping by the coffee shop for that explanation. Tomorrow."

Well, that wasn't going to calm her down.

CHAPTER TWENTY-THREE
MAYA

Maryland 1996

MAYA WANDERED ABOUT the drugstore with the basket hooked on her elbow. She tried to ignore the store's music taunting her, Alanis Morissette going on about free advice not taken. She grabbed a bottle of shampoo. Then she decided she needed more eyeliner. She chose a new lipstick.

She passed the feminine hygiene aisle and headed toward the snack area. Nothing sounded good, but she grabbed a can of barbecue Pringles anyway. *Chocolate would be nice*, she thought. She grabbed a bag of peanut butter cups and lingered awhile debating the merits of plain vs. peanut M&M's.

She couldn't avoid it anymore. She headed back to feminine hygiene and threw in a couple boxes of tampons. For good luck, Maya told herself. Finally, as casually as she could, she grabbed a handful of pregnancy tests and bolted for the checkout.

She was breathing heavily as she headed for her car and somehow made it home. Mr. and Mrs. Mehta had taken a few days off to take their children to the beach, so Maya had some time off, too. Her aunt and uncle and cousin were all at work. She would have the house to herself. She locked the door to the bathroom anyway.

Fingers shaking, she fumbled, but managed to open the first test. Maya inhaled deeply, taking in the familiar scent of soap and bleach mixed with the floral scent of cherry-blossom air freshener, forcing herself to calm down and read the instructions.

She read them three times to be sure she got it right. She peed on the stick, set it on the counter and pulled out another test. She repeated the process five times. She wasn't sure why she chose five—it just seemed like a good number and it ruled out the possibility of a tie.

She paced the small bathroom, intermittently biting her nails and running her fingers through her hair until time was up for the last test. Her stomach fluttering dangerously, she took a step closer to the counter. She stopped. She couldn't look. This wasn't happening. But she knew it was.

With new resolve, or maybe acceptance—it didn't matter—she walked quickly to the counter for confirmation of the answer she already knew. Five pregnancy tests each told her she was having Sam's baby.

Her head spun and she held the counter to keep from falling. What little she had eaten that day threatened to come up, so she grabbed her belly and slowly slid down the wall to the bathroom floor as her tears fell.

Her fingers trembled as she ran a hand through her hair again, the coldness of the tile seeping through the worn mat and causing her to shiver. What was she going to do? How would she tell her mother, her family? Having sex before marriage was bad enough. But getting pregnant before marriage was advertising to the whole world your complete lack of morality and what an awful job your parents had done in raising you. Her mother had had it hard as a single mom, but society had sympathy for her. After all, her husband (the dog!) had left her alone with a child. Her stomach churned. There would be no such sympathy for her. The polite ones would avert their eyes and whisper behind her back. The others would stare and actively shun her. Not to mention she had plans for her life. Things she wanted to do. A child didn't factor in, not now. She leaned her head onto her knees and cried.

She had to tell Sam. Unbidden, the look on his face when Bridget had told him she thought she was pregnant popped into her mind. He had been kind, concerned. She thought of his gentleness. The sobs subsided; she took a few calming breaths and concentrated on the warmth in his eyes and how his smile lit up her heart.

Sam loved her. He would stand by her. This thought in mind, she peeled herself off the bathroom floor. Of course he would. A small voice that sounded like her mother poked at her, reminding her that men were highly unreliable. She ignored it. She caught her bleak reflection in the mirror. Puffy, red-rimmed eyes, her brown skin ashen, her hair a rat's nest.

Maya turned on the water and washed up. She would go tell Sam right now. As she slowly brushed her hair and contemplated the conversation, the phone rang. She dropped the brush and left the bathroom to answer it. It was her mother.

Maya gathered herself together. "Hey, Mum."

"Maya, how are you?" She continued without waiting for an answer. "Mrs. Chen from across the street was just telling me how much she misses your brownies, so I had to call." Her pride and happiness bubbled through the phone and Maya's vision blurred, the lump in her throat making it hard for her to breathe. Her mother would be so disappointed.

"I know you'll be home in a week, but everyone has missed you so!"

It took everything Maya had to keep her tears back. She couldn't even manage a "Mmm-hmm."

"Maya? Is everything all right?" Her mother's voice was filled with concern. "Maya? Maya? Maya, say something."

Maya hung up the phone and dissolved into fresh tears. Her mother would never understand. She had to see Sam. It was 11:00 a.m. He was at one of his many jobs and wouldn't be free until evening. They had made plans to meet at the park. She'd have to wait until then. She walked down to the kitchen and did what came naturally: she started to bake.

Before she knew it, four hours had passed, and as Maya was just starting a round of chocolate chip cookies, she heard the front door open, and suddenly her mother was standing in the kitchen.

"Maya?" She continued their conversation from the morning as if four hours and two hundred twenty-five miles had not passed.

"Mum." Maya forced a smile onto her face, but knew she wasn't fooling anyone. This was her mother. "What are you doing here?"

"You tell me." Her mother's gaze was fierce. She had come for answers. "I called you back many times, but you did not pick up. What has happened?"

"Nothing, Mum. Stop being so dramatic." Maya rolled her eyes for effect, knowing it was futile.

Her mother put down her purse and glanced around

the kitchen. Brownies, muffins and now cookies covered the countertop. She pursed her lips and studied her daughter. Without a word, she walked upstairs. Maya heard her mother enter the bathroom, and the blood drained from her head. *No, no, no!* In her distraction, she hadn't gotten rid of any of the evidence. She tried to force her feet to move, or call out to her mother, but she was frozen with fear. The silence as her mother came back down was the loudest Maya had ever experienced.

"You didn't stop seeing that boy, did you?" The accusation was clear.

Maya remained silent. The answer was obvious.

"I warned you. I told you no good would come of it." Her mother's voice was calm and hard. Maya wished she would yell.

"Have you told him?"

Maya swallowed tears and shook her head.

"Fine. Get yourself together. We'll talk elsewhere. I don't need my brother coming home in the middle of this."

Maya nodded and twenty minutes later they were seated at the back of a coffee shop, staring into coffees that were getting cold.

"So, Maya, I suppose you were right. This boy was your mistake." Her mother's voice was firm and unforgiving. "How did you let this happen?"

"I don't know." Somewhere in the car ride, Maya had found her voice. Angry tears welled up in her eyes. "I love him. He loves me."

Her mother shook her head, her voice full of hostility. "You know that means nothing," she said. "He will not stay around and take care of you or this child. And do you really want him to? Never knowing if he stayed for you or out of a sense of duty?"

Sunita reached for Maya's hand, pity suddenly in her eyes. "Your father left us with nothing. You know this. You cannot depend on a man—only yourself."

"No, Mum. Sam is different," Maya beseeched her mother. "He really loves me. I know it."

"You don't think your father loved me?" Her mother dropped her hand, her nostrils flaring, her eyes hard. "We ran away together. Left the country! Left our parents, our families!" She leaned toward her daughter. "All so that we could be together. That was love." Her voice turned bitter. "And look how that ended."

Maya watched a young woman walk by the coffee shop. She was laughing, and her eyes lit up as a young man approached and kissed her. Was it only yesterday that Maya had felt that carefree, that light? An image of Bridget's frightened face flashed through her mind. Was that how she looked like, now? Frightened? And exactly how many other girls were there, right now, who had this same problem?

Her mother gently turned Maya's gaze back to her. "Unreliable, Maya. Men are unreliable." She sighed, her eyes pained from a lifetime of living with the knowledge that her love was not good enough, and worried that her daughter would suffer the same fate. "Maya, honey. At least if you don't tell him, he can't abandon your child, the way your father abandoned you."

SAM SUGGESTED A picnic dinner in the park that very night. It was just as good a place to tell him about the baby as any. Her mother was wrong. Sam would stand by her, she was sure. Mostly.

She pulled into the parking lot as Sam had instructed. He had been very specific about where she should park. The evening was warm and sticky, a typical August day in Maryland. She paced the sidewalk, allowing the scent of the lake to calm her while she waited for him. She wanted this baby, no matter that it wasn't part of the plan. There had to be a way to make it work.

She paced a few more minutes and checked her watch. It wasn't like Sam to be this late—or even late at all. She walked a bit farther around the parking lot, and sure enough, the powder blue Honda Civic was there. But no Sam. Puzzled, she looked around, and wandered down the path that circled around the lake.

She heard them before she saw them. Hushed voices, Sam's deep voice low and agitated, Bridget's high-pitched and urgent.

Maya froze. What were they doing here? Sam did not look happy; he actually looked angry. Before she could decide whether to interrupt them or wait by the car, Sam's gaze landed on her, almost as if he could sense her presence. He looked relieved to see her, but did she see guilt flash across his face?

He turned back to Bridget, and shook his head. She turned and upon seeing Maya, she grabbed her bag and turned on her heel, stomping away from Sam and toward Maya. She paused as she passed Maya to shake her head at her, and Maya could see that she had been crying. What was happening? Had Bridget gotten the results of her test?

Before Maya could speak, Bridget continued walking away from her, and Sam came to stand by her. Maya was watching Bridget disappear around the corner when she felt Sam's lips on her cheek. She leaned into him, as much from habit as for comfort. It had only taken one season to get used to him.

"Hey." He wrapped his arms around her.

"Hey." She let herself melt into him for a moment, inhaling the clean, masculine scent of him as she turned to face him. His hair was slightly damp from his shower, his face smooth from a recent shave. "What was that all about?"

"Just drama. Don't worry about it." Sam's lips were soft and gentle when they touched her own, and her eyes filled with tears at how much she loved him. She deepened their kiss and Sam responded in kind by pulling her into him, until finally he pulled away, laughing. "We may need to get a room."

"Was that about the pregnancy?"

His eyes darkened as he glanced in the direction that Bridget had stomped away from them. In the next instant, his brown eyes filled with amusement. "Maya, I did not invite you out here to talk about Bridget." He bit his bottom lip and looked her in the eye. "She found me waiting for you—and I promise I will tell you all about it, but right now, I have dinner." He enthusiastically produced a basket, grabbed her hand and led the way. Sounds of children playing and the scents of lake water and sunscreen filled the air as Sam searched for a spot of grass worthy of their dinner. He stopped at a small clearing with a few trees for shade that opened with a breathtaking view of the sunset over the lake. "I've been waiting for this all day."

All signs of the fact that Bridget had been here were gone from him, and he was completely focused on her. But Maya couldn't shake the feeling that something was up.

Dinner consisted of *dhokla*, an Indian lentil cake, steamed and served with sweet and spicy chutneys, as well as fruit and wine. Maya offered to help lay it out, but Sam wouldn't have it. She stood while he worked and stifled the urge to tap her foot nervously. Once he seemed finished, she prepared to sit.

"No." Sam held her hands. "Don't sit. Not yet." Maya raised her eyebrows at him, but remained standing. "Close your eyes."

"Sam, really?" Maya was getting irritated with his games. She needed to talk to him.

"Come on, Maya." Sam was insistent. "Just one minute, I promise."

She rolled her eyes. "Fine." She closed her eyes. He seemed to walk away and return.

"Okay. Open them."

Maya opened her eyes to find Sam down on one knee. Her hands flew to her belly and her breath caught. He had a small box in his hand and his dimple was in full display. "So, Maya." Amusement and the sun added a golden spark to his normally melty brown eyes. "Heads, we get married. Tails, we break up." He opened the box to reveal the small coin sitting where a ring should be.

Maya's heart began to race, and then her blood began to boil, even as she felt it drain from her head. She had just seen his ex-girlfriend stomp off, crying, with no explanation from Sam. If Bridget was pregnant, too, they'd all be tied together forever, and *this* was how he planned their future? And who knew how many other girls there were? It was one thing to toss a coin to decide which movie to see, she thought, but marriage? If the coin turned up tails, they were supposed to break up?

"Is Bridget pregnant?" She spit the words out.

Sam's eyes widened. "What?" Confusion took over his face. "What does that have to do with anything?"

He wasn't answering the question. Sam couldn't *really* love her. He might love her now, but what about in the future when he had all these other responsibilities? Would he love her then, or would she just be another responsibility he had to take care of? No. Maya wasn't going to let her child be something on a checklist. Men *were* unreliable. With this realization, she wiped away her tears.

"Maya." His voice was tender. "I love you and I—"

"Sam Hutcherson, are you out of your mind?" She shrieked at him, vaguely registering the hurt and surprise in his eyes. She turned on her heel and ran full tilt back to her car. He was calling to her, running after her. She couldn't listen. She fumbled with her keys, then finally got in her car. Sam was outside her window, saying something, but she couldn't hear him for all her sobbing. The car screeched as she pulled out and raced home.

It was close to impossible to see through her tears. She couldn't tell him about the baby. She just couldn't. He wasn't ready to be a father. He was just a boy. Her stomach hurt. She couldn't breathe. He would leave her, just like her father left—just like her mother had said. Well, he wouldn't get the chance. She'd leave him first.

CHAPTER TWENTY-FOUR
SAM

New York 2012

SAM FOUND HIS way to the back entrance of the coffee shop that led to Maya's apartment, and rang the bell. He'd told Paige he had a meeting, and he'd promised to meet her and his parents later so they could go to the appointment with the cake decorator together.

First, he needed answers from Maya. He was getting them today. Right now.

Sam missed a beat before speaking when Maya opened the door. Her hair was down, one rogue piece falling to the side of her face. He used to wonder how it was that whether her hair was up or down, that one piece always wanted to lie on the side of her face. His hand moved as if from muscle memory to tuck that strand back behind her ear, like he had done so many times before. Instead, he pushed his hand deep into his pocket. She was dressed simply in leggings and a sweatshirt, but he'd never seen a more beautiful woman.

"Hi." She tucked the hair back as she stepped aside, avoiding his eyes.

"Hi." Sam stepped in and followed her up the steps,

doing his best to ignore the traces of honeysuckle that floated back to him. "How's Samantha doing?"

She opened another door, and the honeysuckle was replaced by the warm scent of that orange coffee he remembered so well. "Oh, she's fine. She's resilient." Maya ducked into the kitchen as he stepped in and automatically slipped off his shoes. "I made coffee—this is the only coffee I had. Don't read too much into it."

Sam looked around the apartment. Samantha—his daughter!—was growing up here. Maya had grown up here, too. A sectional sofa took up much of the small space, along with an easy chair and some lamps.

A coffee table in the middle was piled with photo albums. The walls were covered with pictures of Samantha and her many awards. Framed newspaper clippings about the bakery were scattered here and there. Closer inspection revealed how the bakery had evolved to include the gourmet coffee roastery it had today. An open doorway behind him led to the kitchen, and a short hallway to his left led to the bedrooms.

Sam tossed his overcoat and suit jacket on the armchair and glanced down that hallway. The door to the master was partway open, which left Maya's unmade bed visible. Sam quickly looked away and occupied himself with the nearest framed picture of his daughter. She was very young in the photo, but he could see himself in her even then. His heart grew heavy.

Maya came up behind him. "She's about fifteen months here."

His pressed his lips together, unable to even force a smile. "Yeah."

She handed him a mug of coffee and moved to the

sofa. "Come sit." She set her coffee on the table and motioned for Sam to join her.

Sam set his jaw and sat beside Maya on the sofa. He put his coffee down without taking a sip. Maya looked at him sideways, and then reached across him for one of the albums. His body stiffened. She smelled of honeysuckle and cinnamon and something he remembered as distinctly *Maya*. She opened an album and handed it to Sam.

"I thought you might want to see some of Samantha's baby pictures or videos." Maya glowed and began flipping through the pages.

"This is the day she was born." The scene was in a hospital room: a ragged and spent Maya holding an infant Samantha.

The fresh-faced young girl in the photo was the Maya from his youth. Sam closed his eyes against the memory of this girl defiantly proclaiming that she had never loved him.

Sam nodded, tightening his lips as he returned to the past. Maya and her mother had documented Samantha's upbringing well. Each page was colorful, painstakingly arranged with clever captions and important date stamps.

Maya turned the page and continued to narrate. "Maya." He cut her off. "Could I just look through them?" He didn't even bother to keep his tone gentle.

She appeared a bit taken aback. "Oh, sure." She fidgeted for a moment, before handing the album to Sam. "Of course." He sat back in the sofa, crossed one ankle over the other knee and returned his attention to the album.

Samantha was two in the next few photos. Curly dark

hair, light brown skin, her smile all chubby cheeks and scrunchy nose, Sam grinned at the wonder she was, even then. A few pages later she was five, her first day of kindergarten in a school uniform, her dark brown eyes alight with excitement. Sam skipped a page or two and suddenly she was seven, in a soccer uniform. Her curly, dark hair was tied up in a bushy ponytail. She was wearing a keeper jersey. Sam's agitation grew.

"She played soccer since she was this little?" Sam's voice was abrupt. "Is it true, why she's not playing? That she's too busy to play?"

"Um, no." Maya flushed. "She started at this new high school." She hesitated, but then met his gaze. "She's on partial scholarship there, but still, the tuition—" she put one hand out, palm up "—versus the soccer fees—" she did the same with the other hand and moved them up and down, as if weighing them. "I, well—I couldn't do both." She picked up her coffee and appeared to be very interested in drinking it.

Sam narrowed his eyes at her and returned to the albums. Now Samantha was ten, her hair in two braids as she accepted a ribbon at a school science fair. Her mischief-filled eyes reached across the years to him in the next photo, as she was caught eating batter from the big mixer in the bakery.

Her intensity heated the next page as she concentrated on decorating her first custom cake. Her innocence grabbed him as she lit the traditional *diya* for Diwali, completely attired in her traditional Indian clothes. He smiled at the little girl and reached out to touch her face. But it was just a picture.

In the next album, Samantha was twelve and all

dressed up in her first high heels, curly hair tamed and cascading around her face. Her skin had taken on a creamier hue that closely matched his skin tone. A man Sam didn't recognize stood next to her. He wore a suit and tie and upon closer inspection, Sam noticed a flower corsage on his daughter's wrist. He turned to Maya for explanation.

"Oh, that's Ajay. Ami's husband?" She avoided his eyes as she mumbled. "Father-daughter dance."

Sam's throat tightened, and he needed to loosen his tie even as he glared at Maya before he roughly tossed aside that album for the next.

Now she was thirteen and dressed for an Indian wedding. He could see traces of the young woman she would become. Tears burned behind his eyes as he continued to turn pages. More school awards, higher-level soccer, parties and everyday things. Things he hadn't been allowed to share. Or even know about.

"Sam?" Maya's face filled with apprehension. "Sam, are you okay?"

Sam turned toward Maya, nostrils flaring; one tear escaped. He raised a trembling finger to catch it. "No, Maya. How could I possibly be okay?"

Maya looked confused. "I thought you might want to see her growing up."

Sam stood and turned on Maya. "*This* is watching her grow up?" His heart pounded, heat rose up in waves. "These are pictures, Maya. Moments. Frozen in time." He raised his voice, the injustice of having his own child kept from him finally given release. "This is all I get. Pictures."

"I wanted to tell you so many times. I picked up the

phone countless times over the years. I wrote emails I never sent. The more time that passed, the harder it became. What could I possibly say to you that wouldn't result in you looking at me the way you are now?" She lifted her chin, almost defiant. Almost, but not quite. "I knew I couldn't keep her from you indefinitely. She's too smart, too curious. I figured eventually, she would do what I didn't have the courage to do." Her voice was soft, resigned.

"You should have." He growled at her.

"There are a lot of things I should have done."

The pain on her face softened him for a moment. Unbidden, he was assaulted by memories of the last time he kissed her. It was almost sixteen years ago, but he could still feel the sun on his skin and smell the water from the lake. She had had tears in her eyes. And then it hit him. "That day, at the lake. You knew you were pregnant." Sam narrowed his eyes at her, his heart pounding, grim realization beginning to set in. "You didn't say anything, but when I proposed to you, you ran."

"*That* was a proposal?" Maya's defiance turned angry. She stood and leaned toward him, her voice low and dangerous. "You presented me with that *coin*." A tremor shook her words. "And said—" she paused and steadied her voice "—you said, 'heads, we get married, tails, we break up.'" She spit his words back at him with venom. "How was I supposed to agree to that?" She backed away from him, her breath heavy. "I was pregnant." Her lips trembled.

"Which I did not know." Sam moved in closer to her, his voice harsh.

"How was I supposed to tell you?" Maya's voice

caught. "Only minutes before, you were cozying up to Bridget. And you wouldn't tell me why! I thought she was always going to be around!"

"Bridget? Are you serious? She was *lying*! In any case, how could you *not* tell me?" He nearly vibrated with agitation, and he was unmoved by the tears in her eyes. "Damn it, Maya! You had *our child* without me— without even *telling* me."

"You were too immature to handle it." Maya stood firm.

"You never even gave me a chance!"

"Your 'proposal' told me I didn't need to!"

Sam watched as she swallowed her tears, even as he pushed back against the burn behind his own eyes. "I came back for you, two days later—" He couldn't even finish, he clenched his jaw and ran an angry hand through his hair. He hadn't let himself remember *that* day in almost sixteen years.

"I remember." She avoided his eyes, lowering her head.

Sam stared at her, anguish filling his belly. He leaned close enough for the tears on her lashes to stir something inside him. He ignored it as he all but hissed through gritted teeth. "Are you telling me that you kept Samantha from me all these years because of *how I proposed to you*?" His heart, his stomach, wrenched at this knowledge. *Who was this woman whom he loved, but did not know at all?* He couldn't breathe.

Maya gaped back at him. She tried to speak.

"No!" His voice boomed as he stepped back from her. He held his hands up in front of him. "Don't bother." He snatched up his coats and gloves, slipped on his shoes. "You didn't even give me a chance." Tears continued to burn behind his eyes. "You were supposed to have faith in me. *We belonged to each other.*" He grabbed her hand and pushed an object into it. "Remember?"

He turned on his heel and thundered down the steps just as his phone dinged. It was probably the text from Paige telling him where to meet her. He ignored it as thoughts of the photos and the lifetime he had missed filled his head, and he stalked out into the biting cold.

CHAPTER TWENTY-FIVE
MAYA

New York 2012

MAYA STOOD MOTIONLESS in her apartment and listened to Sam's thundering footsteps as he stormed off. When the bottom door slammed, she brought her attention to the object in her hand. She knew what it was the instant he put it there. She just didn't know why. She held it up to the light. The coin was old, tinged slightly green. She turned it this way and that.

Heads, we get married, tails, we break up. Heads, we see your movie, tails, we see mine. The words echoed in her ear, deafening her when the secret of the coin was revealed to her. The whole world stopped, leaving Maya in a vacuum, the only sound her rapidly pounding heart, which quickly filled with remorse. *It couldn't be.*

She squeezed the coin in her hand, tighter and tighter until the coin pressed uncomfortably into her hand, and her nails dug into her skin. She opened her hand to verify the truth. She stared down at the coin and flipped it over, her head, her limbs, joining her heart, heavy with regret and opportunities lost.

On one side, the profile of a man who must've been of some importance to be immortalized on a coin. A head. On the flip side, the other profile of the same man.

Another head. *Heads, we do what you want, tails, we do what I want.* Always.

Tears threatened again as a heavy sob built from her depths. What had she done? She quelled the sob before it broke, dragging her into a well of lament and despair. Tears would have to wait. She had a meeting with a bride in fifteen minutes. Maya tore her gaze away from the coin and fortified herself before heading into the bathroom. She needed this wedding contract. What was done was done.

She couldn't change the past. Even if she wanted to.

CHAPTER TWENTY-SIX
SAM

New York 2012

SAM LEANED AGAINST the cold brick building outside Maya's apartment, letting his head fall hard against it. The crisp air was refreshing, but his stomach was in knots. So that was it. Sarcastic laughter built inside him. It was almost like sixteen years hadn't even passed. She still drove him insane.

So Maya had kept Samantha from him because of that coin? No—it didn't make sense. Something else must have happened during those two days. Unless... unless what she had said to him that day had been true.

She had never really loved him.

Sam stood upright and tried to shake the painful memory from his head. He needed to focus if he was going to meet Paige and his parents for that cake tasting. He checked the text from Paige and his whole body went rigid with disbelief. His heart hammered in his chest. *How is that even possible?*

Paige had texted him the address of Sweet Nothings. It took him a full sixty seconds to process that she wanted him to meet her *here*. For a moment he considered returning upstairs, giving Maya a heads-up.

The moment passed in a wave of renewed anger at

her. No, they would just have to deal with whatever happened in the next hour. He straightened his tie and put on his suit jacket and overcoat, closing his eyes and inhaling deeply. The crisp air cooled his anger, but did nothing for the ache in his chest. No matter, he'd have to deal with that later.

Right now he had to deal with the fact that the cake designer his fiancée was enthralled with was none other than the mother of his child.

CHAPTER TWENTY-SEVEN
SAM

Maryland 1996

THE SUNLIGHT WAS painful even through his eyelids. Thankfully, they seemed to be sealed shut. The fuzziness in his mouth would eventually demand to be taken care of, but there wasn't any rush. He knew instinctively that if he moved, one thousand tabla players would use his head for a drum. Sam had always been mesmerized by the speed and accuracy of the tabla players' hands; he just didn't need them in his head right now. Rays of sharp light continued to bore through his eyelids, and from a distance, he heard someone calling out to him.

"Sammy! Ah, jeez, Sammy. What happened?"

Sam did not respond. Couldn't, even if he'd wanted to.

"Sammy?" Even with his eyes closed, Sam could see the furrow between his father's eyebrows grow with concern. "Sammy!"

His eyes were spared the sun's needle rays as his father moved closer and blocked the light. Sam tried to open his eyes. Bad idea. He closed them again, but unfortunately that was enough to start the tabla players inside his head, and the fuzz in his mouth was growing. He tried to move his arm and was rewarded with aching pain all throughout his body, causing him to groan. He unglued his eyes and found he was on the sofa.

"There you are." His father was shaking his head. He leaned down to give his son a hand to sit up. Sam's every muscle protested this, but his stomach protested the most. "C'mon, now." His father pulled an empty bottle from Sam's grip and shoved a bucket in front of him, just in time.

Sam emptied the poisonous liquid contents of his stomach, much to the joy of the drummers in his head. He actually welcomed the rhythmic, pounding pain. It took away from the crater in his chest that just got bigger every time he thought about Maya. Which was constantly.

"Well, at least you drank the good stuff." His dad forced a chuckle, but concern still laced his words. "I take it that it didn't go well."

Sam shook his head. *Oohh. Big mistake.* "The coin. She didn't understand." It was all he could do to get the words past the desert landscape of his throat.

His dad shoved a glass in front of him. "Drink this. Electrolytes."

Sam drank down the whole glass, decreasing the fur in his mouth by a fraction. Images from the night before flashed before him. Maya had looked amazing. They had shared that amazing kiss, he put out the picnic dinner and proposed with the coin. The idea was that she would've picked it up, and seen the ring underneath— and she would also learn the secret of the coin. It had made sense in his head, was maybe even romantic, but now, it seemed a bit ridiculous. Especially since she'd flipped out and run. Tears burned again, putting his head in a vise. The crater grew bigger.

"Let's go, Sammy." His father grunted as he pulled Sam up by the armpits. "Let's get you in the shower. Give it a day or so, then go explain. She'll understand."

John helped his son get in the shower, and Sam stood there and willed the water to bring him relief. To show him the way to make all this right with Maya. Somehow, he'd hurt her, and he had no idea what he'd done. Whatever it was, he'd fix it.

He turned off the shower and toweled off, his head still pounding. He threw on sweats and a T-shirt and fell asleep on top of his bed, wet hair and all. The whole universe was looking down on him from his ceiling, and he wondered yet again how the hell he had screwed this up. Agitated voices broke through his fog, and he opened his eyes to listen.

"He has to at least explain to her about the coin."

"No, he does not. If she really cared, she would not be so harsh. Good riddance to her, I say." Sam's mother sounded relieved.

"Hema, he's in love with her. And she's in love with him. They can fix this. There must be some other reason she was upset. He needs to make amends and find out."

"He cannot be in love with her—she's not right for him, for the kind of future he promises to have. I've held my tongue the whole summer and let him have his little romance—but now it is over. *I* did not even think he was serious about marrying her—how could she think so? She's wise. The best thing she can do for him is leave."

"Hema, he loves her and he's going to fight for her. You better get used to the fact that she will be your daughter-in-law."

"Humph. We will see."

At the sound of his father's optimism, Sam smiled

to himself. *He's right. It'll be fine.* He'd go see Maya tomorrow and straighten all this out. But right now, he needed to silence the drums in his head.

CHAPTER TWENTY-EIGHT
SAM

New York 2012

SAM FIDGETED OUTSIDE the bakery, waiting, so he could catch Paige before she went in. He had to at least tell her that the cake designer she loved so much was his ex-girlfriend. He could break the news about Samantha when they got home. His parents would recognize Maya, too. But they hadn't known she was pregnant back then any more than he had. He'd tell them about Samantha later, as well.

Paige and his parents pulled up in a cab. They gazed around at the storefront, eyes wide, huge smiles on their faces. He walked over quickly, calling out to Paige as he approached.

She turned to him, beaming. "Great, you beat us here! Oh, my goodness, Sam! Do you see this place? So quaint, so perfect."

"Yeah, it's great." He spared the store a cursory glance before he took her hands and planted a peck on her cheek. "Can I talk to you, quick?"

"Sam, we're late. It'll have to wait." She admired the sign and the floor-to-ceiling windows. "I love it! I just knew I would."

His mother took Paige's hands from Sam's as she presented her cheek to him for her kiss. Sam automatically obliged. "Let her go for a minute. We have important things to do." She wrapped an arm around Paige, as if she really were her daughter, and guided her toward the bakery. Paige leaned into his mother's embrace and continued her chatter.

His father clapped Sam on the back. "How you doing, son?"

"Great, Dad." An automatic reply as he tried to get his fiancée's attention while she continued to gush over the storefront. "Seriously, Paige. Just one minute."

She smiled at him as if he were a little boy. "I'll give you all the minutes you want after this. I simply *must* have this woman make our cake." With that, she followed his mother through the front door. Even the door chime made her giddy.

His dad laughed as he guided Sam through the door. "Don't get in the way of a woman and her wedding plans."

Sam shoved his sweaty hands into his pockets as he followed his father through the door and mumbled, "You have no idea."

They entered Sweet Nothings to the glorious aroma of baking cakes and fresh coffee. It was almost after hours, but Julie was still there. Paige approached her. "Hello. I'm Paige Doyle and I'm here to see—" she pulled out her phone "—Maya Rao. The appointment may be under the name of my art gallery since my assistant made the call."

Julie smiled at Sam in recognition. Paige was not paying attention to anything except the shop, so she failed to notice the sudden thickness in the air as Sam's parents recognized Maya's name. Sam could feel, more than see, his father turn to him. Sam focused on Paige.

Before Julie could go back to get her boss, Maya came through the door from the kitchen. She'd changed into slacks and crisp chef's whites, her hair bound in its ponytail. Sam could appreciate the fact that her smile seemed forced and that there was no real light in her eyes, but he doubted anyone else could see that. She walked around to the front of the display cases. "Hi, I'm Maya R—" She addressed Paige and froze as she caught sight of Sam's father, then his mother, and finally, her jaw clenched as she laid eyes on Sam.

"Hello, Maya, I'm Paige Doyle, and this—"

"Maya Rao." Sam's father cut her off and advanced toward Maya with open arms. "I can't believe my eyes." His voice was filled with the same warmth it had always held for Maya. Sam couldn't stop his own smile or the warm feeling he experienced as his father embraced Maya like a long-lost daughter. When his dad finally released her, there were tears in Maya's eyes. "Let me look at you." He held her at arm's length, but didn't let her go. "How have you been all these years?"

Maya brushed her tears aside, a love-filled smile taking over her face. "I'm doing just fine, Uncle, thanks."

Sam's father shook his head at her, in that way that older men do when they've seen something unique. He turned to address his wife. "Hema, what a small world it is."

Sam's mother stood firmly beside a very bewildered Paige, her lips in a line. "True. Who would have thought it would be Maya making Sam's wedding cake?"

Sam curbed his instinct to reprimand his mother for her coldness. She had never been fond of his dating Maya, but he wasn't dating her now. Once out of Sam's father's embrace, Maya's body stiffened, and she put distance between her and Sam's family.

Paige spoke up. "Umm, what's going on here?" She glanced back at Maya, then looked from Sam's father to his mother, before finally settling her bewildered gaze on Sam.

"Well, Paige." Sam approached her, taking her hands in his. He absently fingered her engagement ring as he looked her in the eye. "This is what I was trying to tell you before we came in. Maya and I dated briefly when I was in law school."

Maya flinched behind Paige. Sam avoided her eyes.

Paige freed herself from Sam's hands and turned to face Maya. "This is *that* Maya?"

Maya squared her shoulders and smiled widely. "Well, yeah, Sam and I dated—but it was a long time ago, and we were basically children." Maya dismissed their entire relationship with a wave of her hand. *Not the first time she'd done that.* "That's in the past and I really do have some wonderful ideas—"

"I'm sorry, but could you excuse me one moment?" Paige turned back to Sam. "Your mom and dad are clearly surprised. But you don't seem to be. How did you know before we walked in that this shop was hers?"

Before Sam could speak, a young girl burst through the door from the kitchen, carrying a tray full of cake samples. "Here are the samples you asked for, Mom."

Sam's stomach hit the ground as Samantha took in Paige and his parents. Her gaze landed on Sam and she lit up. Any other time, Sam would have relished the joy on her face. "Hey, Dad. Oh my God! Is Mom making your wedding cake?"

"Dad?" Just when Sam didn't think Paige's eyes could get much bigger, they did.

"Sammy?" His father's soft voice was riddled with confusion.

His mother said nothing. Her eyes were fixed on Maya. Maya, in turn, was completely focused on her daughter.

Paige narrowed her eyes in Samantha's direction. "Wait, you're that new intern…" She turned back to Sam, fire in her eyes. "You told me she was your *intern*! What's going on here?"

"First, I want you to know, that I didn't know myself until two weeks ago."

"Are you—are you saying she's really your *daughter*?" Paige spit out the last word.

"Yes." He knew he had hurt her by keeping the secret, but there was nothing he could say right now to fix that.

"Why did you lie to me when I met her?" Paige's voice rose.

"I was still trying to figure all this out, trying to get answers. I didn't know what to tell you." Sam bored his gaze into her, silently imploring her to believe him. "My parents are finding out right now, too."

Paige faced Sam's father.

"He's telling the truth. Hema and I are hearing this for the first time, just like you. Isn't that right, Hema?" He looked at his wife. She allowed a stiff nod, and a small smile. "And if Sammy says he found out two weeks ago, then he found out two weeks ago. Though when he was going to share this with the rest of us is a mystery."

Samantha's angry glare burned into Sam, and he

"I didn't *let* her, or at least at the time, it didn't seem like I was letting her..." He drifted off, and Maya recognized a lace of regret. "I went back for her. Once. But...she wasn't having it." He paused. "I wish I had gone back again. Then maybe I'd at least have found out about you."

Doubtful. She flipped the coin through her fingers, noting the identical head on each side. Tears burned behind her eyes. *She should have trusted him.*

"Didn't you love her?" Curiosity was getting the best of Samantha. There was hardly a trace of teenage sarcasm.

"Well, yes."

Maya snapped out of her revelry.

"At the time."

An unexpected letdown as Maya's heart fell into her stomach. Well, what the hell did she expect? That he still loved her now? Ridiculous.

"Well then I don't understand how—"

"Samantha, all that doesn't matter now. All that is... past. I want to be in your life. I don't need or want that test at all."

"Yeah, you do." Maya stood and entered the room. "You need it for proof for the media, once you make your bid. Better to just have it, otherwise they'll come after Samantha."

Sam stood. "I'll take care of the media."

Maya shared a look with her daughter. Samantha nodded at her mother. "No, it's all right. I'll do it." She looked from Maya to Sam, a slow grin filling her face. "So, by the way, were those my grandparents?"

CHAPTER THIRTY
SAM

Maryland 1996

IT WAS MIDMORNING and already sticky outside. The sun mocked him with its happy yellow color and blinding brightness. Whatever it seemed to promise, it would only deliver another sweltering hot August day. Sam parked in front of Maya's uncle's house and left the cool of the car for the heavy, clammy air.

He knocked and waited on the porch. This was where she had first kissed him. He could still feel her lips as she had firmly kissed him, surprising him. He could still smell the honeysuckle scent of her as it had mingled with the cigarette smoke and smell of fresh grass at that concert.

Maya opened the door and Sam's stomach knotted as she stepped out. His hands shook, so he shoved them in his pockets. Her hair was neatly tied in a ponytail and her eyes appeared sunken and hard, devoid of the love he had seen in them only two days ago, and she was surprisingly pale. The lips he could so clearly remember kissing him were set in a hard line. He tried to sound casual, but he knew his voice sounded lost. "Can we walk?"

"Here is fine." Sam shivered from her tone, despite

turned away from her, only to face the question and doubt on Paige's face. Maya had taken more than a few steps back, and currently appeared to be trying to melt into a wall behind Paige. He tried to ignore her. "Paige, I haven't seen Maya in over sixteen years. She approached me two weeks ago, out of the blue, for legal help with Samantha."

"What gall!" His mother had finally found her voice.

"Mom!" Sam silenced her and returned to his fiancée. "When I found out Samantha was mine, I couldn't refuse."

"So you knew Maya was pregnant and you left her?"

"No, I never knew she was pregnant." He shot a glare at Maya.

Paige glanced at Maya over her shoulder and then redirected her gaze back at Sam. "How do you know her daughter is yours?"

Sam furrowed his brow. "What do you mean? Of course she's mine."

"You did a paternity test?"

"No." He caught Maya's eye, and images of Samantha winning prizes, playing soccer and growing up flashed before him. "But maybe you're right," he said, still focused on Maya, his hands balled into fists. The possibility that she could have been with someone else while she was with him was nauseating, even after all this time. But the image of Samantha at her father-daughter dance with someone else broke his heart in a whole other way. "It might be wise to have some documentation on file for when this eventually goes public, when I run for Congress. Make sure she's mine." In the same instant it took Sam to regret the wound he created in Maya's eyes, he heard the cake platter crash to the floor behind him, as Samantha stormed off.

He closed his eyes and swore under his breath before calling out her name, but it was too late to take the words back. They were floating around in the air around them, affecting each person uniquely. The pain in Maya's eyes cut him, but the fact that he'd hurt Samantha had him undone. He stepped around the cake splatter and was through the door before Maya caught up to him.

"Leave her alone," Maya growled at him. "Don't you think you've done enough?"

CHAPTER TWENTY-NINE
MAYA

New York 2012

SAM SWIVELED BACK to Maya. "Don't I think *I* have done enough? You were the one with the big secret!" He moved closer to her, his voice rising, his angry heat hitting her in waves. "Don't you *dare* tell me I've done 'enough'! Should I have told my fiancée and parents sooner? Probably—but really, it's only been two weeks. You kept this secret for *sixteen years*! And you never would have told me except for that fact that you needed something."

The pain in his face hit Maya harder than his angry insinuation that Samantha wasn't his. Her sympathy and guilt must have shown, because he softened. "I didn't mean to hurt her. I need to fix this. So either help me, or get out of my way."

Sam marched through the back of the shop, his overcoat flailing behind him like a cape, and out the back door. Maya hurried to keep up with his long strides. She found him pounding on the outside door to her apartment, calling Samantha's name and her gut instantly went back to the last time she heard him pound a door. The memory made her nauseous.

"Damn!" He kicked the brick next to the door.

"If you're done throwing a fit…" Maya dangled the key and waited for him to step aside.

She barely had the door open before he brushed by her and stopped. He was close enough for her to feel the heat from his body and to take in traces of his cologne. She stepped back.

"Thanks." He turned and took the steps up two at a time until he reached her apartment. He waited for her to reach the top.

Maya shrugged as she approached him. "Don't thank me. You haven't experienced a teenage fit yet."

This elicited a small smile. "Niki used to throw really good ones."

At the mention of her young charge's name, Maya was filled with shame and regret, and she looked away from Sam again. She opened the door to her apartment, and he entered, slipping off his shoes once more, and casually tossing his overcoat on the same armchair. He headed straight for the bedroom with the closed door and knocked.

"Go away, Mom. I'm fine." Samantha's voice was thick with tears.

"It's not Mom." Sam pressed his lips together.

"Mom? Mom? Are you out there?" She sounded like she did when she was little.

Maya moved closer to the door. "Yes."

"Tell Mr. Hutcherson we appreciate his help, but we no longer need his services." And there was the teenage sass.

The depth of pain on Sam's face was so unexpected, so real, Maya actually felt sorry for him. He never could hide his feelings. She spoke again to the door. "Can you at least talk to him?"

Silence.

"Samantha?" Sam's voice was hoarse. He cleared his throat and leaned in toward the door with his head bowed. "I did promise that I would tell Paige about you, and I didn't. I'm sorry. It's not because I'm embarrassed about you or that I don't want you—I do. I really do. I just wanted to keep you to myself for a bit. I mean, I missed fifteen years of your life." He cut his eyes to Maya and she flinched. "In any case, I should've told her." He leaned his shoulder against the door and faced Maya. "And I don't really want that paternity test."

Maya raised her eyebrows. Of course he didn't. The Sam she had known...well, the Sam she had known sixteen years ago wouldn't have needed it, either. Good to know some things hadn't changed.

He pressed his forehead against the door. "Samantha?"

More silence.

He pushed his hand against the door and slowly pushed himself upright. He ran his fingers through his hair, avoiding Maya's gaze. By the time he looked at her again, his jaw was set, but his sadness was reflected in the set of his mouth and in the dimness in his eyes. "Well, I guess you were right to keep her from me, considering it took me all of two weeks to mess it up."

Maya couldn't help it. She wanted to be angry with him for agreeing to the paternity test, especially in front of Samantha. But the man standing in front of her was not a would-be congressman trying to protect himself. He was a man who just found out he was a father and was being shot down for things he'd said in anger and pain. Much of which she had caused.

"She'll come around." Maya smiled. "Trust me. She's stubborn and she's a teenager. A difficult combination."

"I don't know. I mean, she's right to be angry."

The coin weighed heavy in her pocket. "So are you." She couldn't look at him.

Sam shrugged. "Yeah, well. I'll deal with that later." He glanced back at the door. "Mind if I wait it out a bit?"

"Sure." Maya slid down the wall on the side of the door and sat on the floor. "Get comfy."

Sam took off his suit jacket and slid down his wall, and they sat on either side of the closed door. He loosened his tie and rolled up his shirtsleeves, all the while avoiding Maya's gaze.

"It was nice to see your dad." Maya grinned at Sam. One beat too many passed before she hastily added, "And your mom."

This did not go unnoticed. "It's okay. I know she wasn't as kind to you as she should've been."

Her whole body tensed. *What did he know? What had his mother said to him?* "What do you mean?"

Sam just stared at her, a question on his face. "You know... I never liked the way she talked to you—even though I told her—" Sam broke eye contact. "Anyway, seems as though sixteen years didn't change anything. But not to worry, I will be having a chat with her. Samantha is her grandchild. She'll have to accept that." He threw his head back against the wall. "Assuming our daughter ever speaks to me again."

At the words *our daughter*, a thrill blazed through Maya before she could stop it. There was no need to get excited about Sam sharing something with her— even if it was *their daughter*. Shit. She couldn't help it.

"I always thought she just didn't like the fact that you

tried to change your life plans while we were together."
But Maya knew that, in truth, Hema-auntie had never
thought Maya was good enough for Sam.

Sam remained silent.

"But you must've really wanted the politics, since
here you are."

"It's been a long time. Things change. People change."
Sam's voice roughened. "She was diagnosed with cancer."

"What? When?" Maya sat upright. She might not
have been a fan of Hema's, but she certainly didn't wish
her ill.

"Right at the end of…" His voice trailed off, but
Maya heard him. "Right after you left." He paused and
cleared his throat. "She's fine now."

"I'm sorry to hear that." Maya paused. "I mean I'm
sorry she had cancer, not that she's fine now."

Sam chuckled, an unexpected low rumble that released the tension building in the air around them. "I
know what you meant."

Maya met his eyes and for the first time, she saw
something other than pain and anger. She was drawn
into him and was startled at the sound of the door opening. Before she could say anything, Sam was on his feet.

Samantha opened the door, but then stomped back
into her room. She grunted as she turned and plopped
down on her bed. She folded her arms across her chest
and pointedly faced away from Sam, looking out the
window.

Sam glanced at Maya, wide-eyed, eyebrows raised,
clearly out of his element, his experiences with Niki
notwithstanding. She jutted her chin toward Samantha in encouragement. He pressed his lips together and

stepped into the room, as wary as if he were stepping into an unfriendly courtroom.

The room was small, and he instantly filled it with his broad shoulders and long legs. He straddled the desk chair and rested his arms on its back, facing her. Maya took her spot again, seated outside the door.

Silence. Then both father and daughter spoke at the same time.

"I'm really sorry."

"Why didn't you go after *her*?"

"After who?" Sam asked.

"Paige. The redhead—you know, your fiancée?" Sarcasm ran thick through her voice.

Sam refused to take the bait. "I came after you."

Maya smiled, impressed. Maybe he had learned something from Niki's teenage years. She pulled the coin from her pocket.

Maya heard the smirk in her daughter's voice. "You've been sitting here all this time because I was mad at you?"

Sam sighed, his voice calm, almost tender. "I've been sitting here all this time because I hurt you, and that's the last thing I wanted to do."

Silence again. Maya was rooting for Sam. It was not very often that Samantha was rendered speechless. The coin became heavier in her hand.

"Why did you let my mom break up with you?" Samantha's voice was soft, almost cautious. "You know, back then?"

Maya fingered the coin, turning it around and around. He'd had no choice. Maya had seen to that.

"Why did I let…? What did she tell you?" He was gruff, and Maya pictured his anger.

"Nothing. She never told me *anything*."

"I didn't *let* her, or at least at the time, it didn't seem like I was letting her…" He drifted off, and Maya recognized a lace of regret. "I went back for her. Once. But…she wasn't having it." He paused. "I wish I had gone back again. Then maybe I'd at least have found out about you."

Doubtful. She flipped the coin through her fingers, noting the identical head on each side. Tears burned behind her eyes. *She should have trusted him.*

"Didn't you love her?" Curiosity was getting the best of Samantha. There was hardly a trace of teenage sarcasm.

"Well, yes."

Maya snapped out of her revelry.

"At the time."

An unexpected letdown as Maya's heart fell into her stomach. Well, what the hell did she expect? That he still loved her now? Ridiculous.

"Well then I don't understand how—"

"Samantha, all that doesn't matter now. All that is… past. I want to be in your life. I don't need or want that test at all."

"Yeah, you do." Maya stood and entered the room. "You need it for proof for the media, once you make your bid. Better to just have it, otherwise they'll come after Samantha."

Sam stood. "I'll take care of the media."

Maya shared a look with her daughter. Samantha nodded at her mother. "No, it's all right. I'll do it." She looked from Maya to Sam, a slow grin filling her face. "So, by the way, were those my grandparents?"

CHAPTER THIRTY
SAM

Maryland 1996

IT WAS MIDMORNING and already sticky outside. The sun mocked him with its happy yellow color and blinding brightness. Whatever it seemed to promise, it would only deliver another sweltering hot August day. Sam parked in front of Maya's uncle's house and left the cool of the car for the heavy, clammy air.

He knocked and waited on the porch. This was where she had first kissed him. He could still feel her lips as she had firmly kissed him, surprising him. He could still smell the honeysuckle scent of her as it had mingled with the cigarette smoke and smell of fresh grass at that concert.

Maya opened the door and Sam's stomach knotted as she stepped out. His hands shook, so he shoved them in his pockets. Her hair was neatly tied in a ponytail and her eyes appeared sunken and hard, devoid of the love he had seen in them only two days ago, and she was surprisingly pale. The lips he could so clearly remember kissing were set in a hard line. He tried to sound casual, but he knew his voice sounded lost. "Can we walk?"

"Here is fine." Sam shivered from her tone, despite

the heat of the day. Maya squinted in the sun and tilted her head. "What do you want, Sam?" Under her gaze, he became aware of the fact that he hadn't shaved, or slept, or really even eaten in two days.

You. He ran a nervous hand through his hair. "I need to explain about the other night." A strand of her hair escaped the ponytail. Sam automatically reached out to tuck it behind her ear. She stepped back out of his reach. His rejected hand hung frozen for a second or two before he willed it back to his pocket.

"Nothing to explain." Maya didn't sound angry or disappointed or anything. Her voice was devoid of emotion. How could that be? He studied her face and Sam could see her eyes were red and there were dark circles under them. The flat voice continued, "It's pretty clear to me that whatever we had this summer was just a way for you to pass the time."

Sam's eyes flew open wide and he felt a flush of adrenaline. He edged closer to her. If he could touch her, she'd know what she was saying was ridiculous. "What? How did you get...no! That's not..." She backed away from him, almost as if afraid. He stopped. "You can't really believe that!" He knew he was blabbering. "I know I've had other girlfriends in the past, but they didn't mean anything compared to how I feel about you."

"You know, Sam." Maya smirked at him. "You don't have to explain it to me. I get it. It's not—" she paused and took a deep breath. She looked him directly in the eye. "It's not like I was in love with you or anything."

The blood drained from his head and he grabbed the railing, her words a physical blow. "What are you saying? When we were in Virginia—" He stumbled on the words, his eyes darting wildly. "This whole summer… you said…" *Why was she saying these things?*

Maya raised her eyebrows at him, amusement filling her face. "You said things, too, Sam. Doesn't make them true."

Sam was speechless. It was a lie? The whole summer, what he thought they had meant to each other…none of it was real?

"Goodbye, Sam." She cleared her throat. "The summer's over, so…"

"No, Maya. Let me explain. The coin—"

She shook her head. "I don't care about that coin." She swallowed. "Or you."

Sam stepped close enough to her to be enveloped by her honeysuckle scent. It made him light-headed and he longed to feel her body against his and undo whatever it was that he had done. He knew his eyes were frenzied and his voice was severe. There was only one way to get the truth. "Tell me you don't love me." He leaned in, daring her, through gritted teeth, "Say it." There was no way she could say the words. He knew it.

Her face was stoic. She squared her shoulders and lifted her chin. "I don't love you."

Sam stared at Maya in disbelief as a wave of nausea flooded over him. She turned and gracefully walked back into the house without so much as a goodbye. He stood on the porch, paralyzed.

Once, when Sam was five, Arjun had been very angry and had kicked a soccer ball at him with all his might. The ball hit young Sam dead in the belly, the force throwing him backward to the ground. The wind was knocked out of him, his head pounded from hitting the dirt and he had the metallic taste of blood in his mouth. Sam did not cry, but he remembered wondering how someone he loved could hurt him so.

What happened next occurred in a fog. He pounded on the door, called out to her. An older woman with skin the same color as Maya, and eyes as fierce as the depths of night, stepped out and told him to leave. She repeated herself until Sam finally turned on his heel, leaped down the two porch steps and headed toward his car.

If she didn't love him, there was no reason for him to stay. He tapped the coin in his pocket. It had never steered him wrong. Until now.

CHAPTER THIRTY-ONE
SAM

New York 2012

SAM HESITATED FOR a beat just before turning the knob to enter his apartment. He'd barely just made peace with Samantha, and now he had to face Paige. And his parents. No doubt all three of them were here waiting for him. He walked into his apartment and confirmed what he already knew.

"Hello, everyone." He tossed his key on the hall table and headed for the bar. His mother was murmuring to Paige, who threw furtive looks in his direction as his mother continued to pat her hand. He needed at least two fingers of bourbon for this conversation. "Dad, bourbon?" he called out.

"Uh, no, son. We were just leaving." He stood. "C'mon, Hema. Let the kids talk."

His mother did not budge.

"How about it, Mom? Bourbon?" Sam grinned at her as only sons could to their mothers when they knew they were in trouble. He sipped. The liquid was cool, almost soothing.

His mother finally stood and faced her son. "Don't you grin at me like that, young man!" Suddenly Sam felt like he was eight years old and had broken a dish, or like he was sixteen and had had a fender bender. Or maybe he was twenty-three and had fallen in love with the wrong girl. "Start talking."

"It's pretty clear, Mom. Maya was pregnant when we broke up." He shrugged in a grand gesture of sarcasm and nonchalance as he took a gulp of soothing bourbon. "She didn't tell me, and she went on her merry way." Paige's eyes were red-rimmed. That was his fault. He softened and moved toward her. "Paige, I'm sorry I didn't tell you—"

His mother blocked his way, his fiancée's guard. "You can apologize to her later. Tell me, what reason did that Maya give for keeping this secret?"

Sam had rarely seen his mother so agitated. Her words shook, and her Indian accent got thicker with her mounting rage. Pretty soon, she'd give up on English altogether.

"Mom, calm down. You can't get all worked up like this." Sam looked to his father for support.

"He's right. Take it easy, Hema. I'm sure Sammy got all the answers he needed. He's right—getting this worked up is not good for you."

Hema turned on her husband. "You two always play the cancer card to get me to back down. I've been fine for years!" She approached Sam, her eyes wild. He couldn't remember the last time he'd seen her so upset. "What. Reason. Did she give?"

Sam downed his bourbon and set down the glass. "She said—" He hesitated as he looked to Paige. Her sad eyes brimmed with tears, her bottom lip trembled. Her normally perfect red tresses were flat and tucked uncharacteristically behind her ears. Guilt stabbed at him. He answered his mother, unable to turn away from Paige. "She said it was because of Bridget and that coin."

Paige was confused. "What coin?"

"Bridget was trying to get you back. Not to mention she was lying," Sam's dad said.

"Yeah, but I was twenty-three. I was stupid and I didn't handle it well. I never told Maya what Bridget was up to—she assumed the worst." Sam remembered it well. He had been annoyed that Bridget wouldn't just let him be. He'd known she wasn't pregnant, but he had wanted to focus on Maya at the time.

"Doesn't seem like enough for her to keep your daughter from you." John sounded confused. "There's got to be more."

"That's all she said." Sam shrugged and dropped his arms.

"I thought you explained about that coin." His dad's brow was furrowed. "Didn't you go back?"

The pain on Paige's face was killing him. She didn't need to be hearing all this. But he answered his father. "I did. She wouldn't listen." He flicked his eyes toward his father. "You remember?"

John touched his nose. "Of course."

"Well, if that's all it took for her to keep this from you, then it is just as well she left." His mother gathered her things, seemingly satisfied. She turned to Paige and smiled, almost triumphant. "She was never right for him the way you are, dear."

"What coin?" Paige repeated herself.

"It was Arj—my brother's. He had this old coin he used to toss around. He gave it to me the day he—he gave it to me. Turned out to be a two-headed coin." Sam glanced at his dad, avoiding his mother's eyes. "I used it a few times, for…things, and she got pissed. She didn't know it was two-headed."

"Can I see it?"

"I…uh, I don't have it." Sam could feel his father's surprise and avoided his gaze.

"So, now what?" John asked.

"So, now you have a grandchild." Sam's laugh was weak.

His dad's eyes lit up, even as he shook his head in disbelief. "I can't…" He stopped and swallowed and Sam noticed tears in his father's baby blues. "That's fabulous!"

His mom went pale. "What do you mean?"

"I mean Samantha's my daughter, so she's your granddaughter. And she's pretty amazing."

"But she's also Maya's."

"So?" Sam narrowed his eyes at his mother.

"So, do you think I'm going to accept Maya's daughter after what she did to you? After she broke your heart like that?"

"Yes, I do." Sam was firm. "She's not just Maya's daughter, she's mine, as well. So I expect you to accept her."

"We'll see about that." His mother stormed to the door. "Come, John. It's time to go."

John turned to Sam, a silent, don't-worry-she'll-come-around look in his eye. He hugged his son tight, an almost giddy look on his face as he whispered, "A granddaughter!" He waved to Paige and they left.

Sam went to his fiancée. "Finally."

Paige nodded.

"I'm really sorry. I should have told you from the

beginning, but honestly, I could barely get my head around it..."

She walked toward their bedroom without speaking.

"Paige, talk to me."

She turned before she opened the door. "I know you're sorry, and ultimately, I'll understand that you needed a few days to 'process.'"

"So then why do feel like I'm sleeping on the sofa tonight?"

"Because when it came down to it, you went after your daughter with *her*, and left *me* standing there." She walked into the bedroom and shut the door.

CHAPTER THIRTY-TWO
MAYA

New York 2012

MAYA LIT THE cotton-and-butter wick on the last diya and looked around to check her handiwork. The coffee shop was bathed in soft light from the flickering diya, as it was every year for Diwali. Aromas of onion, garlic and garam masala from tonight's dinner of palak paneer, chicken tikka and fresh naan wafted down to her all the way from her mother's apartment. She and her mother always closed the shop on this day to celebrate the coming of the new year. It used to be just her, her mom and Raju-kaka, along with Ami and her family. Deepak-mama and his family had come on occasion, but it wasn't always convenient for them to make the trip from Maryland. She would miss them again this year. As the years passed, Ajay started to join them, along with his family. When they'd added fireworks, the neighbors had wanted in on the fun. Now, their annual Diwali gathering was highly anticipated in the neighborhood, and they usually maxed out the capacity of the coffee shop.

After everything was in place, Maya dashed upstairs to put on her sari and help Samantha into her outfit. This year, Maya had donned a burgundy chiffon sari with a smattering of beadwork. Simple, elegant, yet festive. Samantha was wearing a *chaniya choli*—a short blouse and floor-length skirt with a half-length sari wrapped around her—also in burgundy. Maya was leaning toward the mirror to properly center her *chandlo*, when Samantha paused in the doorway.

"Here, let me help you with that." Samantha rushed in and took the tiny adhesive jewel and centered it on Maya's forehead. "Gorgeous! *Nani* wanted me to tell you to hurry because people are here."

"Well, let's go then." Maya grabbed a tray of food and went down to the shop to greet her guests. Her mother and Raju-kaka were already mingling with everyone, just as they should be. They looked so natural together, greeting everyone with a "Happy Diwali!" and their hands clasped together in front of them in namaste.

Raju-kaka kept a protective hand on the small of her mother's back, and she allowed him to direct her in this way. This small gesture added to Maya's lightness in the spirit of the holiday, and she caught Raju-kaka's eye. He winked at her, handsome as ever in his cream *sherwani* tunic and matching cream bottoms, with a bright blue scarf that conveniently matched the exact shade of her mother's sari. She carried the warm tray to a table near the counter where they had set up a buffet table and returned to her mother and Raju-kaka. She bent down to touch their feet for blessings, as was the custom. As always, they stopped her halfway, insisting that the gesture of respect was not necessary. Her mother hugged her tight and joined in the laughter surrounding her. Raju-kaka glowed, unable to tear his eyes from his love.

People milled about, chatting and laughing, the festive beat of the tablas and Bollywood music providing the track for their fun. Maya pushed aside her troubles from the week and lived in the moment. Thoughts of Sam were pushed away. Or at least pushed to the back of her mind.

Diwali was the eve of the new year. It was the celebration of light over dark. Historically, this was the day that Ram and his wife, Sita, along with his brother, Laxman, returned to their hometown of Ayodhya after having been banished to the jungle for fourteen years. For Maya, it had been the first time anyone had celebrated the fact that she was pregnant with Samantha. A young girl, pregnant out of wedlock, no sign of the father—in her world, this was unheard of. She had felt banished herself. Sure, her mother was a single mother—but at least she had been married. Sunita had been convinced that Maya's future was bleak, and her uncle and aunt had just looked upon her with disappointment dripping from their very beings.

But that Diwali, she had been three months pregnant, and panic was setting in, because she was starting to show. Raju-kaka had taken her into his arms and told her it was a new beginning. He scolded Sunita, and told her to get over herself, that Maya shouldn't be treated like an outcast for falling in love—especially by her own mother. It was the only time Maya had ever seen Raju-kaka angry with her mother.

Sure enough, after that Diwali, things turned around. It still wasn't easy, but Maya had held her head up and dealt with whatever came her way. She had come to terms with giving up some dreams, but she had found new ones and had never looked back. It was that Diwali that she had had the idea to modernize the bakery her mother had run, and add the coffee roastery. Her mother had insisted on keeping some baked goods, and eventually they'd evolved into what Maya had today.

Maya closed her eyes and told herself that this, too, was a new beginning, and she simply had to move on from Sam, just like she had all those years ago. It was the hardest thing she'd ever done, and if she was honest with herself, she never had moved on—she'd simply pushed Sam and every feeling that went with him into a small corner of her mind. But like an overstuffed cupboard, her feelings had burst out with a vengeance, and now every cell in her body was filled with him. That was when she heard Samantha's voice.

"Dad! You came!"

"Hi, sweetheart. You remember Paige?"

"Yeah, sure." Samantha's voice was easygoing and friendly, as if teenage girls met their father's fiancées every day. "It's really nice to officially meet you."

Light laughter eased whatever tension there may have been, but Maya's body tensed. She knew Samantha had invited them, but Maya didn't think they would actually show.

She turned toward Sam's voice and her breath caught. She had never had occasion to see Sam in his Indian clothes, and she wished she hadn't now. He stood tall, his broad shoulders filling out a navy silk sherwani, with a gray scarf that he had simply hung around his neck. He was smiling at Samantha, and Maya had a full and complete view of his dimple and perfect teeth, not to mention the love in his eyes as he wrapped his daughter in a hug.

Against everything she knew was right, Maya melted, and tears filled her eyes. The navy showed off

Sam's brown skin tone, and the silk stretched pleasantly over his muscles as he hugged his daughter. As if he could feel her gaze, he looked up and found Maya watching him. Something soft flickered in his brown eyes before they turned hard again, in a way Maya was becoming familiar with. She averted her gaze and blinked back tears as if she had been caught doing something wrong.

"Mom!" Samantha called out as she walked over. "Look who's here."

Maya forced a casual smile onto her face. "I can see. Happy Diwali, Sam. Paige, it's good to see you. I'm glad you were both able to join us."

"Happy Diwali, Maya." Sam sounded formal, as if they'd never met before. Clearly the fact that Maya agreed to the paternity test had not swayed Sam from his general anger at her.

Paige glanced sideways at Sam before smiling at Maya. "Thanks for having us. I did some reading about Diwali, and this celebration seemed a wonderful way to start anew."

Maya couldn't help smiling at Paige. "You're right, of course. It is Diwali, after all—new beginnings and all that." She worked to keep her eyes averted from Sam, and so concentrated on the sari Paige had donned for the occasion. It was a navy blue silk with a gray border, and it matched Sam's outfit perfectly. But it was slipping from her shoulder.

"I have a surprise for Samantha." Sam's voice dragged Maya's gaze back to him.

"Whoa? Really?" Samantha's face lit up.

"Well." Sam looked so happy it was like he was the one getting the surprise. "I heard all about how you don't play soccer anymore, so I signed you up for a team again. And since you've missed some time, I'll give you some goalie training myself."

He'd done what? Maya stiffened.

"What? Dad, that's amazing!" Samantha's face mirrored Sam's for a moment, and she threw her arms around his neck. "Thank you, thank you, thank you." She hugged Maya.

"Um, Samantha, can you take Paige into the kitchen and help her with her sari?" Maya pointed to Paige's shoulder. "Your sari is slipping—Samantha can help you pin it."

Paige appeared grateful as Samantha led her back toward the kitchen.

Maya narrowed her eyes at Sam. "What did you do?"

He flicked his gaze away for a second and folded his arms across his chest before staring her firmly in the eyes. "I paid the soccer fees."

"You did *what*? Without even talking to me about it?" Maya glowered as she leaned toward him. He smelled of soap and sandalwood, and Maya had to force herself to ignore how badly she wanted to lean even closer into him and wrap herself up in his scent like she used to do.

"What? I'm supposed to talk to you about everything I want to do for her?" His voice was filled with indignation, but it seemed to peter out at the end as if he was just now hearing his own words.

Her eyes widened. "Yes! That's what parents do!"

"I wouldn't know that since I've only been a parent for a month." Now he was just being snarky.

Heat rose into Maya's face. "Is that what this is?" She lowered her voice to speak in an undertone, as some of her guests had started to look her way. "Are you getting back at me by paying her soccer fees behind my back?"

He uncrossed his arms and smirked as he looked away from her. "Don't be ridiculous."

Maya's mouth gaped open. "I think that's exactly what you did." She stepped closer to him as she poked a finger into his chest. He really did smell good. "I think you know you should've come to me first, but you're pissed and you didn't care!"

Sam did not speak.

Maya took his silence as a triumph. "Listen." Her gaze was steady. "I can't turn back time. I can't stop you from being angry. However, I *am not* going to pay for my mistake for the rest of our lives. And I'm certainly not going to let you use it as an excuse to do things behind my back. Even nice things."

She poked a finger into his very firm chest again. "If we're *both* going to be her parents, then we need to be able to discuss things related to her. Can you do that?"

He rubbed the area she'd poked, as if she'd really hurt him, and the edges of his mouth turned up as he nodded in agreement.

"Okay." She bit her bottom lip. "Good. In that case, thank you." Adrenaline was pumping through her body, but civility was called for here, so she made every effort to calm her voice. "Soccer makes her very happy, and I hated taking it away from her." She glanced at him. "And I think she'll benefit from you training her. So, thank you."

Sam just stared at her, those big brown eyes studying her face. The smile that had started formed instead into a tight line before he turned away from her to join the festivities. "Don't thank me. I'm her father."

Maya was left standing there as he made his way around the room, ending up face-to-face with Sunita and Raju-kaka. After a moment of Maya's mom glaring at him, Sam bent down to touch her feet. She allowed him to finish the gesture, and when he stood, Maya noted his crooked smile, as her mother had to reach up to place her hand on his head to offer her blessings.

Maya turned away before she was caught staring again and headed into the kitchen. Soft laughter reached her as she saw Samantha trying and failing at pinning Paige's sari.

"Hi. Here, let me get it." She approached Paige, and Samantha stepped aside.

"The material is too soft, I can't get the pleats right."

Maya nodded and studied the other woman. "Did you do this yourself?"

Paige nodded. "YouTube."

Maya half smiled. "Well, it's a great first attempt. But Samantha is right, with this material, it can be challenging. Do you mind?" She reached for the material on Paige's shoulder.

"No. Please."

Maya gathered the material and started to remove part of the sari so she could rewrap it. "Samantha, you can go. I'll get this."

"Okay. So, Paige-auntie, great seeing you. And I will definitely take you up on that offer," Samantha called as she returned to the party.

What was she talking about? Maya turned to Paige, the question on her face.

"I offered to help with her with her art history homework." Paige's green eyes were huge. "If that's okay with you."

Maya continued to wrap the sari on Paige. "Yeah. Sure. Why not?" She pinned the pleats to the blouse at the shoulder before stepping back to inspect her work. The navy blue did amazing things to Paige's eyes, and she was stunning in the sari now that it was secured properly. "Actually, that's very kind. I'm sure none of this is easy for you."

Paige smiled. "Well, I guess we have to make the best of it. And Samantha is great." She paused. "I told him to discuss the soccer fees with you first. But you know Sam. Once he gets an idea…"

Maya nodded, her mouth set in a line. "It's fine." No, she didn't really know Sam. Though there was a time she thought she had. "There's a full-length mirror on a door in the back if you want to take a look and freshen up."

"Great." Paige nodded at Maya and went in search of the mirror.

No sooner did Paige leave than Hema-auntie entered the kitchen. Maya was pleasantly surprised at the absence of lavender scent that usually accompanied the older woman. Hema-auntie was not dressed in a sari, but rather in a simple red-and-gold embroidered kurta top and dress pants. "Hello, Maya."

The sound of Hema-auntie's voice was enough for Maya's shoulders and back to tense, and her jaw to clench. Maya glanced over her shoulder. Paige was in the bathroom in the back. She hadn't been alone with Hema-auntie in over fifteen years.

Hema-auntie took a few steps toward Maya. Her smile was nothing like her son's. It was something that was done with only her lips; her eyes were not involved in the gesture. "It's been a long time, Maya. Truthfully,

I did not think I would ever see you again. In fact, that was part of our agreement, was it not?" Her black eyes flashed with hard amusement.

Maya said nothing.

"I mean, you took the check. Yet here you are today."

"You know I never cashed it." Maya surprised herself with the confidence in her voice. Young Maya would have fallen apart by now.

"True, but Sam does not know about any of this." The smile disappeared. "If he finds out what happened all those years ago…"

Maya shrugged. "I have no desire to hurt anyone. Your secret is safe."

"What secret?" Paige had returned from freshening up and looked from Maya to Hema, her features betraying that she'd heard more than she should have. Maya shot a look at Hema-auntie, daring her to tell her future daughter-in-law what she was capable of.

"Oh, nothing. We were simply discussing the possibility of Maya making your cake, but not telling Sam. It might be—awkward—for him."

Paige looked again from Hema-auntie to Maya, clearly not buying it. "Yes, it would be awkward."

"But I don't mind." Maya blurted out. *What?* "I mean, it's a pretty high-profile wedding, it could mean a lot of business for me." She stopped and addressed Paige. "If you're okay with it, of course."

"Are you sure?" Paige's eyes lit up. "I mean I love your work, but if it's weird, I get it."

"Yes, I'm sure. I have some sketches, and we can look at them this week if you want." *What was she getting herself into? Was she actually going to make Sam's wedding cake?*

Paige smiled. "I'd really love that. Thank you." She hugged Maya, and Maya returned the hug. If things were different, they might have been friends.

"Well, now, that's settled." Hema-auntie grinned, but kept her gaze on Maya for a beat too long. She motioned to Paige. "Come, we'll have some food. I understand Maya is quite the cook as well as baker."

Paige followed Hema-auntie to the door, glancing back at Maya with a puzzled look on her face. Maya's heart sank. How much had she really heard?

CHAPTER THIRTY-THREE
MAYA

Maryland 1996

MAYA SHUT THE door behind her and leaned against it as a wave of nausea overcame her. How had she been able to tell Sam she didn't love him? She would never know. What she did know was that she wasn't going to wait for him to resent her and then abandon their child. She'd spent her childhood waiting for her father to return to her. He never had. She couldn't risk putting her child through that.

The vibrations from his fist pounding against the door shivered all the way through her. He called out to her, his voice at first strong and demanding, but eventually giving way to desperation. It was the love in that desperation that ripped open her heart. Her hand flew to the knob. All she had to do was open the door.

She'd tell him she'd made a mistake. That she was sorry she'd hurt him. She'd tell him about the baby, and they could be together. All she had to do was walk out there and tell him that she'd lied, that she really did love him—that they belonged with each other—and the pain in her chest would go away. And the pain she was putting him through would go away, too. She turned the knob just as her mother's hand covered hers.

Sunita's eyes met Maya's, and she nodded her head to indicate that Maya should step aside. A fresh wave of nausea sent Maya running for the bathroom. She collapsed on the bathroom floor and retched the contents of her stomach into the toilet. She thought she could still hear him calling out to her.

Long after her stomach was empty, long after Sam's voice could no longer be heard, she continued to retch as sobs racked her body. She doubled over on the cold tile of the bathroom floor and cried, hoping the pain would leave her.

It never did.

CHAPTER THIRTY-FOUR
SAM

New York 2012

"Mom! Seriously, she's your granddaughter!" Sam ran a hand through his hair. His mother was going to be the death of him. "It doesn't matter how you feel about Maya. Samantha is *my* daughter."

His mother pressed her lips together and scanned the room. Sam let his words hang in the air. This was going to be his first weekend with Samantha, and he had asked his parents to come up so they could all get to know each other. His father was thrilled beyond belief that he had a grandchild, and even Paige was warming up to the idea of a teenager being around. She already had a strategy involving Samantha that would help his campaign. But his mother—his mother could not or would not get past the fact that Samantha was Maya's daughter. Well, that was too bad. She was going to have to.

"Come on, Mom. You're coming with me to get her from school."

"What? I'm what?"

Sam held out her coat. "Yep. And we're walking."

"Walking? All the way? How far is it? I'm an old lady, young man."

Sam opened the door. "Let's go." There was no

room for argument in his voice, and behind his mom, Paige's mouth gaped open, while his father shook in silent laughter.

"Have fun!" his dad called out, his laughter following them as Sam shut the door.

The brightness of the sun and clear blue skies had fooled him into wearing only his leather jacket. He blew on his hands, rubbing them together and shoving them into his pockets against the November chill. He turned to his mother. "This way." Her pace was slower than his, but certainly not old-lady-like. She threw him irritated looks and mumbled under her breath in Gujarati, but did not turn around to go back.

They arrived just as the final bell rang, and stepped to the side of the walkway to avoid the swarm of students. Most of the crowd dissipated, and there was no sign of Samantha. Sam scanned the steps and down the walkway, to the two sets of double doors, as a young couple holding hands exited the building and started walking down the steps. He looked past the couple to see if Samantha was behind them—but then he did a double take.

"Isn't that her, holding hands with that boy?" His mother squinted through her glasses.

"No. Couldn't be." He stepped closer. But it was. A slight pounding started in his ears. He widened his stance, folded his arms across his chest and waited. *Who was this boy? Why was he holding his daughter's hand?* Samantha and the boy were so enthralled with one another, they failed to notice that Sam was in their way. Just as they were about to collide with him, he cleared his throat.

"Dad!" Samantha's eyes lit up, her smile easy. The boy dropped her hand as his eyes widened. "And *Dadi*!"

His mother stiffened. Sam would have chuckled at hearing his mother referred to as a grandmother, except that he was absorbed with checking out the hoodlum standing next to his daughter.

Samantha greeted her father with a hug that he did not return. She tried to hug Hema, too, but was met with the same resistance. Samantha pulled back and raised an eyebrow at her father. "Hey, Dad. What's up?" She followed his gaze to the boy and turned back to him. "Oh, uh, Dad, this is Will. Will Waters, this is my dad, Sam Hutcherson, and my grandmother, Hema."

Will was almost eye to eye with Sam, and he remained wide-eyed as he shuffled his feet. He smiled, extending a shaky hand to Sam. "Um…nice to meet you, sir." He nodded to Sam's mother. "Ma'am."

Hema smiled. "Hello, Will."

Sam could not move or speak. He was filled with a sudden and complete dislike of this young man. His eyes were too blue and his dark hair was too…something. From the corner of his eye, he noted that Samantha was looking back and forth between him and this boy.

Will hesitated, then awkwardly placed his ignored hand back in his pocket. He managed to stammer out a goodbye to Samantha, and a wave at the still silent Sam. "Uh, well, bye." His eyes flicked to Samantha before he rushed off.

As soon as Will was out of earshot, Sam's mother dissolved into laughter. "Talk about not liking your children's choices!"

Sam looked at her, incredulous. "What? I was fine."

"Oh my God, Dad! Could you have been more rude?" Samantha was glaring at him.

"I was not rude. I was checking him out."

His mother practically guffawed, as if a guffaw was something she actually ever did. "Yes, maybe. But you were rude about it."

Samantha turned to her grandmother. "Thank you. Thank you very much."

"It must have been quite embarrassing for young Samantha, here."

"It really was." His daughter glared accusation up at him.

"Who is he?" Sam needed answers.

Samantha blushed as she shrugged. "I told you. Will Waters."

Sam gawked at her. Did she just swoon a bit when she said his name? "Who *is* he?"

She averted her eyes to a passing bus, pretending to squint into the sun. "Kind of my boyfriend," she mumbled.

"Kind of? What does that mean?" Sam flashed back to being a sixteen-year-old boy himself, and what he remembered did nothing to calm him.

She sighed and glanced sideways at her grandmother. "It means he just asked me to be his girlfriend two days ago and I can only see him at school."

Sam frowned at her. "Why?"

"Because to go on an actual date, I'd have to tell Mom, and I'm not going to do that. And neither are you."

"What? Maya doesn't know? Why not?" Sam liked this less and less.

"You've met my mom, right? She'll freak." She threw up her arms for effect. "I don't know how many times

I heard the story about *her* high school boyfriend, and the lecture she got from *Nani*." She rolled her eyes. "I didn't think you would freak. You seem—normal. Can you not tell her? I'll tell her when I'm ready. Please?"

Sam was silent as he contemplated this. It didn't feel right. Maya might actually freak out. But was that really a bad thing? But then, maybe the truth should come from Samantha.

"Come on, Sam. It's not a big deal. She seems a sensible girl. Let her tell her mother in her own time." His mother had stopped laughing.

Sam did a double take at his mother. She winked at Samantha, and Sam nearly fell over.

"Fine. As long as you do tell her." He remembered Maya's younger self. "No sneaking around to see him."

"Why? Did Maya have to sneak around to see you?" His mother was enjoying this way too much. Sam did not answer.

Samantha's eyes popped open. "Did she? Oh my God!"

"It really isn't any of your business," Sam growled.

His mother and his daughter feigned shock at the reprimand. Sam turned on his heel and started to walk. "Let's go. Dad and Paige are waiting for us."

"Hey, Dad!"

Sam turned around and walked back to where Samantha and his mother had stayed put. "Yes?"

"Don't you think you should call Uber or something? You can't make *Dadi* walk all the way back in the cold."

His mother didn't even try to hide her gloating as Sam tapped his phone and called for a car. "Smart and considerate girl we've got here, Sammy."

Twenty minutes later, they exited the Uber. Sam simmered the entire trip, while Samantha and his mother found they had much in common. Not the least of which was a love of teasing Sam. They also realized that they both loved to cook.

"I taught your father how to cook. He's pretty good." Hema beamed.

"Really, Dad?"

"Hmm? Yeah. Why so surprised?" He narrowed his eyes at her. He really should just send Maya a text about Will.

"Samantha, let's see what you can do. How about we cook dinner together?" Sam couldn't believe it. His mother sounded excited to spend time with her granddaughter. When had she changed her mind?

Samantha's whole face lit up. "That would be great, *Dadi*!"

Sam's mother nodded toward the kitchen. "Go see what they have, and we'll come up with a menu." She grabbed Sam's arm while Samantha entered the kitchen, greeting his father and Paige on the way. "Sam," his mother whispered, "don't break your daughter's confidence by telling Maya about this Will. I'm sure it's harmless."

Sam stared down at his mother. "You're enjoying her."

"Well, yes." His mother didn't meet his eyes. "She's intelligent and funny—I mean she *is* my grandchild." She shrugged her shoulders as if she had never resisted the idea. It was the first time she'd actually looked happy to be a grandmother.

Sam sighed, and agreed against his better judgment. "Okay, *fine*. I won't say anything."

CHAPTER THIRTY-FIVE
MAYA

New York 2012

IT WAS TWO weeks before Christmas and the coffee shop was hopping. People doing their Christmas shopping in the cold always needed a break, and hot coffee was always the remedy. Maya and her mother baked extra cookies this time of year for the crowd, and the specialty cake orders increased every year. Her sense of accomplishment and pride generally made up for the lack of sleep and accompanying exhaustion, but this year, her focus waned. There was no question in her—or anyone else's—mind as to why.

Ami leaned against the counter. "I heard Sunita-auntie finally went out with Raju-kaka." She wiggled her eyebrows.

Maya grinned. "About time, don't you think? I saw her before they left. She actually ditched the traditional salwar kameez for a skirt and top—very modest, of course—and get this—heels!"

"Go, Auntie!" Ami grabbed one of the cookies Maya was packing up for her.

"Do you have to do that every time?" Maya let out an irritated breath.

"Makes me feel like I'm getting away with something." Ami took a bite and moaned. "I keep you as my best friend for these cookies alone. So, Christmas." She flashed her eyes at Maya. "What are you doing?"

"Well, Samantha is going to Maryland with her dad for a few days." Maya avoided her friend's eyes. "So I'll be here." Heat rose to her face for no comprehensible reason.

"You still love him." Ami was nothing if not blunt.

"Huh? What? We're not even talking about him. No." She fumbled with the box. "Ouch."

"What's that? Paper cut?" Ami arched a perfect eyebrow.

"Yeah. So? Don't read into it."

"Don't read into the fact that you still love Sam and the mere mention of it has you fumbling and cutting yourself?"

Maya ignored her friend as she searched for a Band-Aid. Truth was, now that Sam was back, thoughts of him invaded her waking and sleeping hours. Not to mention that Samantha adored him, and he seemed to adore her back. That gave Maya warm, fuzzy feelings she could do without.

"He's getting married." Ami's other talent was stating the obvious.

"I know. I'm making the cake."

"So either fight for him or move on."

"He's clearly in love with Paige, and I actually kind of like her." She fastened the Band-Aid around her finger, and murmured, "I had my chance. It's gone."

"When are you going to tell him whole truth of why you left? You have proof."

"Never. I'm never going to tell him. What purpose would that serve?"

"Well, he could stop being pissed at you."

"But he'll be hurt. Not to mention, Samantha also loves Sam's mom. And I'm not taking that away from my daughter." She sighed and fussed with the pens near the register. "Either way, Ami, it was my decision to keep his child from him. I should've known he would love being a father, and I did not." This conversation was dragging her heart into her stomach. She couldn't keep going back to this.

Ami pointed a chocolate-covered finger at Maya and spoke through a mouthful of cookie. "You need to start dating again." It was nearly closing time, and only a few customers remained. Ami leaned on the counter by the register and licked the chocolate from her finger.

Maya delivered her best eye roll and continued to box up Ami's treats. This was an old discussion and she was tired of it. Evasion was in order. "How do you eat like that and stay so thin?" Maya asked.

"Don't change the subject," Ami said. "It wouldn't kill you to consider—"

"Hey, Maya! How's it going?" The door chime and a friendly male voice interrupted their conversation. Maya and Ami turned to see who had entered.

"Well, well, well. What have we got here?" Ami positively purred, just loud enough for Maya to hear.

Maya turned deliberately from Ami to the customer. "Hey, Leo. Doing well, thanks." She smiled. "Large house coffee and three extra special chocolate chip cookies?"

Leo winked at Maya. "You know me so well." His gaze lingered on her, causing her to flush and break eye contact. She turned to fill his coffee and pack the cookies, then took the package to the register.

"Well, you make it easy. Same order every time."

Ami scooted over slightly to allow Leo room near the register, but didn't leave. She almost leered at him. He nodded at her, but focused his attention on Maya. "It gives me an excuse to come and see you." His eyes were hopeful. "What do you say, Maya? How about dinner?"

"Leo." Maya raised an eyebrow with exaggerated patience.

"Lunch?" he pressed.

She shook her head at him.

"Coffee, then. Surely you can do a cup of coffee?" He leaned on the counter, his grin sexy and inviting. Another woman would have melted. But Maya was unmoved.

She sighed and ignored Ami's encouraging look. "Honestly, you flatter me. But—" she handed him his box and took his money "—my answer is the same as always. I don't date."

Ami gawked.

Leo chuckled softly. Again, it was probably sexy to other women. "Can't blame a guy for trying." He took his change and turned to leave. At the door he turned to look at Maya. "Maybe you'll change your mind someday."

"Goodbye, Leo." Maya was friendly, but firm. He opened the door and walked out.

Ami rounded on Maya. "What's wrong with *him*? Did you not *see* him?" She leaned her elbows on the counter and gazed dreamily at Maya. "Have you ever seen eyes *that blue*?" Her grin turned salacious. "And I swear I could see muscles through his coat." Ami sighed and waved her hands at Maya without waiting for an answer. "Do you have something against completely hot guys—" at this she widened her eyes "—who *like* you and *ask you out*?"

"Aren't you married?" Maya tried to laugh it off. Leo *was* quite attractive.

Ami simply shrugged. "I'm not dead," she said. "I can certainly appreciate an attractive man—even if you can't."

Maya sighed. "I'm just not interested. I don't date." She stared back at Ami. "Don't you remember all the disasters I've had over the years?" Ami had tried to set her up with various men over the years, but Maya could never bring herself to feel anything for them.

"Yes. But now Sam is back and *you know* he's moved on. So maybe that's enough for you to move on, as well."

"Sam being back has nothing to do with it." She ignored that annoying little voice inside her head that said, *Yeah, right.*

"Maya, save me the denial. You and I both know I'm right. Admit it, this Leo guy is cute. I saw you blush."

"But…okay. He's kind of cute."

"Yes! Yes, he is."

"But he asks me out every time he comes in here. Isn't that weird?"

Ami rolled her eyes. "No! That's *persistent*. Go out with him. One date. What could it hurt?" She softened and placed her hand on top of Maya's. "It's time to move on. You deserve a life outside your daughter and this shop."

Maya recalled another boy who had been persistent, and the memory warmed and saddened her all at once. She was living in the past and it had to stop. She locked the door and began to close up for the evening.

CHAPTER THIRTY-SIX
SAM

Maryland 2012

SAM TOSSED ASIDE his covers and turned over his pillow.
He lay on his back and stared up at the glow-in-the-
dark stars and planets on the ceiling. Even the universe
seemed intent on robbing him of sleep. He gently heaved
himself out of his childhood bed, grabbed a sweatshirt
against the December chill, and softly made his way
downstairs past the kitchen to the bar. He poured himself two fingers of his father's best bourbon and made
his way to the sofa in the dark. He started to take his
regular seat on the far end, and jumped up when he
hit feet.

"Samantha?" He squinted at the form on the sofa.

"Yeah, Dad. It's me." She shifted her feet and sat up.

"Can't sleep?" He sat down beside her.

"I miss Mom."

Good thing it was dark enough that Samantha
couldn't see his face. His own lack of sleep was due
to memories of Maya that continued to invade his
thoughts. Same woman, keeping them both awake.

Samantha covered herself with a blanket. Sam sipped
the bourbon. It warmed him. "Haven't you ever been
away from her?"

"Not at Christmas."

"What do you usually do?"

Even though it was dark, Sam could tell his daughter was grinning. "Well, Sejal-*masi* and their family usually come up and we open presents first thing Christmas morning. Then Mom and I go to church while they cook brunch."

"Mom takes you to church?" Sam could not hide the surprise in his voice. A lightness filled him. There was only one reason for Maya to have done that all these years. He smiled to himself. But why should that be a source of happiness for him? He forced the grin away, but the lightness remained.

"Well, yeah. I figured out years ago, it had something to do with my dad—you. I just never got her to admit it. She and *Nani* used to argue about it sometimes. *Nani* thought it wasn't necessary."

He couldn't believe it. And he certainly couldn't let himself think too deeply about what it might mean. He was engaged, for God's sake.

"Tell me how you and Mom met." Samantha interrupted his thoughts.

"Oh, I don't think we should talk about all that."

"Please! She never tells me anything."

He was already starting to unravel. Thoughts of Maya interrupted his day and his night; he waffled between excitement when he was going to see her and anger at her for keeping Samantha from him all this time. Talking about their past had the potential to undo him.

In the dim light, Samantha widened her eyes in a plea, and Sam caught a glimpse of his brother in her smile. It gripped his heart and for just that second, Sam had proof that his brother had actually existed and was still with them in some form. Sam melted. If going down this road would undo him, then he would be undone. He swallowed a large sip of bourbon, relishing the burn as it made its way down.

"You know, she didn't like me very much when we first met. She wouldn't even talk to me unless she had to. But the first thing I remember about her was how beautiful—"

"What's going on here?" Hema turned on a light, making Sam and Samantha squint in the sudden brightness. "Is it the Can't-Sleep-Midnight-Crew?" Her hand flew to cover her mouth as if she had revealed a long-time family secret. Which she kind of had.

Sam's heart stopped. The Can't-Sleep-Midnight-Crew was what his mother used to call him and Arjun when she would catch them stealing midnight snacks. That she had referred to her dead son was nothing short of a Christmas miracle.

"What's the Can't-Sleep-Midnight-Crew?" Samantha's grin widened, and she scooted closer to Sam to make room for her grandmother on the sofa. She was all over that forbidden middle cushion, but his mother did not say a thing.

Sam's mother remained frozen in her spot, her eyes glazed over. "Mom?" Sam sat straight up. "Mom? Are you okay?" He started to stand.

"Oh my." His mother shook her head and motioned for Sam to stay seated. "I'm sorry, I don't know what came over me. I haven't used that phrase since... since..." She scanned the room as if it was written somewhere how long it had been.

"It's okay, Mom. Here, sit next to Samantha." Sam spoke slowly, his gaze on her face.

"Oh, of course, Samantha." His mother smiled, as if seeing her granddaughter in the room for the first time. She sat down next to her grandchild.

Samantha looked to Sam for an explanation. He gave a quick shake of his head, indicating that she should drop it.

"The Can't-Sleep-Midnight-Crew is what I used to call your father and his…his brother, whenever I caught them sneaking ice cream and junk food in the middle of the night." His mother placed her hand on top of Samantha's as if she could gain strength from it.

This time it was Sam who couldn't speak. His mother continued, slowly at first, but with more ease as Samantha showed genuine interest in her father's youth, as well as in Arjun, the uncle she'd never meet. Samantha clasped her grandmother's hand in her own and never relaxed her grip.

Sam remained quiet as his mother conversed with his daughter. At times, the older woman's eyes filled with tears, but somehow, his daughter knew what to say and how to say it.

"You know, not a day goes by, even after all these years, that I do not think of my Arjun." Her voice trembled, but she composed herself. "But I see him in you, Samantha. And I feel like I have a part of him back."

Tears burned in Sam's eyes, and for the first time in a long time, he did not feel as though he was competing with his brother. A lightness fell over him, the likes of which he hadn't experienced in a long time.

"It's a terrible thing to lose a child."

"And to lose a dad."

"What do you mean? You have your father, now." She looked at her hands for a moment.

"I'm talking about my mom." She looked her grandmother in the eye. "My mom's father chose to leave them—she doesn't even know if he's alive or not. At least you know that Arjun-kaka loved you, and it wasn't his choice to leave."

Sam had never seen his mother rendered quite this speechless. Silence was loud in the air as his mother had a kind of war with herself.

It was still dark out when his father joined them. Sam's father told stories about Sam as a boy, and Samantha gobbled them up. Sam sank into the sofa, sipped his bourbon and allowed the warmth of his family to envelop him in a way that it hadn't for almost twenty-five years.

Just before sunrise, Paige peeked in and retreated to the kitchen before returning with a tray of mugs, bringing the aroma of fresh coffee with her. She smiled at Sam as she curled up in the chair across from him, her hands wrapped around a steaming mug. Her attention was on Hema and Samantha as their conversation continued.

Sam hadn't heard his mother laugh like this since Arjun was alive. Both Sam and John just watched as Samantha unknowingly revealed a woman that both Sam and his father had thought was lost to them forever. The glow on his mother's face was a direct result of Samantha's presence. His mother could have been this happy all these years, if Maya hadn't kept Samantha from them, and anger soured the moment of bliss. He shoved the anger away for another day. Today, he wanted to enjoy his parents' happiness.

Sam traded his empty bourbon glass for a mug of coffee and tried to catch his fiancée's eye, but she was focused on his mother. Concern grew on her face as she quietly watched the exchange between grandmother and granddaughter.

They laughed and talked while the sun came up on Christmas morning, at which point Samantha stood and stretched. "Aren't we going to church?"

Sam's mother stared at her, speechless. Sam stood and shrugged at his mother. "Apparently, Maya takes her to church every Christmas."

Something flickered in his mother's eyes, but before Sam could place it, the laughter was back. "Well then, we better get dressed."

Back in his room with Paige, Sam plopped down on his bed as she prepared to shower.

"I haven't seen your mother this happy—ever," she said.

Paige was right. Sam did not respond; he felt the anger returning.

"I mean, don't you think it's great how Samantha seems to be able to bring out the best in your mom? She's even talking about your brother."

Sam remained silent.

"Sam?" Paige wrapped her arms around him. "What's the matter?"

Sam pulled out of her arms. "Imagine if my mom had had Samantha for the past fifteen years. She could have been this happy all along." His heart hammered and blood pulsed in his head. "*Maya* robbed my family of this."

Paige stepped back from him, her eyes blazing.

"Your mother is truly happy for the first time in years, and all you can think about is Maya?"

"Of course, I'm thrilled to see my mom and dad happy." Sam set his jaw. "That's not what I meant, and you know it."

"Do I?" She looked disgusted as she went for her shower.

By the time Sam finished getting dressed, Paige was already downstairs. He hadn't stayed up all night in years, so he headed to the kitchen for another cup of coffee. His mother and Paige were speaking in hushed tones in the kitchen and he caught the tail end of their conversation.

"He blames Maya completely." Paige sounded worried.

"As he should."

"But Mom, that's not…"

"It doesn't matter, beti. Trust me. This is best." His mother was firm, ending the discussion as he entered the kitchen.

"Talking about me again?"

"Only the best things, beta." His mother patted his cheek. "Now grab that coffee to go and let's get in the car. Where is that granddaughter of mine?"

CHAPTER THIRTY-SEVEN
MAYA

New York 2013

Maya approached the back entrance to her apartment carrying a large package while trying to balance multiple grocery bags, one of which included the eggs she needed to bake today. She fumbled and strained with the packages as she reached for her key.

"Hey, Maya." Sam's voice startled her. She dropped the bag with the eggs and teetered as she tried not to drop the package. Sam caught her, his hands on her back, before she fell. He was dressed for work, precisely tailored dress coat over what must be a nicely fitted designer suit and he smelled so completely masculine—like leather and soap—it was all Maya could do to not lean into him.

"What the hell, Sam? Sneak up on people much?" Maya grabbed for the bag that had the eggs.

"I wasn't trying to scare you." His touch was all at once foreign and familiar, and when he removed his hands from her, she felt a sense of loss.

She inspected the bag. "The eggs look broken. Shit."

"At least you didn't break. You're welcome." He pressed his lips together and gave a small shake of his head.

"I would've been fine if you hadn't startled me."

Sam just stared at her. It was really not fair that he

be so handsome when he was clearly so angry with her. She found the key and opened the door. "Why are you here? Samantha is in school."

Sam picked up the package and the bags with ease and followed her up the stairs. "I need a copy of Samantha's birth certificate for soccer registration. She told me to stop by today. Didn't she tell you?"

"No. She probably forgot." Her phone dinged as they entered the apartment. Maya glanced at it as she put down the bag she carried. "No, here's the text now."

"Where do you want these?" Sam stood in the entrance, holding everything that Maya had been carrying.

Maya grabbed the bag that had the eggs and motioned Sam toward the dining table. "You can put that stuff there."

She took out the cartons and opened each one. One carton was totaled, but the others seemed usable. She sighed. "Well, at least I can get some baking done."

"Don't you get a shipment of baking supplies? So you don't have to go out and buy eggs?"

"I do, but the eggs didn't come in the last shipment. Or in the shipment before that. I've called and stopped payment, so as of now, I have a new supplier, but that shipment isn't due for a few days."

"Well, let me know if you need help with that. Like legal help."

"I'll be fine." Her words were harsher than she intended.

"Fine."

Silence, during which they looked everywhere but at each other.

Sam shoved his hands into his coat pockets. "Can I have that birth certificate?"

"Oh, yes. It's back here." Maya walked toward the bedroom, keenly aware that Sam was behind her. At least she'd made her bed today. The papers were in a small safe in her closet. She pushed aside clothing and kneeled down to punch in the combination for the safe, Sam still behind her.

"Did you just put in 0525?"

"Why are you looking at my code?" Maya snapped at him. She opened the safe and pulled out a bulging folder and started rummaging through papers.

"That's my birthday," Sam murmured, the hostility gone from his voice.

Maya ignored him. "How was your Christmas?"

Sam joined her on the floor. "It was great having Samantha with us. You should have seen my mom. I don't think I've ever seen her happier."

The accusation in his voice was loud and clear. Maya cringed but did not look up from her paper search.

"My dad, too." Sam softened his voice. "He was just so…content."

Maya's heart ached at this. Uncle had never been anything but kind to her, and she had thanked him by keeping his grandchild from him.

"Even talked to my dad about taking on some more pro bono type cases. So if you know anyone who needs legal counsel…"

Maya snapped her head up. "What? You mean like helping out the little guy?" She couldn't help the huge grin that spread across her face. "That's awesome."

"Thanks." Sam's nod was curt, but if she was not mistaken, there was true gratitude and excitement in his eyes. Not that she was looking.

"Actually, Mrs. Chen from across the street is having

trouble with the company that is holding her lease. She's a smart lady, but language is a problem. Her daughter usually helps with that, but she's away at school…"

"I'll talk to her." Sam actually grinned.

It was much nicer to see him smiling. She did her best to ignore any happy thoughts about him. "Ooh! And Lorenzo, the owner of the Italian market, is having an issue with one of his suppliers, too." She was failing.

"Okay, great. I'll talk to him, too." Sam leaned against the wall and stretched his legs out. "Thanks."

"Sure." Maya returned to her pile of papers. She tossed aside a thick stack of papers. "What's this doing in here?" She continued her search for the birth certificate. Only the sound of shuffling papers broke the silence.

"Are you expanding the coffee shop?"

Maya looked up to find Sam deep into the stack of papers she had put aside. "Um, yeah. It's the next logical step."

"You buying next door and taking down walls, and all that?"

"Mmm-hmm."

He flipped through the stack, scanning, grunting here and there. Maya forgot about the birth certificate as she watched him. "Is something not right with that agreement? I had my lawyer look over it, he said it looked great."

"You have a lawyer?"

"Well, I have a lawyer I go to before I sign papers."

"You just got these last week." He pointed to the date. "I could have looked at them for you."

"Oh, uh, well. I know." She went back to her search.

"You've done enough." She stared him down. "And you're always mad."

"Well, mad or not, I can take care of this kind of thing for you." His voice was still distant, but less angry. "Your guy missed a few things."

"What?" Maya dropped her pile and crawled over to Sam. "Where?"

She leaned over him to see. Sam pointed out a few places that would eventually cost Maya extra money. Why did it have to feel so good to be close to him?

"Damn it! And I paid him already." Maya closed her eyes. She couldn't afford to keep wasting money like this.

"I can fix it." His voice became soft and kind, almost the way Maya remembered it, except now a bit deeper, older. "And you can pay me in those chocolate chip cookies you used to make."

Maya risked a glance at him. "Okay. Chocolate chip cookies, it is." She looked down at her stack. "Ah! Here it is." She handed it to Sam. "I have a copier in the shop." She started to gather up the disarray of papers and put them back in the safe, when they slipped from her hands, falling everywhere. "Oh, crap. I don't have time for this."

Sam set the certificate down and laughed, helping Maya gather the papers.

"Let's just get all this stacked together. I'll have to organize it later. I need to get some things into the oven and my eggs are sitting out." She frantically gathered papers, trying to make an even stack. Sam gathered the smaller things that had escaped, making a smaller pile of sorts. Before Maya had a chance to register what Sam was doing, he had stopped moving, clutching a small piece of paper in his hands. *No-no-no-no!*

"What's this?"

The sight of Sam holding that particular piece of paper paralyzed Maya. Her heart hammered while her arms hung, useless, by her side. She willed them to grab that slip of paper, but even as they tried to comply, Sam moved out of her reach.

"Sam, give it back to me." Her voice cracked.

It was a check, made payable to Maya Rao, in the amount of ten thousand dollars. It was signed by Hema Hutcherson. And the date. The date was… "This is the day before I came to see you again. After the proposal fiasco." He looked up at her, pain and confusion lining his features. "What is this?" It was a demand.

Maya remained frozen to her spot. "Nothing. Just forget about it. It's inconsequential." She grabbed for it again. He easily pulled it out of her reach.

"I'll be the judge of that, Maya." His voice was gruff. "Tell me. Tell me now." A renewed anger was beginning to ooze from him. But there was a touch of fear in his face, too. Like he had figured out what the check was about and didn't want to accept it.

"Fine. But remember, you asked. You demanded to know." Maya looked him in the eye. If he wanted to know, fine.

CHAPTER THIRTY-EIGHT
MAYA

Maryland 1996

"MAYA, IT'S A mistake to tell him. He may stay for a bit, but he will run. Trust me." Her mother's voice held fourteen years of disappointment, resentment and loss. But Maya held firm. Sam should at least know he had a child. She would make it clear that he was under no obligation to her. Especially if Bridget was pregnant, too. No way Maya wanted to be tied to *her* for the rest of her life. She grimaced inwardly. You really couldn't make this shit up. Who got two girls pregnant in the same summer? Her mother was starting another round with Maya when the doorbell rang.

Grateful for the disturbance, Maya peeked through the window and her body tensed. What was Sam's mother doing here? She took a deep breath and put a smile on her face as she answered the door. "Auntie! What a surprise." Her eyes were still red-rimmed and swollen from crying, but she hoped Hema-auntie wouldn't notice.

"Maya." Hema-auntie's smile only reached her lips. Her eyes were black coal, though there were bags under them, as if she hadn't been sleeping well. Her skin also seemed to lack some of the rosy glow Maya had remembered from meeting her before.

"Won't you come in?" Maya's stomach lurched as she caught the scent of lavender when Hema-auntie passed. She led her into the family room where her mother was sitting.

"Mum, this is Hema Hutcherson, Sam's mother." Maya's voice trembled so she cleared her throat in a vain attempt to steady it. "Auntie, this is my mother, Sunita Rao."

Her mother stood and nodded to Hema-auntie. "Hello." She wasn't cold as ice, but she was clearly not going to spare any warmth for Sam's mother.

Hema-auntie matched her mother's nod. "Hello."

Ever the hostess, Maya's mother did not miss a beat, inviting Hema-auntie to have a seat and offering water or tea.

"Actually, this is not really a social call. I was hoping to have a word with Maya." She rested her eyes on Maya. "Alone."

The corners of her mother's mouth curved into the semblance of a smile. "Of course. I'll leave you to it, then." She turned to Maya as she left. "I'll just be upstairs, should you need anything."

Maya sat across from Hema-auntie and waited. Hema-auntie moved slowly, almost as if she were in pain. Maya had always had the feeling that Sam's mother was not fond of her, but she didn't know what she had done to offend her, except date her son.

Oh.

"Maya." She wasn't so much cold as she was businesslike. "The summer is over, your employment at my brother's house will come to an end in a few days and you will return home."

Maya's heart pounded. "Yes. That's true."

"You have had an enjoyable summer with my son, but that is going to end. Now. Go home. Forget you came here." Her steady gaze remained focused on Maya.

Blood drained from Maya's head and she had a sense of falling. She reached for her glass of water. "I'm sorry, what?"

"You heard me. You come from different worlds. You had your summer fun, and he had his. So, put it behind you. Go back to Queens." She spoke as if this were the most obvious conclusion of things. As if she were telling a ten-year-old that the party was over and it was time to go home.

Maya gripped the side of the chair to steady herself. Surely she had misunderstood this woman. "I don't understand."

"What's to understand?" Her tone was impatient, as if Maya were daft. "You are not the type of woman my son needs. He's going to *be* somebody someday." She squared her shoulders and lifted her chin. "*You* are just a *girl*. It's not personal—I'm sure you are lovely. But you grew up the daughter of a single immigrant mother in *Queens*. You don't have the upbringing or the connections that my son will need to move forward with his ambitions."

The words hit her like a punch in the stomach. Her breath became short. She searched Hema-auntie's eyes and found only disapproval. Had she planned on leaving Sam? Yes. Then why did her insides scramble to hear his mother confirm it? Maybe she didn't want to leave him. Maybe it wasn't right for her. Or for him.

"Did he tell you he loves you?"

Maya's face must have revealed the answer.

"He *thinks* he does." Sam's mother chuckled, but without humor. "But did you not notice that he had a different girl on his arm three months ago?" Hema-auntie waved her hand dismissively. "He thought he loved her, too."

Maya's stomach dropped and she placed a protective hand on her belly. It was a small gesture, easily over-looked. But women have been making this small gesture since the beginning of time. Women *knew.*

Hema-auntie's eyes flew open as she took in the gesture. She flicked her gaze to Maya's face. Whatever she saw there brought her hand to her mouth. "Oh my," Hema-auntie whispered and looked at Maya's belly. "You are pregnant." She met Maya's eyes. "And Sam does not know."

Maya pressed her lips together. Silence filled the room for a long moment as all the information in the air was digested.

Hema-auntie took a few steps closer to Maya and placed her small cold hand on Maya's cheek as if talking to a small child. "Surely you did not think you were the only one?" Maya broke her gaze and Hema-auntie's voice filled the air. "Oh dear, you did." She looked Maya up and down. "How naive."

Maya's stomach turned and the taste of bile coated the back of her throat. Was she talking about Bridget? Had Hema-auntie made the same visit to Bridget's house? She clenched her jaw and forced her chin up.

"See, my dear, you are no one special. When the time does come for Sam to marry, I will see to it that the woman is…appropriate." She stepped back and opened her purse, taking out her checkbook. "Something that you are not.

"You are free to tell him about your baby, but where would that leave you? He may marry you, he may not." Hema-auntie frowned and shrugged as she took out a pen and scrawled on a check. "In either case, Sam has a sense of responsibility, so more likely than not, he'll try to take care of you and that child."

She paused as she turned sad eyes on Maya. "But what happens five or even ten years from now when he realizes that you and your child stole all of his dreams? His real dreams? Sure, right now he thinks he can save the world as a small, two-bit lawyer working for the people—but that won't last. And that's your influence, anyway. He never spoke of that until you came along." She raised a triumphant eyebrow. "Will he think he loves you then? Or will he turn bitter?" She moved closer, and Maya nearly gagged again when her nostrils were overcome with the sickly floral scent of lavender perfume. "He may even leave. Abandoning not only you, but your child. What kind of life is that?"

Maya knew exactly what kind of life that was. She felt the air leave the room. She fumbled for a seat, and Hema-auntie continued to talk, but Maya couldn't hear her. She was right, of course. Sam would feel *obligated* to stay with her. He would eventually abandon not only her, but her child, too. She couldn't knowingly put her baby through that.

Hema-auntie handed her a slip of paper. "Maya.

Maya! Did you hear me?" Maya took the paper. "Take this check." Her voice was harsh. "It should be enough to take care of things however you see fit." She made a point to look into Maya's eyes. "And if you tell Sam I did this, he won't believe you."

CHAPTER THIRTY-NINE
SAM

New York 2013

SAM THUNDERED AWAY from Maya's apartment, deaf to the sounds of traffic, blind to the world around him. The only sound—his own blood pulsing in his head. The only sight—the movie of Samantha's life, playing in his mind.

A life he had missed.

By the time he realized that he'd forgotten the birth certificate, he was a block away from the subway, standing in front of an empty building with a for lease sign in the window. He leaned against the glass wall, not seeing the people pass him by while he played back the scene Maya had just narrated to him. He still had the check in his pocket. He took it out, and a snippet of a conversation he'd overheard at Christmas came to him. His heart broke again.

Rage flowed through him and he barely remembered taking the subway home. Suddenly, he found himself in his apartment, and Paige was asking why he was home from work. Why was she home? Then he remembered. She had wedding things to do. His mother was here.

"Where is my mother?" he growled.

"I'm right here, dear." His mother emerged from the

spare bedroom. "What's wrong, Sam? You look like you've seen a ghost."

His heart pounding in his chest, he produced the check from his pocket and slammed it down on the island. Both Paige and his mother jumped at the sound. His mother paled. "Where did you get that?" It was barely a whisper.

"I found it."

"She gave it to you, didn't she?" His mother actually had the guts to spit the words out as if Maya had done something wrong. "That little—"

"Watch it." It was something between a growl and a hiss as something feral reared its head inside him.

"What did she tell you?"

"She told me everything." He barely moved his lips.

She softened. "You have to understand, Sam. You were young. She was young. You two hardly knew each other…"

"It wasn't your decision." It was taking all his restraint not to blow up at her.

"I tried to stay out of it." His mother raised her chin. "When she turned down your proposal, I thought it was over. That you could move on… But then your father convinced you to see her again. I couldn't let that happen. I couldn't stand by and watch you throw your life away for the wrong girl." She squared her shoulders, but her lips trembled, ever so slightly. "So I went to see her. I was just going to scare her off. But then I found out she was pregnant. I knew you'd never leave her if you knew. I knew you would honor your responsibilities. So I did it for you. I wrote her that check and sent her on her way." Her voice cracked ever so little, even as she fought to maintain her stance. "I did it for your future."

This was so backward to him, he let go of his restraint. "Is that what you thought? That I would 'honor' my responsibilities?" Sam paced, his voice getting louder. He ran a hand through his hair, loosened his tie. "I loved her. I was ready to spend the rest of my life with her—baby or not. Do you have any idea what I went through when she left—no explanation, no goodbye, no nothing?"

"She would have ruined you. All those dreams of a political career would have been gone once you settled for the quiet life she was dragging you into. I saved you." No mama bear could have been a match for his mother. Even with Sam almost shouting at her, she wouldn't back down. "Don't you see? She was wrong for you. You need someone like Paige, someone who can be there for you and has a stomach for a life in politics."

"Those were never my dreams." He spit the words out. He turned to Paige. Tears were already streaming down her face. "How long have you known?"

Paige wiped her eyes with shaking fingers. "I, um, I figured it out at Diwali." She looked him in the eye. "I heard them talking. Maya swore she would never tell you. She didn't." Paige shook her head, swallowed. "She didn't want to hurt you." Fresh tears fell down her cheeks and she pressed her lips together as she wiped them away.

Sam glared at Paige for a moment, turmoil brewing inside him. She was supposed to love him. But she had kept the secret, too. He turned his back on her and returned to his mother. "Your own grandchild, Mother."

"It was a sacrifice I was willing to make."

"That's how you see this? A sacrifice? Something for the 'greater good'?" Sam threw up his arms and shook his head in disbelief. "So I guess you won't mind if I never let you see Samantha again."

"You wouldn't." There was a tremor in her words and she gripped a chair. Her eyes were moist, but that didn't stop him.

"Wouldn't I?" Sam sneered. "I am *your* son, after all. What about Dad? Is he in on this?" He'd lose his mind if he found out his father had known, too.

"Of course not, this is not something he would—" His mother stopped, attempted to gather herself. "No, he does not know. And he does not need to know." She wavered. "Please."

"You cannot ask me anything. Not. One. Thing. You saw to it that I didn't even know I had a child."

"Maya kept the secret, too. For sixteen years." Paige's voice behind him was almost a whisper.

Sam did not turn to face her. "I am aware. Don't think I'll forget that anytime soon."

Sam's mother approached him. "Can't we just put this in the past?"

"Oh, I see. You want me to forgive you, to put in the past that you tried to pay off the woman I love. You played on her fear of abandonment and you got her to keep from me that she was carrying my child. A child that grew up without me. A child that I would have loved as much as I love Maya." Sam was out of breath but he continued. "Then you and my fiancée conspire to continue to keep the truth from me? Why?" He turned to face Paige and was stopped by the hurt in her eyes.

Sadness surrounded her. "You still love her."

"No. That's not what I said."

"Yes, it is, Sam. And it doesn't matter. I can see it. I have been seeing it. Every time she's around." She turned and fled toward the bedroom. "And even when she's not."

"Don't let her go, Sam." His mother pleaded with him.

"I'm letting you both go." He picked up his jacket and walked out, letting the door slam behind him.

He spent the night in a hotel, and when he returned in the morning, both his mother and fiancée were gone. Paige's abandoned engagement ring caught the sunlight, a rock sitting on an island.

CHAPTER FORTY
SAM

Maryland 1996

IF SHE DIDN'T love him, if she could actually say those words, there was no reason for him to stay. He tapped the coin in his pocket and stared at the closed door. He had pounded on the door to get her back, but only her mother had come out. Sunita had made it abundantly clear that Maya no longer needed or wanted him, and then, for the second time in the span of thirty minutes, a woman had slammed a door on him.

Sam turned on his heel and leaped down the porch steps. He headed for his car, expecting the burn of hot tears behind his eyes or a painful lump in his throat, but they didn't come. A deafening pounding filled his ears, robbing him of rational thought. He put the car in gear and sped off away from her, leaving behind a trail of burning rubber.

He found himself parked at the soccer field, feeling like he'd been punched in the stomach, while a large pit expanded in his chest. In the dwindling crowd of players, he noted three of his college-bound strikers, getting in the last bit of time together before moving on to their respective universities.

Andy was sprawled out in the grass and Mohit and

Kevin were taking turns blocking shots at the goal. A few older players were doing sprints and passes; a lone striker took shots on an unattended goal.

Sam opened the car door and was assaulted by Maryland's suffocating August heat. He dug around the trunk until he found his cleats. The tightness of them—the pressure on his feet—that's what he needed to feel, what he would prefer to feel. No need for shin guards or pads or gloves today. There was nothing left to protect.

Sam gave the trunk a satisfying slam and one of the boys turned toward him. "Hey, guys! It's Coach!"

Mohit let the ball in the goal as his focus shifted to Sam. "Hey!" He motioned to Kevin as he jogged over to his coach.

Sam greeted the boys, though his attention was concentrated on the lone striker.

Mohit followed Sam's gaze. "It's just Nikhil—let him be, Coach. He's still sore about that save you made."

Nik kicked the ball right at Sam. Sam caught it with ease and waited as Nik sauntered over.

Nik paused a few feet from Sam. "Well, if it isn't the famous Hutcherson." Nik raised his voice, narrowed his black eyes and spread his arms out wide as if he had a grand audience.

"What do you want, Nik?" Mohit turned his body so he was standing between his coach and Nik. His arms hung by his side, every muscle and tendon tensed and ready to explode as necessary. The other boys followed suit.

"Oh, not to worry, kid." Nik's mouth was smiling, but his words were sharp. "I don't want trouble. Just a chance to prove that Hutcherson here isn't all that everyone thinks he is." He set his lips in a hard line and froze his gaze on Sam. "Last year's championship was mine, and you know it."

Sam forced a smile and spread his own arms. Going head-to-head against a guy who hated him was just what he needed. "Are you fucking serious right now? I made that save because you are not as unstoppable as you think." Nikhil Amin had an ego the size of a stadium, and Sam knew how to play him. "I made that save because I'm better, Amin."

The boys were aghast at Sam's words, but Sam saw the anger simmering in Nikhil, and that's all he needed.

"Bring it, if you have it." He turned his back on Nikhil, and in just a few strides, had reached the goal. The boys followed close behind, confused by Sam's behavior.

"At least get gloves, Coach," Mohit whispered, his eyes slightly panicked.

Sam waved him off. That pit in his chest was starting to fill with cement.

Nikhil Amin was a technical finisher, a player that was so powerful, he was almost guaranteed to get the ball past the goalie. The only time he'd failed was last year's championship game. Sam had been in the goal.

Sam positioned himself on the goal line, ignored the boys' anxious pleas and focused on Nik. From the corner of his eye, he saw the boys huddle together, and then Kevin ran off in the direction of the pay phone.

Nikhil grinned at Sam, his eyes cold and metallic, as he placed the ball on the ground. He licked his lips and started his run. All of Sam's senses were focused on the ball.

At first, Sam blocked shot after shot. The ball carried Nik's frustration, and his shots were wild but powerful.

Each sting of the ball on Sam's bare hands matched the sting of Maya's words.

Their summer flashed before him. Nik's shots started coming harder and faster. Sam tried to shake off the memories.

Sam dove hard left, and remembered how she would tuck her hair behind her ear. He missed the ball and hit the ground hard. Blood oozed from a scraped elbow. His shirt was soon soaked with sweat as the sun continued to beat down on him, and as he imagined the coolness of her hands on his face before she kissed him, he dove to the right and banged his shoulder on the goalpost.

Dirt mixed with the sweat and blood on his knees. The ball came off Nik's foot from a shot inside the box and hit Sam full in the stomach. The wind knocked out of him, Sam fell back into the goal and took a minute, prone on the ground, to catch his breath.

"Coach! Coach! Are you all right?"

Sam heard pounding feet and started to push himself up. He licked his lips and tasted the metallic tang of blood. "I'm fine!"

"Here," Mohit said, offering him a bottle of water.

Sam slapped it away. "Again." He spat out blood and grabbed the goalpost to help himself up. The hot aluminum scorched his already swollen hands—he just squeezed the bar harder.

Sam could still hear her voice. *I don't love you.* He was on his knees, clinging to the heated aluminum, willing himself to stand when a sharp pain exploded in his face and he was forced onto his back. His world suddenly became blurred and a searing pain coursed through his face and head. Nik had kicked from the penalty line, hitting Sam in the face. He barely registered the blood dripping from his nose as everything went black.

He woke a few minutes later to find himself still in the nightmare. Mohit was yelling instructions to the other two, and Kevin was trying to keep Andy from attacking Nik.

From behind the goal, he heard a familiar voice. "It's okay, boys. Go on home. I got him." The voice paused, but still the angry voices pounded his head.

"Boys!" John Hutcherson boomed over them. The boys fell silent. "Don't lay a hand on Nik." He raised his voice slightly. "You better go, Nik. I can only hold them back so long."

Sam felt his father kneel down beside him. "C'mon, Sammy. Let me see." Sam forced himself to a sitting position and met his father's gentle blue eyes. Dr. Hutcherson pulled a handkerchief from his pocket and held it expertly against Sam's nose. The pain made Sam lightheaded, but he refused to cry out. He held the handkerchief in place. His father laid his hand on Sam's chest and spoke softly to his son. "It's broken for sure."

The sound of his father's voice, the strength of his hand supporting him broke the last of Sam's control. Sam felt the burn of tears from behind his eyes and deep within his stomach. A painful lump filled his throat and the tears finally came. He leaned forward on his knees and rested his head on his father's shoulder. Sobbing made it harder to breathe.

But who needed to breathe?

CHAPTER FORTY-ONE
MAYA

New York 2013

MAYA WOKE UP extra early on Saturdays in January to roast coffee beans, as well as to blend the cloves, cardamom, cinnamon, black pepper and ginger needed for her chai masala. There was no chai-flavored syrup in her Indian-style tea; she made the spice mix the same as her mother, and her mother before her. And since chai had become all the rage, she couldn't make the spice mix fast enough. She'd sold out over Christmas, so now was the time to replenish. The kitchen smells reminded her of childhood, and her thoughts turned to her Deepak-mama and Sejal. Her mother joined her and filled her in on her most recent "date" with Raju-kaka from the night before.

"He was a complete gentleman, Maya. Opening doors for me, pulling out chairs." Her mother nearly glowed.

Raju-kaka had been opening doors and pulling out chairs for Sunita for thirty years, but only now had Sunita decided to notice. Maya simply smiled and nodded, glancing at the clock. Samantha was due back from Sam's around noon, but it was only ten thirty now. She shook her head, as if doing so would get rid of her nervous anticipation at seeing Sam, and focused her attention on what her mother was saying, all the while stirring the coffee beans and checking if the spices were blended fine enough. She had barely spoken to him in the past week since he'd found out about the check.

Customers lined up, and Maya lost herself in the preparation of the chai masala and coffee, so before she knew it, Samantha and Sam were walking toward the shop.

Maya's breath caught when he came into view, just as it always did and she berated herself yet again for it. But damn if he didn't make jeans and a long-sleeved T-shirt look *good*. It must be unseasonably warm today, because he carried his leather jacket. He and Samantha were intense in conversation, and Maya found herself smiling at how easily they got along. Sam pulled out his phone and showed it to Samantha. Her eyes lit up.

They stopped just outside the entrance to the coffee shop but didn't come in, as if they were waiting for something. Sure enough, a cab pulled up, and from it emerged a stunning young woman. Her dark hair was in a ponytail and she, too, wore jeans and a T-shirt. She smiled broadly upon seeing Sam and wrapped her arms around him as he lifted her off her feet in a hug. He put her down and kissed her cheek. Maya forgot her customers and became enthralled by what was unfolding outside her window.

Sam kept his arm around the woman and turned to Samantha. Samantha extended her hand but the woman bypassed it and hugged her. Maya's heart dropped into her stomach. They made quite the attractive family. Well, it certainly didn't take him long, did it? It had hardly been seven days since he and Paige had broken up, according to Samantha. But honestly, introducing every woman he dated to his daughter was not going to be healthy for Samantha. No, Maya could not stand for this.

Sam put his hand on the doorknob to enter the shop and Maya rushed to occupy herself. "Well, I just thought you two should finally meet." Sam was smiling. "Samantha is very interested in people who are important to me."

Really? This woman was already important to him? They hadn't seen her yet, so Maya slipped into the kitchen. Why did he have to bring his little chippy here?

"Maya, I'm going up. Raj is coming to get me in a few minutes. Can you close up?"

"Sure, Mum. Go ahead." Maya barely registered her mother's words.

"She's probably finishing up in the kitchen. She was making chai masala today," Maya heard Samantha say. "Come on back. I'm sure she'd love to see you."

They were coming into the kitchen! Maya froze with horror, recovering just in time to rip off her hairnet and fluff her hair in the small mirror.

"Mom! Mom! You'll never guess who Dad just introduced me to!" The excitement in Samantha's voice grated on Maya. She'd *just met* this woman! Sam and the young woman were just behind Samantha. Sam still had his arm draped on the woman's shoulders and he was beaming. If Maya weren't so irritated with him, his smile would've made her stomach flutter. The woman standing next to him was actually more of a girl—way too young for Sam. *What the hell was he thinking?*

Maya couldn't contain herself. "Well, it looks like he's brought around a young girlfriend." She turned to

Sam and tried to burn holes in him with her eyes. Honestly, Maya hadn't seen him this happy since...well, in a long time. Her face got hot and she didn't even care that the girl was standing right there.

"Honestly, Sam. Do you even think before you act?" She moved toward him. "If you want to have a girlfriend that's actually young enough to be your daughter, that is certainly your business, but to introduce her to *our* daughter?" Maya poked a finger into Sam's chest and he looked at her like she was a crazy woman.

"Seriously, Maya. Calm down!" Sam's eyes were wide with surprise. "She's not my girlfriend."

"Oh, a date then?" Maya was incredulous. Had he just rolled his eyes at her? She poked her finger harder, nearly hurting herself as she came up against hard muscle. "How is that any better?"

"It's not! Stop poking me." He was clearly getting irritated.

"I. Will. Not." She accented each word with a poke. "I saw you hugging and kissing her! In front of our daughter! This is irresponsible, but what did I expect, anyway?" The warmth in her face was causing her to sweat a little as she realized that she might be getting a little shrill. Whatever.

"Maya." He folded his arms across his chest and looked down at her through his lashes. "You might want me to explain." He spoke to her from between clenched teeth.

"Oh, let's hear it!" She stepped back.

"Well, actually, maybe I should." The young woman looked to Sam for permission.

Sam grinned broadly. He spread open his arms and took a few steps back from Maya. "Please do."

The young woman turned her huge, chocolate-brown eyes on Maya and smiled. "Maya, I suppose it has been a long time. Close to sixteen years."

Maya narrowed her eyes and looked closely at the woman for the first time. There was something familiar about her. She stepped closer to her.

"It's me, Maya. It's—"

"Niki!" Maya covered her mouth with her hand as realization hit. "Oh, Niki. It's really you! You're so grown up!" She laughed even as tears spilled from her eyes. "Oh, I'm an idiot, going on like I did!"

Niki gave Maya a hug. "Oh, we've missed you! That summer with you was one of our favorites." Niki pulled back. "But then you left so suddenly…" She looked from Sam to Samantha. "I suppose it all makes sense now. And no, you're not an idiot—I take every chance I can to yell at Sammy."

Maya flushed and was thankful that Sam was standing behind her where she didn't have to see his I-told-you-so face. She nodded to Niki. "Yes, well. I'm sorry for how I left things with you and Ben and your parents. It really was thoughtless. I was young and scared and—"

"No, no. Don't." Niki gave a vigorous shake of her head and wiped tears from her own eyes. "Don't give it another thought. It's all in the past." She glanced over Maya's shoulder at Sam. "We can all start over. Now we have Samantha, too."

Niki's words hung in the air, almost palpable. A beat too late, Maya answered her, "Sure, of course." She had been holding Niki's hands and now she dropped them. "Listen, since it's Saturday, we'll be closing in a few minutes. I do have a cake meeting, but it's not for another hour. Stay and have lunch here."

Niki smiled broadly, and Maya was taken aback by the similarity in Niki's and Sam's smiles. "That sounds wonderful. We haven't eaten yet and it would be nice to catch up."

Sam had edged toward the door and was rapidly moving the pull tab of his jacket zipper up and down. "Well, I'll just leave you girls to it, then." He made a move to leave.

Samantha stopped him. "Dad, you can stay! You didn't eat yet, either. That's okay, right, Mom?"

Maya finally looked in Sam's direction, but was still unable to meet his eyes, her earlier antics still fresh in her mind. "Of course Sam can join us. There's always plenty of food." Sam silently nodded his acceptance.

"Samantha—" Maya pointed to the back. "Why don't you get some sandwiches together? I'll close up and bring coffee."

Samantha pulled Niki to the back of the kitchen to work on the sandwiches. Sam lingered with Maya.

"Nice, Maya." He raised his eyebrows at her and shook his head. "Assuming I had a girlfriend—" his voice was terse as he leaned back against the counter, arms folded across his chest "—that age."

Maya had to force herself to look away from the way his T-shirt stretched over the muscles in his arms. "Well, what was I supposed to think?" She started the coffee maker and closed her eyes but the image remained. *Oh boy.*

Sam blew air out of his mouth. "Oh, I don't know. How about assuming that I *wouldn't* bring random women around my daughter, especially since my fiancée just left me? Or that I might want someone closer to my own age, as opposed to my daughter's?" He unfolded his arms and leaned back on them. "But then again, I guess thinking the best of me isn't necessarily natural for you." There was more than a touch of venom in his words, but it was matched by a touch of sadness.

She frowned. "That's not true."

"Really? Then why the big show?"

She turned away from him and opened a cupboard door so he couldn't see her flush. She spoke into the cupboard. "If I didn't trust you, there's no way I'd let you take Samantha all the time—father or not." She peeked around the cupboard door. He was silently nodding agreement.

He looked in her direction and she ducked behind the cupboard door again. "What are you looking for?"

"Coffee mugs. The extras are up here." She stood on tiptoe to try to reach the top shelf. She got a finger on one and tried to pull it toward her.

"Here, I'll get it." He was immediately behind her, his warmth and traces of cologne filling the space behind her. His body pressed against her back as he reached over her to get the mugs, and it was all Maya could do not to melt back into him.

Honestly, this had to stop.

He grabbed four mugs. "Here you go." She heard the smile in his voice.

She hesitated before turning around, waiting for him to step back. Instead, he leaned down toward her, his breath on her ear. "You weren't *jealous,* were you?"

"What?" She spun around too fast, her body grazing hard muscle. *Oh God.* She quickly sidestepped, and tried to breathe Sam-free air and gather herself. "Nah—

don't think so much of yourself, Sam." The pitch of her voice was too high, and she was speaking too fast. But she couldn't stop herself. "If I was jealous, that might imply that I was still in love with you." *What was she saying?*

Sam snapped his eyes to hers. "Are you?"

"Am I what?" She needed to get out of this conversation.

"Are you still in love with me?" He had captured her in his gaze as if her answer could change the course of the universe.

"No." It wasn't any easier to force the lie from her mouth than it was the first time she'd said it. She thought for an instant that disappointment flashed across Sam's face. But before she could confirm it, Sam once again hardened his gaze. She took the mugs and returned to the coffee maker. "Niki has grown up to be quite a beautiful young lady."

He cleared his throat. "Yes, she has. She's doing her master's in education at NYU."

Maya busied herself with the cream and sugar for the coffee. From the corner of her eye, she saw Sam filling a plate with cookies.

"She's focusing on early childhood development. Largely, I think, from your influence on her that summer." He paused and she turned back to face him.

"She didn't stop talking about you for a very long time." His jaw was tight and his knuckles were white from gripping the counter. "The way you left…"

She couldn't tear her gaze away from him. Did she imagine it, or were there tears in his eyes?

"She was seven. It was hard to make her understand."

Another person she'd harmed. "I know I hurt people—and not just you. But I can't change that."

"Maybe, but you had sixteen years to try to make that right—and you didn't."

Tears burned behind her eyes, but she wouldn't cry in front of him, not again. She swallowed her tears and the burn subsided. "I tried. Every birthday, every milestone." She folded her arms tight across her chest, willing herself to stay composed. "I must have picked up the phone a hundred times the first year of her life, to tell you what cute and new thing she did."

"But...?" His eyes were still hard, but for the first time since all this started, Maya knew he was really listening.

"But then I would remember how it felt to sit by the window all day on a Saturday, willing my father to come back to us. Or the hole in my belly as I searched the crowd for him at my dance recitals, only to be disappointed and having to paste a smile on my face and dance. I remembered what it felt like when I finally realized that he wasn't coming home." Her nose prickled, tears were inevitable now. "That he didn't care enough."

As she spoke, Sam inched closer to her. The hardness in his eyes had melted into something tender, and when that lone tear escaped from Maya's eyes, he wiped it away. His touch was achingly gentle, causing more tears to fall. "You know it wasn't your fault he left."

"Don't be ridiculous, Sam. I'm a grown woman. Of course I know that."

"It wasn't your fault he left." He repeated himself as he studied her face, with some surprise. "Have you felt, all this time, that your father left because of you?"

Something hard flashed in his eyes and he clenched his jaw, his nostrils flared.

"No. Of course I understand—" Maya attempted a smile, but she couldn't hold it as her lips quivered.

"You may 'understand', but that's different from what you feel." The edge in his voice held her. "Didn't your mother ever tell you that it wasn't your fault? That he left because of himself and nothing you did?"

Maya shook her head. If she said anything, she'd break down.

"Damn it, Maya." A new look in Sam's eyes that she'd never seen before. It looked like pity. He moved closer, as if to put his arms around her. Every cell in her body wanted to be held by him. To inhale him. To feel protected in his arms like she once had. To love and be loved by him. But not if he pitied her. Hell, no.

She stepped away. "Don't." She put her hands up between them. "I do not need pity from you. I told you that once and it still applies."

"I'm not pitying you, and I never have."

"Yes, you are. It's all over you." She hardened her gaze. "And I don't want it."

Sam worked his jaw as he shook his head at her. "It's *not* pity. It's—" He fisted his hands and moved away from her. "Never mind."

Maya couldn't read his face, but every muscle in his body was tense.

"But I will say one thing. We're not all the same." His hands were still clenched.

"Who?"

"Men. We're not all the same. You should've given me a chance."

A new emotion had found its way into Sam's face,

and Maya didn't like it much more than whatever had just been there. It was disappointment.

She turned back to the coffee maker. Nothing would ever change his mind. He would never love her again. She was surprised to realize that there was a significant part of her that had actually thought that might be possible. "Here's your coffee." Her hand trembled as she gave him his mug and she almost spilled the coffee.

"Careful, now." He reached out to take the mug from her and his fingers grazed hers, sending a thrill through her. Damn it.

A loose strand of her hair tumbled forward into her face. As she automatically reached to tuck the rebel lock behind her ear, Sam's hand had started to come up, as well. She tucked the rogue piece of hair back and found Sam's hand frozen in midair.

Maya shifted her gaze up and caught Sam watching her. She weakened as his eyes softened and held hers for a moment. He opened his mouth as if to speak. Then, just as fast as it had come, the softness left his eyes and he closed his mouth without saying a thing. He closed his hand, quickly returning it to his side.

Maya inhaled, as if doing so would calm her heart. The fact that he smelled like *Sam* wasn't helping.

Sam sipped the coffee and frowned. "What happened to the coffee?"

She tried to look him in the eye. "I, uh—I ran out of the other stuff and didn't make more." She stepped away from him. "This is a new blend I roasted last week."

His frown deepened as he met her eyes. "It's great." He took another sip. "It's just not, you know, the other stuff."

She raised her eyebrows at him. "Well, we've had the

other stuff for years. We're overdue for a change." Her voice hardened and her body stiffened as she looked at him. "Time to move on."

Sam again opened his mouth to speak, but Niki and Samantha returned. They were laughing and they produced a plate of sandwiches. "Come on, you two. We're hungry," Niki called out to them.

"You all go sit down. I'll just shut down a few things here." Maya quickly stepped away from Sam, as if she'd been caught doing something wrong, and headed toward the ovens.

During lunch, Niki and Sam told stories about her and Ben growing up. Samantha radiated joy and clearly adored this big-sister-auntie she'd found. Maya relaxed for a moment into that feeling of family, laughing and smiling easily. She caught Sam's eye, his glance rested on her, easy and familiar. Maya reminded herself of his earlier anger and disappointment. She hardened her gaze and looked away.

"So, tell me about Ben." Maya sipped her coffee.

"Ben is currently in Africa, doing his Doctors Without Borders type thing." Niki rolled her eyes and looked at Sam. Sam laughed.

"What?" Maya looked to Niki.

Sam answered. "Well, he's been there for over six months. Usually, the docs go for about a week or two."

"It's a girl." Niki shook her head. "He's hiding from a girl." She giggled and Sam laughed along with her.

The door chimed and all heads turned. It was Leo. He was here for the cake meeting. Ami was right: he really was quite handsome. Maya set down her coffee. "I'm sorry. My appointment is here. But take your time, finish up. I just have to show some sketches."

Sam pressed his lips into a straight line and all the laughter left his face. "I'll bet," Sam murmured. The table shook from Sam's leg jostling beneath it, and Niki threw him a glare.

Maya didn't understand Sam's sudden change in mood, but it wasn't her problem. She walked over to Leo. "Hi. So glad you could make it."

"Of course, Maya. Wouldn't miss my chance."

"Great, we can sit right here." She guided him to the opposite side of the shop. The coffee shop was small, so it was more for the appearance of privacy. "I've drawn up some sketches." Leo sat down and Maya joined him, opening her sketchbook. They went over cake ideas for his niece's sweet sixteen. Maya felt his gaze on her, and for the first time, allowed herself to enjoy the attention. He really did have the most amazing blue eyes. She caught Sam's gaze on her over Leo's shoulder and shifted her seat so she couldn't see him.

Leo finally settled on a three-tiered "lopsided" cake, which would add whimsy to the party. Maya walked him to the door.

"So, Maya, what do you say? Dinner sometime?"

Her automatic "No" was on her lips, when she heard Ami's voice in her head. *Time to move on.* She glanced over Leo's shoulder and found Sam glaring in her direction. Smoldering was more like it. "Um, yeah, sure. That sounds nice." And it did.

Leo was unable to hide his surprise or his pleasure. "Really? Great. How about Friday, 8:00 p.m.? I'll come by here to get you."

"Okay. I look forward to it."

Leo left, and Maya turned back to find Sam, Samantha and Niki staring at her.

Sam spoke first. "You're going out with that guy?" It was an accusation.

"Well, yes." Maya squared her shoulders and looked him in the eye.

"Do you think that's wise? I mean, Samantha here is impressionable."

"I'm good." Samantha grinned at her mother. "Have fun. He's a really nice guy."

Sam glared at his daughter. "Come on, Niki. Let's go."

CHAPTER FORTY-TWO
SAM

New York 2013

SAM IGNORED THE buzz of the phone in his pocket and turned up the collar of his coat against the wind. He wound his way through the mass of people that made up the motion of the New York City streets. The buzzing stopped and he relaxed some. Within half a block, the buzzing started again. This time he pulled out his phone. *Mom.* He sent it to voice mail. Another half block and the buzzing started yet again. With a groan, Sam pulled out his phone, ready to send it to voice mail, but the screen read *Dad.* He tapped his phone and put it to his ear, not breaking his stride.

"Hey, Dad." Sam forced some lightness into his voice.

"Don't you 'Hey, Dad' me, young man!" His father's voice was unusually stern. "Why aren't you taking your mother's calls? And is your wedding off or on?"

"Don't worry about it. And as far as Paige goes, I'll take care of it."

"What do you mean take care of it? Your mother is worried sick about you."

"Dad, I really can't do this right now. I'll call you later and you can yell at me then." Sam tapped off the phone. He'd pay for that, but right now he had more immediate concerns.

He slid his phone into his pocket just as he reached the door of The Dream Bar. Paige was already waiting at their regular table. He stopped to whisper to the bartender. After leaving the coffee shop the other day, he had called Paige. His run-in with Maya had made it clear to him what he needed to do. He needed to move on. He fingered Paige's engagement ring in his pocket.

She looked up when he approached. "Hey, you." Her eyes were swollen and tired.

"Hey." He stood there, suddenly awkward with the woman he had planned to spend his life with.

"You're late." She smirked. Punctuality was a pet peeve of his.

Sam laughed. "Sorry. I was meeting with my real estate agent, and time got away from me."

She motioned to a chair opposite her. "Have a seat."

Sam sat and ordered a bourbon. Paige sipped her dirty martini. "Why am I here, Sam?"

He placed the ring on the table in front of her. "I want to apologize for being an ass."

Her eyes saddened. "I should have told you what I overheard on Diwali."

Sam shrugged one shoulder. "Yeah, well… But I know why you didn't. I'm sorry I was so harsh on you. You're intelligent, and funny and beautiful, and I do love you."

"But…" Paige twirled her drink, suddenly very interested in what was inside her glass.

"But we lie to each other."

Her eyes filled almost instantly with tears and she nodded her head in agreement. "Couples should not lie to one another." Her breath caught as tears dripped down. She hastily wiped them away. "Especially if they're getting married."

Sam sipped his bourbon as she gathered herself. Even though he had expected tears, they still made him feel terrible. No matter that this was best for both of them. The thick liquid added to the heaviness of the moment. He held her hand across the table. She pulled it away. "Don't, Sam. Don't be nice to me. Not when I need to hate you for a while."

They stared at each other, letting the awkwardness build.

"I don't know what I want anymore." Sam leaned toward her and she stared him in the eye.

"Quite frankly, Sam, I have been thinking. I deserve more." Her voice got stronger. "I deserve someone who looks at me the way you look at Maya."

"I'm angry because I missed out on my daughter, and I don't look at Maya—"

"Save it, Sam. If you don't see, you don't see it." She shook her head at him as if he were a young child. Silence fell between them, during which they both sipped from their glasses. "Why do you have a real estate agent?"

Sam grinned at her, happy for a moment. "Fresh start. The one thing I do know is what I want to do with my law degree. I quit my job and I'm opening up my own practice. And I'm going to get to know my daughter."

"What about Congress—all the work you did for that?" Paige took an olive out of her drink and popped it in her mouth.

"You're the candidate, not me. Everything we did came from you. You should run."

She raised an eyebrow and tilted her head as if considering this possibility for the first time. "Would I have your vote?" A smile twitched at her lips.

"Depends on what your stances are." He smiled at her.

She nodded and the smile broke through. She looked pointedly at the ring. "You wouldn't dare be asking me back, would you?"

Sam shook his head slowly. "Do you really want me to?"

"No." Her answer was firm, but her eyes betrayed her. "I do love you, but you're not good for me."

He gulped at his drink. "Like I said, fresh start. You love that ring. You had it designed to your specifications. It's yours."

She laughed but her eyes glistened with tears again.

Sam covered her hand with his. She tried to pull back, but Sam held firm. "You go back to the apartment. I found a new place. I'll come get the rest of my things while you're at work."

"That's not necessary. I'll just move in with my dad for a bit longer."

Sam chuckled. "No one wants that. I suspect one week has been more than a lifetime for you both." He downed his drink and stood. "Drinks are on me." He bent down and kissed her cheek. "Goodbye, Paige."

"Goodbye, Sam."

CHAPTER FORTY-THREE
SAM

New York 2013

EARLY FEBRUARY BROUGHT Samantha into Manhattan for a soccer tournament. Samantha would spend the weekend with Sam, and Maya would attend the games when she could. The week before Valentine's Day was always busy at the shop.

Clear skies and bright sun did nothing to warm the air that Saturday afternoon as Sam and Samantha walked to the soccerplex. They had tied their game the night before, so today's game was important if the team was to advance in the tournament.

Sam found himself checking his watch as game time approached. No sign of Maya. Good. He'd be able keep a clear head. Not that Maya clouded his head. Not at all.

The teams hit the field. He looked toward the entrance. Still not here. *Why did he even care?*

The game started and Sam took his regular seat, two rows in on the bleachers, closer to the goal than midfield. The girls came out aggressively, and he was soon engrossed in the first minutes of the game. Sam was unaware that Maya had entered the arena until she was standing in his line of sight.

She had on dark jeans with a cream-colored, fitted

wool coat and carried something under her arm. Dark
hair cascaded in waves down her back and she bit her
bottom lip as she flicked her eyes about, looking for
him. Sam waited for irritation to kick in, but tonight it
did not. Instead, he found himself remembering how
soft her hair felt in his fingers, and the soft pinch when
she bit his lips. *What?*

He was shaking his head, trying to clear those memories, when she turned and saw him. He quickly looked
away so as not to get caught gazing at her, but watched
from the corner of his eye as she climbed over the first
two rows to where he was sitting.

"Hi. Did I miss anything?" She faltered a bit as she
climbed over the second row. Must be the high heels.
Sam offered his hand to steady her. She ignored it and
sat down, leaving space between them. He slowly lowered his unwanted hand.

"Um, not too much. They just started. No one scored
yet." He studied her. Had he forgotten how beautiful
she was? Or had he just stopped noticing?

Maya was waving her hand in front of him.

"What?" He furrowed his brow in question.

"You're staring like you were the first time we met,"
she said.

Heat crept up his face. "Oh, I just—sorry." He slowly
turned his gaze away from her to focus on the game. Samantha made a great save by plucking the ball out of the
air as the offensive player tried to head it into the goal.

"Yes! That's my girl!" Sam cheered. He turned excit-
edly to Maya. "Did you see that? Did you see *our girl*
take that goal away?"

Maya was laughing. "That was *incredible*." She
grabbed his arm. "Who knew she could jump that high?

It has to be all that time you spent training her. She plays a lot like you did."

Sam grinned, enjoying her touch. She hastily released his arm and returned her attention to the game.

Samantha's team scored before the end of the first half, so they were up 1–0 at halftime. But in the last seconds of the second half, the opposing striker got a breakaway. Samantha ran up to meet her, but she second-guessed herself for just a split second. The delay cost her, and the striker easily deked her and scored.

Maya grabbed Sam's arm with both hands. "*No!* It's down to penalty kicks now, right?"

Again, Sam relished her touch. He laughed. "Yes. Our Samantha against five of their best strikers."

Maya paled and covered her eyes with her hands. "I can't watch. I can't watch." She peeked at him through her fingers. "In case you were wondering—I can *never* watch PKs."

He remembered. Sam relaxed into his amusement. "She'll be fine. We've practiced this—and true, the odds are against the goalie—but she'll be fine as long as she doesn't hesitate. Or second-guess herself."

Maya's eyes widened behind her fingers, and Sam melted. The once or twice she had seen him play in a game, she had done the same thing. It was as endearing now as it had been then.

"Oh, God, Sam." She nearly squealed.

A hush fell over the stadium, and Sam turned to face the field. Samantha's team shot first, but the other goalie punched it out of play. Now, Samantha was in the goal, the other team's striker was gearing up. She took the shot. "Left!" Sam whispered. Samantha did just that and plucked the ball out of the air.

Maya cheered with the crowd, but covered her face once Samantha was protecting again. Each team had five shots apiece. Each team got the ball past the opposing keeper two times. The opposing keeper saved the last attempt by Samantha's team. The opposing team put up their last striker. If they made this, they would win. Samantha took her spot in front of the goal. If she saved this, there would be another round of PKs.

Sam glanced at Maya. What he could see of her face was pale, her eyes were huge behind her hands. It suddenly struck him that she had sat through these moments—and many more—over the past fifteen years, alone. She had raised this wonderful young woman on her own. Forget the reasons why. Samantha was incredible, because Maya was incredible. Without thinking, he reached out, rested a reassuring hand on Maya's arm, and leaned closer to her ear. "I'm sorry it took so long for me to say it, but you've done a fabulous job raising her."

He felt her relax and she dropped her hands. The anxiety in her eyes was replaced by a softness she hadn't seen in years. Before she could say anything, he nodded his head toward the field. "Last one."

They both turned back to the field, just as the striker hit the ball. "Jump!" Sam whispered. But Samantha hesitated, jumping just a fraction of a second too late and missing the save. The other team scored, winning the game.

"What was *that*?" Maya turned horrified eyes on Sam.

"Well," Sam said, his voice calm and matter-of-fact,

"she hesitated." He gave a small shrug. "She hesitated, and she lost the save. It's something she needs to work on." He looked Maya in the eye and his voice softened. "Something all keepers have to work on—not hesitating."

She briefly held his gaze, then turned away from him.

Sam continued to watch her a moment, then cleared his throat and stood. He offered his hand again. This time she took it. "Come on, we'll meet her on the sidelines."

They waited together for Samantha to come off the field. Maya released his hand as soon as they were off the bleachers. She didn't say much and Sam couldn't think what to say. Finally, Samantha walked over.

"Nicely done, sweetheart." Maya gave her daughter a hug.

"I'm all sweaty, Mom. Don't hug me. You'll get all gross for your date."

"What?" Sam snapped at Maya as his stomach formed a knot. "You have another date?" Alarms started going off inside his head.

Maya turned to him, eyes frozen. "Yes, I do."

"Same guy?"

"Not that it's any of your business, but yes."

"How many dates have you had?" He couldn't stop himself.

Maya inhaled deeply. "Okay. Time for me to go." She turned to Samantha. "Great game. I should be able to make your game tomorrow." She kissed her daughter and widened her eyes in mock sympathy. "Have fun with your dad."

"Sam." She grimaced at him and left.

Sam narrowed his eyes at Maya as she walked away. No wonder she looked so good today.

"Dad. Dad!" Samantha waved her hand in front of his face. "Come on. I need food and a shower."

"Yeah, okay." He started to walk.

"Dad." Samantha stopped. "This way."

"Yeah, okay." He switched direction and followed her lead.

They left the soccerplex and headed for the subway. "How many times has your mom gone out with that guy? She just went out with him last week." He wasn't even going to try to pretend he didn't want to know.

Samantha smirked at him. "This will be the third date."

"What?" His breath became more jagged.

"Unless you count the fact that he shows up at the coffee shop every few days and has Mom make her special chai."

Sam stopped walking. Sirens in his head again as nausea washed over him. "What, like you mean, in the morning?" Now, he could hardly breathe. "He's not... I mean, he couldn't already be...never mind." He shoved his hands in his pockets and hunched over as he continued to walk.

Samantha raised her eyebrows at him. "Are you wondering if he's ever *already there in the morning*?" She covered her mouth to hide her smile. "Pathetic, really— asking your teenage daughter." She finally succumbed to her laughter.

Sam scowled at her and continued walking. It really was pathetic.

"Come on, Dad." She caught up to him and hooked

her arm through his. "If she were going to let him 'stay over,' she'd send me to *Nani*'s, and she hasn't." Samantha grinned at her father. "Although, I *am* spending tonight here with you." She raised one eyebrow, a twinkle in her eye.

Sam's heart sank.

CHAPTER FORTY-FOUR
SAM

New York 2013

SAMANTHA WAS CHATTERING on about the game, complaining about biased calls by the referee, analyzing and overanalyzing the details of each play. Normally, Sam loved this part as well, but today he was still reeling from the knowledge that Maya was going out with *that* guy. Again. Distracted as he was, he nearly tripped over a huge object in the middle of his small entrance hall.

"What is this?" Samantha gawked at the filthy brown canvas duffel bag. "It wasn't here when we left."

This bag could mean only one thing. Sam grinned and pressed his index finger to his lips. Samantha complied, and followed his gaze.

Sure enough, there was someone sleeping on his sofa. Sam grabbed a pillow from the chair and threw it at the form on his sofa. The young man bolted up and looked around. "What the hell?"

Sam cackled.

Ben jumped off the sofa and grabbed Sam in a hug. "Sammy!"

Sam returned the hug with gusto and then took a step back to examine his cousin. "You took the time to shave and get a haircut this time."

Ben rubbed his face. "Well, a haircut, anyway. You know how the ponytail drives my mom nuts. For the shave, I just used your razor." He chuckled.

"Consider that razor yours now." Sam grimaced in that way that big brothers did to their little brothers when they used their stuff.

Ben's hair and skin color were the same as Sam's, except that Ben's hair was straight, and when he traveled, he tended to let it grow and pull it back in a ponytail. But Sam knew Ben hadn't gotten a haircut for his mother.

"You came here first?" Sam wrinkled his brow at Ben. "Do I even want to know how you got in—I just moved here."

Ben gave him his best do-you-really-want-to-know look. "Just enjoy the surprise."

Before Sam could introduce Samantha, Ben had taken note of her. He directed his words to Sam, all the while looking at Samantha. "And of course I came here before going to Maryland! I got the family gossip and had to see what my big brother was up to. And clearly, it's a good thing I stopped by." He grinned at Samantha. "You could not possibly be the daughter I'm hearing about! Way too pretty to have this guy as your dad."

Samantha rolled her eyes as she shook his hand. "Nice to meet you. You must be Ben-kaka. But I thought you were in Africa. Hiding from a girl."

Ben laughed—almost a guffaw, really. "Niki does not waste any time." He wiped his eyes. "It's all true, but I don't do details." He jerked his head in Sam's direction. "Does he feed you?"

"I could eat."

Ben slammed his hands down on the small island. "Sammy, we *need* New York pizza."

"Yeah, okay." Butterflies invaded his belly as he watched Ben and Samantha. Unlike Niki, Ben would say just about anything. No filter. Sam picked up his phone and ordered the pizza, then got two beers and a Gatorade from the fridge.

Ben and Samantha were making small talk, and Sam joined them on the sofa. He handed Samantha the Gatorade. "Want to shower first? Pizza will be a bit."

"Sure." She stood and considered Ben. "Do you have any stories about my dad?"

Ben chortled. "Of course!" Samantha started to leave for her shower when Ben called out, "Maya is your mom, right?"

"Why?" She narrowed her eyes at Sam. "Are there a bunch of us to keep track of?"

Sam threw Ben a glare, but addressed his daughter. "Of course not. Go get your shower."

After Samantha left the room, Ben turned on ESPN. "She looks just like you."

"So I've been told."

"What's with all the boxes?" Ben indicated the piles of open and unopened boxes that were scattered around. "Unpack and move in already."

"It's fine the way it is." Sam opened the beers and handed one to Ben. "I unpacked the essentials."

They did the cursory clinking of the bottles, but before Sam could take a sip, Ben stopped him. "Wait. First, a toast." Sam rolled his eyes. "To my big brother for causing so much family drama that my mother doesn't even care that I've been in Africa for close to nine months." Ben cackled.

"Technically, I did not *cause* drama." Sam chuckled softly. "She came to me."

"Whatever. Better you than me. Where were you?" He tilted his head toward the bathroom. "Her soccer game?"

"Yes. She's a goalie." Sam could not help the ear-to-ear grin that took over his face in fatherly pride. "I just wish I'd known her when she was little. She's all grown up. She'll be sixteen in a couple months."

"News flash—fifteen isn't grown up. Don't you remember me at fifteen? A lot of growing up still to be done."

Sam nodded as he remembered Ben's adventurous teen years. He smiled. "How many times did I have to bail you out of jail?"

Ben laughed. "Twice. But come on, is it my fault the protests got out of hand? Don't make it sound like the Howard County police had a cot for me." Ben took a swig of his beer and grinned into the past.

"Do you remember—" Sam darted his eyes toward the bathroom, as he lowered his voice and leaned toward Ben.

"Yes." Ben rolled his eyes and started laughing. Thus began a round of recounting Ben's minor offenses as a growing teen.

"See?" Ben spread his arms wide again. "All of that is behind me. Thanks to your tutelage, I am now a productive member of society."

Sam settled back into his chair, comfortable and content. Ben had always had that effect on him, even as a child. "That you are." He waited a beat before continuing. "I heard from Niki that Divya is looking for you."

"I heard that, too." Ben's voice was flat and the mischievous grin was history. He looked down at his hands for a moment, before countering, "I also heard about Maya."

"What about Maya?" Sam tried to keep his voice neutral. He checked the bathroom again.

"You tell me. She's your daughter's mother."

"Nothing to tell."

"Oh, come on." Ben leaned in toward Sam, his face filled with anticipation. "Give me something. She's still hot, right? I mean, she still looks good, right?"

Ben was on the edge of his seat, his eyes filled with all the excitement and anticipation of a teenage boy waiting to hear the details of hot date. Sam grinned broadly. "Better." It was the truth.

Ben threw himself back on the sofa. "I knew it."

The door buzzer interrupted, letting them know the pizza had arrived. Ben opened two more beers as Sam got the pizza. He set it on the island and went down the hall to get Samantha. She was fast asleep on top of her bed, her hair still wrapped in a towel. She looked like a little kid. Kind of reminded him of Niki when she was that age. Maybe Ben was right: maybe Samantha wasn't quite all grown up. He wrapped a blanket around her and gently shut the door.

Ben had already downed one slice. "Um, sorry. I was so hungry and it smelled so good."

"No problem." Sam helped himself to a slice. "She's out cold. You'll have to hang with her tomorrow."

Ben nodded, his mouth full.

Sam finished his first slice and reached for another. "How was Africa?"

Ben lit up. "Amazing! Sammy, next time I go, you have got to come." He sipped his beer. "There's nothing like it. The work is—" he paused and smiled at something Sam couldn't see "—rewarding. I know it's cliché, but that's the only word. They think you're helping them, but those kids, they're helping you." He picked up another slice.

"It's a great place to hide, too." Sam pushed a bit.

Ben shrugged, avoiding Sam's gaze. "If that's what you need." He busied himself with eating his pizza.

"Do they feed you at all over there?" Maybe time to lighten up a little.

"Yes. But it's not this. If I could take this pizza with me, life would be perfect." He closed his eyes and chewed slowly, savoring his food.

Sam considered asking him more directly about Divya, but decided to save it for later. He finished his second beer.

Ben swallowed and wiped his mouth with the back of his hand. "I can't believe you're someone's dad!"

"That makes two of us." Sam settled back and enjoyed his beer while he caught Ben up on Samantha and whatever Niki hadn't told him. Ben continued to work on both pizzas and got himself another beer.

"So, you're pissed because Maya kept Samantha from you all these years?"

Sam was silent.

"So, what happened to Paige?"

"It wasn't going to work out."

"Yeah, I could see that. With Maya back in the picture, no other woman has a chance, huh, Sammy?"

"Maya is not back in the picture."

Ben froze, the pizza slice halfway to his mouth. "Well, why the hell not? What is the matter with you?"

"Nothing is the matter with me. Did you not hear the

part about how she never even told me she was *pregnant with my child*?" Sam hushed his voice and glanced down the hall to be sure he wasn't overheard.

"I also heard about how your mom helped that along. Did it ever occur to you that you would've known about Samantha if you'd ever actually gone after Maya?"

"I went after her, Ben." Sam closed his eyes and sighed heavily. "You know that."

"One time, Sammy," Ben snapped. "One time."

Sam watched him go to the kitchen. *Humph.* Ben never snapped at him. "She said there was no point. She said she didn't—" He rubbed his face with his hands. Sam really didn't want to repeat it. Even after all these years. Even though he knew his mother put her up to it. He *couldn't* repeat it.

"And you just let her go." Ben gestured with his hands. "The love of your life." His eyes darkened as he shook his head at his cousin and took his seat. "Even *I* knew you bought her a ring after your second date, and you didn't even fight for her."

Sam looked up from his hands to glower at his cousin. "My mom was *sick,* and I went back to school. Things happen."

"Not good enough! All these years, you knew where she was. Not once did you go to her." Disappointment flowed from Ben's eyes and voice. "Not *once!*" As if that weren't enough, Sam was treated to Ben's best withering look. "Just as well you didn't know about your daughter."

Sam's head pounded and his knuckles turned white from gripping the arm of the chair. Anyone else and Sam wouldn't have bothered with restraint. His next words were a growl from the back of his throat. "What the fuck could you *possibly* know about it?"

Ben stared him down. "What's to know? You can be as mad as you want, just make sure some of that anger is focused toward yourself. You can't lay it all on Maya." Ben examined Sam more closely and raised his eyebrows. "You became so focused on becoming this hard-ass lawyer with the uptown girl and all the trimmings, I'm surprised you ever gave her another thought. So if you didn't know about your daughter, maybe it was for the best."

Sam continued to fume as he considered Ben's words. The truth was that it had been easier to get lost in school and work and moving forward than to think about Maya and what he had lost. Everything he had done was so he didn't have to think about her.

But he always had, anyway.

"Listen, Sammy." Ben's voice softened. "You're the best older brother, which is why I thought that one day you would go and find her, and…" He fidgeted with his bottle.

"And *what*?"

"I know it sounds silly, but I was just a little kid. I always thought that at some point, you would man up and fight for her… I thought you'd bring her back *home*."

Sam was silenced and loosened his grip on the seat. *Home*. That was exactly how he had thought of Maya. When he was with her, he was home. Ben lay down on the sofa and closed his eyes. The only sound was the quiet murmurings of the ESPN announcer.

Sam gulped down the last of his beer. "She's seeing someone." The words needed to be pushed out of his mouth. They hung like a weight in the air.

"What does that mean?" Ben asked without turning or opening his eyes.

"It means she went on a few dates with the same guy." Sam sighed deeply. "He shows up every other day at her coffee shop, and she's out with him now, and Samantha's sleeping over here, so…" The thought of Maya *with* some other guy burned him. Nauseated him. Actually, it made him want to punch something. All these years, whenever he thought about her, and on some level, he always did, he never thought of her in terms of being with someone else. She was always *his*. He picked at the label on the bottle. He was always *hers*. "What if I'm too late?"

Ben groaned as he sat up to face Sam. "Oh, yeah." He held out both hands, palms up. He looked at one. "Father of her child, madly in love with her." He brought it down as if it was heavy with weight. He looked at the other hand. "Went on a few dates with some random guy." He raised his eyebrows and tightened his lips. "Yeah, you're right. No competition." He shook his head in frustration and started to lie back down. "Just let her go again. You can't win that fight."

"Is that what you did with Divya? Did you *fight* for her?" It felt good to let off some of that frustration.

"As a matter of fact, I did," Ben responded calmly as he sat back up to face Sam. "However, *I* am not the Boy Scout you are, so by the time she came around, I had already screwed it up." He turned to lie back down, shifting on the sofa getting comfortable. "Nice try, though."

Silence again, during which Sam thought Ben had fallen asleep. He started to get up when Ben spoke with his eyes closed. "Listen, bhaiya."

Ben hadn't called him bhaiya in ages.

"The first thing you need to do is admit you still want her, and then go get her. If you don't—trust me, you'll find out just how great a hiding place Africa is."

CHAPTER FORTY-FIVE
SAM

Maryland 1996

HIS MOTHER HAD been diagnosed with cancer.

Sam leaned forward on his elbows with his face in his hands and winced from the pain. His nose was broken and his body was black-and-blue, but the pain grounded him. Right now, he'd give anything for Maya's gentle touch or whispered assurance. But her comfort was gone to him forever.

His mother had collapsed that morning. Sam and his father had brought her to the hospital, where ten hours later, they'd gotten their answer. His father was currently consulting with colleagues about the best course of action.

He didn't notice his father's approach until he felt a hand on his shoulder. Sam looked up into the eyes of a much older man. The usual blue twinkle of amusement had given way to a darker worry, and Sam stood in an instant, ready for whatever his father had to say.

"Just tell me, Dad."

His father nodded. "It's CLL. Chronic lymphocytic leukemia."

"What does that mean?"

"It means she has a treatable form of cancer. It means that she has to take a pill, but she can expect to beat it."

"What kind of timeline?" Sam forced his voice into the same clinical, detached tone his father used.

"Hard to say. But it's not too advanced, so we can be hopeful that she has many years to come."

"I'll transfer closer to home. Maybe defer this next semester."

"Sammy, that's not necessary." He laid a hand on Sam's shoulder. "Right now, you need a meal and some sleep. It's been two days since you saw Maya…"

"Don't." Sam pulled his shoulder away from his father. "Can I see her?"

"Sure." His father sighed and rested weary eyes on Sam. "She's going to be fine. No need to make any rash decisions."

Sam nodded and walked down the hall to his mother's room. He knocked and let himself in. "Hey, Mom."

His mother was five feet tall and all of a hundred pounds dripping wet, but he had never thought of her as frail. Machines beeped and burped, providing an eerie soundtrack. As he looked at her tiny frame being swallowed by the bed, a new pit grew in his stomach. Her brown skin, usually radiant with her inner fire, was ashen, and upon closer inspection, Sam could see how thin she had become. He hadn't noticed because he had been preoccupied with Maya. Tears burned behind his eyes. He forced them away.

"Hi, son." She smiled and her voice was weak.

"So, Dad tells me you're attention-seeking again." He forced a chuckle.

She waved a hand. "What about you? With that face?" She managed a crooked smile.

Sam rolled his eyes at her. "You had to one-up me."

"Your father worries too much, and he exaggerates."

"He does. But not this time." Sam sat down and leaned his elbows on the bed as he took her frail hand in his. "I have a great idea." He smiled hugely, as if his idea was earth-shattering. "I'll transfer out of Columbia Law to UMD Law. That way, I'll be closer to home. It'll give me a chance to meet people and build clientele so when I start my practice, I'll be ready to roll."

His mother pulled her hand away from his, and furrowed her brow. "Are you still chasing that idea? I would have thought you would have come to your senses by now. You were made to be in politics, Sam. Look at you—tall, good-looking, intelligent, charming. All you need is the right training and contacts."

Sam breathed deeply. "Mom, I told you, that's not really what I want. I want to help people. Like we were helped when Arjun—"

"Don't!" Her voice was sharp enough to throw Sam back. "Don't." She sank farther away from him. "You *promised* me that you would do what he could not. You were on that path until that *girl* distracted you. Since when do you let anything, even a girl, get in the way of your dreams?"

Sam took in the sallow tone of his mother's skin, the gray in her hair, and his heart broke. The beeping increased as his mother's heart rate went up. The sound tore at him.

There was no future with Maya—what did it matter what he did with his life? At least this way, he'd be making his mother happy. "You're right, Mom. I made you a promise and I'm going to keep it. But that means I'll need to go back to school in New York. That's where all the contacts are."

Her eyes lit up and she broke into a smile. "That's my boy! I knew you would see sense." She tried to sit up. "Oh, I'm so happy. You are going to make our dreams come true." She beamed at him, but Sam had the sense that she wasn't really seeing him at all. And a part of him knew that when she said "our dreams," she wasn't really talking about him, either. No matter. At least he'd made one person happy.

CHAPTER FORTY-SIX
SAM

New York 2013

"I CAN'T BE in the same house as your mother right now." Sam's father quickly brushed past him and into the apartment. "I know you have Ben here now, so I'll just take the sofa." He set down his suitcase next to the door and turned to face Sam.

"I'm sorry, what?" A pit formed in Sam's stomach as he digested the dark circles under his father's eyes, not to mention the tousled hair and unshaved beard.

"You heard me." His father nodded at the bar. "You still got the good bourbon I gave you?" He plopped himself on the sofa. "Just grab two glasses and the bottle."

Sam did as he was told, the pit in his stomach growing. What had his mother done now? He settled down in the chair across from his father and poured them each two fingers of straight bourbon.

His father grabbed his glass and, before Sam had even sipped his own bourbon, he downed it. Since when did his father do shots?

Sam's father reached for the bottle and poured himself another drink. Sam sipped his drink in a deliberate fashion and waited until his father was prepared to talk. He didn't have to wait long.

"Your mother told me about that check."

Sam frowned. Why would she tell him? "What did she tell you?"

"She told me that she tried to pay Maya to leave you alone and not to tell you she was pregnant."

Sam was surprised that she'd told the truth. "That is true."

"She said that's why you won't take her calls."

Sam shrugged. Had another gulp of bourbon.

"She kept Samantha from me, too." His dad sighed, a sad, almost helpless thing.

Sam stared into his near-empty glass. "Not just her. Maya participated in that, too."

His father sipped his drink and settled more comfortably into the sofa. "Maya was young, impressionable. Scared."

It was Sam's turn to polish off his drink. He reached for the bottle. "Doesn't make it right."

"Maybe not. But sometimes it helps if we understand why." His father stared him down.

"Do you understand why?"

His father frowned. "Your mother put all of her hopes and dreams for Arjun onto you. She didn't know how else to handle his death. When that was threatened, she took care of it. She honestly thought she was doing what was best for you."

"Yet here you are. With a suitcase." Sam didn't even try to keep the bitterness from his voice.

"Here I am. She robbed you of a child, and me of a grandchild. Not easy to forgive that, no matter her intentions." He drank a little more. "But she is my wife. And damn if she doesn't drive me crazy. I love her."

"It's not only us. Samantha grew up without a father. She didn't have you in her life as a grandfather. She deserved to have all of that." The bourbon burned as Sam downed it. He poured another as the familiar anger built again.

"Maya did the best she could. Samantha is feisty and intelligent. And you're in her life now. I don't see Maya standing in your way."

Sam grunted. *True.*

His father set down his empty glass and stretched out. "Can't choose who you fall in love with, sometimes. Your mom and I have been through a lot. If we made it through Arjun's death, we can make it through just about anything. I just need a few days to sort through things."

"Stay as long as you like. Ben will take the sofa." Sam concentrated on the bottom of his glass, as if the answers to his questions were actually somewhere in there. How was his dad even able to consider forgiving his mother?

"Did you really tell your mother she couldn't see Samantha?"

"I was pissed." He looked up at his father. "But I wouldn't do that to Samantha."

"She's probably the best thing that has happened to your mother in a long time." John leaned toward his son, his elbows on his knees. "Your mother carried around a lot of anger over Arjun's death. To some extent, she still does." He paused, his mouth set in a grim line. "But it was that anger that fueled her to hand that check to Maya—it was that need to control that which she could not. You're more like your mother than you think. Don't let your anger over the fact you missed Samantha's childhood rule the rest of your life."

Sam leaned forward on his knees, staring at his hands. "It's just that every time I see her, I'm reminded of what I missed."

"Are you talking about raising Samantha, or your missed life with Maya?"

Sam looked up into his father's eyes and exhaled. "Yes."

CHAPTER FORTY-SEVEN
MAYA

New York 2013

As SHE CLEANED up the shop at the end of the day, Maya glanced out the window and was stunned to see Hema-auntie approaching. Maya stiffened, just as she did all those years ago when Hema-auntie had come to her uncle's house. Her stomach fluttered as she waited for the door to open, but it did not. When she peeked outside, she saw Hema-auntie walking away from the coffee shop, back the way she had come. Curiosity overruled her butterflies, and Maya dropped her rag and rushed to open the door.

"Auntie?"

Hema-auntie stopped and turned toward her.

"Auntie," Maya started again, "why don't you come in?"

Hema-auntie took a couple tentative steps toward Maya. "I, um. Well, I don't really know." She stopped. "It was foolish of me to come here. I have no right…"

"At least warm up with a cup of coffee or chai. I insist."

Hema-auntie looked at Maya with a grateful smile. "That would be wonderful. Thank you."

Maya held the door open for Sam's mother, and then

led her back into the bakery kitchen. "Here, have a seat while I make chai."

"Oh, don't go to any trouble. Coffee is fine."

"It's no trouble. Please, sit." Maya motioned to a small table she had set up in the back for when she needed a quick break. "Maybe a bit more spice, since it's so cold?"

Hema-auntie nodded and removed her coat and sat while Maya filled a small pot just about halfway with water to boil. She added her homemade chai masala, enhancing it with a bit of grated fresh ginger. She put in loose tea leaves, more than a pinch, less than a handful, and turned to face Hema-auntie while she waited for the mixture to come to a soft boil.

Hema-auntie watched Maya carefully before finally speaking. "Maya, what I did, I did for my son." No one could accuse Hema Hutcherson of not getting to the point. "At the time, I believed what I was doing was right." She raised her chin and made eye contact with Maya.

The chai simmered, but Maya could not bring herself to break eye contact with this woman who had terrified her all those years ago. Tears shimmered in Hema-auntie's eyes, even as she set her lips in a firm line.

"After Arjun was taken from me, I shut down. Don't get me wrong, I loved Sam—how could one *not* love Sam?" She paused to smile at something Maya couldn't see. Her smile withered into a frown when she began speaking again. "But I was never the same, and I knew that Sam suffered for that. My way of loving Sam was to push him…to push him to fulfill his brother's dreams. Because, you see, that way I could have them both." She smiled again, but it wasn't a happy thing. "Selfish,

I know. And saying it out loud, it sounds ridiculous—even to myself. Imagine knowing you should love your child more, but not knowing how to do it." She stopped for a moment, staring at Maya. One lone tear escaped. Hema-auntie did nothing to stop its trail down her face.

Maya's body tensed, her mind and heart at war. Young Sam had craved his mother's love, and the only way she could give it was to push him to be like Arjun. Yet how could she judge this woman, who had lost a child? The thought of losing Samantha made her feel like all the blood had been drained from her body—no parent should have to navigate such black waters.

"I know that what I did was wrong—and that I hurt so many people. Especially you and Sam." She swallowed hard. "And Samantha." More tears rolled down her face. She reached a shaky finger to wipe them.

Maya handed her a tissue. She turned to the chai mixture, which was now emitting the warm aroma of cinnamon and cardamom mixed with the sharp scent of peppercorn. She poured some milk into the pot, until the mixture was the medium brown color of a walnut.

"Sugar?"

"If you like it."

Maya sprinkled sugar with an experienced hand. While she waited for the mixture to come to a rolling boil, she turned back to Sam's mother, who was blotting her eyes and fighting for her composure.

"I thought I should at least explain to you why I did what I did. You were young, and I took advantage. I apologize for what I did to you all those years ago. For what I did to my son." A small sniffle escaped her. "I don't know what I was thinking, coming here. I should go." She stood and gathered her coat.

"No. Wait. The chai is ready." Maya turned off the heat and strained the chai into two mugs. She handed one to Hema-auntie and sat down, motioning for Sam's mother to join her. The older woman remained standing for a moment, seemingly—and uncharacteristically—unsure of what to do.

"Please, sit." Maya motioned once again to the chair. "If I haven't bitten you yet, I probably won't."

This elicited a small but grateful smile that transformed Hema-auntie's face. "It's more than I deserve, but the chai smells wonderful." She removed her coat and sat down, wrapping her hands around the mug. She inhaled deeply before taking her first sip. "This is wonderful, Maya, thank you." Her gaze rested on Maya's, warm and grateful. It was clear she was talking about more than just the chai.

"Well, the ultimate decision to keep Samantha from Sam was mine, so there's more than enough blame to go around. Thankfully, I'm not that young girl anymore." Maya sipped her chai, and enjoyed for a moment how the cardamom and cinnamon hit her tongue and the way the milky liquid warmed her.

"I was not a young girl. I let my own ambitions and needs get in the way of what truly mattered, and that was my son's happiness. The truth is—" she paused, and Maya could have sworn she was swallowing back more tears "—you were the key to his happiness." Hema-auntie regained her composure and finished her chai. Maya was dumbstruck by her words. *She* was the key to Sam's happiness? Well, not anymore.

"You probably still are." It was as if Hema-auntie could read her mind. She fixed Maya in her gaze. "I hope that one day you will see fit to accept my apology." She stood and gathered her coat.

Maya was struck for the first time at how small and fragile Sam's mother seemed. She had always seemed so powerful, so strong. But here she was, trying to right the wrongs of her past—and why? Suddenly it was clear.

"Auntie, do you want to stay for dinner? Samantha says she hasn't seen you in a while."

Hema-auntie looked away from Maya, suddenly preoccupied with buttoning her coat. "Sam doesn't want me to see her."

"Oh, I'm sure he didn't mean that. He was probably just angry. And I am her mother, after all. Stay for dinner. Tell Uncle to join us, as well. Samantha will be thrilled. Did he come up with you?"

Tears filled Hema-auntie's eyes again. "I suspect he's been staying with Sam for the past few days. When I told him about that check, he packed a bag and left."

"You told him?"

Hema-auntie nodded. "Yes. The truth was out, and I couldn't leave him in the dark. Even though I knew he would be angry with me." She swallowed hard, and this time, Maya saw tears for sure. "I love him. But he's never left like this before."

Silence. Maya had no idea how to process this new side of Sam's mother. Though maybe it wasn't that new.

Hema-auntie turned to leave again. "Thank you for the invitation for dinner, but—"

"Apology accepted." Sometimes Maya blurted things out and she instantly regretted them. This was not one of those times. This happened to be one of those times she was grateful she could blurt things out without overanalyzing.

"What?"

"You heard me. I accept your apology. Now we'll move on." Maya smiled and reached out for Hema-auntie's coat. This woman had lost one son years ago, and now her other son wouldn't talk to her. Her husband had left, and she had been banned from seeing her granddaughter. Maya might not have been able to do anything about Arjun, Sam and John, but she could certainly allow a grandmother to see her grandchild. "You'll have dinner here, with us."

"So I suppose all that 'We're both her parents and we need to consult with each other about matters regarding her' only applies to me." Sam's voice boomed through the kitchen as he walked back to them. "*You* can do whatever the hell you want, apparently."

Maya had been so distracted by this new version of Hema-auntie that she hadn't heard the door chime. She now turned to face Sam, and found his father standing next to him, looking grim-faced.

Sam stood tall and broad-shouldered, filling the small room like he filled up any space he was in. Eyes flaming, his mouth in a tight line, he stared Maya down, not even acknowledging his mother's presence.

"It's *dinner*. I'm not running away with her." Maya faced him. "And you didn't consult with me, either."

"It's dinner with my mother, who I decided does not get the grandmother privileges that she so easily tossed aside."

"Sam, she apologized. To *me*. We have to give her a chance."

Sam's eyes flicked momentarily to his mother and softened for an instant, before they hardened again, and he turned back to Maya. "No, we don't. Second chances aren't always offered."

Maya moved closer to him and lowered her voice to a hiss. "We're not talking about *me*, we're talking about your mother. I believe she is truly regretful of her actions, and I believe her apology is sincere." Maya stood as tall as she could and squared her shoulders. "And besides, Samantha misses her. It's not fair to deprive her of her grandmother."

Sam said nothing.

"You and Uncle are welcome to stay, as well."

Before Sam could say no, his father spoke. "Thank you—that would be wonderful." Sam's father had gone, unnoticed, over to stand by his wife. Tears streaming down her face, Hema-auntie allowed her husband to pull her close. Maya was frozen as the woman who had intimidated her for years sobbed into her husband's shoulder. He murmured softly as he held her.

Maya couldn't help but smile. Sam's parents had lost a son, built a life together and now Uncle had discovered that his wife had lied to him and their son all these years about a granddaughter, and still, they connected. Still, they loved each other. Still, they needed each other. She wiped a tear from her cheek and turned to find Sam watching his parents, as well. His jaw was clenched, but he looked resigned to what was happening.

Hema-auntie calmed down a little and Uncle looked at Sam and Maya over her head, the twinkle back in his blue eyes. "Sammy, you were never going to keep your mother from Samantha anyway, so why argue with Maya about it now? Especially when she's right."

Sam closed his eyes, resigned. "Yeah, okay. Dinner

it is." He opened his eyes and addressed the room. "For Samantha's sake."

"Whatever." Maya rolled her eyes as if she didn't care, but her gut was hollow, and her heart felt empty. She might have once been important to Sam's happiness, but she had thrown away her chance and now it was time for her to move on. Away from Sam.

CHAPTER FORTY-EIGHT
SAM

New York 2013

THE WEEKEND AFTER Valentine's Day, Maya was signed up for an accelerated workshop on wedding cakes. The workshop was in Manhattan, so she'd stayed with Ami. Samantha had asked to spend the weekend with Sam, and he was thrilled to have this much time with his daughter. Ben had gone to see his parents, but would return later that night.

Sam picked her up from school Friday afternoon, and this time, there was no sign of the boy she'd been with the last time he'd picked her up. "Where's Will?"

"Around." She shrugged and kept walking.

"Did you ever tell your mom about him?" Sam studied the top of her head as she avoided his gaze.

"Um, sure." Another quick shrug and no eye contact.

"She was okay with it?" Sam tilted and twisted his head to get a look at her face.

"Well, you know, she asked a lot questions, but she's on board." She finally looked up at him with a tight smile.

Sam regarded her with doubt. *Note to ask Maya about this.* No, he was not trying to come up with reasons to talk to Maya. This was legit.

"Okay, then. We have practice, then we can do whatever you want to do."

"Great." She glanced up at him, her smile tentative. "Listen, I know we have a big weekend planned, but I have a group project due Monday, and the group wants to get together tonight to work on it for a couple hours. Then I'm free."

"Oh, uh, sure." Sam hid his disappointment. Homework was homework. "You're welcome to invite them over. I'll move the boxes."

"No, that's okay. We're going to meet at Stacy's." She texted him the address. It was a few blocks from his apartment. "Why do you still have boxes? It's been, like, two months."

"I just do." It was his turn to avoid her eyes. "Is *Will* in this group?"

"Uh, no." She turned her gaze away from him and frowned. "He has soccer tonight anyway."

"Did you guys break up or something?" Sam tried and failed to get her to look at him.

"No, of course not." She finally turned to him and rolled her eyes. "Sometimes we don't agree on stuff." Her tone indicated that she really didn't want to talk about it.

Sam frowned, but decided he had all weekend to find out what was bothering her, so he let it go. "Okay, I'll drop you off after dinner."

"You're the best!" She threw her arms around him.

"You probably say that to all your parents."

After a fabulous practice and a delicious, home-cooked meal, Sam dropped his daughter off in the lobby of Stacy's building.

Back in his apartment, he glanced at his watch. 8:00

p.m. Maya was probably finished with the day's work and heading over to Ami's. Unless Leo was joining her. His stomach clenched, and he found his hands balled into fists. He could just call her, ask if she'd heard about Will.

He picked up his phone and scrolled for her number. No. That was probably a conversation better had in person. Besides, she could do what she wanted, right? If she wanted Leo, he could have her. At the thought of Leo having her, Sam stood and paced his apartment. He grabbed his jacket and was about to go to Ami's, but stopped himself. *Idiot.* He was supposed to be happily hanging out with their daughter. Sam grinned to himself. *That's right, Leo, I have a child with her. Compete with that.* He grimaced at his own juvenile thoughts and opened his laptop to do research.

A couple hours passed and Sam was considering sending Samantha a text to see how her project was going, when there was a pounding at his door. Someone was calling to him from the other side.

"Mr. Hutcherson! Are you there? It's Will and I have Samantha!" Panic laced the boy's voice. More banging. "Mr. Hutcherson? Please be there!"

Sam's stomach did a flip as he bolted to the door. He opened it to find Samantha leaning on Will, her hair tousled and eyes half shut. She was barely able to stand.

"What did you do to her?" Sam shouted at the boy as he grabbed Samantha from him. She reeked of alcohol.

Will's eyes flew open. "Nothing, Mr. Hutcherson. I swear. I got a text from Lisa, and she was like this when I got to Stacy's. I didn't know what to do, so I brought her here."

"Sit!" Sam motioned to Will, as he pointed at the sofa. Samantha was babbling.

"Aww, hey, it's Sammy!" She giggled. "Don't yell at good William."

Sam gaped at her, aghast. "She's drunk!"

"I know!" Will looked nervous as he noted Sam's clenched fists. "I told her not to go."

"Hey, Sammy! Hey, Dad!" She put her index finger to her mouth. "Don't tell my mom. She'll freak." She doubled over in laughter.

Sam placed Samantha on the sofa and took out his phone to call Maya. She picked up on the second ring.

"Hey, Sam." There was a smile in her voice that any other time, he might've been happy to hear.

"Maya. Are you still in Manhattan?" He couldn't keep his voice neutral.

"Yes, I just finished dinner with Ami." Concern filled her voice. "What's going on, Sam? Did she have another allergic reaction?"

"Um, no. Nothing like that, but you might want to come over here." He hesitated. There was not a gentle way to say it. "Samantha's drunk." A small part of him did spark to life when he registered that she wasn't with Leo.

"What?" Concern turned to anger. "Did she go to that party?" She was yelling into the phone as if she were talking to Samantha herself.

Sam was not fazed by her anger. "Party? She told me she was going to work on a school project!" He glared at Samantha on the sofa next to Will. She was trying to kiss him and Will was doing his best to keep her under control, all the while throwing fearful and furtive glances in Sam's direction.

"On a Friday night, Sam?" His stomach plummeted at the exasperation in her voice. "Really?"

Oh. His grip on the phone tightened as he realized he'd been played. "Just come over, okay? We can talk about how gullible I am later." First anaphylactic shock, now this. He was the worst parent ever. Maya would definitely never leave him alone with Samantha after this.

"Be there in fifteen." She disconnected.

He tapped his phone with such violence, it was as if he was punishing it for his own naivete.

Sam grabbed a bottle of Gatorade from the kitchen and handed it to Samantha. He got her to take a few sips.

"Oh, Dad. I don't feel so good." Her voice was small and she seemed to forget Will as she reached for Sam.

"Okay, up you go." He stood to help her up to the hallway bathroom. Will held her other side. They made it down the hallway and to the door of the bathroom, when Samantha vomited all over the floor and herself, and also managed to get the two of them. Sam grimaced; his reflexes must not be what they used to be.

"Fantastic, Samantha." He closed his eyes. "Lucky for you, I'm used to this."

He nodded to Will as he finally just picked Samantha up and carried her into the bathroom. "Don't you go anywhere," Sam growled at him. "I'm not done with you yet."

Will turned pale.

Samantha was crying now; the tears smeared her makeup and made black streaks down her face. Sam cleaned her up the best he could when she vomited again. At least this time, she made it to the toilet.

"Dad. Please." She hiccuped and tried to wipe her face. "Don't tell Mom."

"She'll be here any minute." Sam crouched down to where she was seated on the bathroom floor.

"What? You called her?" Samantha's indignation amused Sam, because she was in a lot of trouble. "I can't believe you did that. She'll kill me." Her eyes were frantic and she pouted like a petulant toddler. "How could you do that?"

"Well, she is your mother—"

"She'll never let me out again! I thought I could trust you!" She narrowed her eyes at him and spit out her words with as much venom as she could muster in her present state. "I hate you."

It actually might have been painful for Sam to hear his daughter proclaim her hate for him, except for the fact that she was drunk, she'd lied to him and, quite frankly, he wasn't too thrilled with her right now, either. There was a knock at the bathroom door.

"Sam? It's me." Maya's voice came through the door.

Sam stood and opened the door.

She covered her mouth with her hand as she wrinkled her nose. "She got you, huh?"

He nodded somberly.

"Who's that boy?" Maya spoke through her hand. "He's got vomit on him, too. He was cleaning the floor out here."

"That's Will."

"Who's Will?"

Sam turned back to Samantha, jaw clenched. "Will Waters, her boyfriend."

"Her *what*?" Maya's voice rose in pitch as she looked from Sam to Samantha.

Sam narrowed his eyes at Samantha and shook his head in disappointment. He sighed and turned to Maya.

"I'll get her clothes so you can change her and we'll put her to bed." He frowned as he raised his eyebrows. "Then we can catch up."

While Maya took care of Samantha, Sam used the shower in his room to clean up. He emerged from the bathroom, a towel wrapped around his waist, to find Samantha passed out, half in, half out of his bed, and Maya futilely trying to get her all the way in.

"Need some help?" He started toward Samantha.

"Sure." Maya turned to face him and quickly turned away, using her hand to shield her eyes. "Pants, Sam! Put on pants."

"Oh, yeah. Right." He grinned at her back as he quickly slipped on jeans and discarded the towel. "Okay."

She cautiously removed her hand and turned toward him. "Fine." She cleared her throat and appeared to be trying to suppress a smile. "Um, you get her legs."

"Actually, I got her." He motioned for Maya to step aside. She stepped back, but he was acutely aware of her presence as he bent over and picked up his daughter like a baby, settling her comfortably in the bed.

"Thanks." Maya reached over and pulled the covers over Samantha. "She just stumbled in here and passed out, and I, uh, couldn't move her."

Maya was looking everywhere but at him.

He studied her a moment. "Are you okay?"

"Yeah, sure. I'm fine." She managed brief eye contact. "Why wouldn't I be?"

"No reason." He smirked. The flush on her skin captivated him, and he couldn't look away.

Maya cleared her throat. "I suppose we deal with this boy now."

"Is he still here?"

Maya inhaled deeply. "Apparently, you told him to stay." She dipped her head at him, and wildly waved in the direction of his torso. "But you might want to, um… well, put on a shirt first." She was suddenly interested in Samantha's blankets. "And you're still wet—your hair…" The wave became an abstract motion in the direction of his head.

"Right." He toweled off and pulled on an old concert T-shirt.

Maya smiled. "You still have that?"

"Hell, yeah. It's Hootie. Come on."

She actually laughed. A real, genuine sound that reminded him of summer—*that* summer. "Nothing wrong with Hootie, but that shirt has seen better days." Her gaze lingered a bit longer than necessary, and when he caught her looking, she flushed again.

He opened the door and allowed her to walk through first. The scent of honeysuckle wafted by as she passed him and he was momentarily frozen in the doorway.

She took a few steps and turned back to him. "Aren't you coming?"

"Oh, yeah—of course." He gathered himself and followed her out.

"Teenagers." She treated him to her crooked smile and shook her head.

Will was sitting on the edge of his chair when the two of them came out. Sam noticed that the floor was clean and that Will had done the best he could to clean himself off, too. He had cleats on his feet, and was still wearing his shin guards. Will started to stand as they approached.

Sam motioned for him to stay seated. He folded his arms across his chest and looked down at Will on the sofa. "What happened?" It was a demand, no doubt. But this boy had just brought home his intoxicated daughter. Sam would be nice when it was warranted.

Will threw an apprehensive glance at Maya.

"I'm her mother." She extended her hand to him.

He shook her hand. "Nice to meet you, Mrs. Hutcherson. Oh, cr—I'm sorry, it's Mrs. Rao, like Samantha. Sorry." Color rose to his face and he wiped his hand on his shorts.

Sam and Maya deftly avoided looking at one another by concentrating on Will. Maya sat down across from Will, while Sam continued to stand. Sam felt a gentle tug on his T-shirt, and looked down to see Maya nodding at him to sit. Sam bit the inside of his cheek and glowered in Will's direction, but sat down next to her.

"Fine, okay." Will began. "There was a party at Paul Jameson's and Brittany Stevenson was going."

Sam and Maya both groaned at the mention of the girl's name.

Will's smile was sardonic. "Yeah, I know, right?"

Sam glared at him. Will cleared his throat and continued, "So, anyway, Brittany dared Samantha to show up. I told her it wasn't worth it and I didn't think she should go. Brittany always brings alcohol to these parties and they get out of hand. And I didn't want her to get into any more trouble." He looked away for a split second. "She was kind of mad at me about that."

Sam grunted acknowledgment. He'd known something was up with Samantha and Will.

Will leaned toward them and held his hands out for emphasis. "See, Brittany never got over the whole shoplifting thing and has had it out for Samantha all year.

That whole marijuana in Samantha's locker thing...
everyone *knows* Brittany put it there."

Sam saw fury in Will's eyes and paid closer attention to the boy.

Will continued, his voice rough with anger. "Brittany totally deserved that punch Samantha gave her. It
was awesome." The boy looked past Sam and Maya and
seemed to get lost in the memory.

Maya gently elbowed Sam. He cut his eyes to her
just as the edges of her mouth turned up into a ghost
of a smile.

"Continue," Maya encouraged Will.

"Oh, yeah. So, Samantha said there was no way she
was going to back down from Brittany. Especially since
Brittany kept going on about how Samantha was only
allowed back at school because of *gym equipment*." Will
shook his head in bewilderment. "Not sure what all that
is about. Brittany's probably just making things up to
get to Samantha."

Sam shifted uncomfortably in his seat.

"Samantha wouldn't listen to anyone. So, she went
to the party and Lisa went with her. A little past nine, I
got a text from Lisa to hurry up and come over there."
He pulled out his phone and showed it to Sam. "You
can check my phone if you want."

Sam took the proffered phone, and sure enough the
text from Lisa was there. He handed it back to Will.

"When I got there, Lisa told me Brittany had challenged Samantha to some kind of drinking contest. So,
she'd had about four shots when Lisa got scared and
texted me to come get her. And I saw beer there, but no
one knew if Samantha had had any or not. That's all I

know." Fear and apprehension flickered over his face and he flicked his gaze between them.

"Why weren't you at the party?" Maya asked.

"I had soccer practice until 9:15. I saw the text from Lisa as soon as I was done, and raced over there. I didn't know what else to do." His words tumbled over each other in their effort to provide the answer required.

"No, that's fine, Will. You did the right thing bringing her here." Sam was forced to concede that the boy's story was legit. "How did you know where I was?"

"It's on her phone. And I live in this building, too. Twenty-third floor."

Fantastic. What were the odds? "Yeah. Okay. You can go." He caught Maya's eye and they stood in unison.

Will stood and put his hands in his pockets as he passed them. "Well, good night." He ducked his head and looked at Maya, blue eyes wide with concern. "She'll be all right?"

"She'll be fine." Maya walked Will to the door, but not before Sam received an elbow to the ribs and a mild glare.

Sam pursed his lips together. Message received. He offered his hand to Will. "Listen, Will. Thanks for bringing her home. And for looking out for her." He flicked his eyes to Maya. "Her mother and I really appreciate it."

Will shook Sam's hand, maybe with more enthusiasm than was necessary. "Sure thing, Mr. Hutcherson. Anything for Samantha."

Sam couldn't help but smile softly. "I know the feeling."

No sooner had Maya shut the door on Will, than Sam collapsed on the sofa and threw his head back. He pressed the palms of his hands into his eyes. "I'm really bad at this, Maya."

She sighed as she collapsed beside him. Along with the flowery scent of her perfume, she brought the warm aroma of burnt sugar. "Well, yeah."

"Great. Is that supposed to make me feel better?"

"No." She pulled his hands away from his eyes. Her cool touch soothed every part of him. "You just haven't been doing this very long." She blew air out of her mouth. "And anyway, I knew she wanted to go to that party. I just didn't think she'd try to play *you*. I should've at least warned you." She shook her head. "Next time we'll be better prepared."

"She said she hated me." Sam sounded more wounded than he intended.

Maya chuckled. "Well, that's a good start. If she doesn't hate me once a month, I feel like I'm not doing my job correctly."

"She hates me for calling you. Like *I* wouldn't be mad she showed up drunk at my door with her boyfriend. I screwed that up, too. I should've at least given you a heads-up. She said she was going to tell you about Will months ago. And I believed her. Just like I believed she was going to 'study' tonight." He dropped his head in embarrassment.

Maya nodded her head in understanding. She took his hand in both of hers and squeezed firmly. "You've only been doing this for a few months. You're still like a buddy to her. She's not used to having a real father any more than you're used to having a teenage daughter." She trailed off at the end as if she realized again why that was true and attempted to pull her hands away from his.

Sam held on to one of her hands.

"I get why you came to me for help with Samantha's school situation." He turned on the sofa so he was facing her, and softened his voice. "When Will showed up with Samantha in that condition and I thought he'd done something to her—" he narrowed his eyes and almost growled with the memory "—I would've done anything to keep her safe."

He held her gaze a beat too long. She looked away and slipped her hand back.

"So, 'gym equipment'?" She was suspicious.

Rightfully so.

Sam cleared his throat. "Um, well." He hung his head. "Okay, here's the thing." He turned back to Maya, knowing she was going to be mad. "I was able to intimidate Byron into dropping those charges against Samantha, and the juvenile courts responded to my name and connections. But Mrs. Pappenberger—" Sam exhaled and shook his head "—that woman did not respond to intimidation or connections or anything."

"Not even your charms?" Maya snickered.

"Nothing worked." Sam raised his arms in exasperation. "Until she happened to mention that the school hadn't had new gym equipment for fifteen years." Sam peeked at Maya through his lashes. "So, I wrote a check—but I insisted on being anonymous. Byron must have found out."

Maya's eyes widened. "Are you serious? You had to pay her off?" There was a touch of anger in her words. "Why didn't you say anything?" Her words were coming fast and hard. "You should've told me. I never expected—money—that's not why I came to you."

"Whoa, I know that." *Great.* He'd known she would

be mad. Sam placed his hand on hers. "Don't be upset—
I wanted to tell you, but then you got upset over the soccer fees…" He trailed off, but was hopeful when she
didn't pull away from him. "Besides, we had to get the
school to back down. I was still in shock about finding
out Samantha existed—I would've done anything you
asked. I couldn't let you down." It was Sam's turn to
ramble. "Writing a check was something I could do—
at the very least I could offer her money."

"Sam." Maya was sharp, her voice a shocked whisper. "Is that what you…" She forced him to look at her.
"You have a lot more to offer her than money." She
clasped his hand in hers, as if trying to transfer strength
to him. "And you absolutely have not let me down."

She smiled at him, her crooked smile. It was a simple thing, but her eyes glowed, her cheeks flushed, and
it reached all the way into the part of him that had always belonged to her, and he couldn't remember why
he was angry with her, or why he had let her go in the
first place. He was unable to tear himself away from
that smile, even though he knew his face revealed everything in his heart. There was, simply, nothing to be
done about that. She was as lost in him as he was in her.
There was nothing to hide behind here.

Something flickered in her eyes and the spell was
broken. "I should go. Our daughter is passed out in
your bed and it's late." She stood. "I'll just catch a cab
back to Ami's."

Sam hurriedly stood. "Look, it's too late to be running around. You don't have to go." Without thinking,
he took a step closer to her. "Stay." He was close enough
to glimpse the hesitation in her eyes.

Her voice was strained, but she was looking right at him. "Oh, no. I don't want to put you out."

That rebellious piece of hair fell to her face. On instinct, Sam reached out to tuck it back behind her ear. This time she let him. Her hair was soft, silken, just like he remembered. He had the sudden urge to run his fingers along her jawbone, pull her close...

Without removing his hand, he stepped closer. Her breath came faster, but she didn't move. He rested his hand on her cheek, so lightly, it was almost as if he was touching her with only the heat from his skin. He leaned into her. Heat from her body warmed him and he shifted his gaze from her eyes to her lips. She wasn't pulling away, but then—*bang, bang, bang*—on the door.

Maya jumped away from him at the sound, and he was forced to release her. He scrunched his eyes shut and made a fist with the fingers that had just been touching Maya's hair. That could only be one person. He opened his eyes. "Don't go anywhere."

He jogged to the door and opened it just a crack. Sure enough, there was Ben, his motorcycle helmet tucked beneath his arm. Sam spoke in a harsh whisper. "Go to a hotel." He started to shut the door. Ben put a foot in and stopped it.

"What's going on, Sammy? I thought you said you had Samantha this weekend. I want to hang out with her."

Sam tried to shut the door again. "Really, Ben. I'll pay for it."

"Sam? Who's there?" Maya called out.

Ben's eyes widened, his grin full of glee. "Is that— is that Maya?"

Sam tried to make his nod as meaningful as possible and pleaded, "Now can you go?" Wasn't there supposed to be some kind of guy code that required Ben to leave right now?

Guy code or no guy code, Ben laughed out loud and called out to Maya anyway. He pushed the door open just as she approached. He tossed Sam his helmet and smirked as he brushed past him to greet Maya.

Maya assessed Ben for minute, her eyes cautious. Ben waited while she studied him. She raised a tentative hand to brush hair from his face and her face lit up. Sam thought he would melt from her beauty. "I know those eyes—Ben!"

Ben reached down and enveloped her in a bear hug that lifted her off her feet. He kissed her cheek and winked at Sam over her head. "Maya! I heard you were back."

"Yes, I suppose so." Maya's laughter matched Ben's. "Look at you! All grown up!"

As the two of them got caught up, Sam waited, his arms folded across his chest. He glowered at Ben behind Maya's back. Ben shrugged innocence.

"It's great seeing you, Ben." Maya picked up her bag. "But I better get going." She caught Sam's eye and he was rewarded with a small smile. She averted her eyes to Ben. "I have an early class."

"No, no, no! You can't go! I just got here." Ben put his arm around Maya's shoulders and guided her back to the sofa. "I'll bet Sammy here hasn't even offered you a glass of wine yet."

Sam jumped in. "Well, our teenage daughter just came home drunk and is currently passed out, so wine was not a priority."

Ben spread his arms wide and laughed. "Oh, well

why didn't you say so?" He turned to Maya. "In that case, you *have* to stay over."

Sam glared at him.

"Don't you remember, Sammy? My first hangover?" Ben turned back to Maya and cleared his throat. "I may have been a bit underage."

Sam grinned at the memory. Ben had been just fourteen.

"Anyway, Sammy took me in, but the next morning…"

"Fed him greasy bacon, eggs, hash browns…"

"Prepared with the noisiest pots and pans you've ever heard." Both Sam and Ben laughed at the memory.

Sam turned to Maya, still laughing. "That's what I was getting to when Ben arrived." As he focused on those honey eyes, she held his gaze for a moment.

"Is it?"

"Mmm-hmm."

Maya turned to Ben. "That actually sounds really great. God knows Samantha could use that lesson. I'm just not prepared to stay over. All my stuff is at Ami's."

"Not a problem." Ben jut his chin to Sam. "As I'm sure you know, Sammy's dad is a doctor. I'm sure our Boy Scout here is prepared with an extra set of scrubs. Right, Sammy?"

"Uh, yeah. As a matter of fact, I am."

"It's settled!" Ben clapped his hands together. "Awesome! Let me get changed." Ben rummaged through Sam's boxes until he found a change of clothes and headed for the bathroom.

Left alone again, Maya turned to Sam. "It's okay. I don't want to be in the way."

"Nonsense. You won't be." He cleared his throat.

"You can sleep in my bed." He closed his eyes, grimacing, and ducked his head. "What I mean is, you can sleep *with Samantha* in my bed." He held his hands in an I-mean-no-harm manner, as the heat rose to his face. "I'll take the bed in her room."

"What about Ben?"

"Ben sleeps on the floors of mud huts in Africa. He slept out here when Dad stayed over." Sam dismissed that whole thing with a shrug. "And you really don't want to miss the show in the morning."

"How are your mom and dad?"

Sam shoved his hands into his jeans pockets. "Fine. Dad went home after that day in the coffee shop, and they're working things out."

"What about you and your mom?" She regarded him with genuine concern. Even after everything.

"What can I say, Maya? She loves Samantha and Samantha loves her. Mom will spend her life regretting what she sacrificed in terms of her granddaughter. It seems cruel to add to that." Sam grinned at her. "You're avoiding the question. Staying or not?" Every part of him wanted to step closer to her, touch her. But he held himself back, lest he scare her away.

Maya bit her bottom lip and Sam sensed victory. She finally grinned back at him, her eyes twinkling with amusement. "I do like the way you think. I certainly wouldn't want to miss the intoxicating aroma of greasy eggs and bacon and potatoes at the crack of dawn." She laughed, and Sam wanted to listen to that sound all day. "I assume your pots and pans are just as noisy as they were for Ben?"

She was staying over! Sam couldn't help the huge smile that took over his face. "Oh, yeah they are."

Sam threw off the covers and stretched out on his back. His feet hung over the edge of the bed. What had he been thinking when he bought this bed? He thought he'd never be the one sleeping in it. He tried to distract himself with thoughts of work—getting new clients and deciding where to open up the new office—but every thought evaporated into smoke and the only thought that remained was of Maya sleeping in the next room, in *his* bed.

He got out of bed and was in front of his bedroom door, his heart thumping against his chest, before he had a chance to think too much about it. He knocked softly, but no answer. The thumping slowed. Just as well. What was he thinking would happen anyway? He turned to go back to the spare room, when the door opened. Maya stood there in his olive green scrubs, her hair pleasantly tousled, looking wide-eyed and awake, and Sam went weak from how beautiful she was.

"Hey." She leaned on the door. "Can't sleep, or do you need a shirt?" How was it that she could be so sassy in the middle of the night?

He missed a beat before speaking, since his words were caught in his throat. "Can't sleep."

"Me, either." The door did not budge.

"How about a drink?" Sam tilted his head toward the kitchen.

"What about Ben?"

"He sleeps like the dead."

"Okay, but you're going to have to put this on." She rolled her eyes as she grabbed a T-shirt from his room and tossed it to him.

Sam poured them each two fingers of bourbon. Maya held hers and leaned against the kitchen counter.

"HERE'S TO TEENAGERS." Sam raised his glass and Maya raised hers as well, a smile playing at her lips. They both drank. Maya swallowed hers easily. "I don't think I knew you were a bourbon drinker."

"Lots of things you don't know about me." The smile made a full show of it, even lighting her eyes.

"I'd like to know all those things." Sam gripped her gaze in his. The smile faded, replaced by caution. "Anyway—" He changed the subject so she didn't run off. "I found a place in Queens that I really like for the practice." He spoke in hushed tones, a sliver of moonlight their only light.

"In Queens?" Every part of her, her face, her voice, her gaping mouth, looked like she was overflowing with excitement at this news. It was everything Sam could do to not kiss her. "Samantha will be thrilled."

"Well." Sam found his voice after a moment. "Let's not say anything until I can make it official. I'm signing papers this week." He took another sip of the warming liquid. Actually, he had still been deciding between that place and a place in Manhattan, but when her eyes lit up like that, he'd made his decision. It was the best thing to do. For Samantha, of course. They sipped in silence for a moment; the moonlight silhouetted Maya's profile and Sam was taken back to the first time he saw her like that. It had been the night of their first movie together. The night he fell in love with her.

Maya continued to sip her bourbon slowly, looking a bit more relaxed. "You know, I'm very proud of you. It isn't easy to make a huge career change. Here you are, going after what you always wanted."

"Well, it's time I did things for the right reasons. And if we're handing out compliments, then bravo to you for forgiving my mother." Another solid sip. "You make it look easy."

"It's actually not that hard when you see her with Samantha. She's a different person."

"My dad would say she's the woman he fell in love with." Sam surprised himself at his own lack of skepticism.

"He may be right." It was clear she still believed in true love.

The bourbon was warm and relaxing. A sense of peace fell over him, and for the first time since that summer, Sam was calm, in the moment. There was, in fact, nowhere he'd rather be, than right here, right now, with Maya. "Although that practice isn't necessarily the only thing I'm going after." He dropped his voice to a whisper and held Maya's gaze.

Her eyes widened, and her body grew tense. "About what happened earlier tonight…"

"What about it?" He moved slightly closer to her.

"It's a good thing nothing happened." She drank again, avoided his eyes.

"Is it?" he whispered, but didn't move. His entire focus right now was on her lips. He tried to remember what it felt like to kiss her, but the memory of it failed him while she stood in front of him.

"Well, yes." She fidgeted with her glass, trying not to look at him, but no matter where she looked, her eyes ended up on his. "I'm seeing someone."

Sam nodded. "True, but a few dates hardly—" He spoke slowly, studying her. If he was not mistaken, her gaze kept falling to his mouth, even while she held her glass between them.

She licked her lips. "It's more than a few dates."

The moonlight shifted to her face. He was close enough to see her eyes darken, but not close enough to feel her breath. Sam's gaze shifted from her eyes to her lips. Right then, he didn't care that she was seeing someone, or that Ben slept mere feet away. Right then, he realized that he had been missing her for sixteen years.

"Samantha doesn't know everything that I do." She was still talking. "And anyway, he asked me to go away with him next weekend." She took a large swallow of bourbon. "And I said yes."

He snapped his gaze back to her eyes. The bourbon did nothing to keep his insides from quaking. Somehow, he was able to keep his voice calm. "You've been dating him for hardly a month."

Maya downed the remainder of her drink. "What I do is really none of your concern." She put down her glass and brushed past him. He gently grabbed her arm.

"I never should have let you leave." Frustration added desperation to his voice. He didn't care. "I should have come back for you again and again, until we were back together. I *wish* that I had come back for you." If he could hold her, she would know. She would know that he belonged to her—always had and always would. She would know that she belonged with him.

Something in her softened, her breath quickened. She looked at his hand on her arm, and gently pulled free of him. "Don't beat yourself up about it, Sam. I had my mind made up." Without looking at him, she started back to his bedroom.

"Did you really?" He turned so he could see her.

She hesitated midstep before continuing to bed.

Sam poured himself another finger of bourbon, but this time, the drink failed to calm him.

Ben's sleepy voice interrupted his thoughts. "Looks like you actually might have to fight for her."

SAM FOUND SLEEP only in the wee hours of the morning. The thought of Maya with another man had gnawed at his insides, making sleep all but impossible. He woke to hushed voices and the inviting scent of coffee from the kitchen. Ben and Maya were laughing over their morning brew. Ben's feet dangled from where he was seated on the counter, and Maya leaned against the granite next to him. They looked like they'd known each other their whole lives. Maya laughed as she squeezed Ben's hand, and Sam was visited by the warm feeling that he was watching his family. He walked over to the coffeepot.

Maya studied Ben's face. "You look just like Sam, except his hair has curls. And the eyes. You have your mom's green eyes. Other than that, you could be brothers."

Sam poured himself a cup of coffee. "We are."

His warm feeling was cooled by Maya's tight smile, and he absently gulped the hot coffee.

"Morning." She stifled a yawn.

Sam's mouth was slightly scalded and he tried to be subtle while sucking in some cool air. "Didn't—didn't you sleep well?" More cool air.

"No, I slept fine. Bourbon is great for sleep." She stifled another yawn.

Sam carefully sipped his coffee and shrugged, amused that she was lying. Her hair was in a ponytail, and she was wearing her clothes from last night. She was stunning.

Ben had silently watched this exchange, and now rolled his eyes as he mumbled something inaudible. He clapped his hands together, and then spoke loud enough for all to hear. "Ahh, Sammy! What d'ya say we get this show on the road?" Ben cackled with glee.

The three of them spent the next thirty minutes making as much noise as possible while they cooked the greasiest breakfast they could. Halfway through, Samantha finally emerged, her hair tousled, and alternately holding her head and her belly. "What is happening?" She groaned. "Dad? *Mom?*"

Maya hugged her daughter. "Not feeling so great, huh?"

Sam folded his arms across his chest and leaned back against the counter. "Must've been some study session last night." He narrowed his eyes at her. "Get your project done, did you?"

"What?" Samantha appeared to be supremely confused as she plopped down at the island and rested her head on it.

Maya kissed her daughter on the head. "I have to get to class. You'll be in good hands here."

Maya waved goodbye to Ben and rushed out the door. Sam quickly followed, barefoot, in his haste.

"I'll come get her after class." Maya pushed the elevator call button.

"Actually, I need to go into Queens to speak to my real estate agent."

"On a Saturday?"

"The sooner the better."

Silence. Sam moved closer to Maya, rested his hand on her cheek. "Maya, don't go."

She tensed and removed his hand. "I have to go to class, Sam."

"Don't go away. With him."

The elevator door opened, and she stepped in. "It's what I want." She pressed the button for the lobby.

Something in the defiant way she threw those words at him spurred Sam into action. He stepped into the elevator just as the doors closed. "Are you sure?" His voice was low, almost a growl. They were alone. He had thirty-one floors to find out how sure she was. He reached behind her and released her hair from the ponytail. Thirty floors. Her breath caught as her hair cascaded in waves of dark silk over his hand. He threaded his fingers into the soft strands, cupping the back of her head. Twenty-nine.

"Sam…" It was a whisper.

He leaned down. "Don't. Say. Anything." He said the words softly onto her lips as he pressed his mouth against hers. His kiss was gentle, not pressing. She opened her mouth and he pulled back slightly in case she was going to protest, but then she pressed her mouth to his and kissed him back. This kiss was different than kisses on the porch, making out in the car, or even the early passion of the bed-and-breakfast. This kiss was about forgiveness and new beginnings. This kiss was about falling in love again.

When she did not push him away, his kiss became more insistent. Maya responded by pressing closer to him. He deepened their kiss, drinking in the honeysuckle fragrance of her, mixed with coffee on her lips, intoxicated by the essence that was Maya. She clung to him, her arms around him, pulling him even closer. He lifted her up and she automatically wrapped her legs around his waist. He brushed his mouth along the soft skin on her neck, and a low moan in her throat vibrated against his lips. He grinned against her lips as

he pressed her against the elevator wall, his hands on
her bottom, their bodies melting into each other. She
loved him. It was right there in her kiss.

They weren't the kids they used to be all those years
ago. So while everything was familiar, it was also new.
Sam was so lost in Maya, that when the elevator halted
and the familiar ding sounded, it came to him as if from
a tunnel. His time was up.

Suddenly Maya was scrambling to stand, her cheeks
pleasantly flushed, her voice agitated. "Damn it, Sam.
Let me down."

Sam let her down, taking his time to remove his
hands from her body. He finally stepped away from
her, giving her space. He could still taste her.

"I—*we*—cannot do that." She furrowed her brow as
she put her hair back in its ponytail.

"Apparently, yes, we can."

"I don't know what the hell *that* was, but I'm still
going away with Leo." She stomped out of the elevator.
The doors started to close.

Sam threw out his arm to stop the doors from closing. "Do you love him?" he called out. She turned
around, eyes wide. He held her gaze, daring her to answer. He removed his arm and the doors began to close.
"Because—" The doors shut. "I love you," he said to
his reflection in the closed doors.

Sam bit his lip and paced the empty elevator as it
ascended back to his apartment. He smiled to himself.
She wasn't very sure. Not at all.

Sam burst back into his apartment to find Ben and
Samantha exactly where he'd left them. Ben smirked at
him. "Had to take her down in the elevator, did you?"

"She cannot go away with that guy."

Samantha lifted her head, and both she and Ben stared at him. "So, what're you going to do, Sammy?"

It wasn't until he actually said the words out loud that he knew them to be true. But now that he knew that he loved her, he couldn't possibly imagine his life without her. Everything was suddenly very clear. She loved him. He knew it. She was just scared. He was not going to let her run from him twice in a lifetime. He handed Samantha a bottle of Gatorade. "Drink up. We need to get to my jeweler. And then see your grandmother."

Samantha looked more puzzled. "*Nani?* What do you want with her?"

"I have to ask her something. Something I should have asked her a long time ago."

CHAPTER FORTY-NINE
MAYA

New York 2013

THE ELEVATOR DOORS shut and Maya just stood there. Her lips were swollen from that kiss—she could still feel Sam's lips on hers, as well as the heat from his body. He couldn't just kiss her and then say…what *did* he say? Because, what? Did he think he could kiss her *like that* and she'd go running to him like some lovesick Bollywood heroine? No. Just because her body responded to him that way did not mean that they should be together. That was just biology. Though she didn't melt like that when Leo kissed her. *Not at all.*

Her phone buzzed and she was startled from her thoughts. It was Ami. How was last night? The insinuation was loud and clear, even through text. She ignored it and rushed to catch a cab to Ami's to change before class.

Maya hopped into the shower while Ami dealt with her toddler twin boys. *Thank goodness for those mischief-makers!* She dressed quickly so as to make a getaway, but Ami cornered her while she was doing her makeup. There was no way to lie when Ami turned her "truth serum" stare your way.

"What do you mean, he kissed you?" Ami almost screeched, her eyes wide.

Maya slipped on her clogs and grabbed her backpack. "I have to get to class." She walked past Ami and out into the small living area. Manhattan apartments were tiny, which Maya had always loved, but today, she needed a place to hide. And there was nowhere to go. Not if Ami had a say.

"Well, did he say anything?"

"What happened to the little monsters?" Maya looked around as if finding the twins was her life's ambition.

"Ajay took them to soccer." Ami was still in flannel pajamas, wearing her thick-rimmed glasses, with her hair up in a messy bun. There was egg stuck to her shirt and possibly ketchup splatter on her bottoms, but with her arms folded across her chest like that, she was as intimidating as any courtroom lawyer. "Maya! What is happening?"

Maya dropped her backpack and busied herself pouring coffee into a to-go cup, in an attempt to avoid Ami's stare down. The warm scent of the coffee was comforting (she had roasted the grounds at her own shop, after all!), but she knew that if she didn't answer her friend's questions, she'd never get to class. "He said… I don't know what he said. He can't just kiss me and think I'll come running. I mean what does that mean, anyway?"

"What does *what* mean?" An expression of sheer confusion colored Ami's face.

"I can't…" Maya shook her head.

"You kissed him back!" She pointed a finger at Maya and covered her gaping mouth with her other hand.

Maya looked away, but a smile poked through her grimace.

"And you liked it!"

"No! No, I did not." A flush warmed her face as her traitorous body revealed her lie.

"You are such a liar! Well, he sure as hell took his time, didn't he?" She giggled. "So what's the problem?"

"You're the one who told me to go on with my life and date and blah-blah-blah."

"True. But that was when Sam was being an ass." Ami started to gather breakfast dishes and pile them in her sink. Maya started to wash them.

"I'm seeing someone, remember?"

"Leave the dishes, Maya." Ami waved her hand and butted Maya out of the way. "So you're in love with Leo?" Ami's eyebrows shot high into her forehead.

"Leo is easy." Maya stepped back and picked up her backpack again.

"Because you don't love him. So you have nothing to lose. With Sam, you stand to lose everything." Ami turned off the water and gave Maya her full attention.

"I can't do that again." Maya shook her head against the prickle of tears behind her eyes.

"Maya—there are no guarantees—but I do know that every man is not your father. Sam is a good man. That's why you fell for him in the first place. Trust your heart." Ami's voice was soft, yet firm. The way it had been when she'd told Maya that having a baby was a good thing.

"But what if it doesn't work? What if we're not good together? What if he decides I'm too messed up, and he can't deal?"

"Do you love him?"

Maya shook her head no, even as her vision blurred and disloyal tears filled her eyes.

Ami grabbed Maya by the shoulders as if to shake her. "What if you're great together, and he's crazier than you?"

"I have to go." Maya attempted to free herself from Ami's grip.

Ami let go. "You could lose everything with Sam, it's true. But think of what you could gain."

CHAPTER FIFTY
MAYA

New York 2013

MAYA HAD TOLD Samantha she'd needed to run an errand in Manhattan and would return in an hour or so. Four hours had passed, and Samantha had texted her no less than fifty times about her ETA. She'd lied and said she'd gone to get her hair done. The truth was, she'd run her errand and then gone to Sam's apartment and found it empty. Not even Ben was there.

The thought of going back to her apartment made her so lonely, she had wandered around Manhattan for a bit, then gone back to Sam's apartment. She really needed to talk to him. He still wasn't there. It was the bitter chill left in the air after the sun set that sent her back to Queens. It had been three days since that kiss in the elevator, and she hadn't spoken to Sam since. She wasn't sure if Sam's plans about the practice in Queens had worked out, or if he had changed back to the Manhattan location.

She relived that kiss for the millionth time. It had taken every bit of self-control to walk away from him the night before, but she had then lain awake *in his bed*, chiding herself for pushing him away. Morning had brought logic, and she was momentarily grateful that she had shown restraint. That had lasted until he had entered the kitchen, in his muscle-clinging old Hootie T-shirt and pajama bottoms. His curls were disheveled, possibly from a night of tossing and turning, and his jaw had that glorious morning scruff. Combine all that with the molten way he looked at her, and sexy wasn't enough to describe it. He was so openly happy to see her, that when he'd burned himself on coffee, Maya was slightly heady from the power she seemed to have over him. Power that she clearly handed right back to him when he kissed her in the elevator. *Did she really wrap her legs around him?*

She exited the subway station and hunched over against the cold. It was already dark, and businesses were starting to close, dimming their lights. It was a slower time of year, so her mother would have closed the shop a few hours ago.

She stopped at the space Sam wanted for his practice. The For Lease sign was gone. She clapped her hands in front of her and did a little jump. He'd done it! She looked around as if he might be right there to share the joy, but the street was empty. She cupped her hands around the window and peeked in. She could imagine a secretary's desk (she would be an elderly, motherly woman—or, better yet, a man) and a waiting area, with Sam's office in the back. She could almost see him leaning back in his chair, long legs stretched out on his desk as he talked on the phone, defending the little guy. She was bursting with pride. She tried to call him. Straight to voice mail.

She continued to amble her way to the coffee shop. She was about half a block away when she noticed a glow coming from near the shop. She quickened her pace and the glow appeared to be fire. Not huge flames, but a glow. The shop was glowing. She ran the remaining half block and tried the door. It was open. She pushed the door open to the sound of the chime and entered to find the source of the glow.

The shop was blanketed in candlelight. Many of the flames had died or were dying, but a good amount were strong and offered enough light for Maya to make her way to the far side of the shop. The scent of her orange coffee floated out to her from the kitchen. Light flickered and bounced off the glass cases, giving the illusion of movement.

Three small café tables had been pushed together, and on top of them was a sleeping Sam. He was wearing dark jeans and his shoes were still on. His arms were folded across his chest, muscles straining the fabric of a crisp, white button-down shirt. She had been here before. Sleeping Beauty. If she kissed him right now, would he wake up? Her shoes clicked on the floor and Sam started.

He carefully sat up, slowly moving his neck to release stiffness, and looked around, gaining his bearings as he registered Maya's presence. "You're here." His voice was sleepy, but his curls had been tamed, and in the candlelight, he looked at her with that same molten look that had always weakened her.

Maya nodded. "So are you."

Pure pleasure radiated from him in the flickering light. "I've been here."

She grinned at him, her stomach fluttering. "I can see that. What's going on?"

He hopped down from the table, his enthusiasm that of a young boy. He spread his arms wide, looked around the shop. "Every time I try this with you—" he dropped his arms and laughed "—you're late and I end up falling asleep." He ran a hand through his hair, dislodging just the right amount of curls.

"I was out." She bit her bottom lip.

"Yeah, where?"

There was clear apprehension in his voice. Yet here he was. Waiting for her. All day. In a candlelit coffee shop. "At your place."

He widened his grin and stepped closer to her. "Why?"

Maya pressed her lips together. If she told him, she would be baring herself open to him. He stepped close enough for her to smell his cologne and feel the heat from his body.

He studied her intensely for a long moment. Before she could answer, he closed the distance between them and took her face gently in both of his hands and kissed her. Without thought, Maya melted into him, kissing him back. This was not the elevator kiss. This was tender, questioning. She started to deepen their kiss when he pulled away.

"Tell me where you were." His voice was like gravel in honey.

Her heart pounded. "I went to talk to Leo."

Sam cocked an eyebrow and whispered, "Tell me you told him no."

"I told him no." She grinned into his hands.

He smiled all the way out to that dimple, and it made her body flutter. "Maya, I have been an idiot. I was so caught up in what I'd lost that I almost couldn't see what I had. I never should have let you go all those years ago. I loved you then. I love you now. And I loved you all the time in between. When I'm with you, I'm home."

Warm brown eyes glistened at her. And then he was down on one knee. Her heart stopped.

"I should have done this correctly sixteen years ago." His voice was husky and he sounded confident, but his fingers trembled as he reached into his pocket. Sam pulled out a dazzling diamond ring. Her heart was pounding so loudly she could swear he heard it.

He held the ring out to her, swallowed hard. "Maya, I have loved you from the minute I opened the door that summer. All I've ever wanted was you. I want us to have breakfast together and argue about what boy our daughter is dating, and whose turn it is to do the dishes. I want to live every day together and grow old with you." His next words were whispered. "Marry me, Maya. Come *home*."

Tears warmed her eyes as she took in his words and that astounding ring. It was gorgeous: a huge diamond with seemingly infinite little diamonds on the sides and band. She would be a fool to turn it down.

She didn't want it.

She bit her bottom lip and bent down to whisper in his ear, "Where is it, Sam?"

Sam raised an eyebrow at her. "Where is—?" He inhaled deeply. "Maya, you can't be serious." He was clearly trying not to laugh, but his lip twitched, giving him away. "I'm down here on one knee—"

"I can see that." Maya pursed her lips as she stepped yet closer to him. She leaned her leg against his and inhaled sharply as his muscles supported her. She bent down, brushing her cheek against his and whispered again, "Where. Is. It?" She pulled back to find the answer in his eyes.

Sam finally let out a breath as he shook his head at

her. His smile was intimate when he reached back into his pocket and pulled out a considerably smaller, yet equally dazzling, diamond ring. *This* was a single diamond, maybe one karat, on a simple gold band.

This diamond was smaller, but it shone brighter. True love would do that.

"That's the one." She rested her fingers on his face. "I love you. I don't know how not to love you." She leaned her body into him, and he wrapped his arms around her, supporting her on his knee as she pulled him to her to kiss him again. He tasted of peppermint, and she drank in the familiar scent of him.

The kiss bared her soul to his. He was hers, and she had finally claimed him. His heart beat against hers, and he pulled her closer. She was his, too.

She pulled back, reached into her pocket, and pulled out the coin. Her heart light, she held it out for Sam to see. "Heads, we get married, tails, we break up."

EPILOGUE
SAM

New York—Twelve Years Later

SAM STOOD ON the sideline next to his team, his arms folded across his chest. The slight evening chill was refreshing after a warm spring day and he inhaled the familiar scent of wet grass. The only sign of his nervousness was the fingernail he was chewing. Without turning, he cut his eyes to his assistant coach, who was actively pacing the sidelines and calling out her instruction to the players. She was also eating—again.

"All right, that's fine, goalie!" She clapped her hands as she chewed and swallowed. "Just shake it off." Samantha absently rested a hand on her expanded belly as she paced the sideline, her trademark bushy ponytail bouncing with every step.

The other team had just scored, tying up the game in overtime. This meant penalty kicks. The goalie looked to his coach. Only Sam could see the panic in the goalie's honey-colored eyes. Sam unfolded his arms and smiled at the boy.

Maya was in the front row of the bleachers, just behind the team bench. She was sitting with his parents, her mother and stepfather, and Niki. Sam turned to her and caught her eye. Her eyes widened with apprehension. He nodded. *I know, I know. But he'll be fine.*

"Dad." A hand on Sam's shoulder drew his attention away from Maya. Will handed him a slip of paper. "Dad, here's a list of their best strikers and what foot they use." He pointed to five that he had grouped together. "These are most likely the ones they'll use."

Sam grinned at Will and patted him on the shoulder. "I knew having a striker in the family would pay off someday." He glanced at his daughter. "Can't get her to sit still, huh?"

Will sighed. "The only way we were going to miss this game is if she was in active labor." He looked sideways at Sam. "And even then, she'd probably be coaching from the hospital." He shook his head. "Is the little guy ready?"

Sam shrugged. "We'll see."

Movement behind the goal turned Sam's gaze. Ben was pacing back and forth. Sam motioned for him to come over to the bench. No spectators were allowed behind the goal. Ben ended his vigil and jogged back to the bleachers to join the family.

A groan from Samantha's direction had Sam and Will turning to her. She was holding her belly. Sam started toward her, but before he could take even a second step, Will was at her side. A movement from the bleachers caught his eye. Maya was standing and looking in Samantha's direction, as well. Their eyes met and Sam took a second step toward their daughter. Maya widened her eyes and shook her head. *No.* She jutted her chin in Samantha's direction.

Sam turned to see Will and Samantha talking softly. Will had his hand on Samantha's belly, the sunlight glinted off his wedding ring, and he carried a worried expression. Samantha tossed her head, her lips set in a grim line. Will motioned toward a chair, and seemed to be mildly glaring at her. Samantha held her hands up in surrender as she started to sit down. She stopped and smiled at Will, then kissed him. He shook his head and chuckled as he handed her a water bottle.

Sam caught Maya's eye again, a small smile playing at his lips. Maya met his eyes and grinned as she shrugged. *She was fine.*

Sam's smile broadened to fill his face and he nodded to his wife. *Okay.* He held her gaze for an extra moment. Even after all these years, she still made his heart quicken.

The referee's whistle jolted them back to the game.

Sam motioned to Samantha and Will to call in the team while the referee prepped for penalty kicks. The boys responded immediately to their assistant coach, and she high-fived each one of them as they reached the bench.

This was the final championship game of the under-ten boys' soccer. Sam stood before the team and grinned from ear to ear. "You guys are amazing! What a game—and against a really good team." The boys were tired, but most managed some eye contact and a couple even smiled. The goalie's eyes never strayed from him.

"Okay. So you all know the drill—can't end championship games in a tie. So, we get to pick five of you to each take a shot on goal. It's you against the goalie. They get five shots on us, too."

He glanced at the keeper. The boy's eyes were huge, his dark, curly hair plastered to his skull with sweat. "But I am confident, as you all should be, that we can make those goals."

All of the boys turned to look at their keeper. One of them, a short blond striker, smiled at him, and turned to Sam. "Coach, we only need to make one, because nothing gets past our goalie. He's The Wall."

All the boys cheered the goalie's name in unison.

The boy grinned as he stood and the team got louder. Ben fist-bumped him. "Nothing gets by you."

Samantha ruffled his damp hair. "Listen, kid—you'll be great. Goaltending is in your blood."

Sam looked over the boy's head at Maya. He nudged his keeper. "Your mom wants you."

The boy rolled his eyes at his coach. "Dad!"

Sam flashed his eyes at him. *"Your mom wants you."*

The keeper grudgingly turned and gave his mom a thumbs-up. Maya grinned from ear to ear and returned the thumbs-up.

As their son started back to the field, Sam chuckled to himself as Maya covered her eyes and hid her face in his father's shoulder. She never could watch penalty kicks.

The boy hesitated on the sideline. Sam draped an arm around his son's shoulders and looked down into his eyes. "You know, no matter what happens out there, your mother and I love you and are proud of you. You've worked hard all season, and it shows. This—" Sam indicated the field "—this is just a game."

"Yeah, yeah." The boy stared straight ahead and

waved a dismissive hand. He had heard all this before. "I know." He tapped the pocket of his shorts.

Sam smiled to himself. "What does the coin say, Arjun?"

Arjun looked up and gave his father a sly grin. "Heads, we win. Tails, they lose."

* * * * *

RECIPES
CILANTRO CHUTNEY

CHUTNEY IS ONE of those things that you can't possibly get wrong. Proof of this is in my real-life story of being assigned to make chutney by my mother-in-law shortly after I was married. I had no idea how to make chutney, but I remembered a few things I had seen my mother do. I didn't want to admit my lack of knowledge, so I simply asked my mother-in-law how *she* made chutney, because my mom added such and such ingredients. I believe my mother-in-law saw right through me, but kindly played along. I fumbled along, and threw ingredients into a blender, and voilà, chutney! It was so yummy, I became the family chutney maker. Bear that in mind as you make your own, unique chutney!

2–3 handfuls of cilantro, washed
(wash by floating in a medium-sized bowl, so all the sand etc. sinks to the bottom and the cilantro floats to the top)

1–2 handfuls of salted, roasted nuts of choice
(peanut, almonds, cashews—whatever you like)
Cashews will make the chutney creamier, if that's what you like—I do! I am currently using cashews.

3–5 cloves of garlic, peeled
(not from a jar or frozen—use fresh!)

Lemon juice

½–1 finely chopped jalapeño pepper
(depends on the heat of the pepper, as well as how
spicy you want the chutney)

Salt (to taste)

1. Place cilantro, nuts, garlic and jalapeño (start with ½) into a blender or smoothie maker of your choice. You may have to add a bit of water. Blend until it is the consistency you like. If it is not coming together, add a bit more water.

2. Add lemon juice. A couple squirts from a bottle, or the juice of half a lemon if using fresh. Mix.

3. Taste it. Does it need salt? Add a pinch or two. Mix.

4. Taste it again. Does it feel like something is missing? Add a bit more lemon juice. Mix.

Serve with samosa. Or use as a spread in a chutney sandwich. Add sliced cucumber, sliced tomato and sliced onion. If you like, add a slice of cheese. I prefer the sandwich on toasted bread to avoid sogginess.

CHAI

MAYA SERVES CHAI when Hema visits the bakery looking for forgiveness. It's a cold day, and the warm spices and milk make this a comforting drink on such a day. I chose chai in the scene as opposed to coffee, for many reasons. Not the least of which is that the coffee scent is associated with Sam.

But I mostly chose chai because a bit of effort is required to make it, and I have always associated the smell of chai with family. When I was growing up, my mom would make chai when all the family was together in the summer. She would add fresh mint, and that aroma still takes me back to those carefree days. When I first got married, my in-laws seemed to love when I made chai, and it always made me feel loved and part of my new family.

By the end of this scene, Hema and Maya have started their journey as part of a family, so chai just seemed the right choice of drink.

The thing to know about chai is that it's a very individual thing, like coffee. People have preferences for how they take their chai. Some like it strong and dark, while others prefer a more milky tea. Sweetness is always an issue. You can avoid this by simply not adding sugar while it boils, and allowing everyone to add their own sugar. Some like it spicy, some like it mild.

The best way to figure out what you like is to simply try different versions and see which you like the best.

The differences in some chai start with the makeup of the chai masala (spice mixture that makes chai *chai*). The basic ingredients are cinnamon, cardamom, peppercorn, nutmeg, cloves and ginger. Chai masala can be bought or homemade. I use homemade versions from my mother and mother-in-law.

I personally enjoy chai in the summer when fresh mint grows. I add the fresh mint before I add milk. Very refreshing! Some people will also add fresh grated ginger at this juncture—also yummy!

I imagine that when Maya makes chai for Hema, she adds just a bit more spice as it is a cold day outside, and the strong aroma and taste is warming and comforting. Here is a basic chai recipe. As I said, variations occur!

1. Fill a small/medium pot with enough water for about 2 cups of chai (this amount depends on the size of your cup).

2. Add 2–3 spoons of tea, and about 1 small spoon of chai masala (more if you like more spice, less if you prefer less spice).

3. Let the mixture come to a soft boil.

4. Add milk until the chai is the color you like (less milk if you like strong chai, more if you like a milkier flavor).

5. Add sugar to taste.

6. Allow this mixture to come to a rolling boil. *Do not step away from the mixture at this juncture, as it may boil over!*

7. Once the mixture has boiled a bit, turn off the stove and strain the chai into two cups. Makes chai for two.

ACKNOWLEDGMENTS

IT TAKES A VILLAGE to do many things and writing a book is one of them. My dream of being a published author would not have come true if it hadn't been for this village of people, each of whom had a role that was instrumental in making this happen.

Ed Barrett (*In a Manner of Speaking*) was a fellow student in an online class I was taking when I first started *Then, Now, Always*, and he was the first person to read this manuscript who didn't already know me. His praise "I'd buy this book and I don't really read romance" was all the encouragement I needed to know I was on the right path.

My cousin Sonia Shah introduced me to Shaila Patel (Joining of Souls series). Shaila changed the course of my writing experience by introducing me to RWA, which in turn led me to my home chapters of MRW and WRW. Shaila, you continue to be hands-on with all my work, from brainstorming to beta reading, and I would be stuck in a quagmire of words and plotlines if not for you! You have my undying gratitude. As does Sonia, for putting us together.

Friends who are family, Dr. Jyothi Rao-Mahadevia (*Finding Balance*) and Kosha Dalal. Kosha, thanks for all of your feedback for the setting in Manhattan and Queens as well as your legal expertise with how Sam's career might have been. Jyothi, as one of my very first readers, my reference for all things medical (and my conduit to the universe), your support was priceless. Thanks to you both for always being there to toast my accomplishments as well as my sorrows.

Family who I would choose as friends, Tina Patel and Hetal Diwan, my sisters-in-law who are sisters to me in all ways (thank God I married your brother)! Thanks for your unwavering support as I set off on this journey, even as I dragged my computer with me on family vacations. I am grateful for your patience in reading various versions as I grew as a writer (and for listening to me drone on and on and on about the process)! We never have enough time together, but you are always ready with wine to hear my latest, and most important, you always have my back.

My brother and sis-in-law, Satyan and Monica Sharma, thanks for being my NYC "base" and coming out with me to celebrate each little accomplishment as I chipped away at my goal. Your unrelenting enthusiasm and wisdom always gave me the energy boost I needed to keep chipping away. I hope I have earned a spot on your "signed by the author" bookshelf! I can't wait for you to read this!

Caroline Phoebus, I'm not even sure how many versions of this book you've read, but your encouragement has been invaluable. Thank you as well for making my website and handling all that computer stuff!

Special heartfelt thanks to Anju and Romi Saini and Neel and Sharada Vibhakar, for reading and listening and supporting over all these years!

Samatha Harris (Madison Square series), your insight over a cup of coffee quite literally changed the course of my story, expanding it and making it better than I could imagine on my own.

Chocolate truffles to all my MRW and WRW peeps, particularly Christi Barth, author of many contemporary romance titles, who came up to me at my very first MRW meeting and basically became my mentor and who currently continues to push me to be a better writer every time we meet.

Can't forget my Desi Girl Peeps, Sonali Dev, Falguni Kothari, Kishan Paul and Soni Wolf. All wildly successful published authors whom I greatly admire and aspire to be like when I grow up. They immediately understood what it meant for me to go down this path and without question helped me navigate the confusing waters of querying and agenting and publication. My heart overflows with gratitude for you.

To both sets of my parents, Ran and Sudha Sharma, and Vasant and Shakuntala Shroff, your never-ending support made this process much smoother.

Thanks to my awesome agent, Rachel Brooks at Bookends Literary. When you actually quoted me to me, I knew you loved Sam and Maya as much as I did, and that I had found my agency home. Brittany Lavery at HQN Books has to be the best editor ever. You showed me how to fine-tune and polish what I had and still remain true to my characters and story! A special shout-out to Beth Phelan for #DVPit, which is how Rachel and I met!

Thanks to both of my children. Anjali, for loving the 750-word short story that was the beginning of *Heads or Tails* and convincing me that this was my novel. Also, thanks for keeping it real and reminding me that I wasn't a hit, yet. Anand (my live-in goalie), thanks for all the soccer tips, and for not being embarrassed to tell your fraternity brothers your mother is a romance author.

Last, but never least, thanks to my husband, Deven Shroff, without whom this journey would never have even started. From the moment I decided to pursue my dreams, your support was steadfast and true, as our love has always been. When you gifted me with my dream computer, you knew this day would come. And then so did I.